Praise for *The Chosen* from the Past Fifty Years

"So entertaining, so full of love and compassion that readers of all persuasions will take it to their hearts. Mr. Potok is writing about two fathers and their sons . . . in a way that will ring just as true in Iowa as in Brooklyn."

—*Publishers Weekly*

"A coming-of-age classic."

—*The Boston Globe*

"Anyone who finds *The Chosen* is finding a jewel. Its themes are profound and universal. . . . It will stay on our bookshelves and be read again."

—*The Wall Street Journal*

"It makes you want to buttonhole strangers in the street to be sure they know it's around. . . . It revives my sometimes fading belief in humanity. Works of this caliber should be occasion for singing in the streets and shouting from the rooftops."

—*Chicago Tribune*

"A fine, moving, gratifying book."

—*Saturday Review*

"A classic story of faith and friendship. Fifty years after publication it is still inspiring."

—Alice Hoffman, *New York Times* bestselling author of *The Dovekeepers, The Museum of Extraordinary Things,* and *The Marriage of Opposites*

"It is a simple, almost meager story . . . yet the warmth and pathos of the dealings between fathers and sons and the understated odyssey from boyhood to manhood give the book a range that makes it worth anybody's reading."

—*The Christian Science Monitor*

ALSO BY CHAIM POTOK

NOVELS
The Chosen (1967)
The Promise (1969)
My Name Is Asher Lev (1972)
In the Beginning (1975)
The Book of Lights (1981)
Davita's Harp (1985)
The Gift of Asher Lev (1990)
I Am the Clay (1992)
Old Men at Midnight (2001)

NONFICTION
Wanderings: Chaim Potok's History of the Jews (1978)
The Gates of November (1996)

PLAYS
Out of the Depths (1990)
The Play of Lights (1992)
The Chosen (with Aaron Posner, 1999)

CHILDREN'S LITERATURE
The Tree of Here (1993)
The Sky of Now (1995)
Zebra and Other Stories (1998)

THE CHOSEN

CHAIM POTOK

Introduction by Rena Potok

SIMON & SCHUSTER

NEW YORK   LONDON   TORONTO   SYDNEY   NEW DELHI

Simon & Schuster
1230 Avenue of the Americas
New York, NY 10020

First Simon & Schuster hardcover edition November 2016

SIMON & SCHUSTER and colophon are registered trademarks of Simon & Schuster, Inc.

For information about special discounts for bulk purchases, please contact Simon & Schuster Special Sales at 1-866-506-1949 or business@simonandschuster.com.

Interior design by Laura Levatino

Manufactured in the United States of America

10 9 8 7 6 5 4 3 2 1

Library of Congress Cataloging-in-Publication Data is available.

ISBN 978-1-5011-4247-5
ISBN 978-1-5011-4248-2 (ebook)

Credits can be found on pages 397–98.

CONTENTS

INTRODUCTION

Rena Potok

CHAIM POTOK WROTE *The Chosen* in 1963–64 while living in Jerusalem. He wrote in longhand, in gray-covered spiral-bound notebooks with lined pages, the kind that were readily found in Israeli stationery stores in the 1960s and '70s. The notebooks are numbered from I through XI and total 757 manuscript pages. On the cover of each notebook, he wrote the chapter number, and at the bottom, in capital letters: "PLEASE RETURN IF FOUND. HANDSOME REWARD WILL BE GIVEN," and the address in English and in Hebrew.

In his youth, Potok attended a yeshiva, an Orthodox Jewish parochial school, where he studied Jewish sacred texts in the morning and secular subjects in the afternoons. On evenings and weekends he read his way through the Western literary canon and wrote fiction. He would study a chapter of a novel the same way he studied a page of Talmud, taking the text apart and trying to figure out how it was put together. Potok's earliest influences were Evelyn Waugh's *Brideshead Revisited* and James Joyce's *A Portrait of the Artist as a Young Man*. These were his first major encounters with Western secular humanism.

Word spread of his curious reading and writing habits, and one day he was stopped on the way out of class by his Talmud teacher. Potok tells the story in "An Invisible Map of Meaning: A Writer's Confrontations": "I hear you want to be a writer," the teacher said. He proceeded to scold the boy: "Isn't it enough that the school has to waste every afternoon of each day on secular studies in order to be licensed by the government? [You] have to add to that, and instead of giving every spare moment to the study of sacred texts, [you are] writing *stories*!"

Among Potok's papers—which are housed in the Kislak Center for Special Collections, Rare Books and Manuscripts, at the University of Pennsylvania—he kept a copy of Elie Wiesel's 1966 article "My Teachers" and underlined the following lines in red ink:

> The "Shelishter Rebbe" told me one day: "Be careful with words, they're dangerous. Beware of them. They beget demons or angels. It's up to you to give life to one or the other. Be careful, I tell you, nothing is as dangerous as to give free rein to words."

These words clearly rang true for Potok, mirroring, as they do, his own childhood experience. How fortunate we readers are that both men so thoroughly ignored the warnings of these teachers!

Potok's yeshiva education had prepared him well for the rigorous writing schedule he imposed on himself during that year in Jerusalem: in the mornings he worked on the novel in the small, cold apartment; the afternoons he devoted to his doctoral dissertation on Solomon Maimon and post-Kantian dialectics at the Hebrew University library. In his adult life, he gave the novel the position of the sacred morning texts of his youth, the dissertation that of the world of afternoon secular studies.

He wrote the first version of *The Chosen* in those notebooks, in the manner that he would adopt for the entirety of his career as a novelist: the first draft of the text he wrote on the right-hand page; revisions and notes for later consideration he wrote on the left-hand facing page—sometimes in different colors, often with arrows pointing wildly at one important change or another. Here and there are rewritten bits Scotch-taped over sections of original text. Meticulous about details, he posed questions to himself in the manuscript for investigation, such as: "Check this: How soon after the Revolution did Russia withdraw from the First World War?"

The manuscript draft of the novel opens with the story of Reb Saunders, the tragic loss of his first family in a pogrom in pre–World War II Poland, and his emigration to the United States with the entire community of his followers. The final draft embeds that material later in the novel as an exposition of Reb Saunders's character, where it has far greater impact and weight. The baseball game—the dramatic scene that sets the entire action of the novel in motion—does not originally begin until page 11 of the manuscript. The original chapter two in the manuscript later became chapter one, which famously begins, "For the first fifteen years of our lives, Danny and I lived within five blocks of each other and neither of us knew of the other's existence."

The title of the novel had its own arc of revisions and iterations: *The Locust Years*, *The Silence*, *The Echoes of Silence*, *The Long Silence of Danny Saunders*—as we can see in the archival material reproduced in the "History, Context, and Criticism" section of this volume. In his warm and witty piece "The Birth of *The Chosen*," which opens this section, Potok's longtime editor and friend Robert Gottlieb tells us how the book got its final title and notes its development from an unwieldy manuscript (which, he told the author, contained not one but two novels) to a runaway bestseller. Gottlieb also sheds light on the longtime appeal of the novel: it introduces gentile and secular Jewish readers alike to the unfamiliar worlds of Hasidism and Orthodox Judaism and, in so doing, explores pervasive and well-known themes of religious conflict, father-son relationships, teenage emotion, the complexities of friendship, and the challenges of rejecting tradition to follow one's own path.

When *The Chosen* was published in 1967, Potok expected his novel to have a small, quiet reception. But then the reviews started to come in, followed by the steady climb up the *New York Times* Best Sellers list, where it stayed for ten months. Other books on the list that year: William Styron's *Confessions of Nat Turner*; Leon Uris's *Topaz*; Thornton Wilder's *The Eighth Day*; Ira Levin's *Rosemary's Baby*; and Jacqueline Susann's *Valley of the Dolls*.

The Chosen is set against two interlocking historical backdrops: World War II and the Holocaust (embodied in the character of Reb Saunders) and Zionism and the founding of the State of Israel (represented by David Malter). The conflict between these men signifies a larger ideological clash between the two diametrically opposed worldviews of Zionism and Messianism: the position that the Jewish state should be founded by men and women, and the belief that it could not be established without divine intervention and the coming of the Messiah. The pain of this conflict manifests itself in the novel in Reb Saunders's forced separation of Danny and Reuven, who must (for a time) endure in their friendship the oppressive silence imposed by Reb Saunders upon his son.

The primary religious and cultural context of *The Chosen* is that of Hasidism and Orthodox Judaism. Potok was intimately acquainted with the world of Hasidism: his mother was a direct descendant of the Rizhener, one of the great Hasidic dynasties of Europe; his father was a follower of the Belzer, another important Hasidic dynasty. In "*The Chosen*: The Hasidim and the Orthodox," Edward Abramson discusses these two contexts and explains that Hasidism was a Jewish spiritual movement that began in eighteenth-century Poland as a reaction to the intellectual strictures of rabbinic Judaism at the time, with its almost exclusive focus on the study of the Talmud (a collection of civil, religious, and ethical laws based on Jewish teaching and interpretation of biblical text). Kathryn McClymond, in "*The Chosen*: Defining American Judaism," goes even further, exploring Hasidism and the world of the novel as contributing importantly to the development of the Jewish American self.

The historical, religious, and cultural contexts of *The Chosen* are the doorway to Potok's lifelong fascination with what he termed "core-to-core culture confrontation," a concept that was the fulcrum of all his writing. This idea found its inception in his youthful forays into the aesthetic realm beyond the boundaries of his strict religious upbringing, and came to full expression after his encounter with a world that could not have been more different.

Potok attended Yeshiva University and then the Jewish Theological Seminary, where he received his rabbinic ordination. He then served for sixteen and a half months as a U.S. Army chaplain in Korea, in a medical battalion and in a combat engineering battalion. Raised to believe that Judaism made a fundamental difference in the world, Potok found himself, in Asia, in a world where Judaism meant nothing and where, to his astonishment, he witnessed deep faith in the heart of pagan idol worship. His cultural encounters in Korea and Japan relativized his Jewishness, Americanness, and Westernness simultaneously, creating a fundamental paradigm shift: he had entered that world with a coherent sense of who he was as a Jew, as an American, and as a Westerner. But in Japan, Korea, and the other parts of Asia he visited as an American soldier, that coherence came undone. The paradigm shift, and its attendant notions of unraveling and reconstituting identity, became the driving force behind his novels.

Out of this fundamental change in his worldview, Potok developed his theory of core-to-core culture confrontation, which he would continue to cultivate throughout his life as a writer. He would come to call this concept the "invisible scaffolding" of all his novels. The three essays published in this volume show the progression of his ideas about culture conflict and their manifestation in *The Chosen* and all the subsequent novels. "Culture Confrontation in Urban America: A Writer's Beginnings" is an early expression of these ideas as they emerged from the urban world of his youth. "The Culture Highways We Travel" focuses on his encounter with Asian religion and culture in Korea, and explains the ascending order of difficult culture confrontations experienced by Danny Saunders, Reuven Malter, and characters from his other novels. "The Invisible Map of Meanings: A Writer's Confrontations" is Potok's seminal piece—the culmination and fullest exposition of his theory.

In "Culture Confrontation in Urban America," Potok uses the term *Zwischenmensch* to define himself and his experience of cultural conflict: "Urban wanderings that result in core-culture confrontations often shape a certain kind of individual. I call that individual a *Zwischenmensch*, a between-person. Such an individual will cross the boundaries of his or her own culture and embrace life-enhancing elements from alien worlds."

Daniel Walden, the preeminent scholar of Potok's work, takes up that self-description and uses it as the basis for an analysis of the author's writing in "Chaim Potok: A Zwischenmensch ('Between Person') in the Cultures." Potok, suggests Walden, was formed by his urban Jewish upbringing in the Bronx and then encountered the umbrella culture of Western secular humanism. As a result, his urban, intellectual, and literary wanderings produced a *Zwischenmensch*—a person, a novelist, occupying the interstitial space between Western secular humanism and religious orthodoxy. In "The Chosen Borough: Chaim Potok's Brooklyn," Joan Zlotnick picks up on these ideas in her discussion of the urban landscape of the Bronx, where Potok grew up, and of Brooklyn, where his novels are set.

In *The Chosen*, a boy from the center of Jewish tradition collides with one of the most significant elements from the model of Western secular humanism: Freudian psychoanalytic theory. Danny and Reuven act out Potok's theory of core-to-core culture confrontation. They are young men concerned with matters of identity, with the development and preservation of the individuated self. Danny, in particular, struggles with a love of his core culture and a love of the umbrella culture, which offers him cultural and intellectual enlightenment. In the course of the struggle, moral values grate against each other and family systems are redrawn as Danny tries to balance the two worlds in which he finds himself irretrievably immersed.

In the friendship between the young men, we see the influence of Evelyn

Waugh; even the novel's early title, *The Locust Years*, echoes Waugh's use of the Greek concept of Arcadia (everlasting youth) as a central theme in *Brideshead Revisited*. In "The Head, the Heart and the Conflict of Generations in Chaim Potok's *The Chosen*," Sam Bluefarb concentrates on Reuven and Danny's friendship and suggests that they are symbolically two halves of a single personality, each searching for its complement—a dynamic he calls a "doppelgänger effect." And in the father-son relationships, Bluefarb sees the conflict of generations and visions of the future with America as the catalyst.

All the critical essays in this volume share a sense of admiration for *The Chosen* and its significant role as an American novel. The final contribution is Hugh Nissenson's reappraisal of *The Chosen* thirty-five years after its publication. His piece was originally given—along with Daniel Walden's essay—as a talk at a symposium at the University of Pennsylvania honoring the memory of Chaim Potok in 2002, five months after his death. We can hear in these two scholars' voices the personal affection and admiration they had for the writer and for the man.

Following on the heels of the novel's success, there have been a number of adaptations of *The Chosen* in various iterations:

In 1977, a radio play created by Shimon Wincelberg was broadcast on *The Eternal Light*, a series on the NBC Radio Network.

The film *The Chosen* was released in 1982; it was produced by Edie and Ely Landau and directed by Jeremy Paul Kagan, with a screenplay by Kagan and Edwin Gordon. It features Maximilian Schell as David Malter, Rod Steiger as Reb Saunders, Robby Benson as Danny Saunders, and Barry Miller as Reuven Malter. Potok served as technical advisor on the film and played a cameo role as the "Talmud teacher." In this volume there are reproductions of photos and other artifacts from the set of the film, from the Chaim Potok Papers at the Kislak Center for Special Collections, Rare Books and Manuscripts.

On January 6, 1988, a short-lived musical based on the book opened at the Second Avenue Theater in New York City. The script was by Chaim Potok; the music was by Philip Springer; the lyrics were by Mitchell Bernard; and the production starred George Hearn, Richard Cray, Gerald Hiken, and Rob Morrow.

In 1999, the novel was adapted for the stage by Aaron Posner and Chaim Potok and directed by Posner. The play was presented by the Arden Theatre Company in Philadelphia from March 18 to April 18 and then at City Theatre in Pittsburgh from April 23 to May 23, 1999. It won the 1999 Barrymore Award for Best New Play. It has since been produced in a great many theaters across the country. In his foreword to the play, Posner shares his personal reflections on directing the play and on his adaptation and collaboration with the author.

In his foreword to the twenty-fifth anniversary edition of *The Chosen*, Potok calls the work a "seemingly fragile raft of a novel; this rarefied weave of signs, symbols, and metaphors; this odd tale of two boys from different backgrounds spinning out their adolescent lives in an arcane realm of Brooklyn homes, streets, playgrounds, libraries, houses of workshop, and academies of learning around the closing years of the Second World War."

Since *The Chosen* was first published in 1967, this "fragile raft of a novel" has sold 3.4 million copies worldwide and has been translated into numerous languages, including Dutch, Italian, French, Hebrew, and Japanese. Its author enjoyed a prolific career of writing, exploring ideas, and asking questions, always cross-referencing texts and ways of reading. And it all started with a story conceived in a small, cold Jerusalem apartment and written in those gray-covered, spiral-bound notebooks more than five decades ago.

Rena Potok
August 2016

Acknowledgments and thanks to David McKnight and Tom Hensle at the Kislak Center for Special Collections, Rare Books and Manuscripts, the University of Pennsylvania Libraries, and to Megan Hogan at Simon & Schuster.

THE CHOSEN

To Adena

To Dr. Israel Charny, Mrs. Jonas Greenfield, Rabbi Raphael Posner, and Dr. Aaron Rosen, all of whom helped with the research, I offer my gratitude.

C.P.

When a trout rising to a fly gets hooked on a line and finds himself unable to swim about freely, he begins with a fight which results in struggles and splashes and sometimes an escape. Often, of course, the situation is too tough for him.

In the same way the human being struggles with his environment and with the hooks that catch him. Sometimes he masters his difficulties; sometimes they are too much for him. His struggles are all that the world sees and it naturally misunderstands them. It is hard for a free fish to understand what is happening to a hooked one.

—KARL A. MENNINGER

True happiness
Consists not in the multitude of friends,
But in the worth and choice.
—BEN JONSON

BOOK ONE

I was a son to my father . . .
And he taught me and said to me,
"Let your heart hold fast my words. . . ."

—Proverbs

BOOK ONE

ONE

FOR THE FIRST FIFTEEN YEARS of our lives, Danny and I lived within five blocks of each other and neither of us knew of the other's existence.

Danny's block was heavily populated by the followers of his father, Russian Hasidic Jews in somber garb, whose habits and frames of reference were born on the soil of the land they had abandoned. They drank tea from samovars, sipping it slowly through cubes of sugar held between their teeth; they ate the foods of their homeland, talked loudly, occasionally in Russian, most often in a Russian Yiddish, and were fierce in their loyalty to Danny's father.

A block away lived another Hasidic sect, Jews from southern Poland, who walked the Brooklyn streets like specters, with their black hats, long black coats, black beards, and earlocks. These Jews had their own rabbi, their own dynastic ruler, who could trace his family's position of rabbinic leadership back to the time of the Ba'al Shem Tov, the eighteenth-century founder of Hasidism, whom they all regarded as a God-invested personality.

About three or four such Hasidic sects populated the area in which Danny and I grew up, each with its own rabbi, its own little synagogue, its own customs, its own fierce loyalties. On a Shabbat or festival morning, the members of each sect could be seen walking to their respective synagogues, dressed in their particular garb, eager to pray with their particular rabbi and forget the tumult of the week and the hungry grabbing for money which they needed to feed their large families during the seemingly endless Depression.

The sidewalks of Williamsburg were cracked squares of cement, the streets paved with asphalt that softened in the stifling summers and broke apart into potholes in the bitter winters. Many of the houses were brownstones, set tightly together, none taller than three or four stories. In these houses lived Jews, Irish, Germans, and some Spanish Civil War refugee families that had fled the new Franco regime before the onset of the Second World War. Most of the stores were run by gentiles, but some were owned by Orthodox Jews, members of the Hasidic sects in the area. They could be seen behind their counters, wearing black skullcaps, full beards, and long earlocks, eking out their meager livelihoods and dreaming of Shabbat and festivals when they could close their stores and turn their attention to their prayers, their rabbi, their God.

Every Orthodox Jew sent his male children to a yeshiva, a Jewish parochial school, where they studied from eight or nine in the morning to four or five in the evening. On Fridays the students were let out at about one o'clock to prepare for the Shabbat. Jewish education was compulsory for the Orthodox, and because this was America and not Europe, English education was compulsory as well—so each student carried a double burden: Hebrew studies in the mornings and English studies in the afternoons. The test of intellectual excellence, however, had been reduced by tradition and unvoiced unanimity to a single area of study: Talmud. Virtuosity in Talmud was the achievement most sought after by every student of a yeshiva, for it was the automatic guarantee of a reputation for brilliance.

Danny attended the small yeshiva established by his father. Outside of the Williamsburg area, in Crown Heights, I attended the yeshiva in which my father taught. This latter yeshiva was somewhat looked down upon by the students of other Jewish parochial schools of Brooklyn: it offered more English subjects than the required minimum, and it taught its Jewish subjects in Hebrew rather than Yiddish. Most of the students were children of immigrant Jews who preferred to regard themselves as having been emancipated from the fenced-off ghetto mentality typical of the other Jewish parochial schools in Brooklyn.

Danny and I probably would never have met—or we would have met under altogether different circumstances—had it not been for America's entry into the Second World War and the desire this bred on the part of some English teachers in the Jewish parochial schools to show the gentile world that yeshiva students were as physically fit, despite their long hours of study, as any other American student. They went about proving this by organizing the Jewish parochial schools in and around our area into competitive leagues, and once every two weeks the schools would compete against one another in a variety of sports. I became a member of my school's varsity softball team.

On a Sunday afternoon in early June, the fifteen members of my team met with our gym instructor in the play yard of our school. It was a warm day, and the sun was bright on the asphalt floor of the yard. The gym instructor was a short, chunky man in his early thirties who taught in the mornings in a nearby public high school and supplemented his income by teaching in our yeshiva during the afternoons. He wore a white polo shirt, white pants, and white sweater, and from the awkward way the little black skullcap sat perched on his round, balding head, it was clearly apparent that he was not accustomed to wearing it with any sort of regularity. When he talked he frequently thumped his right fist into his left palm to emphasize a point. He walked on the balls of his feet, almost in imitation of a boxer's ring stance, and he was fanatically addicted to professional baseball. He had nursed our softball team along for two years, and by a mixture of patience, luck, shrewd manipulations during some tight ball games, and hard, fist-thumping harangues calculated to shove us into a patriotic awareness of the importance of athletics and physical fitness for the war effort, he was able to mold our original team of fifteen awkward fumblers into the top team of our league. His name was Mr. Galanter, and all of us wondered why he was not off somewhere fighting in the war.

During my two years with the team, I had become quite adept at second base and had also developed a swift underhand pitch that would tempt a batter into a swing but would drop into a curve at the last moment and slide just below the flaying bat for a strike. Mr. Galanter always began a ball game by putting me at second base and would use me as a pitcher only in very tight moments, because, as he put it once, "My baseball philosophy is grounded on the defensive solidarity of the infield."

That afternoon we were scheduled to play the winning team of another neighborhood league, a team with a reputation for wild, offensive slugging and poor fielding. Mr. Galanter said he was counting upon our infield to act as a solid defensive front. Throughout the warm-up period, with only our team in the yard, he kept thumping his right fist into his left palm and shouting at us to be a solid defensive front.

"No holes," he shouted from near home plate. "No holes, you hear? Goldberg, what kind of solid defensive front is that? Close in. A battleship could get between you and Malter. That's it. Schwartz, what are you doing, looking for paratroops? This is a ball game. The enemy's on the ground. That throw was wide, Goldberg. Throw it like a sharpshooter. Give him the ball again. Throw it. Good. Like a sharpshooter. Very good. Keep the infield solid. No defensive holes in this war."

We batted and threw the ball around, and it was warm and sunny, and there was the smooth, happy feeling of the summer soon to come, and the tight excitement of the ball game. We wanted very much to win, both for ourselves and, more especially, for Mr. Galanter, for we had all come to like his fist-thumping sincerity. To the rabbis who taught in the Jewish parochial schools, baseball was an evil waste of time, a spawn of the potentially assimilationist English portion of the yeshiva day. But to the students of most of the parochial schools, an inter-league baseball victory had come to take on only a shade less significance than a top grade in Talmud, for it was an unquestioned mark of one's Americanism, and to be counted a loyal American had become increasingly important to us during these last years of the war.

So Mr. Galanter stood near home plate, shouting instructions and words of encouragement, and we batted and tossed the ball around. I walked off the field for a moment to set up my eyeglasses for the game. I wore shell-rimmed glasses, and before every game I would bend the earpieces in so the glasses would stay tight on my head and not slip down the bridge of my nose when I began to sweat. I always waited until just before a game to bend down the earpieces, because, bent, they would cut into the skin over my ears, and I did not want to feel the pain a moment longer than I had to. The tops of my ears would be sore for days after every game, but better that, I thought, than the need to keep pushing my glasses up the bridge of my nose or the possibility of having them fall off suddenly during an important play.

Davey Cantor, one of the boys who acted as a replacement if a first-stringer had to leave the game, was standing near the wire screen behind home plate. He was a short boy, with a round face, dark hair, owlish glasses, and a very Semitic nose. He watched me fix my glasses.

"You're looking good out there, Reuven," he told me.

"Thanks," I said.

"Everyone is looking real good."

"It'll be a good game."

He stared at me through his glasses. "You think so?" he asked.

"Sure, why not?"

"You ever see them play, Reuven?"

"No."

"They're murderers."

"Sure," I said.

"No, really. They're wild."

"You saw them play?"

"Twice. They're murderers."

"Everyone plays to win, Davey."

"They don't only play to win. They play like it's the first of the Ten Commandments."

I laughed. "That yeshiva?" I said. "Oh, come on, Davey."

"It's the truth."

"Sure," I said.

"Reb Saunders ordered them never to lose because it would shame their yeshiva or something. I don't know. You'll see."

"Hey, Malter!" Mr. Galanter shouted. "What are you doing, sitting this one out?"

"You'll see," Davey Cantor said.

"Sure." I grinned at him. "A holy war."

He looked at me.

"Are you playing?" I asked him.

"Mr. Galanter said I might take second base if you have to pitch."

"Well, good luck."

"Hey, Malter!" Mr. Galanter shouted. "There's a war on, remember?"

"Yes, sir!" I said, and ran back out to my position at second base.

We threw the ball around a few more minutes, and then I went up to home plate for some batting practice. I hit a long one out to left field, and then a fast one to the shortstop, who fielded it neatly and whipped it to first. I had the bat ready for another swing when someone said, "Here they are," and I rested the bat on my shoulder and saw the team we were going to play turn up our block and come into the yard. I saw Davey Cantor kick nervously at the wire screen behind home plate, then put his hands into the pockets of his dungarees. His eyes were wide and gloomy behind his owlish glasses.

I watched them come into the yard.

There were fifteen of them, and they were dressed alike in white shirts, dark pants, white sweaters, and small black skullcaps. In the fashion of the very Orthodox, their hair was closely cropped, except for the area near their ears from which mushroomed the untouched hair that tumbled down into the long side curls. Some of them had the beginnings of beards, straggly tufts of hair that stood in isolated clumps on their chins, jawbones, and upper lips. They all wore the traditional undergarment beneath their shirts, and the tzitzit, the long fringes appended to the four corners of the garment, came out above their belts and swung against their pants as they walked. These were the very Orthodox, and they obeyed literally the Biblical commandment *And ye shall look upon it,* which pertains to the fringes.

In contrast, our team had no particular uniform, and each of us wore whatever he wished: dungarees, shorts, pants, polo shirts, sweatshirts, even undershirts. Some of us wore the garment, others did not. None of us wore the fringes outside his trousers. The only element of uniform that we had in common was the small, black skullcap which we, too, wore.

They came up to the first-base side of the wire screen behind home plate and stood there in a silent black-and-white mass, holding bats and balls and gloves in their hands. I looked at them. They did not seem to me to present any picture of ferocity. I saw Davey Cantor kick again at the wire screen, then walk away from them to the third-base line, his hands moving nervously against his dungarees.

Mr. Galanter smiled and started toward them, moving quickly on the balls of his feet, his skullcap perched precariously on the top of his balding head.

A man disentangled himself from the black-and-white mass of players and took a step forward. He looked to be in his late twenties and wore a black suit, black shoes, and a black hat. He had a black beard, and he carried a book under one arm. He was obviously a rabbi, and I marveled that the yeshiva had placed a rabbi instead of an athletic coach over its team.

Mr. Galanter came up to him and offered his hand.

"We are ready to play," the rabbi said in Yiddish, shaking Mr. Galanter's hand with obvious uninterest.

"Fine," Mr. Galanter said in English, smiling.

The rabbi looked out at the field. "You played already?" he asked.

"How's that?" Mr. Galanter said.

"You had practice?"

"Well, sure—"

"We want to practice."

"How's that?" Mr. Galanter said again, looking surprised.

"You practiced, now we practice."

"You didn't practice in your own yard?"

"We practiced."

"Well, then—"

"But we have never played in your yard before. We want a few minutes."

"Well, now," Mr. Galanter said, "there isn't much time. The rules are each team practices in its own yard."

"We want five minutes," the rabbi insisted.

"Well—" Mr. Galanter said. He was no longer smiling. He always liked to go right into a game when we played in our own yard. It kept us from cooling off, he said.

"Five minutes," the rabbi said. "Tell your people to leave the field."

"How's that?" Mr. Galanter said.

"We cannot practice with your people on the field. Tell them to leave the field."

"Well, now," Mr. Galanter said, then stopped. He thought for a long moment. The black-and-white mass of players behind the rabbi stood very still, waiting. I saw Davey Cantor kick at the asphalt floor of the yard. "Well, all right. Five minutes. Just five minutes, now."

"Tell your people to leave the field," the rabbi said.

Mr. Galanter stared gloomily out at the field, looking a little deflated. "Everybody off!" he shouted, not very loudly. "They want a five-minute warm-up. Hustle, hustle. Keep those arms going. Keep it hot. Toss some balls around behind home. Let's go!"

The players scrambled off the field.

The black-and-white mass near the wire screen remained intact. The young rabbi turned and faced his team.

He talked in Yiddish. "We have the field for five minutes," he said. "Remember why and for whom we play."

Then he stepped aside, and the black-and-white mass dissolved into fifteen individual players who came quickly onto the field. One of them, a tall boy with sand-colored hair and long arms and legs that seemed all bones and angles, stood at home plate and commenced hitting balls out to the players. He hit a few easy grounders and pop-ups, and the fielders shouted encouragement to one another in Yiddish. They handled themselves awkwardly, dropping easy grounders, throwing wild, fumbling fly balls. I looked over at the young rabbi. He had sat down on the bench near the wire screen and was reading his book.

Behind the wire screen was a wide area, and Mr. Galanter kept us busy there throwing balls around.

"Keep those balls going!" He fist-thumped at us. "No one sits out this fire fight! Never underestimate the enemy!"

But there was a broad smile on his face. Now that he was actually seeing the other team, he seemed not at all concerned about the outcome of the game. In the interim between throwing a ball and having it thrown back to me, I told myself that I liked Mr. Galanter, and I wondered about his constant use of war expressions and why he wasn't in the army.

Davey Cantor came past me, chasing a ball that had gone between his legs.

"Some murderers." I grinned at him.

"You'll see," he said as he bent to retrieve the ball.

"Sure," I said.

"Especially the one batting. You'll see."

The ball was coming back to me, and I caught it neatly and flipped it back.

"Who's the one batting?" I asked.

"Danny Saunders."

"Pardon my ignorance, but who is Danny Saunders?"

"Reb Saunders's son," Davey Cantor said, blinking his eyes.

"I'm impressed."

"You'll see," Davey Cantor said, and ran off with his ball.

My father, who had no love at all for Hasidic communities and their rabbinic overlords, had told me about Rabbi Isaac Saunders and the zealousness with which he ruled his people and settled questions of Jewish law.

I saw Mr. Galanter look at his wristwatch, then stare out at the team on the field. The five minutes were apparently over, but the players were making no move to abandon the field. Danny Saunders was now at first base, and I noticed that his long arms and legs were being used to good advantage, for by stretching and jumping he was able to catch most of the wild throws that came his way.

Mr. Galanter went over to the young rabbi, who was still sitting on the bench and reading.

"It's five minutes," he said.

The rabbi looked up from his book. "Ah?" he said.

"The five minutes are up," Mr. Galanter said.

The rabbi stared out at the field. "Enough!" he shouted in Yiddish. "It's time to play!" Then he looked down at the book and resumed his reading.

The players threw the ball around for another minute or two, and then slowly came off the field. Danny Saunders walked past me, still wearing his first baseman's glove. He was a good deal taller than I, and in contrast to my somewhat ordinary but decently proportioned features and dark hair, his face seemed to have been cut from stone. His chin, jaw, and cheekbones were made up of jutting hard lines, his nose was straight and pointed, his lips full, rising to a steep angle from the center point beneath his nose and then slanting off to form a too-wide mouth. His eyes were deep blue, and the sparse tufts of hair on his chin, jawbones, and upper lip, the close-cropped hair on his head, and the flow of side curls along his ears were the color of sand. He moved in a loose-jointed, disheveled sort of way, all arms and legs, talking in Yiddish to one of his teammates and ignoring me completely as he passed by. I told myself that I did not like his Hasidic-bred sense of superiority and that it would be a great pleasure to defeat him and his team in this afternoon's game.

The umpire, a gym instructor from a parochial school two blocks away, called the teams together to determine who would bat first. I saw him throw a bat into the air. It was caught and almost dropped by a member of the other team.

During the brief hand-over-hand choosing, Davey Cantor came over and stood next to me.

"What do you think?" he asked.

"They're a snooty bunch," I told him.

"What do you think about their playing?"

"They're lousy."

"They're murderers."

"Oh, come on, Davey."

"You'll see," Davey Cantor said, looking at me gloomily.

"I just did see."

"You didn't see anything."

"Sure," I said. "Elijah the prophet comes in to pitch for them in tight spots."

"I'm not being funny," he said, looking hurt.

"Some murderers," I told him, and laughed.

The teams began to disperse. We had lost the choosing, and they had decided to bat first. We scampered onto the field. I took up my position at second base. I saw the young rabbi sitting on the bench near the wire fence and reading. We threw a ball around for a minute. Mr. Galanter stood alongside third base, shouting his words of encouragement at us. It was warm, and I was sweating a little and feeling very good. Then the umpire, who had taken up his position behind the pitcher, called for the ball and someone tossed it to him. He handed it to the pitcher and shouted, "Here we go! Play ball!" We settled into our positions.

Mr. Galanter shouted, "Goldberg, move in!" and Sidney Goldberg, our shortstop, took two steps forward and moved a little closer to third base. "Okay, fine," Mr. Galanter said. "Keep that infield solid!"

A short, thin boy came up to the plate and stood there with his feet together, holding the bat awkwardly over his head. He wore steel-rimmed glasses that gave his face a pinched, old man's look. He swung wildly at the first pitch, and the force of the swing spun him completely around. His earlocks lifted off the sides of his head and followed him around in an almost horizontal circle. Then he steadied himself and resumed his position near the plate, short, thin, his feet together, holding his bat over his head in an awkward grip.

The umpire called the strike in a loud, clear voice, and I saw Sidney Goldberg look over at me and grin broadly.

"If he studies Talmud like that, he's dead," Sidney Goldberg said.

I grinned back at him.

"Keep that infield solid!" Mr. Galanter shouted from third base. "Malter, a little to your left! Good!"

The next pitch was too high, and the boy chopped at it, lost his bat and fell forward on his hands. Sidney Goldberg and I looked at each other again. Sidney was in my class. We were similar in build, thin and lithe, with somewhat spindly arms and legs. He was not a very good student, but he was an excellent shortstop. We lived on the same block and were good but not close friends. He was dressed in an undershirt and dungarees and was not wearing the four-cornered garment. I had on a light blue shirt and dark blue work pants, and I wore the four-cornered garment under the shirt.

The short, thin boy was back at the plate, standing with his feet together and holding the bat in his awkward grip. He let the next pitch go by, and the umpire called it a strike. I saw the young rabbi look up a moment from his book, then resume reading.

"Two more just like that!" I shouted encouragingly to the pitcher. "Two more, Schwartzie!" And I thought to myself, Some murderers.

I saw Danny Saunders go over to the boy who had just struck out and talk to him. The boy looked down and seemed to shrivel with hurt. He hung his head and walked away behind the wire screen. Another short, thin boy took his place at the plate. I looked around for Davey Cantor but could not see him.

The boy at bat swung wildly at the first two pitches and missed them both. He swung again at the third pitch, and I heard the loud *thwack* of the bat as it connected with the ball, and saw the ball move in a swift, straight line toward Sidney Goldberg, who caught it, bobbled it for a moment, and finally got it into his glove. He tossed the ball to me, and we threw it around. I saw him take off his glove and shake his left hand.

"That hurt," he said, grinning at me.

"Good catch," I told him.

"That hurt like hell," he said, and put his glove back on his hand.

The batter who stood now at the plate was broad-shouldered and built like a bear. He swung at the first pitch, missed, then swung again at the second pitch and sent the ball in a straight line over the head of the third baseman into left field. I scrambled to second, stood on the base and shouted for the ball. I saw the left fielder pick it up on the second bounce and relay it to me. It was coming in a little high, and I had my glove raised for it. I felt more than saw the batter charging toward second, and as I was getting my glove on the ball he smashed into me like a truck. The ball went over my head, and I fell forward heavily onto the asphalt floor of the yard, and he passed me, going toward third, his fringes flying out behind him, holding his skullcap to his head with his right hand so it would not fall off. Abe Goodstein, our first baseman, retrieved the ball and whipped it home, and the batter stood at third, a wide grin on his face.

The yeshiva team exploded into wild cheers and shouted loud words of congratulations in Yiddish to the batter.

Sidney Goldberg helped me get to my feet.

"That momzer!" he said. "You weren't in his way!"

"Wow!" I said, taking a few deep breaths. I had scraped the palm of my right hand.

"What a momzer!" Sidney Goldberg said.

I saw Mr. Galanter come storming onto the field to talk to the umpire. "What kind of play was that?" he asked heatedly. "How are you going to rule that?"

"Safe at third," the umpire said. "Your boy was in the way."

Mr. Galanter's mouth fell open. "How's that again?"

"Safe at third," the umpire repeated.

Mr. Galanter looked ready to argue, thought better of it, then stared over at me. "Are you all right, Malter?"

"I'm okay," I said, taking another deep breath.

Mr. Galanter walked angrily off the field.

"Play ball!" the umpire shouted.

The yeshiva team quieted down. I saw that the young rabbi was now looking up from his book and smiling faintly.

A tall, thin player came up to the plate, set his feet in correct position, swung his bat a few times, then crouched into a waiting stance. I saw it was Danny Saunders. I opened and closed my right hand, which was still sore from the fall.

"Move back! Move back!" Mr. Galanter was shouting from alongside third base, and I took two steps back.

I crouched, waiting.

The first pitch was wild, and the yeshiva team burst into loud laughter. The young rabbi was sitting on the bench, watching Danny Saunders intently.

"Take it easy, Schwartzie!" I shouted encouragingly to the pitcher. "There's only one more to go!"

The next pitch was about a foot over Danny Saunders's head, and the yeshiva team howled with laughter. Sidney Goldberg and I looked at each other. I saw Mr. Galanter standing very still alongside third, staring at the pitcher. The rabbi was still watching Danny Saunders.

The next pitch left Schwartzie's hand in a long, slow line, and before it was halfway to the plate I knew Danny Saunders would try for it. I knew it from the way his left foot came forward and the bat snapped back and his long, thin body began its swift pivot. I tensed, waiting for the sound of the bat against the ball, and when it came it sounded like a gunshot. For a wild fraction of a second I lost sight of the ball. Then I saw Schwartzie dive to the ground, and there was the ball coming through the air where his head had been, and I tried for it but it was moving too fast, and I barely had my glove raised before it was in center field. It was caught on a bounce and thrown to Sidney Goldberg, but by that time Danny Saunders was standing solidly on my base and the yeshiva team was screaming with joy.

Mr. Galanter called for time and walked over to talk to Schwartzie. Sidney Goldberg nodded to me, and the two of us went over to them.

"That ball could've killed me!" Schwartzie was saying. He was of medium size, with a long face and a bad case of acne. He wiped sweat from his face. "My God, did you see that ball?"

"I saw it," Mr. Galanter said grimly.

"That was too fast to stop, Mr. Galanter," I said in Schwartzie's defense.

"I heard about that Danny Saunders," Sidney Goldberg said. "He always hits to the pitcher."

"You could've told me," Schwartzie lamented. "I could've been ready."

"I only *heard* about it," Sidney Goldberg said. "You always believe everything you hear?"

"God, that ball could've killed me!" Schwartzie said again.

"You want to go on pitching?" Mr. Galanter said. A thin sheen of sweat covered his forehead, and he looked very grim.

"Sure, Mr. Galanter," Schwartzie said. "I'm okay."

"You're sure?"

"Sure I'm sure."

"No heroes in this war, now," Mr. Galanter said. "I want live soldiers, not dead heroes."

"I'm no hero," Schwartzie muttered lamely. "I can still get it over, Mr. Galanter. God, it's only the first inning."

"Okay, soldier," Mr. Galanter said, not very enthusiastically. "Just keep our side of this war fighting."

"I'm trying my best, Mr. Galanter," Schwartzie said.

Mr. Galanter nodded, still looking grim, and started off the field. I saw him take a handkerchief out of his pocket and wipe his forehead.

"Jesus Christ!" Schwartzie said, now that Mr. Galanter was gone. "That bastard aimed right for my head!"

"Oh, come on, Schwartzie," I said. "What is he, Babe Ruth?"

"You heard what Sidney said."

"Stop giving it to them on a silver platter and they won't hit it like that."

"Who's giving it to them on a silver platter?" Schwartzie lamented. "That was a great pitch."

"Sure," I said.

The umpire came over to us. "You boys planning to chat here all afternoon?" he asked. He was a squat man in his late forties, and he looked impatient.

"No, sir," I said very politely, and Sidney and I ran back to our places.

Danny Saunders was standing on my base. His white shirt was pasted to his arms and back with sweat.

"That was a nice shot," I offered.

He looked at me curiously and said nothing.

"You always hit it like that to the pitcher?" I asked.

He smiled faintly. "You're Reuven Malter," he said in perfect English. He had a low, nasal voice.

"That's right," I said, wondering where he had heard my name.

"Your father is David Malter, the one who writes articles on the Talmud?"

"Yes."

"I told my team we're going to kill you apikorsim this afternoon." He said it flatly, without a trace of expression in his voice.

I stared at him and hoped the sudden tight coldness I felt wasn't showing on my face. "Sure," I said. "Rub your tzitzit for good luck."

I walked away from him and took up my position near the base. I looked toward the wire screen and saw Davey Cantor standing there, staring out at the field, his hands in his pockets. I crouched down quickly, because Schwartzie was going into his pitch.

The batter swung wildly at the first two pitches and missed each time. The next one was low, and he let it go by, then hit a grounder to the first baseman, who dropped it, flailed about for it wildly, and recovered it in time to see Danny Saunders cross the plate. The first baseman stood there for a moment, drenched in shame, then tossed the ball to Schwartzie. I saw Mr. Galanter standing near third base, wiping his forehead. The yeshiva team had gone wild again, and they were all trying to get to Danny Saunders and shake his hand. I saw the rabbi smile broadly, then look down at his book and resume reading.

Sidney Goldberg came over to me. "What did Saunders tell you?" he asked.

"He said they were going to kill us apikorsim this afternoon."

He stared at me. "Those are nice people, those yeshiva people," he said, and walked slowly back to his position.

The next batter hit a long fly ball to right field. It was caught on the run.

"Hooray for us," Sidney Goldberg said grimly as we headed off the field. "Any longer and they'd be asking us to join them for the Mincha Service."

"Not us," I said. "We're not holy enough."

"Where did they learn to hit like that?"

"Who knows?" I said.

We were standing near the wire screen, forming a tight circle around Mr. Galanter.

"Only two runs," Mr. Galanter said, smashing his right fist into his left hand. "And they hit us with all they had. Now we give them *our* heavy artillery. Now *we* barrage *them*!" I saw that he looked relieved but that he was still sweating. His skullcap seemed pasted to his head with sweat. "Okay!" he said. "Fire away!"

The circle broke up, and Sidney Goldberg walked to the plate, carrying a bat. I saw the rabbi was still sitting on the bench, reading. I started to walk around behind him to see what book it was, when Davey Cantor came over, his hands in his pockets, his eyes still gloomy.

"Well?" he asked.

"Well, what?" I said.

"I told you they could hit."

"So you told me. So what?" I was in no mood for his feelings of doom, and I let my voice show it.

He sensed my annoyance. "I wasn't bragging or anything," he said, looking hurt. "I just wanted to know what you thought."

"They can hit," I said.

"They're murderers," he said.

I watched Sidney Goldberg let a strike go by and said nothing.

"How's your hand?" Davey Cantor asked.

"I scraped it."

"He ran into you real hard."

"Who is he?"

"Dov Shlomowitz," Davey Cantor said. "Like his name, that's what he is," he added in Hebrew. "Dov" is the Hebrew word for bear.

"Was I blocking him?"

Davey Cantor shrugged. "You were and you weren't. The ump could've called it either way."

"He felt like a truck," I said, watching Sidney Goldberg step back from a close pitch.

"You should see his father. He's one of Reb Saunders's shamashim. Some bodyguard he makes."

"Reb Saunders has bodyguards?"

"Sure he has bodyguards," Davey Cantor said. "They protect him from his own popularity. Where've you been living all these years?"

"I don't have anything to do with them."

"You're not missing a thing, Reuven."

"How do you know so much about Reb Saunders?"

"My father gives him contributions."

"Well, good for your father," I said.

"He doesn't pray there or anything. He just gives him contributions."

"You're on the wrong team."

"No I'm not, Reuven. Don't be like that." He was looking very hurt. "My father isn't a Hasid or anything. He just gives them some money a couple times a year."

"I was only kidding, Davey." I grinned at him. "Don't be so serious about everything."

I saw his face break into a happy smile, and just then Sidney Goldberg hit a fast, low grounder and raced off to first. The ball went right through the legs of the shortstop and into center field.

"Hold it at first!" Mr. Galanter screamed at him, and Sidney stopped at first and stood on the base.

The ball had been tossed quickly to second base. The second baseman looked over toward first, then threw the ball to the pitcher. The rabbi glanced up from the book for a moment, then went back to his reading.

"Malter, coach him at first!" Mr. Galanter shouted, and I ran up the base line.

"They can hit, but they can't field," Sidney Goldberg said, grinning at me as I came to a stop alongside the base.

"Davey Cantor says they're murderers," I said.

"Old gloom-and-doom Davey," Sidney Goldberg said, grinning.

Danny Saunders was standing away from the base, making a point of ignoring us both.

The next batter hit a high fly to the second baseman, who caught it, dropped it, retrieved it, and made a wild attempt at tagging Sidney Goldberg as he raced past him to second.

"Safe all around!" the umpire called, and our team burst out with shouts of joy. Mr. Galanter was smiling. The rabbi continued reading, and I saw that he was now slowly moving the upper part of his body back and forth.

"Keep your eyes open, Sidney!" I shouted from alongside first base. I saw Danny Saunders look at me, then look away. Some murderers, I thought. Shleppers is more like it.

"If it's on the ground, run like hell," I said to the batter who had just come onto first base, and he nodded at me. He was our third baseman, and he was about my size.

"If they keep fielding like that we'll be here till tomorrow," he said, and I grinned at him.

I saw Mr. Galanter talking to the next batter, who was nodding his head vigorously. He stepped to the plate, hit a hard grounder to the pitcher, who fumbled it for a moment and then threw it to first. I saw Danny Saunders stretch for it and stop it.

"Out!" the umpire called. "Safe on second and third!"

As I ran up to the plate to bat, I almost laughed aloud at the pitcher's stupidity. He had thrown it to first rather than third, and now we had Sidney Goldberg on third, and a man on second. I hit a grounder to the shortstop and instead of throwing it to second he threw it to first, wildly, and again Danny Saunders stretched and stopped the ball. But I beat the throw and heard the umpire call out, "Safe all around! One in!" And everyone on our team was patting Sidney Goldberg on the back. Mr. Galanter smiled broadly.

"Hello again," I said to Danny Saunders, who was standing near me, guarding his base. "Been rubbing your tzitzit lately?"

He looked at me, then looked slowly away, his face expressionless.

Schwartzie was at the plate, swinging his bat.

"Keep your eyes open!" I shouted to the runner on third. He looked too eager to head for home. "It's only one out!"

He waved a hand at me.

Schwartzie took two balls and a strike, then I saw him begin to pivot on the fourth pitch. The runner on third started for home. He was almost halfway down the base line when the bat sent the ball in a hard line drive straight to the third baseman, the short, thin boy with the spectacles and the old man's face, who had stood hugging the base and who now caught the ball more with his stomach than with his glove, managed somehow to hold on to it, and stood there, looking bewildered and astonished.

I returned to first and saw our player who had been on third and who was now halfway to home plate turn sharply and start a panicky race back.

"Step on the base!" Danny Saunders screamed in Yiddish across the field, and more out of obedience than awareness the third baseman put a foot on the base.

The yeshiva team howled its happiness and raced off the field. Danny

Saunders looked at me, started to say something, stopped, then walked quickly away.

I saw Mr. Galanter going back up the third-base line, his face grim. The rabbi was looking up from his book and smiling.

I took up my position near second base, and Sidney Goldberg came over to me.

"Why'd he have to take off like that?" he asked.

I glared over at our third baseman, who was standing near Mr. Galanter and looking very dejected.

"He was in a hurry to win the war," I said bitterly.

"What a jerk," Sidney Goldberg said.

"Goldberg, get over to your place!" Mr. Galanter called out. There was an angry edge to his voice. "Let's keep that infield solid!"

Sidney Goldberg went quickly to his position. I stood still and waited.

It was hot, and I was sweating beneath my clothes. I felt the earpieces of my glasses cutting into the skin over my ears, and I took the glasses off for a moment and ran a finger over the pinched ridges of skin, then put them back on quickly because Schwartzie was going into a windup. I crouched down, waiting, remembering Danny Saunders's promise to his team that they would kill us apikorsim. The word had meant, originally, a Jew educated in Judaism who denied basic tenets of his faith, like the existence of God, the revelation, the resurrection of the dead. To people like Reb Saunders, it also meant any educated Jew who might be reading, say, Darwin, and who was not wearing side curls and fringes outside his trousers. I was an apikoros to Danny Saunders, despite my belief in God and Torah, because I did not have side curls and was attending a parochial school where too many English subjects were offered and where Jewish subjects were taught in Hebrew instead of Yiddish, both unheard-of sins, the former because it took time away from the study of Torah, the latter because Hebrew was the Holy Tongue and to use it in ordinary classroom discourse was a desecration of God's Name. I had never really had any personal contact with this kind of Jew before. My father had told me he didn't mind their beliefs. What annoyed him was their fanatic sense of righteousness, their absolute certainty that they and they alone had God's ear, and every other Jew was wrong, totally wrong, a sinner, a hypocrite, an apikoros, and doomed, therefore, to burn in hell. I found myself wondering again how they had learned to hit a ball like that if time for the study of Torah was so precious to them and why they had sent a rabbi along to waste his time sitting on a bench during a ball game.

Standing on the field and watching the boy at the plate swing at a high ball and miss, I felt myself suddenly very angry, and it was at that point that for me the game stopped being merely a game and became a war. The fun and excitement was out of it now. Somehow the yeshiva team had translated this afternoon's baseball game into a conflict between what they regarded as their righteousness and our sinfulness. I found myself growing more and more angry, and I felt the anger begin to focus itself upon Danny Saunders, and suddenly it was not at all difficult for me to hate him.

Schwartzie let five of their men come up to the plate that half inning and let one of those five score. Sometime during that half inning, one of the members of the yeshiva team had shouted at us in Yiddish, "Burn in hell, you apikorsim!" and by the time that half inning was over and we were standing around Mr. Galanter near the wire screen, all of us knew that this was not just another ball game.

Mr. Galanter was sweating heavily, and his face was grim. All he said was, "We fight it careful from now on. No more mistakes." He said it very quietly, and we were all quiet, too, as the batter stepped up to the plate.

We proceeded to play a slow, careful game, bunting whenever we had to, sacrificing to move runners forward, obeying Mr. Galanter's instructions. I noticed that no matter where the runners were on the bases, the yeshiva team always threw to Danny Saunders, and I realized that they did this because he was the only infielder who could be relied upon to stop their wild throws. Sometime during the inning, I walked over behind the rabbi and looked over his shoulder at the book he was reading. I saw the words were Yiddish. I walked back to the wire screen. Davey Cantor came over and stood next to me, but he remained silent.

We scored only one run that inning, and we walked onto the field for the first half of the third inning with a sense of doom.

Dov Shlomowitz came up to the plate. He stood there like a bear, the bat looking like a matchstick in his beefy hands. Schwartzie pitched, and he sliced one neatly over the head of the third baseman for a single. The yeshiva team howled, and again one of them called out to us in Yiddish, "Burn, you apikorsim!" and Sidney Goldberg and I looked at each other without saying a word.

Mr. Galanter was standing alongside third base, wiping his forehead. The rabbi was sitting quietly, reading his book.

I took off my glasses and rubbed the tops of my ears. I felt a sudden momentary sense of unreality, as if the play yard, with its black asphalt floor and its white base lines, were my entire world now, as if all the previous years of my life had led me somehow to this one ball game, and all the future years of my life would depend upon its outcome. I stood there for a moment, holding the glasses in my hand and feeling frightened. Then I took a deep breath, and the feeling passed. It's only a ball game, I told myself. What's a ball game?

Mr. Galanter was shouting at us to move back. I was standing a few feet to the left of second, and I took two steps back. I saw Danny Saunders walk up to the plate, swinging a bat. The yeshiva team was shouting at him in Yiddish to kill us apikorsim.

Schwartzie turned around to check the field. He looked nervous and was taking his time. Sidney Goldberg was standing up straight, waiting. We looked at each other, then looked away. Mr. Galanter stood very still alongside third base, looking at Schwartzie.

The first pitch was low, and Danny Saunders ignored it. The second one started to come in shoulder-high, and before it was two thirds of the way to the plate, I was already standing on second base. My glove was going up as the bat cracked against the ball, and I saw the ball move in a straight line directly over Schwartzie's head, high over his head, moving so fast he hadn't even had time to regain his balance from the pitch before it went past him. I saw Dov Shlomowitz heading toward me and Danny Saunders racing to first, and I heard the yeshiva team shouting and Sidney Goldberg screaming, and I jumped, pushing myself upward off the ground with all the strength I had in my legs and stretching my glove hand till I thought it would pull out of my shoulder. The ball hit the pocket of my glove with an impact that numbed my hand and went through me like an electric shock, and I felt the force pull me backward and throw me off balance, and I came down hard on my left hip and elbow. I saw Dov Shlomowitz whirl and start back to first, and I pushed myself up into a sitting position and threw the ball awkwardly to Sidney Goldberg, who caught it and whipped it to first. I heard the umpire scream "Out!" and Sidney Goldberg ran over to help me to my feet, a look of disbelief and ecstatic joy on his face. Mr. Galanter shouted "Time!" and came racing onto the field. Schwartzie was standing in his pitcher's position with his mouth open. Danny Saunders stood on the base line a few feet from first, where he had stopped after I had caught the ball, staring out at me, his face frozen to stone. The rabbi was staring at me, too, and the yeshiva team was deathly silent.

"That was a great catch, Reuven!" Sidney Goldberg said, thumping my back. "That was sensational!"

I saw the rest of our team had suddenly come back to life and was throwing the ball around and talking up the game.

Mr. Galanter came over. "You all right, Malter?" he asked. "Let me see that elbow."

I showed him the elbow. I had scraped it, but the skin had not been broken.

"That was a good play," Mr. Galanter said, beaming at me. I saw his face was still covered with sweat, but he was smiling broadly now.

"Thanks, Mr. Galanter."

"How's the hand?"

"It hurts a little."

"Let me see it."

I took off the glove, and Mr. Galanter poked and bent the wrist and fingers of the hand.

"Does that hurt?" he asked.

"No," I lied.

"You want to go on playing?"

"Sure, Mr. Galanter."

"Okay," he said, smiling at me and patting my back. "We'll put you in for a Purple Heart on that one, Malter."

I grinned at him.

"Okay," Mr. Galanter said. "Let's keep this infield solid!"

He walked away, smiling.

"I can't get over that catch," Sidney Goldberg said.

"You threw it real good to first," I told him.

"Yeah," he said. "While you were sitting on your tail."

We grinned at each other, and went to our positions.

Two more of the yeshiva team got to bat that inning. The first one hit a single, and the second one sent a high fly to short, which Sidney Goldberg caught without having to move a step. We scored two runs that inning and one run the next, and by the top half of the fifth inning we were leading five to three. Four of their men had stood up to bat during the top half of the fourth inning, and they had got only a single on an error to first. When we took to the field in the top half of the fifth inning, Mr. Galanter was walking back and forth alongside third on the balls of his feet, sweating, smiling, grinning, wiping his head nervously; the rabbi was no longer reading; the yeshiva team was silent as death. Davey Cantor was playing second, and I stood in the pitcher's position. Schwartzie had pleaded exhaustion, and since this was the final inning—our parochial school schedules only permitted us time for five-inning games— and the yeshiva team's last chance at bat, Mr. Galanter was taking no chances and told me to pitch. Davey Cantor was a poor fielder, but Mr. Galanter was counting on my pitching to finish off the game. My left hand was still sore from the catch, and the wrist hurt whenever I caught a ball, but the right hand was fine, and the pitches went in fast and dropped into the curve just when I wanted them to. Dov Shlomowitz stood at the plate, swung three times at what looked to him to be perfect pitches, and hit nothing but air. He stood there looking bewildered after the third swing, then slowly walked away. We threw the ball around the infield, and Danny Saunders came up to the plate.

The members of the yeshiva team stood near the wire fence, watching Danny Saunders. They were very quiet. The rabbi was sitting on the bench, his book closed. Mr. Galanter was shouting at everyone to move back. Danny Saunders swung his bat a few times, then fixed himself into position and looked out at me.

Here's a present from an apikoros, I thought, and let go the ball. It went in fast and straight, and I saw Danny Saunders's left foot move out and his bat go up and his body begin to pivot. He swung just as the ball slid into its curve, and the bat cut savagely through empty air, twisting him around and sending him off balance. His black skullcap fell off his head, and he regained his balance and bent quickly to retrieve it. He stood there for a moment, very still, staring out at me. Then he resumed his position at the plate. The ball came back to me from the catcher, and my wrist hurt as I caught it.

The yeshiva team was very quiet, and the rabbi had begun to chew his lip.

I lost control of the next pitch, and it was wide. On the third pitch, I went into a long, elaborate windup and sent him a slow, curving blooper, the kind a batter always wants to hit and always misses. He ignored it completely, and the umpire called it a ball.

I felt my left wrist begin to throb as I caught the throw from the catcher. I was hot and sweaty, and the earpieces of my glasses were cutting deeply into the flesh above my ears as a result of the head movements that went with my pitching.

Danny Saunders stood very still at the plate, waiting.

Okay, I thought, hating him bitterly. Here's another present.

The ball went to the plate fast and straight, and dropped just below his swing. He checked himself with difficulty so as not to spin around, but he went off his balance again and took two or three staggering steps forward before he was able to stand up straight.

The catcher threw the ball back, and I winced at the pain in my wrist. I took the ball out of the glove, held it in my right hand, and turned around for a moment to look out at the field and let the pain in my wrist subside. When I turned back I saw that Danny Saunders hadn't moved. He was holding his bat in his left hand, standing very still and staring at me. His eyes were dark, and his lips were parted in a crazy, idiot grin. I heard the umpire yell "Play ball!" but Danny Saunders stood there, staring at me and grinning. I turned and looked out at the field again, and when I turned back he was still standing there, staring at me and grinning. I could see his teeth between his parted lips. I took a deep breath and felt myself wet with sweat. I wiped my right hand on my pants and saw Danny Saunders step slowly to the plate and set his legs in position. He was no longer grinning. He stood looking at me over his left shoulder, waiting.

I wanted to finish it quickly because of the pain in my wrist, and I sent in another fast ball. I watched it head straight for the plate. I saw him go into a sudden crouch, and in the fraction of a second before he hit the ball I realized that he had anticipated the curve and was deliberately swinging low. I was still a little off balance from the pitch, but I managed to bring my glove hand up in front of my face just as he hit the ball. I saw it coming at me, and there was nothing I could do. It hit the finger section of my glove, deflected off, smashed into the upper rim of the left lens of my glasses, glanced off my forehead, and knocked me down. I scrambled around for it wildly, but by the time I got my hand on it Danny Saunders was standing safely on first.

I heard Mr. Galanter call time, and everyone on the field came racing over to me. My glasses lay shattered on the asphalt floor, and I felt a sharp pain in my left eye when I blinked. My wrist throbbed, and I could feel the bump coming up on my forehead. I looked over at first, but without my glasses Danny Saunders was only a blur. I imagined I could still see him grinning.

I saw Mr. Galanter put his face next to mine. It was sweaty and full of concern. I wondered what all the fuss was about. I had only lost a pair of glasses, and we had at least two more good pitchers on the team.

"Are you all right, boy?" Mr. Galanter was saying. He looked at my face and forehead. "Somebody wet a handkerchief with cold water!" he shouted. I wondered why he was shouting. His voice hurt my head and rang in my ears. I saw Davey Cantor run off, looking frightened. I heard Sidney Goldberg say something, but I couldn't make out his words. Mr. Galanter put his arm around my shoulders and walked me off the field. He sat me down on the bench next to the rabbi. Without my glasses everything more than about ten feet away from me was blurred. I blinked and wondered about the pain in my left eye. I heard voices and shouts, and then Mr. Galanter was putting a wet handkerchief on my head.

"You feel dizzy, boy?" he said.

I shook my head.

"You're sure now?"

"I'm all right," I said, and wondered why my voice sounded husky and why talking hurt my head.

"You sit quiet now," Mr. Galanter said. "You begin to feel dizzy, you let me know right away."

"Yes, sir," I said.

He went away. I sat on the bench next to the rabbi, who looked at me once, then looked away. I heard shouts in Yiddish. The pain in my left eye was so intense I could feel it in the base of my spine. I sat on the bench a long time, long enough to see us lose the game by a score of eight to seven, long enough to hear the yeshiva team shout with joy, long enough to begin to cry at the pain in my left eye, long enough for Mr. Galanter to come over to me at the end of the game, take one look at my face and go running out of the yard to call a cab.

TWO

WE RODE TO the Brooklyn Memorial Hospital, which was a few blocks away, and Mr. Galanter paid the cab fare. He helped me out, put his arm around my shoulders, and walked me into the emergency ward.

"Keep that handkerchief over the eye," he said. "And try not to blink." He was very nervous, and his face was covered with sweat. He had taken off his skullcap, and I could see him sweating beneath the hairs on his balding head.

"Yes, sir," I said. I was frightened and was beginning to feel dizzy and nauseated. The pain in my left eye was fierce. I could feel it all along the left side of my body and in my groin.

The nurse at the desk wanted to know what was wrong.

"He was hit in the eye by a baseball," Mr. Galanter said.

She asked us to sit down and pressed a button on her desk. We sat down next to a middle-aged man with a blood-soaked bandage around a finger on his right hand. He sat there in obvious pain, resting his finger on his lap and nervously smoking a cigarette despite the sign on the wall that said NO SMOKING.

He looked at us. "Ball game?" he asked.

Mr. Galanter nodded. I kept my head straight, because it didn't hurt so much when I didn't move it.

The man held up his finger. "Car door," he said. "My kid slammed it on me." He grimaced and put his hand back on his lap.

A nurse came out of a door at the far end of the room and nodded to the man. He stood up. "Take care," he said, and went out.

"How're you doing?" Mr. Galanter asked me.

"My eye hurts," I told him.

"How's the head?"

"I feel dizzy."

"Are you nauseous?"

"A little."

"You'll be okay," Mr. Galanter said, trying to sound encouraging. "You get a Purple Heart for today's work, trooper." But his voice was tense, and he looked frightened.

"I'm sorry about all this, Mr. Galanter," I said.

"What are you sorry about, boy?" he said. "You played a great game."

"I'm sorry to be putting you to so much trouble."

"What trouble? Don't be silly. I'm glad to help one of my troopers."

"I'm also sorry we lost."

"So we lost. So what? There's next year, isn't there?"

"Yes, sir."

"Don't talk so much. Just take it easy."

"They're a tough team," I said.

"That Saunders boy," Mr. Galanter said, "the one who hit you. You know anything about him?"

"No, sir."

"I never saw a boy hit a ball like that."

"Mr. Galanter?"

"Yes?"

"My eye really hurts."

"We'll be going in in a minute, boy. Hold on. Would your father be home now?"

"Yes, sir."

"What's your phone number?"

I gave it to him.

A nurse came out the door and nodded to us. Mr. Galanter helped me get to my feet. We walked through a corridor and followed the nurse into an examination room. It had white walls, a white chair, a white, glass-enclosed cabinet, and a tall metal table with a white sheet over the mattress. Mr. Galanter helped me onto the table, and I lay there and stared up at the white ceiling out of my right eye.

"The doctor will be here in a moment," the nurse said, and went out.

"Feel any better?" Mr. Galanter asked me.

"No," I said.

A young doctor came in. He had on a white gown and was wearing a stethoscope around his neck. He looked at us and smiled pleasantly.

"Stopped a ball with your eye, I hear," he said, smiling at me. "Let's have a look at it."

I took off the wet handkerchief, opened my left eye, and gasped with the pain. He looked down at the eye, went to the cabinet, came back, and looked at the eye again through an instrument with a light attached to it. He straightened up and looked at Mr. Galanter.

"Was he wearing glasses?" he asked.

"Yes."

The doctor put the instrument over the eye again. "Can you see the light?" he asked me.

"It's a little blurred," I told him.

"I think I'll go call your father," Mr. Galanter said.

The doctor looked at him. "You're not the boy's father?"

"I'm his gym teacher."

"You had better call his father, then. We'll probably be moving him upstairs."

"You're going to keep him here?"

"For a little while," the doctor said pleasantly. "Just as a precaution."

"Oh," Mr. Galanter said.

"Could you ask my father to bring my other pair of glasses?" I said.

"You won't be able to wear glasses for a while, son," the doctor told me. "We'll have to put a bandage over that eye."

"I'll be right back," Mr. Galanter said, and went out.

"How does your head feel?" the doctor asked me.

"It hurts."

"Does that hurt?" he asked, moving my head from side to side.

I felt myself break out into a cold sweat. "Yes, sir," I said.

"Do you feel nauseous at all?"

"A little," I said. "My left wrist hurts, too."

"Let's take a look at it. Does that hurt?"

"Yes, sir."

"Well, you really put in a full day. Who won?"

"They did."

"Too bad. Now look, you lie as quiet as you can and try not to blink your eyes. I'll be right back."

He went quickly out.

I lay very still on the table. Except for the time I had had my tonsils out I had never been overnight in a hospital. I was frightened, and I wondered what was causing the pain in my eye. Some of the glass from the lens must have scratched it, I thought. I wondered why I hadn't anticipated Danny Saunders's going for the curve, and, thinking of Danny Saunders, I found myself hating him again and all the other side-curled fringe wearers on his yeshiva team. I thought of my father receiving the phone call from Mr. Galanter and rushing over to the hospital, and I had to hold myself back from crying. He was probably sitting at his desk, writing. The call would frighten him terribly. I found I could not keep back my tears, and I blinked a few times and winced with the pain.

The young doctor returned, and this time he had another doctor with him. The second doctor looked a little older and had blond hair. He came over to me without a word and looked at my eye with the instrument.

I thought I saw him go tense. "Is Snydman around?" he said, looking through the instrument.

"I passed him a few minutes ago," the first doctor said.

"He had better have a look at it," the second doctor said. He straightened slowly.

"You lie still now, son," the first doctor said. "A nurse will be in in a minute."

They went out. A nurse came in and smiled at me. "This won't hurt a bit," she said, and put some drops into my left eye. "Now keep it closed and put this bit of cotton over it. That's a good boy." She went out.

Mr. Galanter came back. "He's on his way over," he said.

"How did he sound?"

"I don't know. He said he'd be right over."

"It's not good for him to be worried. He's not too well."

"You'll be okay, boy. This is a fine hospital. How's the eye?"

"It feels better. They put some drops in it."

"Good. Good. I told you this is a fine hospital. Had my appendix out here."

Three men came into the room, the two doctors and a short, middle-aged man with a round face and a graying mustache. He had dark hair and was not wearing a gown.

"This is Dr. Snydman, son," the first doctor said to me. "He wants to have a look at your eye."

Dr. Snydman came over to me and smiled. "I hear you had quite a ball game there, young man. Let's have a look." He had a warm smile, and I liked him immediately. He took the cotton off the eye and looked through the instrument. He looked at the eye a long time. Then he straightened slowly and turned to Mr. Galanter.

"Are you the boy's father?"

"I called his father," Mr. Galanter said. "He's coming over right away."

"We'll need his signature," Dr. Snydman said. He turned to the other two doctors. "I don't think so," he said. "I think it's right on the edge. I'll have to have a better look at it upstairs." He turned to me and smiled warmly.

"An eye is not a thing to stop a ball with, young man."

"He hit it real fast," I said.

"I'm sure he did. We're going to have you brought upstairs so we can have a better look at it."

The three doctors went out.

"What's upstairs?" I asked Mr. Galanter.

"The eye ward, I guess. They have all the big instruments up there."

"What do they want to look at it up there for?"

"I don't know, boy. They didn't tell me anything."

Two hospital orderlies came into the room, wheeling a stretcher table. When they lifted me off the examination table, the pain rammed through my head and sent flashes of black, red, and white colors into my eyes. I cried out.

"Sorry, kid," one of the orderlies said sympathetically. They put me down carefully on the stretcher table and wheeled me out of the room and along the corridor. Mr. Galanter followed.

"Here's the elevator," the other orderly said. They were both young and looked almost alike in their white jackets, white trousers, and white shoes.

The elevator took a long time going up. I lay on the stretcher table, staring up out of my right eye at the fluorescent light on the ceiling. It looked blurred, and I saw it change color, going from white to red to black, then back to white.

"I never saw a light like that," I said.

"Which light is that?" one of the orderlies asked.

"The fluorescent. How do they get it to change colors like that?"

The orderlies looked at each other.

"Just take it easy, kid," one of them said. "Just relax."

"I never saw a light change colors like that," I said.

"Jesus," Mr. Galanter said under his breath.

He was standing alongside the stretcher table with his back to the rear of the elevator. I tried turning my head to look at him, but the pain was too much and I lay still. I had never heard him use that word before, and I wondered what had made him use it now. I lay there, staring up at the light and wondering why Mr. Galanter had used that word, when I saw one of the orderlies glance down at me with a reassuring grin. I remembered Danny Saunders standing in front of the plate and staring at me with that idiot grin on his lips. I closed my right eye and lay still, listening to the noise of the elevator. This is a slow elevator, I thought. But how do they get the light to change colors like that? Then the light was bad all over and everyone crowded around me. Someone was wiping my forehead, and the light was suddenly gone.

I opened my right eye. A nurse in a white uniform said, "Well, now, how are we doing, young man?" and for a long moment I stared up at her and didn't know what was happening. Then I remembered everything—and I couldn't say a word.

I saw the nurse standing over my bed and smiling down at me. She was heavily built and had a round, fleshy face and short, dark hair.

"Well, now, let's see," she said. "Move your head a little, just a little, and tell me how it feels."

I moved my head from side to side on the pillow.

"It feels fine," I said.

"That's good. Are you at all hungry?"

"Yes, ma'am."

"That's very good." She smiled. "You won't need this now."

She pushed aside the curtain that enclosed the bed. I blinked in the sudden sunlight.

"Isn't that better?"

"Yes, ma'am. Thank you. Is my father here?"

"He'll be in shortly. You lie still now and rest. They'll be bringing supper in soon. You're going to be just fine."

She went away.

I lay still for a moment, looking at the sunlight. It was coming in through tall windows in the wall opposite my bed. I could see the windows only through my right eye, and they looked blurred. I moved my head slowly to the left, not taking it off the pillow and moving it carefully so as not to disturb the thick bandage that covered my left eye. There was no pain at all in my head, and I wondered how they had got the pain to leave so quickly. That's pretty good, I thought, remembering what Mr. Galanter had said about this hospital. For a moment I wondered where he was and where my father was; then I forgot them both as I watched the man who was in the bed to my left.

He looked to be in his middle thirties, and he had broad shoulders and a lean face with a square jaw and a dark stubble. His hair was black, combed flat on top of his head and parted in the middle. There were dark curls of hair on the backs of his long hands, and he wore a black patch over his right eye. His nose was flat, and a half-inch scar beneath his lower lip stood out white beneath the dark stubble. He was sitting up in the bed, playing a game of cards with himself and smiling broadly. Some cards were arranged in rows on the blanket, and he was drawing other cards from the deck he held in his hands and adding them to the rows.

He saw me looking at him.

"Hello there," he said, smiling. "How's the old punching bag?"

I didn't understand what he meant.

"The old noggin. The head."

"Oh. It feels good."

"Lucky boy. A clop in the head is a rough business. I went four once and got clopped in the head, and it took me a month to get off my back. Lucky boy." He held a card in his hands and looked down at the rows of cards on the blanket. "Ah, so I cheat a little. So what?" He tucked the card into a row. "I hit the canvas so hard I rattled my toenails. That was some clop." He drew another card and inspected it. "Caught me with that right and clopped me real good. A whole month on my back." He was looking at the rows of cards on the blanket. "Here we go." He smiled broadly and added the card to one of the rows.

I couldn't understand most of what he was talking about, but I didn't want to be disrespectful and turn away, so I kept my head turned toward him. I looked at the black patch on his right eye. It covered the eye as well

as the upper part of his cheekbone, and it was held in place by a black band
that went diagonally under his right ear, around his head, and across his
forehead. After a few minutes of looking at him, I realized he had completely forgotten about me, and I turned my head slowly away from him
and to the right.

I saw a boy of about ten or eleven. He was lying in the bed with his head
on the pillow, his palms flat under his head and his elbows jutting upward.
He had light blond hair and a fine face, a beautiful face. He lay there with
his eyes open, staring up at the ceiling and not noticing me looking at him.
Once or twice I saw his eyes blink. I turned my head away.

The people beyond the beds immediately to my right and left were blurs,
and I could not make them out. Nor could I make out much of the rest of the
room, except to see that it had two long rows of beds and a wide middle aisle,
and that it was clearly a hospital ward. I touched the bump on my forehead. It
had receded considerably but was still very sore. I looked at the sun coming
through the windows. All up and down the ward people were talking to each
other, but I was not interested in what they were saying. I was looking at the
sun. It seemed strange to me now that it should be so bright. The ball game
had ended shortly before six o'clock. Then there had been the ride in the cab,
the time in the waiting and examination rooms, and the ride up in the elevator.
I couldn't remember what had happened afterwards, but it couldn't all have
happened so fast that it was now still Sunday afternoon. I thought of asking
the man to my left what day it was, but he seemed absorbed in his card game.
The boy to my right hadn't moved at all. He lay quietly staring up at the ceiling, and I didn't want to disturb him.

I moved my wrist slowly. It still hurt. That Danny Saunders was a smart
one, and I hated him. I wondered what he was thinking now. Probably gloat-
ing and bragging about the ball game to his friends. That miserable Hasid!

An orderly came slowly up the aisle, pushing a metal table piled high
with food trays. There was a stir in the ward as people sat up in their beds. I
watched him hand out the trays and heard the clinking of silverware. The man
on my left scooped up the cards and put them on the table between our beds.

"Chop-chop," he said, smiling at me. "Time for the old feed bag. They
don't make it like in training camp, though. Nothing like eating in training
camp. Work up a sweat, eat real careful on account of watching the weight, but
eat real good. What's the menu, Doc?"

The orderly grinned at him. "Be right with you, Killer." He was still three beds away.

The boy in the bed to my right moved his head slightly and put his hands down on top of his blanket. He blinked his eyes and lay still, staring up at the ceiling.

The orderly stopped at the foot of his bed and took a tray from the table. "How you doing, Billy?"

The boy's eyes sought out the direction from which the orderly's voice had come.

"Fine," he said softly, very softly, and began to sit up.

The orderly came around to the side of the bed with a tray of food, but the boy kept staring in the direction from which the orderly's voice had come. I looked at the boy and saw that he was blind.

"It's chicken, Billy," the orderly said. "Peas and carrots, potatoes, real hot vegetable soup, and applesauce."

"Chicken!" the man to my left said. "Who can do a ten-rounder on chicken?"

"You doing a ten-rounder tonight, Killer?" the orderly asked pleasantly.

"Chicken!" the man to my left said again, but he was smiling broadly.

"You all set, Billy?" the orderly asked.

"I'm fine," the boy said. He fumbled about for the silverware, found the knife and fork, and commenced eating.

I saw the nurse come up the aisle and stop at my bed. "Hello, young man. Are we still hungry?"

"Yes, ma'am."

"That's good. Your father said to tell you this is a kosher hospital, and you are to eat everything."

"Yes, ma'am. Thank you."

"How does your head feel?"

"It feels fine, ma'am."

"No pain?"

"No."

"That's very good. We won't ask you to sit up, though. Not just yet. We'll raise the bed up a bit and you can lean back against the pillow."

I saw her bend down. From the motions of her shoulders I could see she was turning something set into the foot of the bed. I felt the bed begin to rise.

"Is that comfortable?" she asked me.

"Yes, ma'am. Thank you very much."

She went to the night table between my bed and the bed to my right and opened a drawer. "Your father asked that we give you this." She was holding a small, black skullcap in her hand.

"Thank you, ma'am."

I took the skullcap and put it on.

"Enjoy your meal," she said, smiling.

"Thank you very much," I said. I had been concerned about eating. I wondered when my father had been to the hospital and why he wasn't here now.

"Mrs. Carpenter," the man to my left said, "how come chicken again?"

The nurse looked at him sternly. "Mr. Savo, please behave yourself."

"Yes, *ma'am*," the man said, feigning fright.

"Mr. Savo, you are a poor example to your young neighbors."

She turned quickly and went away.

"Tough as a ring post," Mr. Savo said, grinning at me. "But a great heart."

The orderly put the food tray on his bed, and he began eating ravenously. While chewing on a bone, he looked at me and winked his good eye. "Good food. Not enough zip, but that's the kosher bit for you. Love to kid them along. Keeps them on their toes like a good fighter."

"Mr. Savo, sir?"

"Yeah, kid?"

"What day is today?"

He took the chicken bone out of his mouth. "It's Monday."

"Monday, June fifth?"

"That's right, kid."

"I slept a long time," I said quietly.

"You were out like a light, boy. Had us all in a sweat." He put the chicken bone back in his mouth. "Some clop that must've been," he said, chewing on the bone.

I decided it would be polite to introduce myself. "My name is Reuven Malter."

His lips smiled at me from around the chicken bone in his mouth. "Good to meet you, Reu—Reu— How's that again?"

"Reuven—Robert Malter."

"Good to meet you, Bobby boy." He took the chicken bone from his mouth, inspected it, then dropped it onto the tray. "You always eat with a hat on?"

"Yes, sir."

"What's that, part of your religion or something?"

"Yes, sir."

"Always like kids that hold to their religion. Important thing, religion. Wouldn't mind some of it in the ring. Tough place, the ring. Tony Savo's my name."

"Are you a professional prizefighter?"

"That's right, Bobby boy. I'm a prelim man. Could've been on top if that guy hadn't clopped me with that right the way he did. Flattened me for a month. Manager lost faith. Lousy manager. Tough racket, the ring. Good food, eh?"

"Yes, sir."

"Not like in training camp, though. Nothing like eating in training camp."

"Are you feeling better now?" I heard the blind boy ask me, and I turned to look at him. He had finished eating and was sitting looking in my direction. His eyes were wide open and a pale blue.

"I'm a lot better," I told him. "My head doesn't hurt."

"We were all very worried about you."

I didn't know what to say to that. I thought I would just nod and smile, but I knew he wouldn't see it. I didn't know what to say or do, so I kept silent.

"My name's Billy," the blind boy said.

"How are you, Billy? I'm Robert Malter."

"Hello, Robert. Did you hurt your eye very badly?"

"Pretty badly."

"You want to be careful about your eyes, Robert."

I didn't know what to say to that, either.

"Robert's a grown-up name, isn't it? How old are you?"

"Fifteen."

"That's grown-up."

"Call me Bobby," I said to him. "I'm not really that grown-up."

"Bobby is a nice name. All right. I'll call you Bobby."

I kept looking at him. He had such a beautiful face, a gentle face. His hands lay limply on the blanket, and his eyes stared at me vacantly.

"What kind of hair do you have, Bobby? Can you tell me what you look like?"

"Sure. I have black hair and brown eyes, and a face like a million others you've seen—you've heard about. I'm about five foot six, and I've got a bump on my head and a bandaged left eye."

He laughed with sudden delight. "You're a nice person," he said warmly. "You're nice like Mr. Savo."

Mr. Savo looked over at us. He had finished eating and was holding the deck of cards in his hands. "That's what I kept telling my manager. I'm a nice guy, I kept telling him. Is it my fault I got clopped? But he lost faith. Lousy manager."

Billy stared in the direction of his voice. "You'll be all right again, Mr. Savo," he said earnestly. "You'll be right back up there on top again."

"Sure, Billy," Tony Savo said, looking at him. "Old Tony'll make it up there again."

"Then I'll come to your training camp and watch you practice and we'll have that three-rounder you promised me."

"Sure, Billy."

"Mr. Savo promised me a three-rounder after my operation," Billy explained to me eagerly, still staring in the direction of Tony Savo's voice.

"That's great," I said.

"It's a new kind of operation," Billy said, turning his face in my direction. "My father explained it to me. They found out how to do it in the war. It'll be wonderful doing a three-rounder with you, Mr. Savo."

"Sure, Billy. Sure." He was sitting up in his bed, looking at the boy and ignoring the deck of cards he held in his hands.

"It'll be wonderful to be able to see again," Billy said to me. "I had an accident in the car once. My father was driving. It was a long time ago. It wasn't my father's fault, though."

Mr. Savo looked down at the deck of cards, then put it back on top of the night table.

I saw the orderly coming back up the aisle to collect the food trays. "Did you enjoy the meal?" he asked Billy.

Billy turned his head in the direction of his voice. "It was a fine meal."

"How about you, Killer?"

"Chicken!" Tony Savo said. "What can be good about chicken?" His voice was flat, though, now, and all the excitement was out of it.

"How come you left the bones this time?" the orderly asked, grinning.

"Who can do a ten-rounder on chicken?" Tony Savo said. But he didn't seem to have his heart anymore in what he was saying. I saw him lie back on his pillow and stare up at the ceiling out of his left eye. Then he closed the eye and put his long hairy hands across his chest.

"We'll lower this for you," the orderly said to me after he took my tray. He bent down at the foot of the bed, and I felt the head of the bed go flat.

Billy lay back on his pillow. I turned my head and saw him lying there, his eyes open and staring up, his palms under his head, his elbows jutting outward. Then I looked beyond his bed and saw a man hurrying up the aisle, and when he came into focus I saw it was my father.

I almost cried out, but I held back and waited for him to come up to my bed. I saw he was carrying a package wrapped in newspapers. He had on his dark gray, striped, double-breasted suit and his gray hat. He looked thin and worn, and his face was pale. His eyes seemed red behind his steel-rimmed spectacles, as though he hadn't slept in a long time. He came quickly around to the left side of the bed and looked down at me and tried to smile. But the smile didn't come through at all.

"The hospital telephoned me a little while ago," he said, sounding a little out of breath. "They told me you were awake."

I started to sit up in the bed.

"No," he said. "Lie still. They told me you were not to sit up yet."

I lay back and looked up at him. He sat down on the edge of the bed and put the package down next to him. He took off his hat and put it on top of the package. His sparse gray hair lay uncombed on his head. That was unusual for my father. I never remembered him leaving the house without first carefully combing his hair.

"You slept almost a full day," he said, trying another smile. He had a soft voice, but it was a little husky now. "How are you feeling, Reuven?"

"I feel fine now," I said.

"They told me you had a slight concussion. Your head does not hurt?"

"No."

"Mr. Galanter called a few times today. He wanted to know how you were. I told him you were sleeping."

"He's a wonderful man, Mr. Galanter."

"They told me you might sleep for a few days. They were surprised you woke so soon."

"The ball hit me very hard."

"Yes," he said. "I heard all about the ball game."

He seemed very tense, and I wondered why he was still worried.

"The nurse didn't say anything to me about my eye," I said. "Is it all right?"

He looked at me queerly.

"Of course it is all right. Why should it not be all right? Dr. Snydman operated on it, and he is a very big man."

"He operated on my eye?" It had never occurred to me that I had been through an operation. "What was wrong? Why did he have to operate?"

My father caught the fear in my voice.

"You will be all right now," he calmed me. "There was a piece of glass in your eye and he had to get it out. Now you will be all right."

"There was glass in my eye?"

My father nodded slowly. "It was on the edge of the pupil."

"And they took it out?"

"Dr. Snydman took it out. They said he performed a miracle." But somehow my father did not look as though a miracle had been performed. He sat there, tense and upset.

"Is the eye all right now?" I asked him.

"Of course it is all right. Why should it not be all right?"

"It's not all right," I said. "I want you to tell me."

"There is nothing to tell you. They told me it was all right."

"Abba, please tell me what's the matter."

He looked at me, and I heard him sigh. Then he began to cough, a deep, rasping cough that shook his frail body terribly. He took a handkerchief from his pocket and held it to his lips and coughed a long time. I lay tense in the bed, watching him. The coughing stopped. I heard him sigh again, and then he smiled at me. It was his old smile, the warm smile that turned up the corners of his thin lips and lighted his face.

"Reuven, Reuven," he said, smiling and shaking his head, "I have never been good at hiding things from you, have I?"

I was quiet.

"I always wanted a bright boy for a son. And you are bright. I will tell you what they told me about the eye. The eye is all right. It is fine. In a few days they will remove the bandages and you will come home."

"In only a few days?"

"Yes."

"So why are you so worried? That's wonderful!"

"Reuven, the eye has to heal."

I saw a man walk up the aisle and come alongside Billy's bed. He looked to be in his middle thirties. He had light blond hair, and from his face I could tell immediately that he was Billy's father. I saw him sit down on the edge of the bed, and I saw Billy turn his face toward him and sit up. The father kissed the boy gently on the forehead. They talked quietly.

I looked at my father. "Of course the eye has to heal," I said.

"It has a tiny cut on the edge of the pupil, and the cut has to heal."

I stared at him. "The scar tissue," I said slowly. "The scar tissue can grow over the pupil." And I felt myself go sick with fear.

My father blinked, and his eyes were moist behind the steel-rimmed spectacles.

"Dr. Snydman informed me he had a case like yours last year, and the eye healed. He is optimistic everything will be all right."

"But he's not sure."

"No," my father said. "He is not sure."

I looked at Billy and saw him and his father talking together quietly and seriously. The father was caressing the boy's cheek. I looked away and turned my head to the left. Mr. Savo seemed to be asleep.

"Reb Saunders called me twice today and once last night," I heard my father say softly.

"Reb Saunders?"

"Yes. He wanted to know how you were. He told me his son is very sorry over what happened."

"I'll bet," I said bitterly.

My father stared at me for a moment, then leaned forward a little on the bed. He began to say something, but his words broke into a rasping cough. He put the handkerchief in front of his mouth and coughed into it. He coughed a long time, and I lay still and watched him. When he stopped, he took off his spectacles and wiped his eyes. He put the spectacles back on and took a deep breath.

"I caught a cold," he apologized. "There was a draft in the classroom yesterday. I told the janitor, but he told me he could not find anything wrong. So I caught a cold. In June yet. Only your father catches colds in June."

"You're not taking care of yourself, abba."

"I am worried about my baseball player." He smiled at me. "I worry all the time you will get hit by a taxi or a trolley car, and you go and get hit by a baseball."

"I hate that Danny Saunders for this. He's making you sick."

"Danny Saunders is making me sick? How is he making me sick?"

"He deliberately aimed at me, abba. He hit me deliberately. Now you're getting sick worrying about me."

My father looked at me in amazement. "He hit you deliberately?"

"You should see how he hits. He almost killed Schwartzie. He said his team would kill us apikorsim."

"Apikorsim?"

"They turned the game into a war."

"I do not understand. On the telephone Reb Saunders said his son was sorry."

"Sorry! I'll bet he's sorry! He's sorry he didn't kill me altogether!"

My father gazed at me intently, his eyes narrowing. I saw the look of amazement slowly leave his face.

"I do not like you to talk that way," he said sternly.

"It's true, abba."

"Did you ask him if it was deliberate?"

"No."

"How can you say something like that if you are not sure? That is a terrible thing to say." He was controlling his anger with difficulty.

"It seemed to be deliberate."

"Things are always what they seem to be, Reuven? Since when?"

I was silent.

"I do not want to hear you say that again about Reb Saunders's son."

"Yes, abba."

"Now, I brought you this." He undid the newspapers around the package, and I saw it was our portable radio. "Just because you are in the hospital does not mean you should shut yourself off from the world. It is expected Rome will fall any day now. And there are rumors the invasion of Europe will be very soon. You should not forget there is a world outside."

"I'll have to do my schoolwork, abba. I'll have to keep up with my classes."

"No schoolwork, no books, and no newspapers. They told me you are not allowed to read."

"I can't read at all?"

"No reading. So I brought you the radio. Very important things are happening, Reuven, and a radio is a blessing."

He put the radio on the night table. A radio brought the world together, he said very often. Anything that brought the world together he called a blessing.

"Now, your schoolwork," he said. "I talked with your teachers. If you cannot prepare in time for your examinations, they will give them to you privately at the end of June or in September. So you do not have to worry."

"If I'm out of the hospital in a few days, I'll be able to read soon."

"We will see. We have to find out first about the scar tissue."

I felt myself frightened again. "Will it take long to find out?"

"A week or two."

"I can't read for two weeks?"

"We will ask Dr. Snydman when you leave the hospital. But no reading now."

"Yes, abba."

"Now, I have to go," my father said. He put his hat on, then folded the newspaper and put it under his arm. He coughed again, briefly this time, and stood up. "I have to prepare examinations, and I must finish an article. The journal gave me a deadline." He looked down at me and smiled, a little nervously, I thought. He seemed so pale and thin.

"Please take care of yourself, abba. Don't get sick."

"I will take care of myself. You will rest. And listen to the radio."

"Yes, abba."

He looked at me, and I saw him blink his eyes behind his steel-rimmed spectacles. "You are not a baby anymore. I hope—" He broke off. I thought I saw his eyes begin to mist and his lips tremble for a moment.

Billy's father said something to the boy, and the boy laughed loudly. I saw my father glance at them briefly, then look back at me. Then I saw him turn his head and look at them again. He looked at them a long time. Then he turned back to me. I saw from his face that he knew Billy was blind.

"I brought you your tefillin and prayer book," he said very quietly. His voice was husky, and it trembled. "If they tell you it is all right, you should pray with your tefillin. But only if they tell you it is all right and will not be harmful to your head or your eye." He stopped for a moment to clear his throat. "It is a bad cold, but I will be all right. If you cannot pray with your tefillin, pray anyway. Now, I have to go." He bent and kissed me on the forehead. As he came close to me, I saw his eyes were red and misty. "My baseball player," he said, trying to smile. "Take care of yourself and rest. I will be back to see you tomorrow." He turned and walked quickly away up the aisle, small and thin, but walking with a straight, strong step the way he always walked no matter how he felt. Then he was out of focus and I could no longer see him.

I lay on the pillow and closed my right eye. I found myself crying after a while, and I thought that might be bad for my eye, and I forced myself to stop. I lay still and thought about my eyes. I had always taken them for granted, the way I took for granted all the rest of my body and also my mind. My father had told me many times that health was a gift, but I never really paid much attention to the fact that I was rarely sick or almost never had to go to a doctor. I thought of Billy and Tony Savo. I tried to imagine what my life might be like if I had only one good eye, but I couldn't. I had just never thought of my eyes before. I had never thought what it might be like to be blind. I felt the wild terror again, and I tried to control it. I lay there a long time, thinking about my eyes.

I heard a stir in the ward, opened my right eye, and saw that Billy's father had gone. Billy was lying on his pillow with his palms under his head and his elbows jutting outward. His eyes were open and staring at the ceiling. I saw nurses alongside some of the beds, and I realized that everyone was preparing for sleep. I turned my head to look at Mr. Savo. He seemed to be asleep. My head was beginning to hurt a little, and my left wrist still felt sore. I lay very still. I saw the nurse come up to my bed and look down at me with a bright smile.

"Well, now," she said. "How are we feeling, young man?"

"My head hurts a little," I told her.

"That's to be expected." She smiled at me. "We'll give you this pill now so you'll have a fine night's sleep."

She went to the night table and filled a glass with water from a pitcher that stood on a little tray. She helped me raise my head, and I put the pill in my mouth and swallowed it down with some of the water.

"Thank you," I said, lying back on the pillow.

"You're very welcome, young man. It's nice to meet polite young people. Good night, now."

"Good night, ma'am. Thank you."

She went away up the aisle.

I turned my head and looked at Billy. He lay very still with his eyes open. I watched him for a moment, then closed my eye. I wondered what it was like to be blind, completely blind. I couldn't imagine it, but I thought it must be something like the way I was feeling now with my eyes closed. But it's not the same, I told myself. I know if I open my right eye I'll see. When you're blind it makes no difference whether you open your eyes or not. I couldn't imagine what it was like to know that no matter whether my eyes were opened or closed it made no difference, everything was still dark.

THREE

ASLEEP, I HEARD A SHOUT and a noise that sounded like a cheer, and I woke immediately. There was a lot of movement in the ward, and loud voices. I wondered what was happening, there was so much noise and shouting going on and a radio was blaring. I began to sit up, then remembered that I was not yet permitted to sit and put my head back on the pillow. It was light outside, but I could not see the sun. I wondered what the noise was all about, and then I saw Mrs. Carpenter walking sternly up the aisle. She was telling people to stop all the shouting and to remember that this was a hospital and not Madison Square Garden. I looked over at Billy. He was sitting straight up in his bed, and I could tell he was trying to make out what was going on. His face looked puzzled and a little frightened. I turned to look at Mr. Savo, and I saw he was not in his bed.

The noise quieted a little, but the radio was still blaring. I couldn't make it out too clearly because every now and then someone would interrupt with a shout or a cheer. The announcer was talking about places called Caen and Carentan. He said something about a British airborne division seizing bridgeheads and two American airborne divisions stopping enemy troops from moving into the Cotentin Peninsula. I didn't recognize any of the names, and I wondered why everyone was so excited. There was war news all the time, but no one got this excited unless something very special was happening. I thought I could see Mr. Savo sitting on one of the beds. Mrs. Carpenter went over to him, and from the way she walked I thought she was angry. I saw Mr. Savo get to his feet and come back up the aisle. The announcer was saying something about the Isle of Wight and the Normandy coast and Royal Air Force bombers attacking enemy coast-defense guns and United States Air Force bombers attacking shore defenses. I suddenly realized what was happening and felt my heart begin to beat quickly.

I saw Mr. Savo come up to my bed. He was angry, and his long, thin face with the black eyepatch made him look like a pirate.

"'Go back to your bed, Mr. Savo,'" he mimicked. "'Go back to your bed this instant.' You'd think I was dying. This is no time to be in bed."

"Is it the invasion of Europe, Mr. Savo?" I asked him eagerly. I was feeling excited and a little tense, and I wished the people who were cheering would be quiet.

He looked down at me. "It's D-day, Bobby boy. We're clopping them good. And Tony Savo has to go back to his bed." Then he spotted the portable radio my father had brought me the night before. "Hey, Bobby boy, is that your radio?"

"That's right," I said excitedly. "I forgot all about it."

"Lucky, lucky us." He was smiling broadly and no longer looked like a pirate. "We'll put it on the table between our beds and give it a listen, eh?"

"I think Billy will want to hear it, too, Mr. Savo." I looked over at Billy.

Billy turned and stared in the direction of my voice. "Do you have a radio here, Bobby?" He seemed very excited.

"It's right here, Billy. Right between our beds."

"My uncle is a pilot. He flies big planes that drop bombs. Can you turn it on?"

"Sure, kid." Mr. Savo turned on the radio, found the station with the same announcer who was coming over the other radio, then got into his bed and lay back on his pillow. The three of us lay in our beds and listened to the news of the invasion.

Mrs. Carpenter came up the aisle. She was still a little angry over all the noise in the ward, but I could see she was also excited. She asked me how I was feeling.

"I'm feeling fine, ma'am."

"That's very good. Is that your radio?"

"Yes, ma'am. My father brought it to me."

"How nice. You may sit up a little if you wish."

"Thank you." I was happy to hear that. "May I pray with my tefillin?"

"Your phylacteries?"

"Yes, ma'am."

"I don't see why not. You'll be careful of the bump on your head, now."

"Yes, ma'am. Thank you."

She looked sternly at Mr. Savo. "I see you're behaving yourself, Mr. Savo."

Mr. Savo looked at her out of his left eye and grunted. "You'd think I was dying."

"You are to remain in bed, Mr. Savo."

Mr. Savo grunted again.

She went back up the aisle.

"Tough as a ring post," Mr. Savo said, grinning. "Turn it up a bit, Bobby boy. Can't hear it too good."

I leaned over and turned up the volume of the radio. It felt good to be able to move again.

I got the tefillin and prayer book out of the drawer of the night table and began to put on the tefillin. The head strap rubbed against the bump, and I winced. It was still sore. I finished adjusting the hand strap and opened the prayer book. I saw Mr. Savo looking at me. Then I remembered that I wasn't allowed to read, so I closed the prayer book. I prayed whatever I remembered by heart, trying not to listen to the announcer. I prayed for the safety of all the soldiers fighting on the beaches. When I finished praying, I took off the tefillin and put them and the prayer book back in the drawer.

"You're a real religious kid, there, Bobby boy," Mr. Savo said to me.

I didn't know what to say to that, so I looked at him and nodded and didn't say anything.

"You going to be a priest or something?"

"I might," I said. "My father wants me to be a mathematician, though."

"You good at math?"

"Yes. I get all A's in math."

"But you want to be a priest, eh? A—rabbi, you call it."

"Sometimes I think I want to be a rabbi. I'm not sure."

"It's a good thing to be, Bobby boy. Cockeyed world needs people like that. I could've been a priest. Had a chance once. Made a wrong choice. Wound up clopping people instead. Lousy choice. Hey, listen to that!"

The correspondent was saying excitedly that some German torpedo boats had attacked a Norwegian destroyer and that it looked like it was sinking. There were sailors jumping overboard and lifeboats being lowered.

"They got clopped," Mr. Savo said, looking grim. "Poor bas—poor guys."

The correspondent sounded very excited as he described the Norwegian destroyer sinking.

The rest of that morning I did nothing but listen to the radio and talk about the war with Mr. Savo and Billy. I explained to Billy as best I could some of the things that were going on, and he kept telling me his uncle was the pilot of a big plane that dropped bombs. He asked me if I thought he was dropping them now to help with the invasion. I told him I was sure he was.

Shortly after lunch, a boy came in from the other ward bouncing a ball. I saw he was about six years old, had a thin pale face and dark uncombed hair which he kept brushing away from his eyes with his left hand while he walked along bouncing the ball with his right. He wore light brown pajamas and a dark brown robe.

"Poor kid," said Mr. Savo. "Been in the ward across the hall most of his life. Stomach's got no juices or something." He watched him come up the aisle. "Crazy world. Cockeyed."

The boy stood at the foot of Mr. Savo's bed, looking very small and pale. "Hey, Mr. Tony. You want to catch with Mickey?"

Mr. Savo told him this was no day to toss a ball around, there was an invasion going on. Mickey didn't know what an invasion was, and began to cry. "You promised, Mr. Tony. You said you would catch with little Mickey."

Mr. Savo looked uncomfortable. "Okay, kid. Don't start bawling again. Just two catches. Okay?"

"Sure, Mr. Tony," Mickey said, his face glowing. He threw the ball to Mr. Savo, who had to stretch his right hand high over his head to catch it. He tossed it back lightly to the boy, who dropped it and went scrambling for it under the bed.

I saw Mrs. Carpenter come rushing up the aisle, looking furious.

"Mr. Savo, you are simply impossible!" she almost shouted.

Mr. Savo sat in his bed, breathing very hard and not saying anything.

"You are going to make yourself seriously ill unless you stop this nonsense and rest!"

"Yes, ma'am," Mr. Savo said. His face was pale. He lay back on his pillow and closed his left eye.

Mrs. Carpenter turned to the boy, who had found his ball and was looking expectantly at Mr. Savo.

"Mickey, there will be no more catching with Mr. Savo."

"Aw, Mrs. Carpenter—"

"Mickey!"

"Yes'm," Mickey said, suddenly docile. "Thanks for the catch, Mr. Tony."

Mr. Savo lay on his pillow and didn't say anything. Mickey went back up the aisle, bouncing his ball.

Mrs. Carpenter looked down at Mr. Savo. "Are you feeling all right?" she asked, sounding concerned.

"I'm a little pooped," Mr. Savo said, not opening his eye.

"You should know better than to do something like that."

"Sorry, ma'am."

Mrs. Carpenter went away.

"Tough as a ring post," Mr. Savo said. "But a big heart." He lay still with his eye closed, and after a while I saw he was asleep.

The announcer was talking about the supply problems involved in a large-scale invasion, when I saw Mr. Galanter coming up the aisle. I turned the radio down a little. Mr. Galanter came up to my bed. He was carrying a copy of the *New York Times* under his arm, and his face was flushed and excited.

"Came up to say hello, soldier. I'm between schools, so I've only got a few minutes. Couldn't've seen you otherwise today. How are we doing?"

"I'm a lot better, Mr. Galanter." I was happy and proud that he had come to see me. "My head doesn't hurt at all, and the wrist is a lot less sore."

"That's good news, trooper. Great news. This is some day, isn't it? One of the greatest days in history. Fantastic undertaking."

"Yes, sir. I've been listening to it on the radio."

"We can't begin to imagine what's going on, trooper. That's the incredible part. Probably have to land more than a hundred fifty thousand troops today and tomorrow, and thousands and thousands of tanks, artillery pieces, jeeps, bulldozers, everything, and all on those beaches. It staggers the mind!"

"I told little Billy here that they were using the big bombing planes an awful lot. His uncle is a bomber pilot. He's probably flying his plane right now."

Mr. Galanter looked at Billy, who had turned his head in our direction, and I saw Mr. Galanter notice immediately that he was blind.

"How are you, young feller?" Mr. Galanter said, his voice sounding suddenly a lot less excited.

"My uncle flies a big plane that drops bombs," Billy said. "Are you a flier?"

I saw Mr. Galanter's face go tight.

"Mr. Galanter is my gym teacher in high school," I told Billy.

"My uncle's been a pilot for a long time now. My father says they have to fly an awful lot before they can come home. Were you wounded or something, Mr. Galanter, sir, that you're home now?"

I saw Mr. Galanter stare at the boy. His mouth was open, and he ran his tongue over his lips. He looked uncomfortable.

"Couldn't make it as a soldier," he said, looking at Billy. "I've got a bad—" He stopped. "Tried to make it but couldn't."

"I'm sorry to hear that, sir."

"Yeah," Mr. Galanter said.

I was feeling embarrassed. Mr. Galanter's excitement had disappeared, and now he stood there, staring at Billy and looking deflated. I felt sorry for him, and I regretted having mentioned Billy's uncle.

"I wish your uncle all the luck in the world," Mr. Galanter said quietly to Billy.

"Thank you, sir," Billy said.

Mr. Galanter turned to me. "They did quite a job getting that piece of glass out of your eye, trooper." He was trying to sound cheerful, but he wasn't succeeding too well. "How soon will you be out?"

"My father said in a few days."

'Well, that's great. You're a lucky boy. It could've been a lot worse."

"Yes, sir."

I wondered if he knew about the scar tissue and didn't want to talk to me about it. I decided not to mention it; he was looking a little sad and uneasy, and I didn't want to make him any more uncomfortable than he already was.

"Well, I got to go teach a class, trooper. Take care of yourself and get out of here soon."

"Yes, sir. Thank you for everything and for coming to see me."

"Anything for one of my troopers," he said.

I watched him walk away slowly up the aisle.

"It's too bad he couldn't be a soldier," Billy said. "My father isn't a soldier, but that's because my mother was killed in the accident and there's no one else to take care of me and my little sister."

I looked at him and didn't say anything.

"I think I'll sleep a little now," Billy said. "Would you turn off the radio?"

"Sure, Billy."

I saw him put his palms under his head on the pillow and lie there, staring vacantly up at the ceiling.

I lay back and after a few minutes of thinking about Mr. Galanter I fell asleep. I dreamed about my left eye and felt very frightened. I thought I could see sunlight through the closed lid of my right eye, and I dreamed about waking up in the hospital yesterday afternoon and the nurse moving the curtain away. Now something was blocking the sunlight. Then the sunlight was back again, and I could see it in my sleep through the lid of my right eye. Then it was gone again, and I felt myself getting a little angry at whoever was playing with the sunlight. I opened my eye and saw someone standing alongside my bed. Whoever it was stood silhouetted against the sunlight, and for a moment I couldn't make out the face. Then I sat up quickly.

"Hello," Danny Saunders said softly. "I'm sorry if I woke you. The nurse told me it was all right to wait here."

I looked at him in amazement. He was the last person in the world I had expected to visit me in the hospital.

"Before you tell me how much you hate me," he said quietly, "let me tell you that I'm sorry about what happened."

I stared at him and didn't know what to say. He was wearing a dark suit, a white shirt open at the collar, and a dark skullcap. I could see the earlocks hanging down alongside his sculptured face and the fringes outside the trousers below the jacket.

"I don't hate you," I managed to say, because I thought it was time for me to say something even if what I said was a lie.

He smiled sadly. "Can I sit down? I've been standing here about fifteen minutes waiting for you to wake up."

I sort of nodded or did something with my head, and he took it as a sign of approval and sat down on the edge of the bed to my right. The sun streamed in from the windows behind him, and shadows lay over his face and accentuated the lines of his cheeks and jaw. I thought he looked a little like the pictures I had seen of Abraham Lincoln before he grew the beard—except for the small tufts of sand-colored hair on his chin and cheeks, the close-cropped hair on his head, and the side curls. He seemed ill at ease, and his eyes blinked nervously.

"What do they say about the scar tissue?" he asked.

I was astonished all over again. "How did you find out about that?"

"I called your father last night. He told me."

"They don't know anything about it yet. I might be blind in that eye."

He nodded slowly and was silent.

"How does it feel to know you've made someone blind in one eye?" I asked him. I had recovered from my surprise at his presence and was feeling the anger beginning to come back.

He looked at me, his sculptured face expressionless. "What do you want me to say?" His voice wasn't angry, it was sad. "You want me to say I'm miserable? Okay, I'm miserable."

"That's all? Only miserable? How do you sleep nights?"

He looked down at his hands. "I didn't come here to fight with you," he said softly. "If you want to do nothing but fight, I'm going to go home."

"For my part," I told him, "you can go to hell, and take your whole snooty bunch of Hasidim along with you!"

He looked at me and sat still. He didn't seem angry, just sad. His silence made me all the angrier, and finally I said, "What the hell are you sitting there for? I thought you said you were going home!"

"I came to talk to you," he said quietly.

"Well, I don't want to listen," I told him. "Why don't you go home? Go home and be sorry over my eye!"

He stood up slowly. I could barely see his face because of the sunlight behind him. His shoulders seemed bowed.

"I *am* sorry," he said quietly.

"I'll just bet you are," I told him.

He started to say something, stopped, then turned and walked slowly away up the aisle. I lay back on the pillow, trembling a little and frightened over my own anger and hate.

"He a friend of yours?" I heard Mr. Savo ask me.

I turned to him. He was lying with his head on his pillow.

"No," I said.

"He give you a rough time or something? You don't sound so good, Bobby boy."

"He's the one who hit me in the eye with the ball."

Mr. Savo's face brightened. "No kidding? The clopper himself. Well, well!"

"I think I'll get some more sleep," I said. I was feeling depressed.

"He one of these real religious Jews?" Mr. Savo asked.

"Yes."

"I've seen them around. My manager had an uncle like that. Real religious guy. Fanatic. Never had anything to do with my manager, though. Small loss. Some lousy manager."

I didn't feel like having a conversation just then, so I remained silent. I was feeling a little regretful that I had been so angry with Danny Saunders.

I saw Mr. Savo sit up and take the deck of cards from his night table. He began to set up his rows on the blanket. I noticed Billy was asleep. I lay back in my bed and closed my eyes. But I couldn't sleep.

My father came in a few minutes after supper, looking pale and worn. When I told him about my conversation with Danny Saunders, his eyes became angry behind the glasses.

"You did a foolish thing, Reuven," he told me sternly. "You remember what the Talmud says. If a person comes to apologize for having hurt you, you must listen and forgive him."

"I couldn't help it, abba."

"You hate him so much you could say those things to him?"

"I'm sorry," I said, feeling miserable.

He looked at me and I saw his eyes were suddenly sad. "I did not intend to scold you," he said.

"You weren't scolding," I defended him.

"What I tried to tell you, Reuven, is that when a person comes to talk to you, you should be patient and listen. Especially if he has hurt you in any way. Now, we will not talk anymore tonight about Reb Saunders's son. This is an important day in the history of the world. It is the beginning of the end for Hitler and his madmen. Did you hear the announcer on the boat describing the invasion?"

We talked for a while about the invasion. Finally, my father left, and I lay back in my bed, feeling depressed and angry with myself over what I had said to Danny Saunders.

Billy's father had come to see him again, and they were talking quietly. He glanced at me and smiled warmly. He was a fine-looking person, and I noticed he had a long white scar on his forehead running parallel to the line of his light blond hair.

"Billy tells me you've been very nice to him," he said to me.

I sort of nodded my head on the pillow and tried to smile back.

"I appreciate that very much," he said. "Billy wonders if you would call us when he gets out of the hospital."

"Sure," I said.

"We're in the phone book. Roger Merrit. Billy says that after his operation, when he can see again, he would like to see what you look like."

"Sure, I'll give you a call," I said.

"Did you hear that, Billy?"

"Yes," Billy said happily. "Didn't I tell you he was nice, Daddy?"

The man smiled at me, then turned back to Billy. They went on talking quietly.

I lay in the bed and thought about all the things that had happened during the day, and felt sad and depressed.

The next morning, Mrs. Carpenter told me I could get out of bed and walk around a bit. After breakfast, I went out into the hall for a while. I looked out a window and saw people outside on the street. I stood there, staring out the window a long time. Then I went back to my bed and lay down.

I saw Mr. Savo sitting up in his bed, playing cards and grinning.

"How's it feel to be on your feet, Bobby boy?" he asked me.

"It feels wonderful. I'm a little tired, though."

"Take it real slow, kid. Takes a while to get the old strength back."

One of the patients near the radio at the other end of the ward let out a shout. I leaned over and turned on my radio. The announcer was talking about a breakthrough on one of the beaches.

"That's clopping them!" Mr. Savo said, grinning broadly.

I wondered what that beach must look like now, and I could see it filled with broken vehicles and dead soldiers.

I spent the morning listening to the radio. When Mrs. Carpenter came over, I asked her how long I would be in the hospital, and she smiled and said Dr. Snydman would have to decide that. "Dr. Snydman will see you Friday morning," she added.

I was beginning to feel a lot less excited over the war news and a lot more annoyed that I couldn't read. In the afternoon, I listened to some of the soap operas—*Life Can Be Beautiful, Stella Dallas, Mary Noble, Ma Perkins*—and what I heard depressed me even more. I decided to turn off the radio and get some sleep.

"Do you want to hear any more of this?" I asked Billy.

He didn't answer, and I saw he was sleeping.

"Turn it off, kid," Mr. Savo said. "How much of that junk can a guy take?"

I turned off the radio and lay back on my pillow.

"Never knew people could get clopped so hard the way they clop them on those soap operas," Mr. Savo said. "Well, well, look who's here."

"Who?" I sat up.

"Your real religious clopper."

I saw it was Danny Saunders. He came up the aisle and stood alongside my bed, wearing the same clothes he had the day before.

"Are you going to get angry at me again?" he asked hesitantly.

"No," I said.

"Can I sit down?"

"Yes."

"Thanks," he said, and sat down on the edge of the bed to my right. I saw Mr. Savo stare at him for a moment, then go back to his cards.

"You were pretty rotten yesterday, you know," Danny Saunders said.

"I'm sorry about that." I was surprised at how happy I was to see him.

"I didn't so much mind you being angry," he said. "What I thought was rotten was the way you wouldn't let me talk."

"That was rotten, all right. I'm really sorry."

"I came up to talk to you now. Do you want to listen?"

"Sure," I said.

"I've been thinking about that ball game. I haven't stopped thinking about it since you got hit."

"I've been thinking about it, too," I said.

"Whenever I do or see something I don't understand, I like to think about it until I understand it." He talked very rapidly, and I could see he was tense. "I've thought about it a lot, but I still don't understand it. I want to talk to you about it. Okay?"

"Sure," I said.

"Do you know what I don't understand about that ball game? I don't understand why I wanted to kill you."

I stared at him.

"It's really bothering me."

"Well, I should hope so," I said.

"Don't be so cute, Malter. I'm not being melodramatic. I really wanted to kill you."

"Well, it was a pretty hot ball game," I said. "I didn't exactly love you myself there for a while."

"I don't think you even know what I'm talking about," he said.

"Now, wait a minute—"

"No, listen. Just listen to what I'm saying, will you? Do you remember that second curve you threw me?"

"Sure."

"Do you remember I stood in front of the plate afterwards and looked at you?"

"Sure." I remembered the idiot grin vividly.

"Well, that's when I wanted to walk over to you and open your head with my bat."

I didn't know what to say.

"I don't know why I didn't. I wanted to."

"That was some ball game," I said, a little awed by what he was telling me.

"It had nothing to do with the ball game," he said. "At least I don't think it did. You weren't the first tough team we played. And we've lost before, too. But you really had me going, Malter. I can't figure it out. Anyway, I feel better telling you about it."

"Please stop calling me Malter," I said.

He looked at me. Then he smiled faintly. "What do you want me to call you?"

"If you're going to call me anything, call me Reuven," I said. "Malter sounds as if you're a schoolteacher or something."

"Okay," he said, smiling again. "Then you call me Danny."

"Fine," I said.

"It was the wildest feeling," he said. "I've never felt that way before."

I looked at him, and suddenly I had the feeling that everything around me was out of focus. There was Danny Saunders, sitting on my bed in the hospital dressed in his Hasidic-style clothes and talking about wanting to kill me because I had pitched him some curveballs. He was dressed like a Hasid, but he didn't sound like one. Also, yesterday I had hated him; now we were calling each other by our first names. I sat and listened to him talk. I was fascinated just listening to the way perfect English came out of a person in the clothes of a Hasid. I had always thought their English was tinged with a Yiddish accent. As a matter of fact, the few times I had ever talked with a Hasid, he had spoken only Yiddish. And here was Danny Saunders talking English, and what he was saying and the way he was saying it just didn't seem to fit in with the way he was dressed, with the side curls on his face and the fringes hanging down below his dark jacket.

"You're a pretty rough fielder and pitcher," he said, smiling at me a little.

"You're pretty rough yourself," I told him. "Where did you learn to hit a ball like that?"

"I practiced," he said. "You don't know how many hours I spent learning how to field and hit a baseball."

"Where do you get the time? I thought you people always studied Talmud."

He grinned at me. "I have an agreement with my father. I study my quota of Talmud every day, and he doesn't care what I do the rest of the time."

"What's your quota of Talmud?"

"Two blatt."

"Two blatt?" I stared at him. That was four pages of Talmud a day. If I did one page a day, I was delighted. "Don't you have any English work at all?"

"Of course I do. But not too much. We don't have too much English work at our yeshiva."

"Everybody has to do two blatt of Talmud a day *and* his English?"

"Not everybody. Only me. My father wants it that way."

"How do you do it? That's a fantastic amount of work."

"I'm lucky." He grinned at me. "I'll show you how. What Talmud are you studying now?"

"*Kiddushin*," I said.

"What page are you on?"

I told him.

"I studied that two years ago. Is this what it reads like?"

He recited about a third of the page word for word, including the commentaries and the Maimonidean legal decisions of the Talmudic disputations. He did it coldly, mechanically, and, listening to him, I had the feeling I was watching some sort of human machine at work.

I sat there and gaped at him. "Say, that's pretty good," I managed to say, finally.

"I have a photographic mind. My father says it's a gift from God. I look at a page of Talmud, and I remember it by heart. I understand it, too. After a while, it gets a little boring, though. They repeat themselves a lot. I can do it with *Ivanhoe*, too. Have you read *Ivanhoe*?"

"Sure."

"Do you want to hear it with *Ivanhoe*?"

"You're showing off now," I said.

He grinned. "I'm trying to make a good impression."

"I'm impressed," I said. "I have to sweat to memorize a page of Talmud. Are you going to be a rabbi?"

"Sure. I'm going to take my father's place."

"I may become a rabbi. Not a Hasidic-type, though."

He looked at me, an expression of surprise on his face. "What do you want to become a rabbi for?"

"Why not?"

"There are so many other things you could be."

"That's a funny way for you to talk. *You're* going to become a rabbi."

"I have no choice. It's an inherited position."

"You mean you wouldn't become a rabbi if you had a choice?"

"I don't think so."

"What would you be?"

"I don't know. Probably a psychologist."

"A psychologist?"

He nodded.

"I'm not even sure I know what it's about."

"It helps you understand what a person is really like inside. I've read some books on it."

"Is that like Freud and psychoanalysis and things like that?"

"Yes," he said.

I didn't know much at all about psychoanalysis, but Danny Saunders, in his Hasidic clothes, seemed to me to be about the last person in the world who would qualify as an analyst. I always pictured analysts as sophisticated people with short pointed beards, monocles, and German accents.

"What would you be if you didn't become a rabbi?" Danny Saunders asked.

"A mathematician," I said. "That's what my father wants me to be."

"And teach in a university somewhere?"

"Yes."

"That's a very nice thing to be," he said. His blue eyes looked dreamy for a moment. "I'd like that."

"I'm not sure I want to do that, though."

"Why not?"

"I sort of feel I could be more useful to people as a rabbi. To our own people, I mean. You know, not everyone is religious, like you or me. I could teach them, and help them when they're in trouble. I think I would get a lot of pleasure out of that."

"I don't think I would. Anyway, I'm going to be a rabbi. Say, where did *you* learn to pitch like that?"

"I practiced, too." I grinned at him.

"But you don't have to do two blatt of Talmud a day."

"Thank God!"

"You certainly have a mean way of pitching."

"How about your hitting? Do you always hit like that, straight to the pitcher?"

"Yes."

"How'd you ever learn to do *that*?"

"I can't hit any other way. It's got something to do with my eyesight, and with the way I hold the bat. I don't know."

"That's a pretty murderous way to hit a ball. You almost killed me."

"You were supposed to duck," he said.

"I had no chance to duck."

"Yes you did."

"There wasn't enough time. You hit it so fast."

"There was time for you to bring up your glove."

I considered that for a moment.

"You didn't want to duck."

"That's right," I said, after a while.

"You didn't want to have to duck any ball that I hit. You had to try and stop it."

"That's right." I remembered that fraction of a second when I had brought my glove up in front of my face. I could have jumped aside and avoided the ball completely. I hadn't thought to do that, though. I hadn't wanted Danny Saunders to make me look like Schwartzie.

"Well, you stopped it," Danny Saunders said.

I grinned at him.

"No hard feelings anymore?" he asked me.

"No hard feelings," I said. "I just hope the eye heals all right."

"I hope so, too," he said fervently. "Believe me."

"Say, who was that rabbi on the bench? Is he a coach or something?"

Danny Saunders laughed. "He's one of the teachers in the yeshiva. My father sends him along to make sure we don't mix too much with the apikorsim."

"That apikorsim thing got me angry at you. What did you have to tell your team a thing like that for?"

"I'm sorry about that. It's the only way we could have a team. I sort of convinced my father you were the best team around and that we had a duty to beat you apikorsim at what you were best at. Something like that."

"You really had to tell your father that?"

"Yes."

"What would have happened if you'd lost?"

"I don't like to think about that. You don't know my father."

"So you practically *had* to beat us."

He looked at me for a moment, and I saw he was thinking of something. His eyes had a kind of cold, glassy look. "That's right," he said, finally. He seemed to be seeing something he had been searching for for a long time. "That's right," he said again.

"What was he reading all the time?"

"Who?"

"The rabbi."

"I don't know. Probably a book on Jewish law or something."

"I thought it might have been something your father wrote."

"My father doesn't write," Danny said. "He reads a lot, but he never writes. He says that words distort what a person really feels in his heart. He doesn't like to talk too much, either. Oh, he talks plenty when we're studying Talmud together. But otherwise he doesn't say much. He told me once he wishes everyone could talk in silence."

"Talk in silence?"

"I don't understand it, either," Danny said, shrugging. "But that's what he said.

"Your father must be quite a man."

He looked at me. "Yes," he said, with the same cold, glassy stare in his eyes. I saw him begin to play absentmindedly with one of his earlocks. We were quiet for a long time. He seemed absorbed in something. Finally, he stood up. "It's late. I had better go."

"Thanks for coming to see me."

"I'll see you tomorrow again."

"Sure."

He still seemed to be absorbed in something. I watched him walk slowly up the aisle and out of the ward.

FOUR

MY FATHER CAME IN a few minutes later, looking worse than he had the day before. His cheeks were sunken, his eyes were red, and his face was ashen. He coughed a great deal and kept telling me it was his cold. He sat down on the bed and told me he had talked to Dr. Snydman on the phone. "He will look at your eye Friday morning, and you will probably be able to come home Friday afternoon. I will come to pick you up when I am through teaching."

"That's wonderful!" I said.

"You will not be able to read for about ten days. He told me he will know by then about the scar tissue."

"I'll be happy to be out of this hospital," I said. "I walked around a little today and saw the people on the street outside."

My father looked at me and didn't say anything.

"I wish I was outside now," I said. "I envy them being able to walk around like that. They don't know how lucky they are."

"No one knows he is fortunate until he becomes unfortunate," my father said quietly. "That is the way the world is."

"It'll be good to be home again. At least I won't have to spend a Shabbat here."

"We'll have a nice Shabbat together," my father said. "A quiet Shabbat where we can talk and not be disturbed. We will sit and drink tea and talk." He coughed a little and put the handkerchief to his mouth. He took off his spectacles and wiped his eyes. Then he put them back on and sat on the bed, looking at me. He seemed so tired and pale, as if all his strength had been drained from him.

"I didn't tell you yet, abba. Danny Saunders came to see me today."

My father did not seem surprised. "Ah," he said. "And?"

"He's a very nice person. I like him."

"So? All of a sudden you like him." He was smiling. "What did he say?"

I told him everything I could remember of my conversation with Danny Saunders. Once, as I talked, he began to cough, and I stopped and watched helplessly as his thin frame bent and shook. Then he wiped his lips and eyes, and told me to continue. He listened intently. When I told him that Danny Saunders had wanted to kill me, his eyes went wide, but he didn't interrupt. When I told him about Danny Saunders's photographic mind, he nodded as if he had known about that all along. When I described as best I could what we had said about our careers, he smiled indulgently. And when I explained why Danny Saunders had told his team that they would kill us apikorsim, he stared at me and I could see the same look of absorption come into his eyes that I had seen earlier in the eyes of Danny Saunders. Then my father nodded. "People are not always what they seem to be," he said softly. "That is the way the world is, Reuven."

"He's going to come visit me again tomorrow, abba."

"Ah," my father murmured. He was silent for a moment. Then he said quietly, "Reuven, listen to me. The Talmud says that a person should do two things for himself. One is to acquire a teacher. Do you remember the other?"

"Choose a friend," I said.

"Yes. You know what a friend is, Reuven? A Greek philosopher said that two people who are true friends are like two bodies with one soul."

I nodded.

"Reuven, if you can, make Danny Saunders your friend."

"I like him a lot, abba."

"No. Listen to me. I am not talking only about liking him. I am telling you to make him your friend and to let him make you his friend. I think—" He stopped and broke into another cough. He coughed a long time. Then he sat quietly on the bed, his hand on his chest, breathing hard. "Make him your friend," he said again, and cleared his throat noisily.

"Even though he's a Hasid?" I asked, smiling.

"Make him your friend," my father repeated. "We will see."

"The way he acts and talks doesn't seem to fit what he wears and the way he looks," I said. "It's like two different people."

My father nodded slowly but was silent. He looked over at Billy, who was still asleep.

"How is your little neighbor?" he asked me.

"He's very nice. There's a new kind of operation they'll be doing on his eyes. He was in an auto accident, and his mother was killed."

My father looked at Billy and shook his head. He sighed and stood up, then bent and kissed me on the forehead.

"I will be back to see you tomorrow. Is there anything you need?"

"No, abba."

"Are you able to use your tefillin?"

"Yes. I can't read, though. I pray by heart."

He smiled at me. "I did not think of that. My baseball player. I will see you again tomorrow, Reuven."

"Yes, abba."

I watched him walk quickly up the aisle.

"That your father, kid?" I heard Mr. Savo ask me.

I turned to him and nodded. He was still playing his game of cards.

"Nice-looking man. Very dignified. What's he do?"

"He teaches."

"Yeah? Well, that's real nice, kid. My old man worked a pushcart. Down near Norfolk Street, it was. Worked like a dog. You're a lucky kid. What's he teach?"

"Talmud," I said. "Jewish law."

"No kidding? He in a Jewish school?"

"Yes," I said. "A high school."

Mr. Savo frowned at a card he had just pulled from the deck. "Damn," he muttered. "No luck nowhere. Story of my life." He tucked the card into a row on the blanket. "You looked kind of chummy there with your clopper, boy. You making friends with him?"

"He's a nice person," I said.

"Yeah? Well, you watch guys like that, kid. You watch them real good, you hear? Anyone clops you, he's got a thing going. Old Tony knows. You watch them."

"It was really an accident," I said.

"Yeah?"

"I could have ducked the ball."

Mr. Savo looked at me. His face was dark with the growth of beard, and his left eye seemed a little swollen and bloodshot. The black patch that covered his right eye looked like a huge skin mole. "Anyone out to clop you doesn't want you to duck, kid. I know."

"It wasn't really like that, Mr. Savo."

"Sure, kid. Sure. Old Tony doesn't like fanatics, that's all."

"I don't think he's a fanatic."

"No? What's he go around in those clothes for?"

"They all wear those clothes. It's part of their religion."

"Sure, kid. But listen. You're a good kid. So I'm telling you, watch out for those fanatics. They're the worst cloppers around." He looked at a card in his hands, then threw it down. "Lousy game. No luck." He scooped up the cards, patted them into a deck, and put them on the night table. He lay back on his pillow. "Long day," he said, talking almost to himself. "Like waiting for a big fight." He closed his left eye.

I woke during the night and lay still a long time, trying to remember where I was. I saw the dim blue night-light at the other end of the ward, and took a deep breath. I heard a movement next to me and turned my head. The curtain had been drawn around Mr. Savo's bed, and I could hear people moving around. I sat up. A nurse came over to me from somewhere. "You go right back to sleep, young man," she ordered. "Do you hear?" She seemed angry and tense. I lay back on my bed. In a little while, I was asleep.

When I woke in the morning, the curtain was still drawn around Mr. Savo's bed. I stared at it. It was light brown, and it enclosed the area of the bed completely so that not even the metal legs of the bed could be seen. I remembered Monday afternoon when I had awakened with the curtain around my bed and Mrs. Carpenter bending over me, and I wondered what had happened to Mr. Savo. I saw Mrs. Carpenter coming quickly up the aisle, carrying a metal tray in her hands. There were instruments and bandages on the tray. I sat up and asked her what was wrong with Mr. Savo. She looked at me sternly, her round, fleshy face grim. "Mr. Savo will be all right, young man. Now you just go about your own business and let Mr. Savo be." She disappeared behind the curtain. I heard a soft moan. At the other end of the ward, the radio had been turned on and the announcer was talking about the war. I didn't want to turn my radio on for fear of disturbing Mr. Savo. I heard another moan, and then I couldn't stand it anymore. I got out of my bed and went to the bathroom. Then I walked around in the hall outside the ward and stared at the people on the street. When I came back, the curtain was still drawn around Mr. Savo's bed, and Billy was awake.

I sat down on my bed and saw him turn his head in my direction.

"Is that you, Bobby?" he asked me.

"Sure," I said.

"Is something wrong with Mr. Savo?"

I wondered how he knew about that.

"I think so," I told him. "They've got the curtain around his bed, and Mrs. Carpenter is in there with him."

"No," Billy said. "She just went away. I was calling him, and she told me not to disturb him. Is it something very bad?"

"I don't know. I think we ought to talk a little quieter, Billy. So we don't bother him."

"That's right," Billy said, lowering his voice.

"Also, I think we'll stop listening to the radio today. We don't want to wake him if he's sleeping."

Billy nodded fervently.

I got my tefillin from the night table and sat on my bed and prayed for a long time. Mostly, I prayed for Mr. Savo.

I was eating breakfast when I saw Dr. Snydman hurrying up the aisle with Mrs. Carpenter. He didn't even notice me as he passed my bed. He was wearing a dark suit, and he wasn't smiling. He went behind the curtain around Mr. Savo's bed, and Mrs. Carpenter followed. I heard them talking softly, and I heard Mr. Savo moan a few times. They were there quite a while. Then they came out and went back up the aisle.

I was really frightened now about Mr. Savo. I found I missed him and the way he talked and played cards. After breakfast, I lay in my bed and began to think about my left eye. I remembered tomorrow was Friday and that in the morning Dr. Snydman was supposed to examine it. I felt cold with fright. That whole morning and afternoon I lay in the bed and thought about my eye and became more and more frightened.

All that day the curtain remained around Mr. Savo's bed. Every few minutes, a nurse would go behind the curtain, stay there for a while, then come out and walk back up the aisle. In the afternoon, the radio at the other end of the ward was turned off. I tried to fall asleep, but couldn't. I kept watching nurses go in and out of the curtain around Mr. Savo's bed. By suppertime I was feeling so frightened and miserable that I could hardly eat. I nibbled at the food and sent the tray back almost untouched.

Then I saw Danny come up the aisle and stop at my bed. He was wearing the dark suit, the dark skullcap, the white shirt open at the collar, and the fringes showing below his jacket. My face must have mirrored my happiness at seeing him because he broke into a warm smile and said, "You look like I'm the Messiah. I must have made some impression yesterday."

I grinned at him. "It's just good to see you," I told him. "How are you?"

"How are *you*? You're the one in the hospital."

"I'm fed up being cooped up like this. I want to get out and go home. Say, it's really good to see you, you sonofagun!"

He laughed. "I *must* be the Messiah. No mere Hasid would get a greeting like that from an apikoros."

He stood at the foot of the bed, his hands in his trouser pockets, his face relaxed. "When do you go home?" he asked.

I told him. Then I remembered Mr. Savo lying in his bed behind the curtain. "Listen," I said, motioning with my head at the curtain. "Let's talk outside in the hall. I don't want to disturb him."

I got out of bed, put on my bathrobe, and we walked together out of the ward. We sat down on a bench in the hallway next to a window. The hallway was long and wide. Nurses, doctors, patients, orderlies, and visitors went in and out of the wards. It was still light outside. Danny put his hands in his pockets and stared out the window. "I was born in this hospital," he said quietly. "The day before yesterday was the first time I'd been in it since I was born."

"I was born here, too," I said. "It never occurred to me."

"I thought of it yesterday in the elevator coming up."

"I was back here to have my tonsils out, though. Didn't you ever have your tonsils out?"

"No. They never bothered me." He sat there with his hands in his pockets, staring out the window. "Look at that. Look at all those people. They look like ants. Sometimes I get the feeling that's all we are—ants. Do you ever feel that way?"

His voice was quiet, and there was an edge of sadness to it.

"Sometimes," I said.

"I told it to my father once."

"What did he say?"

"He didn't say anything. I told you, he never talks to me except when we study. But a few days later, while we were studying, he said that man was created by God, and Jews had a mission in life."

"What mission is that?"

"To obey God."

"Don't you believe that?"

He looked slowly away from the window. I saw his deep blue eyes stare at me, then blink a few times. "Sure I believe it," he said quietly. His shoulders were bowed. "Sometimes I'm not sure I know what God wants, though."

"That's a funny thing for you to say."

"Isn't it?" he said. He looked at me but didn't seem to be seeing me at all. "I've never said that to anyone before." He seemed to be in a strange, brooding mood. I was beginning to feel uneasy. "I read a lot," he said. "I read about seven or eight books a week outside of my schoolwork. Have you ever read Darwin or Huxley?"

"I've read a little of Darwin," I said.

"I read in the library so my father won't know. He's very strict about what I read."

"You read books about evolution and things like that?"

"I read anything good that I can get my hands on. I'm reading Hemingway now. You've heard of Hemingway."

"Sure."

"Have you read any of his works?"

"I read some of his short stories."

"I finished *A Farewell to Arms* last week. He's a great writer. It's about the First World War. There's this American in the Italian Army. He marries an English nurse. Only he doesn't really marry her. They live together, and she becomes pregnant, and he deserts. They run away to Switzerland, and she dies in childbirth."

"I didn't read it."

"He's a great writer. But you wonder about a lot of things when you read him. He's got a passage in the book about ants on a burning log. The hero, this American, is watching the ants, and instead of taking the log out of the fire and saving the ants, he throws water into the fire. The water turns into steam and that roasts some of the ants, and the others just burn to death on the log or fall off into the fire. It's a great passage. It shows how cruel people can be."

All the time he talked he kept staring out the window. I almost had the feeling he wasn't talking so much to me as to himself.

"I just get so tired of studying only Talmud all the time. I know the stuff cold, and it gets a little boring after a while. So I read whatever I can get my hands on. But I only read what the librarian says is worthwhile. I met a man there, and he keeps suggesting books for me to read. That librarian is funny. She's a nice person, but she keeps staring at me all the time. She's probably wondering what a person like me is doing reading all those books."

"I'm wondering a little myself," I said.

"I told you. I get bored studying just Talmud. And the English work in school isn't too exciting. I think the English teachers are afraid of my father. They're afraid they'll lose their jobs if they say something too exciting or challenging. I don't know. But it's exciting being able to read all those books." He began to play with the earlock on the right side of his face. He rubbed it gently with his right hand, twirled it around his forefinger, released it, then twirled it around the finger again. "I've never told this to anyone before," he said. "All the time I kept wondering who I would tell it to one day." He was staring down at the floor. Then he looked at me and smiled. It was a sad smile, but it seemed to break the mood he was in. "If you'd've ducked that ball I would still be wondering," he said, and put his hands back into his pockets.

I didn't say anything. I was still a little overwhelmed by what he had told me. I couldn't get over the fact that this was Danny Saunders, the son of Reb Saunders, the tzaddik.

"Can I be honest with you?" I asked him.

"Sure," he said.

"I'm all mixed up about you. I'm not trying to be funny or anything. I really am mixed up about you. You look like a Hasid, but you don't sound like one. You don't sound like what my father says Hasidim are supposed to sound like. You sound almost as if you don't believe in God."

He looked at me but didn't respond.

"Are you really going to become a rabbi and take your father's place?"

"Yes," he said quietly.

"How can you do that if you don't believe in God?"

"I believe in God. I never said I didn't believe in God."

"You don't sound like a Hasid, though," I told him.

"What do I sound like?"

"Like a—an apikoros."

He smiled but said nothing. It was a sad smile, and his blue eyes seemed sad, too. He looked back out the window, and we sat in silence a long time. It was a warm silence, though, not in the least bit awkward. Finally, he said very quietly, "I have to take my father's place. I have no choice. It's an inherited position. I'll work it out—somehow. It won't be that bad, being a rabbi. Once I'm a rabbi my people won't care what I read. I'll be sort of like God to them. They won't ask any questions."

"Are you going to like being a rabbi?"

"No," he said.

"How can you spend your life doing what you don't like?"

"I have no choice," he said again. "It's like a dynasty. If the son doesn't take the father's place, the dynasty falls apart. The people expect me to become their rabbi. My family has been their rabbi for six generations now. I can't just walk out on them. I'm—I'm a little trapped. I'll work it out, though—somehow." But he didn't sound as if he thought he would be able to work it out. He sounded very sad.

We sat quietly a while longer, looking out the window at the people below. There were only a few minutes of sunlight left, and I found myself wondering why my father hadn't yet come to see me. Danny turned away from the window and began to play with his earlock again, caressing it and twirling it around his index finger. Then he shook his head and put his hands in his pockets. He sat back on the bench and looked at me. "It's funny," he said. "It's really funny. I have to be a rabbi and don't want to be one. You don't have to be a rabbi and do want to be one. It's a crazy world."

I didn't say anything. I had a sudden vivid picture of Mr. Savo sitting in his bed, saying, "Crazy world. Cockeyed." I wondered how he was feeling and if the curtain was still around his bed.

"What kind of mathematics are you interested in?" Danny asked.

"I'm really interested in logic. Mathematical logic."

He looked puzzled.

"Some people call it symbolic logic," I said.

"I never even heard of it," he confessed.

"It's really very new. A lot of it began with Russell and Whitehead and a book they wrote called *Principia Mathematica.*"

"Bertrand Russell?"

"That's right."

"I didn't know he was a mathematician."

"Oh, sure. He's a great mathematician. And a logician, too."

"I'm very bad at mathematics. What's it all about? Mathematical logic, I mean."

"Well, they try to deduce all of mathematics from simple logical principles and show that mathematics is really based on logic. It's pretty complicated stuff. But I enjoy it."

"You have a course in *that* in your high school?"

"No. You're not the only person who reads a lot."

For a moment he looked at me in astonishment. Then he laughed.

"I don't read seven or eight books a week, though, like you," I said. "Only about three or four."

He laughed again. Then he got to his feet and stood facing me. His eyes were bright and alive with excitement.

"I never even heard of symbolic logic," he said. "It sounds fascinating. And you want to be a rabbi? How do they do it? I mean, how can you deduce arithmetic from logic? I don't see—" He stopped and looked at me. "What's the matter?" he asked.

"There's my father," I said, and got quickly to my feet.

My father had come out of the elevator at the other end of the hall and was walking toward the eye ward. I thought I would have to call out to attract his attention, but a few steps short of the entrance to the ward he saw us. If he felt any surprise at seeing me with Danny I didn't notice it. His face did not change expression. But as he came over to us, I saw Danny's face change radically. It went from curiosity to bewildered astonishment. He looked for a moment as though he wanted to run away. I could see he was nervous and agitated, but I didn't have time to think about it, because my father was standing there, looking at the two of us. He was wearing his dark gray, double-breasted suit and his gray hat. He was a good deal shorter than Danny and a little shorter than I, and his face still looked pale and worn. He seemed out of breath, and he was carrying a handkerchief in his right hand.

"I am late," he said. "I was afraid they would not let me in." His voice was hoarse and raspy. "There was a faculty meeting. How are you, Reuven?"

"I'm fine, abba."

"Should you be out here in the hall now?"

"It's all right, abba. The man next to me became sick suddenly, and we didn't want to disturb him. Abba, I want you to meet Danny Saunders."

I could see a faint smile begin to play around the corners of my father's lips. He nodded at Danny.

"This is my father, Danny."

Danny didn't say anything. He just stood there, staring at my father. I saw my father watching him from behind his steel-rimmed spectacles, the smile still playing around the corners of his lips.

"I didn't—" Danny began, then stopped.

There was a long moment of silence, during which Danny and my father stood looking at each other and I stared at the two of them and nothing was said.

It was my father who finally broke the silence. He did it gently and with quiet warmth. He said, "I see you play ball as well as you read books, Danny. I hope you are not as violent with a book as you are with a baseball."

Now it was my turn to be astonished. "You know Danny?"

"In a way," my father said, smiling broadly.

"I—I had no idea," Danny stammered.

"And how could you have?" my father asked. "I never told you my name."

"You knew me all the time?"

"Only after the second week. I asked the librarian. You applied for membership once, but did not take out a card."

"I was afraid to."

"I understood as much," my father said.

I suddenly realized it was my father who all along had been suggesting books for Danny to read. My father was the man Danny had been meeting in the library!

"But you never told me!" I said loudly.

My father looked at me. "What did I never tell you?"

"You never told me you met Danny in the library! You never told me you were giving him books to read!"

My father looked from me to Danny, then back to me. "Ah," he said, smiling. "I see you know about Danny and the library."

"I told him," Danny said. He had begun to relax a bit, and the look of surprise was gone from his face now.

"And why should I tell you?" my father asked. "A boy asks me for books to read. What is there to tell?"

"But all this week, even after the accident, you never said a word!"

"I did not think it was for me to tell," my father said quietly. "A boy comes into the library, climbs to the third floor, the room with old journals, looks carefully around, finds a table behind a bookcase where almost no one can see him, and sits down to read. Some days I am there, and he comes over to me, apologizes for interrupting me in my work, and asks me if I can recommend a book for him to read. He does not know me, and I do not know him. I ask him if he is interested in literature or science, and he tells me he is interested in anything that is worthwhile. I suggest a book, and two hours later he returns, thanks me, and tells me he has finished reading it, is there anything else I can recommend. I am a little astonished, and we sit for a while and discuss the book, and I see he has not only read it and understood it, but has memorized it. So I give him another book to read, one that is a little bit more difficult, and the same thing occurs. He finishes it completely, returns to me, and we sit and discuss it. Once I ask him his name, but I see he becomes very nervous, and I go to another topic quickly. Then I ask the librarian, and I understand everything because I have already heard of Reb Saunders's son from other people. He is very interested in psychology, he tells me. So I recommend more books. It is now almost two months that I have been making such recommendations. Isn't that so, Danny? Do you really think, Reuven, I should have told you? It was for Danny to tell if he wished, not for me."

My father coughed a little and wiped his lips with the handkerchief. The three of us stood there for a moment, not saying anything. Danny has his hands in his pockets and was looking down at the floor. I was still trying to get over my surprise.

"I'm very grateful to you, Mr. Malter," Danny said. "For everything."

"There is nothing to be grateful for, Danny," my father told him. "You asked me for books and I made recommendations. Soon you will be able to read on your own and not need anyone to make recommendations. If you continue to come to the library I will show you how to use a bibliography."

"I'll come," Danny said. "Of course I'll come."

"I am happy to hear that," my father told him, smiling.

"I—I think I'd better go now. It's very late. I hope the examination goes all right tomorrow, Reuven."

I nodded.

"I'll come over to your house Saturday afternoon. Where do you live?"

I told him.

"Maybe we can go out for a walk," he suggested.

"I'd like that," I said eagerly.

"I'll see you, then, on Saturday. Goodbye, Mr. Malter."

"Goodbye, Danny."

He went slowly up the hall. We watched him stop at the elevator and wait. Then the elevator came, and he was gone.

My father coughed into his handkerchief. "I am very tired," he said. "I had to rush to get here. Faculty meetings always take too long. When you are a professor in a university, you must persuade your colleagues not to have long faculty meetings. I must sit down."

We sat down on the bench near the window. It was almost dark outside, and I could barely make out the people on the sidewalk below.

"So," my father said, "how are you feeling?"

"I'm all right, abba. I'm a little bored."

"Tomorrow you will come home. Dr. Snydman will examine you at ten o'clock, and I will come to pick you up at one. If he could examine you earlier, I would pick you up earlier. But he has an operation in the early morning, and I must teach a class at eleven. So I will be here at one."

"Abba, I just can't get over that you've known Danny for so long. I can't get over him being the son of Reb Saunders."

"Danny cannot get over it, either," my father said quietly.

"I don't—"

My father shook his head and waved my unasked question away with his hand. He coughed again and took a deep breath. We sat for a while in silence. Billy's father came out of the ward. He walked slowly and heavily. I saw him go into the elevator.

My father took another deep breath and got to his feet.

"Reuven, I must go home and go to bed. I am very tired. I was up almost all last night finishing the article, and now rushing here to see you after the faculty meeting. . . . Too much. Too much. Come with me to the elevator."

We walked up the hall and stood in front of the double doors of the elevator.

"We will talk over the Shabbat table," my father said. He had almost no voice left. "It has been some day for you."

"Yes, abba."

The elevator came, and the doors opened. There were people inside. My father went in, turned, and faced me. "My two baseball players," he said, and smiled. The doors closed on his smile.

I went back up the hall to the eye ward. I was feeling very tired, and I kept seeing and hearing Danny and my father talking about what had been going on between them in the library. When I got to my bed, I saw that not only was the curtain still around Mr. Savo's bed, there was now a curtain around Billy's bed, too.

I went up to the glass-enclosed section under the blue light where two nurses were sitting and asked what had happened to Billy.

"He's asleep," one of the nurses said.

"Is he all right?"

"Of course. He is getting a good night's sleep."

"You should be in bed now, young man," the other nurse said.

I went back up the aisle and got into my bed.

The ward was quiet. After a while I fell asleep.

The windows were bright with sunlight. I lay in the bed awhile, staring at the windows. Then I remembered it was Friday, and I sat up quickly. I heard someone say, "Good to see you again, Bobby boy. How've you been?" and I turned, and there was Mr. Savo, lying on his pillow, the curtains no longer drawn around his bed. His long, stubbled face looked pale, and he wore a thick bandage over his right eye in place of the black patch. But he was grinning at me broadly, and I saw him wink his left eye.

"Had a bad night, kid. Comes from playing ball. Never could see anything in chasing a ball around."

"It's wonderful to see you again, Mr. Savo!"

"Yeah, kid. Been quite a trip. Gave the doc a real scare."

"You had Billy and me worried, too, Mr. Savo." I turned to look at Billy. I saw the curtains had been pulled back from his bed. Billy was gone.

"Took him out about two hours ago, kid. Big day for him. Good little kid. Lots of guts. Got to give him that three-rounder one day."

I stared at Billy's empty bed.

"I got to take it real easy, kid. Can't do too much talking. Have the old ring post down on my back."

He closed his eye and lay still.

When I prayed that morning it was all for Billy, every word. I kept seeing his face and vacant eyes. I didn't eat much breakfast. Soon it was ten o'clock, and Mrs. Carpenter came to get me. Mr. Savo lay very still in his bed, his eye closed.

The examination room was down the hall, a few doors away from the elevator. Its walls and ceiling were white, its floor was covered with squares of light and dark brown tile. There was a black leather chair over against one of the walls and instrument cabinets everywhere. A white examination table stood to the left of the chair. Attached to the floor at the right of the chair was a large, stubby-looking metal rod with a horizontal metal arm. Some kind of optical instrument formed part of the end of this metal arm.

Dr. Snydman was in the room, waiting for me. He looked tired. He smiled but didn't say anything. Mrs. Carpenter motioned me onto the examination table. Dr. Snydman came over and began to take the bandage off. I looked up at him out of my right eye. His hands worked very fast, and I could see the hairs on his fingers.

"Now, son, listen to me," Dr. Snydman said. "Your eye has been closed inside the bandage all the time. When the last bandage comes off, you may open it. We'll dim the light in here, so it won't hurt you."

I was nervous, and I could feel myself sweating. "Yes, sir," I said.

Mrs. Carpenter turned off some of the lights, and I felt the bandage come off the eye. I felt it before I knew it, because suddenly the eye was cold from the air.

"Now open your eye slowly until you become accustomed to the light," Dr. Snydman said.

I did as he told me, and in a little while I was able to keep it open without difficulty. I could see now through both my eyes.

"We can have the lights now, nurse," Dr. Snydman said.

I blinked as the new lights came on.

"Now we'll have a look," Dr. Snydman said, and bent down and peered at the eye through an instrument. After a while, he told me to close the eye, and he pressed down on the lid with one of his fingers.

"Does that hurt?" he asked.

"No, sir."

"Let's have you on that chair now," he said.

I sat on the chair, and he looked at the eye through the instrument attached to the metal rod. Finally, he straightened, swung the instrument back, and gave me a tired smile.

"Nurse, this young man can go home. I want to see him in my office in ten days."

"Yes, Doctor," Mrs. Carpenter said.

Dr. Snydman looked at me. "Your father tells me you know about the scar tissue."

"Yes, sir."

"Well, I think you're going to be all right. I'm not absolutely certain, you understand, so I want to see you again in my office. But I think you'll be fine."

I was so happy I felt myself begin to cry.

"You're a very lucky young man. Go home, and for heaven's sake, keep your head away from baseballs."

"Yes, sir. Thank you *very* much."

"You're quite welcome."

Outside in the hall, Mrs. Carpenter said, "We'll call your father right away. Isn't that wonderful news?"

"Yes, ma'am."

"You're lucky, you know. Dr. Snydman is a great surgeon."

"I'm very grateful to him," I said. "Ma'am?"

"Yes?"

"Is Billy's operation over yet?"

Mrs. Carpenter looked at me. "Why, yes, of course. It was Dr. Snydman who operated."

"Is he all right?"

"We hope for the best, young man. We always hope for the best. Come. We must call your father and get you ready to leave."

Mr. Savo was waiting for me. "How'd it go, boy?" he asked.

"Dr. Snydman says he thinks I'll be fine. I'm going home."

Mr. Savo grinned. "That's the way to do it, boy! Can't make a career out of lying around in hospitals."

"Are you going home soon, Mr. Savo?"

"Sure, kid. Maybe in a couple of days or so. If I don't go catching any more balls from little Mickey."

"Dr. Snydman operated on Billy," I said.

"Figured as much. Good man, the doc. Got a big heart."

"I hope Billy's all right."

"He'll be okay, kid. Important thing is you're getting out."

An orderly came over with my clothes, and I began to dress. I was very nervous, and my knees felt weak. After a while, I stood there, wearing the same clothes I had worn on Sunday for the ball game. It's been some week, I thought.

I sat on my bed, talking with Mr. Savo, and couldn't eat any of my lunch. I was nervous and impatient for my father to come. Mr. Savo told me to relax, I was spoiling his lunch. I sat there and waited. Finally, I saw my father coming quickly up the aisle, and I jumped to my feet. His face was beaming, and his eyes were misty. He kissed me on the forehead.

"So," he said. "The baseball player is ready to come home."

"Did you hear what Dr. Snydman said, abba?"

"The nurse told me on the telephone. Thank God!"

"Can we go home now, abba?"

"Of course. We will go home and have a wonderful Shabbat. I will take your things from the table."

I looked at Mr. Savo, who was sitting up on his bed, grinning at us. "It was wonderful meeting you, Mr. Savo."

"Likewise, kid. Keep the old beanbag away from those baseballs."

"I hope your eye gets better soon."

"The eye's out, kid. They had to take it out. It was some clop. Didn't want the little blind kid to know, so kept it quiet."

"I'm awfully sorry to hear that, Mr. Savo."

"Sure, kid. Sure. That's the breaks. Should've been a priest. Lousy racket, boxing. Glad to be out of it. Would've been in the war if that guy hadn't clopped me in the head like that years back. Busted up something inside. That's the breaks."

"Goodbye, Mr. Savo."

"Goodbye, kid. Good luck."

I went out of the ward with my father, and out of the hospital.

BOOK TWO

Silence is good everywhere,
except in connection with Torah.

—The Zohar

FIVE

WE TOOK A CAB and on the way home my father handed me my other pair of glasses with a warning not to read until Dr. Snydman told me I could, and I put them on. The world jumped into focus and everything looked suddenly bright and fresh and clean, as it does on an early morning with the sun on the trees, and there was newness everywhere, a feeling that I had been away a long time in a dark place and was now returning home to sunlight.

We lived on the first floor of a three-story brownstone house that stood on a quiet street just off busy Lee Avenue. The brownstone row houses lined both sides of the street, and long, wide, stone stairways led from the sidewalks to the frosted-glass double doors of the entrances. Tall sycamores stood in front of the houses and their leaves threw cool shadows onto the paved ground. There was a gentle breeze and I could hear the leaves moving over my head.

In front of each house was a tiny lawn planted with either morning glories or a hydrangea bush. The hydrangea bush—or snowball bush, as we called it—on our lawn glowed in the sunlight, and I stared at it. I had never really paid any attention to it before. Now it seemed suddenly luminous and alive.

We climbed up the wide stone staircase and came through the vestibule into the long hallway where it was dark and cool, and narrow like the corridor of a railroad car. The door to our apartment was at the end of the hallway, below and to the right of the staircase that led to the two stories above us. My father put his key into the lock, and we stepped inside.

I could smell the chicken soup immediately, and I had only taken two or three steps when Manya, our Russian housekeeper, came running out of the kitchen in her long apron, her man-sized shoes, and with strands of dark hair falling across her forehead from the braided bun on the top of her head, scooped me into her huge arms as though I were a leaf, and smothered me with a hug that pushed the air from my lungs and left me breathless. She planted a wet kiss on my forehead, then held me at arm's length and began to babble in Ukrainian. I couldn't understand what she was saying, but I could see her eyes were moist and she was biting her lips to keep from crying. She released me, and I stood there, smiling and catching my breath, while my father talked to her.

"Are you hungry, Reuven?" my father asked me.

"I'm starved," I said.

"There is lunch on the table. We will eat together. Then you can lie on the porch and rest while I finish typing my article."

Lunch turned out to be a massive affair, with a thick soup, fresh rye bread, onion rolls, bagels, cream cheese, scrambled eggs, smoked salmon, and chocolate pudding. My father and I ate without talking while Manya hovered over us like a protective bear, and afterwards my father went into his study and I walked slowly through the apartment. I had lived in it all my life, but I never really saw it until I went through it that Friday afternoon.

I came out of the kitchen and stood for a moment staring down at the strip of gray carpet that ran the length of the hall. I turned left and walked slowly along the hall, past the bathroom and the dumb-waiter to my left, past the telephone stand and the pictures of Herzl, Bialik, and Chaim Weizmann that hung from the wall on my right, and into my bedroom. It was a long, somewhat narrow room, with a bed against its right wall, a bookcase along its left wall, two closets near the door, and a desk and chair set a bit away from the wall facing the door. To the left of the desk, along the bookcase wall, was a window that looked out onto the alleyway and back yard beyond. The room had been cleaned, the bed carefully made and covered with its green-and-brown spread, and on the desk were my school books arranged in a neat pile. Someone had brought them home for me after the ball game, and there they were, on the desk, as though I had never been away. I went over to the window and stared out at the alleyway. I could see a cat lying in the shade of our wall, and beyond was the grass of our back lawn and the ailanthus tree with the sun on its leaves. I turned, sat down on the window seat, and stared at the *New York Times* war maps I had put on the wall over my bed. There were maps of the North African, Sicilian, and Italian campaigns, and now I would have to add a map of Europe, too. Over the maps was the large picture of Franklin Delano Roosevelt I had cut out of a *New York Times* Sunday magazine section, and next to it was the picture of Albert Einstein I had taken years ago from an issue of *Junior Scholastic.* I looked at my desk. My pens and pencils were neatly tucked into the holder alongside my lamp, and on top of a pile of papers was the recent issue of the WQXR *Bulletin.* I remembered I had wanted to listen to a Tchaikovsky symphony on Sunday night, the night of the ball game which I had been so certain we would win.

At the head of the bed was the door that led to my father's study. The door was closed, and I could hear my father working at his typewriter inside. There was no way to get to the living room except through the study, and I walked around behind my desk, opened the door, stepped inside, and closed it quietly behind me.

My father's study was the same size as my room, but it had no windows. The wall alongside the door was lined with floor-to-ceiling bookcases. Along the opposite wall were curtained French doors bounded by two large Ionic columns. What was left of that wall was also covered with bookcases, as was the wall adjoining it to the right. My father's desk stood near the outside wall of the house, in almost the exact position where I had asked to have my own desk placed. But it was a good deal larger than mine, with dark, polished wood, deep drawers, and a large, green, leather-bordered blotter that covered almost its entire top. It was strewn with papers now, and my father was working intently over his old Underwood typewriter. The study was the darkest room in the apartment because it had no windows, and my father always worked with the desk lamp on, the yellow light bathing the desk and the floor around it. He sat there now, wearing his small, black skullcap and pecking at the typewriter with his index fingers, a thin, frail man in his fifties, with gray hair, gaunt cheeks, and spectacles. I looked at him and suddenly realized that he hadn't coughed once since he had come to take me from the hospital. He glanced up at me for a moment, frowned, then went back to his work. He didn't like me to disturb him while he was at his desk, and I went quietly through the study, walking on the gray rug that covered the floor, then through the French doors into the living room.

Sunlight poured through the three wide windows that faced the street and spread gold across the gray rug, the French-style sofa, the chairs and end tables, the polished, glass-topped coffee table, and along the white walls. I stood near the sofa for a moment, blinking my eyes, which always hurt a little whenever I came from the darkness of my father's study into the brightness of our living room.

The windows were open, and I could hear children playing in the street. A warm breeze came into the room and lifted the lace curtains that fronted the windows.

I stood in that room for a long time, watching the sunlight and listening to the sounds on the street outside. I stood there, tasting the room and the sunlight and the sounds, and thinking of the long hospital ward with its wide aisle and its two rows of beds and little Mickey bouncing a ball and trying to find someone who would play catch with him. I wondered if little Mickey had ever seen sunlight come through the windows of a front-room apartment.

I turned, finally, and went back through the apartment and through the door that led from my father's bedroom onto our wooden back porch. I sat on the lounge chair in the shade that covered the porch and looked out at the back lawn. Somehow everything had changed. I had spent five days in a hospital and the world around me seemed sharpened now and pulsing with life. I lay back and put the palms of my hands under my head. I thought of the baseball game, and I asked myself, Was it only last Sunday that it happened, only five days ago? I felt I had crossed into another world, that little pieces of my old self had been left behind on the black asphalt floor of the school yard alongside the shattered lens of my glasses. I could hear the shouts of children on the street and the sounds of my father's typewriter. I remembered that tomorrow Danny would be over to see me. I lay very still on the lounge chair and thought a long time about Danny.

SIX

THAT NIGHT AS we sat at the kitchen table, with the Shabbat meal over and Manya gone until the morning, my father answered some of my questions about Danny Saunders.

It was a warm night, and the window between the stove and the sink was open. A breeze blew into the kitchen, stirring the ruffled curtains and carrying with it the odors of grass and flowers and orange blossoms. We sat at the table dressed in our Shabbat clothes, my father sipping his second glass of tea, both of us a little tired and sleepy from the heavy meal. There was color now in my father's face, and his cough had disappeared. I watched him sip his tea and listened to the soft rustling of the curtains as they moved in the breeze. Manya had done the dishes quickly after we had chanted the Grace After Meals, and now we sat alone, embraced by the warm June night, the memories of the past week, and the gentle silences of the Shabbat.

It was then that I asked my father about Danny. He was holding his glass of tea in his hands, the bottom of the glass resting upon his left palm, the body of the glass encircled by his right hand, and he put the glass on the white cloth that covered the table, looked at me, and smiled. He sat silent for a while, and I knew his answer would take a long time. Whenever he did not respond immediately to one of my questions, the answer was always a lengthy one. I could see he was arranging it in his mind, so that it would be carefully organized. When he finally spoke, his voice was soft, and the words came out slowly.

He told me he would have to go back a long time into the history of our people in order for me to understand his answer. He asked me if I had the patience to sit and listen quietly, and I nodded. He sat back in his chair and began to speak.

I knew enough Jewish history, he said, not to make him have to start at the beginning. He would start, instead, with the history I had not yet learned in school, with the centuries of horror our people had experienced in Poland. Because it was really in Poland, or, more accurately, in the Slavic countries of eastern Europe, that Danny's soul had been born.

"Poland was different from the other countries of Europe, Reuven. Poland actually encouraged the Jews to come and live and be part of her people. This was in the thirteenth century, during a time when the Jews of western Europe, especially in Germany, were going through terrible persecutions. Jews had been living in Poland before this century, but they were not a very large community. Why did Poland want Jews when almost every other country was persecuting them? Because Poland was a very poor country, with a bankrupt aristocracy and a crushed peasantry. Her upper-class nobles would not engage in work and instead managed to survive by what they could squeeze out of the labor of the serfs. Poland wanted people who would build her economy, organize her affairs, and bring her to life. Jews had a reputation for possessing these abilities, and so the Polish nobles were eager to have Jews settle in their country. They came by the thousands from western Europe, especially from Germany. They ran the nobles' estates, collected the taxes, developed Polish industry, and stimulated her trade. Poland became a kind of Jewish Utopia.

"But the Jews did not only prosper economically. They also built many great academies of learning throughout the country. Every community had its Talmudic scholars, and by the end of the sixteenth century the Jewish academies in Poland had become centers of learning for all of European Jewry.

"And then, Reuven, a great tragedy occurred. It is a tragedy that happens often to anyone who acts as a buffer. The Jews were helping the nobility, but in doing so, in collecting taxes from the serfs and peasants, for example, they were building up against themselves the hatred of these oppressed classes. And the hatred finally exploded into violence. In the borderland east of Ukrainia in Russia, there was a community of Cossacks who were members of the Greek Orthodox Church. This community belonged to Poland, and the Polish nobles, who were Catholics, treated the Cossacks who lived there with cruelty and contempt. They not only taxed the lands and the cattle of the Cossacks but also their churches and religious customs. And who collected these taxes? The Jews. Who had possession of the keys to the Cossack churches? The Jews. Who did the Cossacks need to go to if they wanted to open their churches for a christening service or for a marriage or a funeral? The Jews. All of whom were acting in behalf of the Polish lords.

"Nothing happened for a long time, because the Cossacks, like the Polish peasants, were afraid of the Polish nobles. But in the year 1648, a man named Bogdan Chmielnicki became the leader of the Cossacks, and he led an uprising against Poland. The Jews became the victims of the Polish peasants, who hated them, and of the Cossacks, who also hated them. The revolution lasted ten years, and in that time something like seven hundred Jewish communities were destroyed and about one hundred thousand Jews were slain. When the horror was over, the great Jewish community of Poland had been almost completely destroyed."

My father paused for a long moment. The window curtains moved softly in the cool night breeze. When he spoke again, his voice was low, tense, subdued.

"Reuven, what could our people say to God during the Chmielnicki uprising? They could not thank Him for the slaughter going on before their eyes, and they would not deny His existence. So many of them began to believe the Messiah was coming. Remember, Reuven, that those Jews who believe in the Messiah believe also that just before the Messiah comes there will be an era of great disaster. At the moment when there seems to be no meaning in life, at that moment a person must try to find new meaning. And so thousands upon thousands of Jews in both eastern and western Europe began to look upon the Chmielnicki disaster as the prelude to the coming of the Messiah. They prayed and fasted and did penance—all in an effort to hasten his coming. And he came. His name was Shabbtai Zvi. He revealed himself about the same time as the massacres began. More than half the Jewish world became his followers. Years later, when it turned out that he was a fraud, you can imagine what the effect was. The Chmielnicki uprising was a physical disaster; the false Messiah was a spiritual disaster.

"We are like other people, Reuven. We do not survive disaster merely by appealing to invisible powers. We are as easily degraded as any other people. That is what happened to Polish Jewry. By the eighteenth century, it had become a degraded people. Jewish scholarship was dead. In its place came empty discussions about matters that had no practical connection with the desperate needs of the masses of Jews. Pilpul, these discussions are called—empty, nonsensical arguments over minute points of the Talmud that have no relation at all to the world. Jewish scholars became interested in showing other Jewish scholars how much they knew, how many texts they could manipulate. They were not in the least bit interested in teaching the masses of Jews, in communicating their knowledge and uplifting the people. And so there grew up a great wall between the scholars and the people. It was also a time of terrible superstition. Our people believed that there were demons and ghosts everywhere that tortured the Jew, wracked his body, and terrorized his soul. These fears affected all Jews. But they affected the unlearned masses worst of all. At least the scholar had his pilpul to keep him alive.

"Now, Reuven, if everywhere around you there are forces that wish to harm you, what is it that you can do to help yourself? Of course, you try to destroy those forces. But the masses of Jews did not believe they had the power to do this. Only very skillful people possessed such power, they felt. And so there came upon the scene Jews who claimed to be experts in the chasing away of demons and spirits. Such men were looked upon as saints, and they became very popular in Poland. They claimed that their power came from their ability to manipulate the various letters that spelled out the mystical names of God. That is why they were called Ba'ale Shem—Masters of the Name. To drive away evil spirits they wrote magical amulets, prescribed medicines, performed wild dances, wearing the tallit and tefillin over white robes; they used black candles, sounded the shofar, recited psalms, screamed, pleaded, threatened—anything to drive the evil spirits out of a person who, for example, might be ill, or away from a mother who was about to have a child. To such a level had our people sunk in Poland by the eighteenth century. And here, Reuven, is where my answer to your questions about Reb Saunders's son really begins."

My father paused for a moment and finished his tea. Then he looked at me and smiled. "Are you tired yet, Reuven?"

"No, abba."

"I am not sounding too much like a schoolteacher?"

"I don't mind it when you sound like a schoolteacher," I said.

"It is not a lecture," he said. "I will not ask you questions afterward."

"I want you to go on," I said.

He nodded and smiled again. "I will want some more tea," he said. "But a little later. Now let me tell you about a man who was born in that century, and I think you will begin to have your answer.

"There are many legends about his birth, but I am not interested in telling you legends. He was born about the year 1700 in Poland. His name was Israel. His parents were very poor and not learned, and they both died while he was still a child. The people of his village cared for him and sent him to school. But he did not like school, and whenever he could he would sneak away and escape to the woods where he would walk under the trees, look at the flowers, sit by a brook, listen to the songs of the birds and to the noise of the wind in the leaves. As often as his teachers brought him back, so often did he run away to these woods, and after a while they gave up and left him alone. When he was thirteen, he became an assistant to a schoolmaster, but instead of helping the master teach the little children, he often took them also to the woods where they would sing or stand in silence, listening to the birds in the trees. When he grew older, he became the beadle of the village synagogue. All day long he would sit around, listening to the learned discussions that went on inside the synagogue walls, and at night, when everyone else slept, he would take the holy books in his hands and study them carefully. But it was not the Talmud that he studied, it was the Kabbalah, the books of Jewish mysticism. The rabbis had forbidden the study of the Kabbalah, and so Israel had to study in secret. He married, finally, but almost nothing is known about his wife. She died soon afterward, and Israel, a full-grown man now, became a schoolteacher. He had a wonderful way with children, and he achieved a great reputation as a teacher. He was a kind and gentle person, honest and unaffected, and often people would come to him and ask him to settle their quarrels. He came to be regarded as a wise and holy man, and one day the father of Rabbi Abraham Gershon of the city of Brody came to him and asked him to settle a business dispute he had with another man. He was so impressed with Israel that he offered to give him his daughter Hannah in marriage. Israel agreed, but asked that the betrothal document be kept a secret for the time being. And now, an interesting event occurred. The father of Hannah died, and Israel traveled to Brody, to the house of the great Rabbi Abraham Gershon, Hannah's brother, in order to claim his bride. He was dressed in the clothes of a peasant, torn boots and coarse garments, and you can imagine how shocked the rabbi was when he saw the betrothal agreement in Israel's hands. His sister should marry a peasant? What shame and dishonor that would bring upon the family name! He tried to persuade his sister to reject her father's choice, but somehow Hannah saw something in Israel which the good rabbi of Brody did not, and she refused. After their marriage, Rabbi

Abraham Gershon tried to improve his brother-in-law's education. He began by teaching him Talmud, but Israel seemed very uninterested in Talmud. He made him his coachman, but Israel was a failure at that, too. Finally, the rabbi gave up and ordered his sister and brother-in-law to leave Brody so as not to dishonor his good name, and they left.

"And now, Reuven, you will begin to have the answer to your question. I am sorry I am taking so long."

"Please go on, abba."

"All right. Israel and his wife left Brody and settled in the Carpathian Mountains in a village near Brody. They were very poor, but very happy. Israel earned a living by selling the lime which they dug in the mountains. The Carpathian Mountains are beautiful, and Israel built a little house and spent many days there alone, praying, dreaming, and singing to the great hills. Very often he would remain alone throughout the entire week, and return to his wife Hannah only for Shabbat. She must have suffered terribly because of their poverty, but she believed in him and was very devoted.

"Reuven, it was in these mountains that Israel gave birth to Hasidism. He was there many years, thinking, meditating, singing his strange songs, listening to the birds, learning from peasant women how to heal sickness with grasses and herbs, to write amulets, to drive out evil spirits. The people of the village loved him, and soon his reputation as a holy man began to spread throughout all of Poland. Legends began to grow about him. He was not yet forty, and already there were legends about him. You can imagine what kind of person he must have been.

"His brother-in-law, Rabbi Abraham Gershon, finally regretted his cruelty and asked Israel and Hannah to return to Brody. He acquired a tavern for them to operate, but it was Hannah who really managed it while Israel wandered about in the woods and meadows outside of Brody, meditating. Finally, he began to travel, and he became a Ba'al Shem. He was kind and saintly and godly, and he seemed to want to help people not for the money they paid him but for the love he had for them. And so they came to call him the Ba'al Shem Tov—the Kind or Good Master of the Name. He mingled with the people and talked to them about God and His Torah in plain, simple language that they could easily understand. He taught them that the purpose of man is to make his life holy—every aspect of his life: eating, drinking, praying, sleeping. God is everywhere, he told them, and if it seems at times that He is hidden from us, it is only because we have not yet learned to seek Him correctly.

Evil is like a hard shell. Within this shell is the spark of God, is goodness. How do we penetrate the shell? By sincere and honest prayer, by being happy, and by loving all people. The Ba'al Shem Tov—his followers later shortened his name and called him the Besht—believed that no man is so sinful that he cannot be purified by love and understanding. He also believed—and here is where he brought down upon himself the rage of the learned rabbis—that the study of Talmud was not very important, that there need not be fixed times for prayers, that God could be worshipped through a sincere heart, through joy and singing and dancing. In other words, Reuven, he opposed any form of mechanical religion. There was nothing new in what he taught. You will find it all in the Bible, Talmud, and Kabbalah. But he gave it a special emphasis and taught it at a key time to people who were hungry for this kind of teaching. And these people listened and loved him. Many great rabbis came to mock him and went away converted to his way of thinking. When he died, his followers opened their own synagogues. Before the end of that century, about half of eastern European Jewry consisted of Hasidim, as his followers were called, pious ones. So great was the need of the masses for a new way to approach God.

"There was another man born in that century, Rabbi Elijah of Vilna, a great Talmudist, a genius, and a strong opponent of Hasidism. But even his opposition could not stop Hasidism from growing. It flourished and became a great movement in Jewish life. For a long time there was terrible bitterness between the Mitnagdim, the opponents of Hasidism, and the followers of the Besht. For example, if the son of a Hasid married the daughter of a Mitnaged, both fathers would say Kaddish after their children, considering them to be dead and buried. So great was the bitterness.

"The Hasidim had great leaders—tzaddikim, they were called, righteous ones. Each Hasidic community had its own tzaddik, and his people would go to him with all their problems, and he would give them advice. They followed these leaders blindly. The Hasidim believed that the tzaddik was a superhuman link between themselves and God. Every act of his and every word he spoke was holy. Even the food he touched became holy. For example, they would grab the food scraps he left on his plate and eat them, because the food had become holy through his touch, and they wanted some of this holiness inside themselves. For a while, the tzaddikim were kind and gentle souls, like the Besht himself. But in the next century the movement began to degenerate. Many of the positions of tzaddik became inherited posts, going automatically from father to son, even if the son was not a great leader. Many tzaddikim lived like Oriental monarchs. Some of them were out-and-out frauds, and they exploited their people terribly. Others were very sincere, and a few were even great scholars of the Talmud. In some Hasidic sects, the study of the Talmud became as important as it had been before the time of the Besht. Secular literature was forbidden, and the Hasidim lived shut off from the rest of the world. Anything that was not Jewish and Hasidic was forbidden. Their lives became frozen. The clothes they wear today, for example, are the same Polish-style clothes they wore hundreds of years ago. Their customs and beliefs are also the same as they were hundreds of years ago. But not all of the Hasidic communities are identical, Reuven. The Hasidim of Russia, Germany, Poland, and Hungary are different one from the other. Not very different, but they are different. There are even Hasidic groups that believe their leaders should take upon themselves the sufferings of the Jewish people. You are surprised? But it is true. They believe that their sufferings would be unendurable if their leaders did not somehow absorb these sufferings into themselves. A strange belief, but a very important one, as far as they are concerned.

"Reuven, Reb Saunders is a great Talmudist and a great tzaddik. He has a reputation for brilliance and compassion. It is said that he believes the soul is as important as the mind, if not more so. He inherited his position from his father. When he dies, the position will go automatically to Danny."

My father stopped, looked at me with a smile, and said, "You are not asleep yet, Reuven?"

"No, abba."

"You are a very patient student. I think I am going to have another glass of tea. My throat is a little dry."

I took his glass, poured into it some strong-brewed tea from the teapot, filled it with water from the kettle, then brought it back to him. He put a cube of sugar between his teeth and sipped slowly from the glass, letting the tea soak through the sugar. Then he put the glass down.

"Tea is a blessing," he said, smiling. "Especially to a schoolteacher who must always give long answers to short questions."

I smiled back at him and waited patiently.

"All right," my father said. "I see you want me to continue. Now I am going to tell you another story, also a true story, about a Jewish boy who lived in Poland in the second half of the eighteenth century. As I tell you the story, think of Reb Saunders's son, and you will have your answer.

"This boy, Reuven, was brilliant, literally a genius. His name was Solomon, and later in life he changed his long Polish name to Maimon. When he was young, he found that the Talmud could not satisfy his hunger for knowledge. His mind would not let him rest. He wanted to know what was happening in the outside world. German was by then a great scientific and cultural language, and he decided to teach himself to read German. But even after he learned German he was not satisfied, because the reading of secular books was forbidden. Finally, at the age of twenty-five, he abandoned his wife and child and after many hardships came to Berlin where he joined a group of philosophers, read Aristotle, Maimonides, Spinoza, Leibniz, Hume, and Kant, and began to write philosophical books. It is astonishing how he was able to gobble up complicated philosophical treatises with such ease. He had a great mind, but it never left him in peace. He wandered from city to city, never finding roots anywhere, never satisfied, and finally died at forty-seven on the estate of a kindhearted Christian who had befriended him.

"Reuven, Reb Saunders's son has a mind like Solomon Maimon's, perhaps even a greater mind. And Reb Saunders's son does not live in Poland. America is free. There are no walls here to hold back the Jews. Is it so strange, then, that he is breaking his father's rules and reading forbidden books? He cannot help himself. It is unbelievable what he has read these past few months. You are a brilliant student. I tell you that now very proudly. But he is a phenomenon. Once in a generation is a mind like that born.

"Now, Reuven, listen very carefully to what I am going to tell you. Reb Saunders's son is a terribly torn and lonely boy. There is literally no one in the world he can talk to. He needs a friend. The accident with the baseball has bound him to you, and he has already sensed in you someone he can talk to without fear. I am very proud of you for that. He would never have told you about his library visits if he believed for a moment you would not keep his words a secret trust. And I want you to let him be your friend and to let yourself be his friend. I am certain you and Reb Saunders's son can help each other in such a friendship. I know you, and I know him. And I know what I am saying. And now, Reuven, the lecture is over, I am going to finish my tea, and we will go to bed. What a lecture it has been! Do you want some tea?"

"No, abba."

We sat in silence, while my father sipped from his glass.

"You are very quiet," he said finally.

"It all started with a silly baseball game," I said. "I can't believe it."

"Reuven, as you grow older you will discover that the most important things that will happen to you will often come as a result of silly things, as you call them—'ordinary things' is a better expression. That is the way the world is."

I shook my head. "I just can't believe it," I said again. "This whole week has been like something from another world. The hospital, the people I met there, Mr. Savo, little Mickey, Billy—all because of a ball game."

My father sipped his tea and looked at me over the rim of the glass. He said nothing, but he was watching me intently.

"I don't understand it," I said. "Weeks and weeks go by, one Shabbat follows another, and I'm the same, nothing has changed, and suddenly one day something happens, and everything looks different."

"Different? What do you mean, different?"

I told him how I had felt that afternoon when I had come home from the hospital. He listened quietly, all the while sipping his tea. When I finished, I saw him smile. He put down the glass, sighed, and said, "Reuven, it is a tragedy your mother is not alive to—" He stopped, his voice breaking. He was quiet for a moment. Then he looked at the clock on the shelf over the refrigerator. "It is very late," he said. "We will talk some more tomorrow."

"Yes, abba."

"Reuven—"

"Yes?"

"Never mind. Go to sleep. I am going to sit here for a while and have another glass of tea."

I left him sitting at the kitchen table, staring down at the white cloth.

SEVEN

THE NEXT DAY I met Danny's father.

My father and I woke early so as to be in our synagogue by eight-thirty. Manya came in a little before eight and served us a light breakfast. Then my father and I started out on the three-block walk to the synagogue. It was a beautiful day, and I felt happy to be out on the street again. It was wonderful to be outside that hospital, looking at the people and watching the traffic. When it didn't rain and wasn't too cold, my father and I always enjoyed our Shabbat walks to and from the synagogue.

There were many synagogues in Williamsburg. Each Hasidic sect had its own house of worship—shtibblach, they were called—most of them badly lighted, musty rooms, with benches or chairs crowded together and with windows that seemed always to be closed. There were also those synagogues in which Jews who were not Hasidim worshipped. The synagogue where my father and I prayed had once been a large grocery store. It stood on Lee Avenue, and though the bottom half of its window was curtained off, the sun shone in through the uncurtained portion of the glass, and I loved to sit there on a Shabbat morning, with the gold of the sun on the leaves of my prayer book, and pray.

The synagogue was attended mostly by men like my father—teachers from my yeshiva, and others who had come under the influence of the Jewish Enlightenment in Europe and whose distaste for Hasidism was intense and outspoken. Many of the students in the yeshiva I attended prayed there, too, and it was good to be able to be with them on a Shabbat morning.

When my father and I came into the synagogue that morning, the service had just begun. We took our usual seats a few rows up from the window and joined in the prayers. I saw Davey Cantor come in. He nodded to me, looking gloomy behind his glasses, and took his seat. The prayers went slowly; the man at the podium had a fine voice and waited until each portion of the service had been completed by everyone before he began to chant. I glanced at my father during the Silent Devotion. He stood in his long prayer shawl, its silver trim bathed in sunlight, its fringes dangling almost to the floor. His eyes were closed—he always prayed from memory, except during a Festival or a High Holiday Service—and he was swaying slightly back and forth, his lips murmuring the words. I did not wear a prayer shawl; they were worn only by adults who were or had once been married.

During the Torah Service, which followed the Silent Devotion, I was one of the eight men called up to the podium to recite the blessing over the Torah. Standing at the podium, I listened carefully to the reader as he chanted the words from the scroll. When he was done, I recited the second blessing and the prayer that thanks God when a serious accident has been avoided. As I left the podium and walked back to my seat, I wondered what blessing, if any, I would have recited had my eye been blinded. What blessing would Mr. Savo make if he were a Jew? I asked myself. For the rest of the service, I thought constantly of Mr. Savo and Billy.

Lunch was ready for us when we got home, and Manya kept adding food to my plate and urging me to eat; food was necessary for someone who had just come back from the hospital, she told me in her broken English. My father talked about my work at school. I must be careful not to read until Dr. Snydman gave me his permission, he said, but there was nothing wrong if I attended classes and listened. Perhaps he could help me study. Perhaps he could read to me. We would try it and see. After the Grace, my father lay down on his bed to rest for a while, and I sat on the porch and stared at the sunlight on the flowers and the ailanthus. I sat like that for about an hour, and then my father came out to tell me he was going over to see one of his colleagues.

I lay back on the lounge chair and stared up at the sky. It was a deep blue, with no clouds, and I felt I could almost touch it. It's the color of Danny's eyes, I thought. It's as blue as Danny's eyes. What color are Billy's eyes? I asked myself. I think they're also blue. Both Danny's and Billy's eyes are blue. But one set of eyes is blind. Maybe they're not blind anymore, I thought.

Maybe both sets of eyes are okay now. I fell asleep, thinking about Danny's and Billy's eyes.

It was a light, dreamless sleep, a kind of half-sleep that refreshes but does not shut off the world completely. I felt the warm wind and smelled newly cut grass, and a bird perched on a branch of the ailanthus and sang for a long time before it flew away. Somehow I knew where that bird was, though I did not open my eyes. There were children playing on the street, and once a dog barked and a car's brakes screeched. Someone was playing a piano nearby, and the music drifted slowly in and out of my mind like the ebb and flow of ocean surf. I almost recognized the melody, but I could not be sure; it slipped like a cool and silken wind from my grasp. I heard a door open and close and there were footsteps against wood, and then silence, and I knew someone had come onto the porch, but I would not open my eyes. I did not want to lose that twilight sleep, with its odors and sounds and whispered flow of music. Someone was on the porch, looking at me. I felt him looking at me. I felt him slowly push away the sleep, and, finally, I opened my eyes, and there was Danny, standing at the foot of the lounge chair, with his arms folded across his chest, clicking his tongue and shaking his head.

"You sleep like a baby," he said. "I feel guilty waking you."

I yawned, stretched, and sat up on the edge of the lounge chair. "That was delicious," I added, yawning again. "What time is it?"

"It's after five, sleepyhead. I've been waiting here ten minutes for you to wake up."

"I slept almost three hours," I said. "That was some sleep."

He clicked his tongue again and shook his head. "'What kind of infield is that?'" He was imitating Mr. Galanter. "'How can we keep that infield solid if you're asleep there, Malter?'"

I laughed and got to my feet.

"Where do you want to go?" he asked.

"I don't care."

"I thought we'd go over to my father's shul. He wants to meet you."

"Where is it?" I asked him.

"It's five blocks from here."

"Is my father inside?"

"I didn't see him. Your maid let me in. Don't you want to go?"

"Sure," I said. "Let me wash up and put a tie and jacket on. I don't have a caftan, you know."

He grinned at me. "The uniform is a requirement for members of the fold only," he said.

"Okay, member of the fold. Come on inside with me."

I washed, dressed, told Manya that when my father came in she should let him know where I had gone, and we went out.

"What does your father want to see me about?" I asked Danny as we went down the stone stairway of the house.

"He wants to meet you. I told him we were friends."

We turned up the street, heading toward Lee Avenue.

"He always has to approve of my friends," Danny said. "Especially if they're outside the fold. Do you mind my telling him that we're friends?"

"No."

"Because I really think we are," Danny said.

I didn't say anything. We walked to the corner, then turned right on Lee Avenue. The street was busy with traffic and crowded with people. I wondered what any of my classmates would think if they saw me walking with Danny. It would become quite a topic of conversation in the neighborhood. Well, they would see me with him sooner or later.

Danny was looking at me, his sculptured face wearing a serious expression. "Don't you have any brothers or sisters?" he asked.

"No. My mother died soon after I was born."

"I'm sorry to hear that."

"How about you?"

"I have a brother and a sister. My sister's fourteen and my brother is eight. I'm going on sixteen."

"So am I," I said.

We discovered that we had been born in the same year, two days apart.

"You've been living five blocks away from me all these years, and I never knew who you were," I said.

"We stick pretty close together. My father doesn't like us to mix with outsiders."

"I hope you don't mind my saying this, but your father sounds like a tyrant."

Danny didn't disagree. "He's a very strong-willed person. When he makes up his mind about something, that's it, finished."

"Doesn't he object to your going around with an apikoros like me?"

"That's why he wants to meet you."

"I thought you said your father never talks to you."

"He doesn't. Except when we study Talmud. But he did this time. I got up enough courage to tell him about you, and he said to bring you over today. That's the longest sentence he's said to me in years. Except for the time I had to convince him to let us have a ball team."

"I'd hate to have my father not talk to me."

"It isn't pleasant," Danny said very quietly. "But he's a great man. You'll see when you meet him."

"Is your brother going to be a rabbi, too?"

Danny gave me a queer look. "Why do you ask that?"

"No special reason. Is he?"

"I don't know. Probably he will." His voice had a strange, almost wistful quality to it. I decided not to press the point. He went back to talking about his father.

"He's really a great man, my father. He saved his community. He brought them all over to America after the First World War."

"I never heard about that," I told him.

"That's right," he said, and told me about his father's early years in Russia. I listened in growing astonishment.

Danny's grandfather had been a well-known Hasidic rabbi in a small town in southern Russia, and his father had been the second of two sons. The firstborn son had been in line to inherit his father's rabbinic position, but during a period of study in Odessa he suddenly vanished. Some said he had been murdered by Cossacks; for a time there was even a rumor that he had been converted to Christianity and had gone to live in France. The second son was ordained at the age of seventeen, and by the time he was twenty had achieved an awesome reputation as a Talmudist. When his father died, he automatically inherited the position of rabbinic leadership. He was twenty-one years old at the time.

He remained the rabbi of his community throughout the years of Russia's participation in the First World War. One week before the Bolshevist Revolution, in the autumn of 1917, his young wife bore him a second child, a son. Two months later, his wife, his son, and his eighteen-month-old daughter were shot to death by a band of marauding Cossacks, one of the many bandit gangs that roamed through Russia during the period of chaos that followed the revolution. He himself was left for dead, with a pistol bullet in his chest and a saber wound in his pelvis. He lay unconscious for half a day near the bodies of his wife and children, and then the Russian peasant who tended the stove in the synagogue and swept its floor found him and carried him to his hut, where he extracted the bullet, bathed the wounds, and tied him to the bed so he would not fall out during the days and nights he shivered and screamed with the fever and delirium that followed.

The synagogue had been burned to the ground. Its Ark was a gutted mass of charred wood, its four Torah scrolls were seared black, its holy books were piles of gray ash blown about by the wind. Of the one hundred eighteen Jewish families in the community only forty-three survived.

When it was discovered that the rabbi was not dead but was being cared for by the Russian peasant, he was brought into the still-intact home of a Jewish family and nursed back to health. He spent the winter recovering from his wounds. During that winter the Bolshevists signed the treaty of Brest-Litovsk with Germany, and Russia withdrew from the war. The chaos inside the country intensified, and the village was raided four times by Cossacks. But each of those times the Jews were warned by friendly peasants and were concealed in the woods or in huts. In the spring, the rabbi announced to his people that they were done with Russia, Russia was Esav and Edom, the land of Satan and the Angel of Death. They would travel together to America and rebuild their community.

Eight days later, they left. They bribed and bargained their way through Russia, Austria, France, Belgium, and England. Five months later, they arrived in New York City. At Ellis Island the rabbi was asked his name, and he gave it as Senders. On the official forms, Senders became Saunders. After the customary period of quarantine, they were permitted to leave the island, and Jewish welfare workers helped them settle in the Williamsburg section of Brooklyn. Three years later the rabbi married once again, and in 1929, two days before the stock market crash, Danny was born in the Brooklyn Memorial Hospital. Eighteen months later his sister was born, and five and a half years after the birth of his sister, his brother was born by Caesarean section, both in that same hospital.

"They all followed him?" I asked. "Just like that?"

"Of course. They would have followed him anywhere."

"I don't understand that. I didn't know a rabbi had that kind of power."

"He's more than a rabbi," Danny said. "He's a tzaddik."

"My father told me about Hasidism last night. He said it was a fine idea until some of the tzaddikim began to take advantage of their followers. He wasn't very complimentary."

"It depends upon your point of view," Danny said quietly.

"I can't understand how Jews can follow another human being so blindly."

"He's not just another human being."

"Is he like God?"

"Something like that. He's a kind of messenger of God, a bridge between his followers and God."

"I don't understand it. It almost sounds like Catholicism."

"That's the way it is," Danny said, "whether you understand it or not."

"I'm not offending you or anything. I just want to be honest."

"I want you to be honest," Danny said.

We walked on in silence.

A block beyond the synagogue where my father and I prayed, we made a right turn into a narrow street crowded with brownstones and sycamores. It was a duplicate of the street on which I lived, but a good deal older and less neatly kept. Many of the houses were unkempt, and there were very few hydrangea bushes or morning glories on the front lawns. The sycamores formed a solid, tangled bower that kept out the sunlight. The stone banisters on the outside stairways were chipped, their surfaces blotched with dirt, and the edges of the stone steps were round and smooth from years of use. Cats scrambled through the garbage cans that stood in front of some of the houses, and the sidewalks were strewn with old newspapers, ice cream and candy wrappers, worn cardboard cartons, and torn paper bags. Women in long-sleeved dresses, with kerchiefs covering their heads, many with infants in their arms, others heavily pregnant, sat on the stone steps of the stairways, talking loudly in Yiddish. The street throbbed with the noise of playing children who seemed in constant motion, dodging around cars, racing up and down steps, chasing after cats, climbing trees, balancing themselves as they tried walking on top of the banisters, pursuing one another in furious games of tag—all with their fringes and earlocks dancing wildly in the air and trailing out behind them. We were walking quickly now under the dark ceiling of sycamores, and a tall, heavily built man in a black beard and black caftan came alongside me, bumped me roughly to avoid running into a woman, and passed me without a word. The liquid streams of racing children, the noisy chatter of long-sleeved women, the worn buildings and blotched banisters, the garbage cans and the scrambling cats, all gave me the feeling of having slid silently across a strange threshold, and for a long moment I regretted having let Danny take me into his world.

We were approaching a group of about thirty black-caftaned men who were standing in front of the three-story brownstone at the end of the street. They formed a solid wall, and I did not want to push through them so I slowed my steps, but Danny took my arm with one hand and tapped his other hand upon the shoulder of a man on the outer rim of the crowd. The man turned, pivoting the upper portion of his body—a middle-aged man, his dark beard streaked with gray, his thick brows edging into a frown of annoyance—and I saw his eyes go wide. He bowed slightly and pushed back, and a whisper went through the crowd like a wind, and it parted, and Danny and I walked through, Danny holding me by the arm and nodding his head at the greetings in Yiddish that came in quiet murmurs from the people he passed. It was as if a black-waved, frozen sea had been sliced by a scythe, forming black, solid walls along a jelled path. I saw black- and gray-bearded heads bow toward Danny and dark brows arch sharply over eyes that stared questions at me and at the way Danny was holding me by the arm. We were almost halfway through the crowd now, walking slowly together, Danny's fingers on the part of my arm just over the elbow. I felt myself naked and fragile, an intruder, and my eyes, searching for anything but the bearded faces to look at, settled, finally, upon the sidewalk at my feet. Then, because I wanted something other than the murmured greetings in Yiddish to listen to, I began to hear, distinctly, the tapping sounds of Danny's metal-capped shoes against the cement pavement. It seemed a sharp, unnaturally loud sound, and my ears fixed on it, and I could hear it clearly as we went along. I listened to it intently—the soft scrape of the shoe and the sharp tap-tap of the metal caps—as we went up the stone steps of the stairway that led into the brownstone in front of which the crowd stood. The caps tapped against the stone of the steps, then against the stone of the top landing in front of the double door—and I remembered the old man I often saw walking along Lee Avenue, moving carefully through the busy street and tapping, tapping, his metal-capped cane, which served him for the eyes he had lost in a First World War trench during a German gas attack.

The hallway of the brownstone was crowded with black-caftaned men, and there was suddenly a path there, too, and more murmured greetings and questioning eyes, and then Danny and I went through a door that stood open to our right, and we were in the synagogue.

It was a large room and looked to be the exact size of the apartment in which my father and I lived. What was my father's bedroom was here the section of the synagogue that contained the Ark, the Eternal Light, an eight-branched candelabrum, a small podium to the right of the Ark, and a large podium about ten feet in front of the Ark. The two podiums and the Ark were covered with red velvet. What was our kitchen, hallway, bathroom, my bedroom, my father's study, and our front room was here the portion of the synagogue where the worshippers sat. Each seat consisted of a chair set before a stand with a sloping top, the bottom edge of which was braced with a jutting strip of wood to prevent what was on the stand from sliding to the floor. The seats extended back to about twenty feet from the rear wall of the synagogue, the wall opposite the Ark. A small portion of the synagogue near the upper door of the hallway had been curtained off with white cheesecloth. This was the women's section. It contained a few rows of wooden chairs. The remaining section of the synagogue, the section without chairs, was crowded with long tables and benches. Through the middle of the synagogue ran a narrow aisle that ended at the large podium. The walls were painted white. The wooden floor was a dark brown. The three rear windows were curtained in black velvet. The ceiling was white, and naked bulbs hung from it on dark wires, flooding the room with harsh light.

We stood for a moment just inside the door near one of the tables. Men passed constantly in and out of the room. Some remained in the hallway to chat, others took seats. Some of the seats were occupied by men studying Talmud, reading from the Book of Psalms, or talking among themselves in Yiddish. The benches at the tables stood empty, and on the white cloths that covered the tables were paper cups, wooden forks and spoons, and paper plates filled with pickled herring and onion, lettuce, tomatoes, gefülte fish, Shabbat loaves—the braided bread called challah—tuna fish, salmon, and hard-boiled eggs. At the edge of the table near the window was a brown leather chair. On the table in front of the chair was a pitcher, a towel, a saucer, and a large plate covered with a Shabbat cloth—a white satin cloth, with the Hebrew word for the Shabbat embroidered upon it in gold. A long serrated silver knife lay alongside the plate.

A tall, heavyset boy came in the door, nodded at Danny, then noticed me, and stared. I recognized him immediately as Dov Shlomowitz, the player on Danny's team who had run into me at second base and knocked me down. He seemed about to say something to Danny, then changed his mind, turned stiffly, went up the narrow aisle, and found a seat. Sitting in the seat, he glanced at us once over his shoulder, then opened a book on his stand, and began to sway back and forth. I looked at Danny and managed what must have been a sick smile. "I feel like a cowboy surrounded by Indians," I told him in a whisper.

Danny grinned at me reassuringly and let go of my arm. "You're in the holy halls," he said. "It takes getting used to."

"That was like the parting of the Red Sea out there," I said. "How did you do it?"

"I'm my father's son, remember? I'm the inheritor of the dynasty. Number one on our catechism: Treat the son as you would the father, because one day the son will be the father."

"You sound like a Mitnaged," I told him, managing another weak smile.

"No I don't," he said. "I sound like someone who reads too much. Come on. We sit up front. My father will be down soon."

"You live in this house?"

"We have the upper two floors. It's a fine arrangement. Come on. They're beginning to come in."

The crowd in the hallway and in front of the building had begun coming through the door. Danny and I went up the aisle. He led me to the front row of seats that stood at the right of the large podium and just behind the small podium. Danny sat down in the second seat and I sat in the third. I assumed that the first seat was for his father.

The crowd came in quickly, and the synagogue was soon filled with the sounds of shuffling shoes, scraping chairs, and loud voices talking Yiddish. I heard no English, only Yiddish. Sitting in the chair, I glanced over at Dov Shlomowitz, and found him staring at me, his heavy face wearing an expression of surprise and hostility, and I suddenly realized that Danny was probably going to have as much trouble with his friends over our friendship as I would have with mine. Maybe less, I thought. I'm not the son of a tzaddik. No one steps aside for me in a crowd. Dov Shlomowitz looked away but I saw others in the crowded synagogue staring at me, too, and I looked down at the worn prayer book on my stand, feeling exposed and naked again, and very alone.

Two gray-bearded old men came over to Danny, and he got respectfully to his feet. They had had an argument over a passage of Talmud, they told him, each of them interpreting it in a different way, and they wondered who had been correct. They mentioned the passage, and Danny nodded, immediately identified the tractate and the page, then coldly and mechanically repeated the passage word for word, giving his interpretation of it, and quoting at the same time the interpretations of a number of medieval commentators like the Me'iri, the Rashba, and the Maharsha. The passage was a difficult one, he said, gesticulating with his hands as he spoke, the thumb of his right hand describing wide circles as he emphasized certain key points of interpretation, and both men had been correct; one had unknowingly adopted the interpretation of the Me'iri, the other of the Rashba. The men smiled and went away satisfied. Danny sat down.

"That's a tough passage," he said. "I can't make head or tail out of it. Your father would probably say the text was all wrong." He was talking quietly and grinning broadly. "I read some of your father's articles. Sneaked them off my father's desk. The one on that passage in *Kiddushin* about the business with the king is very good. It's full of real apikorsische stuff."

I nodded, and tried another smile. My father had read that article to me before he had sent it off to his publisher. He had begun reading his articles to me during the past year, and spent a lot of time explaining them.

The noise in the synagogue had become very loud, almost a din, and the room seemed to throb and swell with the scraping chairs and the talking men. Some children were running up and down the aisle, laughing and shouting, and a number of younger men lounged near the door, talking loudly and gesticulating with their hands. I had the feeling for a moment I was in the carnival I had seen recently in a movie, with its pushing, shoving, noisy throng, and its shouting, arm-waving vendors and pitchmen.

I sat quietly, staring down at the prayer book on my stand. I opened the book and turned to the Afternoon Service. Its pages were yellow and old, with ragged edges and worn corners. I sat there, staring at the first psalm of the service and thinking of the almost new prayer book I had held in my hands that morning. I felt Danny nudge me with his elbow, and I looked up.

"My father's coming," he said. His voice was quiet and, I thought, a little strained.

The noise inside the synagogue ceased so abruptly that I felt its absence as one would a sudden lack of air. It stopped in swift waves, beginning at the rear of the synagogue and ending at the chairs near the podium. I heard no signal and no call for silence; it simply stopped, cut off, as if a door had slammed shut on a playroom filled with children. The silence that followed had a strange quality to it: expectation, eagerness, love, awe.

A man was coming slowly up the narrow aisle, followed by a child. He was a tall man, and he wore a black satin caftan and a fur-trimmed black hat. As he passed each row of seats, men rose, bowed slightly, and sat again. Some leaned over to touch him. He nodded his head at the murmur of greetings directed to him from the seats, and his long black beard moved back and forth against his chest, and his earlocks swayed. He walked slowly, his hands clasped behind his back, and as he came closer to me I could see that the part of his face not hidden by the beard looked cut from stone, the nose sharp and pointed, the cheekbones ridged, the lips full, the brow like marble etched with lines, the sockets deep, the eyebrows thick with black hair and separated by a single wedge like a furrow plowed into a naked field, the eyes dark, with pinpoints of white light playing in them as they do in black stones in the sun. Danny's face mirrored his exactly—except for the hair and the color of the eyes. The child who followed him, holding on to the caftan with his right hand, was a delicate miniature of the man, with the same caftan, the same fur-trimmed hat, the same face, the same color hair, though beardless, and I realized he was Danny's brother. I glanced at Danny and saw him staring down at his stand, his face without expression. I saw the eyes of the congregants follow the man as he came slowly up the aisle, his hands clasped behind his back, his head nodding, and then I saw them on Danny and me as he came up to us. Danny rose quickly to his feet, and I followed, and we stood there, waiting, as the man's dark eyes moved across my face—I could feel them moving across my face like a hand—and fixed upon my left eye. I had a sudden vision of my father's gentle eyes behind their steel-rimmed spectacles, but it vanished swiftly, because Danny was introducing me to Reb Saunders.

"This is Reuven Malter," he said quietly in Yiddish.

Reb Saunders continued to stare at my left eye. I felt naked under his gaze, and he must have sensed my discomfort, because quite suddenly he offered me his hand. I raised my hand to take it, then realized, as my hand was going up, that he was not offering me his hand but his fingers, and I held them for a moment—they were dry and limp—then let my hand drop.

"You are the son of David Malter?" Reb Saunders asked me in Yiddish. His voice was deep and nasal, like Danny's, and the words came out almost like an accusation.

I nodded my head. I had a moment of panic, trying to decide whether to answer him in Yiddish or English. I wondered if he knew English. My Yiddish was very poor. I decided to answer in English.

"Your eye," Reb Saunders said in Yiddish. "It is healed?"

"It's fine," I said in English. My voice came out a little hoarse, and I swallowed. I glanced at the congregants. They were staring at us intently, in complete silence.

Reb Saunders looked at me for a moment, and I saw the dark eyes blink, the lids going up and down like shades. When he spoke again it was still in Yiddish.

"The doctor, the professor who operated, he said your eye is healed?"

"He wants to see me again in a few days. But he said the eye is fine."

I saw his head nod slightly and the beard go up and down against his chest. The lights from the naked bulbs on the ceiling gleamed off his satin caftan.

"Tell me, you know mathematics? My son tells me you are very good in mathematics."

I nodded.

"So. We will see. And you know Hebrew. A son of David Malter surely knows Hebrew."

I nodded again.

"We will see," Reb Saunders said.

I glanced out of the sides of my eyes and saw Danny looking down at the floor, his face expressionless. The child stood a little behind Reb Saunders and stared up at us, his mouth open.

"Nu," Reb Saunders said, "later we will talk more. I want to know my son's friend. Especially the son of David Malter." Then he went past us and stood in front of the little podium, his back to the congregation, the little boy still holding on to his caftan.

Danny and I sat down. A whisper moved through the congregation, followed by the rustle of pages as prayer books were opened. An old, gray-bearded man went up to the large podium, put on a prayer shawl, and started the service.

The old man had a weak voice, and I could barely hear him over the prayers of the worshippers. Reb Saunders stood with his back to the congregation, swaying back and forth, occasionally clapping his hands together, and the child stood at his right, swaying, too, in obvious imitation of his father. Throughout the entire service, Reb Saunders stood with his back to the congregation, sometimes raising his head toward the ceiling, or raising his hands to cover his eyes. He turned only when the Torah was taken from the Ark and read.

The service ended with the Kaddish, and then Reb Saunders walked slowly back up the aisle, followed by the child, who was still clinging to his father's caftan. As the child passed me, I noticed his dark eyes were very large and his face was deathly pale.

Danny nudged me with his elbow and motioned with his head toward the rear of the synagogue. He rose, and the two of us followed Reb Saunders up the aisle. I could see the eyes of the congregants on my face, and then feel them on my back. I saw Reb Saunders go to the leather chair at the table near the end window and sit down. The child sat on the bench to his left. Danny led me to the table and sat on the bench to his father's right. He motioned me to sit down next to him, and I did.

The congregants rose and came toward the rear of the synagogue. The silence was gone now, burst as abruptly as it had begun, and someone started chanting a tune, and others took it up, clapping their hands in rhythm to the melody. They were filing out the door—probably to wash their hands, I thought—and soon they were coming back in and finding seats at the tables, the benches scraping loudly as they were moved back and forth. The singing had stopped. Our table filled rapidly, mostly with older men.

Reb Saunders stood up, poured water over his hands from the pitcher, the water spilling into the saucer, then wiped his hands, removed the white satin cloth that covered the challah, said the blessing over bread, cut a section off the end of the challah, swallowed it, and sat down. Danny got to his feet, washed his hands, cut two slices from the challah, handed me one, took one for himself, made the blessing, ate, and sat. He passed the pitcher to me, and I repeated the ritual, but I remained seated. Then Danny cut the remainder of the challah into small pieces, gave a piece to his brother, and handed the plate to the old man sitting next to me. The pieces of challah disappeared swiftly, grabbed up by the men at the table. Reb Saunders put some salad and fish on his plate and ate a small piece of the fish, holding it in his fingers. A man from one of the other tables came over and took the plate. Danny filled another plate for his father. Reb Saunders ate slowly, and in silence.

I was not very hungry, but I made some attempt at eating so as not to insult anyone. Frequently during the meal, I felt rather than saw Reb Saunders's eyes on my face. Danny was quiet. His little brother pecked at the food on his plate, eating little. The skin of his face and hands was almost as white as the tablecloth, drawn tightly over the bones, and the veins showed like blue branches in his face and on the tops of his hands. He sat quietly, and once he began to pick his nose, saw his father look at him, and stopped, his lower lip trembling a little. He bent over his plate and poked at a slice of tomato with a thin, stubby finger.

Danny and I said nothing to each other throughout that entire meal. Once I looked up and saw his father staring at me, his eyes black beneath the thick brows. I looked away, feeling as though my skin had been peeled away and my insides photographed.

Someone began to sing Atah Echad, one of the prayers from the Evening Service. The meal was over, and the men began to sway slowly, in unison with the melody. The singing filled the synagogue, and Reb Saunders sat back in his leather seat and sang, too, and then Danny was singing. I knew the melody and I joined in, hesitantly at first, then strongly, swaying back and forth. At the end of the song, another melody was begun, a light, fast, wordless tune, sung to the syllables cheeree bim, cheeree bam, and the swaying was a little faster now, and hands were clapped in time to the rhythm. Then tune followed tune, and I felt myself begin to relax as I continued to join the singing. I found that most of the melodies were familiar to me, especially the slow, somber ones that were meant to convey the sadness of the singers over the conclusion of the Shabbat, and the tunes I did not know I was able to follow easily, because the basic melody lines were almost all the same. After a while I was singing loudly, swaying back and forth and clapping my hands, and once I saw Reb Saunders looking at me, and his lips curved into a shadow of a smile. I smiled at Danny and he smiled back at me, and we sat there for about half an hour, singing, swaying, and clapping, and I felt light and happy and completely at ease. So far as I could see, Reb Saunders's little son was the only one in the synagogue not singing; he sat pecking at his food and poking at the slice of tomato on his paper plate with his thin, veined hand. The singing went on and on—and then it stopped. I glanced around to see what had happened, but everyone was sitting very still, looking over at our table. Reb Saunders washed his hands again, and others spilled what was left of the water in their paper cups over their hands. The introductory psalm to the Grace was sung together, and then Reb Saunders began the Grace. He chanted with his eyes closed, swaying slightly in his leather chair. After the opening lines of the Grace, each man prayed quietly, and I saw Danny lean forward, put his elbows on the table, cover his eyes with his right hand, his lips whispering the words. Then the Grace was done, and there was silence—a long, solid silence in which no one moved and everyone waited and eyes stared at Reb Saunders, who was sitting in his chair with his eyes closed, swaying slightly back and forth. I saw Danny take his elbows from the table and sit up straight. He stared down at his paper plate, his face expressionless, and I almost had the feeling that he had gone rigid, tense, as a soldier does before he jumps from shelter into open combat.

Everyone waited, and no one moved, no one coughed, no one even took a deep breath. The silence became unreal and seemed suddenly filled with a noise of its own, the noise of a too-long silence. Even the child was staring now at his father, his eyes like black stones against the naked whiteness of his veined face.

And then Reb Saunders began to speak.

He swayed back and forth in the leather chair, his eyes closed, his left hand in the crook of his right elbow, the fingers of his right hand stroking his black beard, and I could see everyone at the tables lean forward, eyes staring, mouths slightly open, some of the older men cupping their hands behind their ears to catch his words. He began in a low voice, the words coming out slowly in a singsong kind of chant.

"The great and holy Rabban Gamaliel," he said, "taught us the following: 'Do His will as if it were thy will, that He may do thy will as if it were His will. Nullify thy will before His will that He may nullify the will of others before thy will.' What does this mean? It means that if we do as the Master of the Universe wishes, then He will do as we wish. A question immediately presents itself. What does it mean to say that the Master of the Universe will do what we wish? He is after all the Master of the Universe, the Creator of heaven and earth, the King of kings. And what are we? Do we not say every day, 'Are not all the mighty as naught before Thee, the men of renown as though they had not been, the wise as if without knowledge, and the men of understanding as if without discernment'? What are we that the Master of the Universe should do our will?"

Reb Saunders paused, and I saw two of the old men who were sitting at our table look at each other and nod. He swayed back and forth in his leather chair, his fingers stroking his beard, and continued to speak in a quiet, singsong voice.

"All men come into the world in the same way. We are born in pain, for it is written, 'In pain shall ye bring forth children.' We are born naked and without strength. Like dust are we born. Like dust can the child be blown about, like dust is his life, like dust is his strength. And like dust do many remain all their lives, until they are put away in dust, in a place of worms and maggots. Will the Master of the Universe obey the will of a man whose life is dust? What is the great and holy Rabban Gamaliel teaching us?" His voice was beginning to rise now. "What is he telling us? What does it mean to say the Master of the Universe will do our will? The will of men who remain dust? Impossible! The will of what men, then? We must say, the will of men who do *not* remain dust. But how can we raise ourselves above dust? Listen, listen to me, for this is a mighty thing the rabbis teach us."

He paused again, and I saw Danny glance at him, then stare down again at his paper plate.

"Rabbi Halafta son of Dosa teaches us, 'When ten people sit together and occupy themselves with the Torah, the Presence of God abides among them, as it is said, "God standeth in the congregation of the godly." And whence can it be shown that the same applies to five? Because it is said, "He had founded his band upon the earth." And whence can it be shown that the same applies to three? Because it is said, "He judgeth among the judges." And whence can it be shown that the same applies to two? Because it is said, "Then they that feared the Lord spake one with the other, and the Lord gave heed and heard." And whence can it be shown that the same applies even to one? Because it is said, "In every place where I cause my name to be remembered I will come unto thee and I will bless thee."' Listen, listen to this great teaching. A congregation is ten. It is nothing new that the holy Presence resides among ten. A band is five. It is also nothing new that the holy Presence resides among five. Judges are three. If the holy Presence did not reside among judges there would be no justice in the world. So this, too, is not new. That the Presence can reside even among two is also not impossible to understand. But that the Presence can reside in one! In one! Even in one! That already is a mighty thing. Even in one! If one man studies Torah, the Presence is with him. If one man studies Torah, the Master of the Universe is already in the world. A mighty thing! And to bring the Master of the World *into* the world is also to raise oneself up from the dust. Torah raises us from the dust! Torah gives us strength! Torah clothes us! Torah brings the Presence!"

The singsong chant had died away. He was talking in a straight, loud voice that rang through the terrible silence in the synagogue.

"But to study Torah is not such a simple thing. Torah is a task for all day and all night. It is a task filled with danger. Does not Rabbi Meir teach us, 'He who is walking by the way and studying, and breaks off his study and says,

"How fine is that tree, how fine is that field," him the Scripture regards as if he had forfeited his life'?"

I saw Danny glance quickly at his father, then lower his eyes. His body sagged a little, a smile played on his lips, and I thought I even heard him sigh quietly.

"He had forfeited his life! His life! So great is the study of Torah. And now, listen, listen to this word. Whose task is it to study Torah? Of whom does the Master of the Universe demand, 'Ye shall meditate over it day and night'? Of the world? No! What does the world know of Torah? The world is Esav! The world is Amalek! The world is Cossacks! The world is Hitler, may his name and memory be erased! Of whom, then? Of the people of Israel! *We* are commanded to study His Torah! *We* are commanded to sit in the light of the Presence! It is for this that we were created! Does not the great and holy Rabbi Yochanan son of Zakkai teach us, 'If thou hast learnt much Torah, ascribe not any merit to thyself, for thereunto wast thou created'? Not the world, but the people of Israel! The people of Israel must study His Torah!"

His voice stormed the silence. I found myself holding my breath, my heart thumping in my ears. I could not take my eyes off his face, which was alive now, or his eyes, which were open and filled with dark fire. He struck the table with his hand, and I felt myself go cold with fright. Danny was watching him now, too, and his little brother stared at him as though in a trance, his mouth open, his eyes glazed.

"The world kills us! The world flays our skin from our bodies and throws us to the flames! The world laughs at Torah! And if it does not kill us, it tempts us! It misleads us! It contaminates us! It asks us to join in its ugliness, its impurities, its abominations! The world is Amalek! It is not the world that is commanded to study Torah, but the people of Israel! Listen, listen to this mighty teaching." His voice was suddenly lower, quieter, intimate. "It is written, 'This world is like a vestibule before the world-to-come; prepare thyself in the vestibule, that thou mayest enter into the hall.' The meaning is clear: The vestibule is this world, and the hall is the world-to-come. Listen. In gematriya, the words 'this world' come out one hundred sixty-three, and the words 'the world-to-come' come out one hundred fifty-four. The difference between 'this world' and 'the world-to-come' comes out to nine. Nine is half of eighteen. Eighteen is chai, life. In this world there is only half of chai. We are only half alive in this world! Only half alive!"

A whisper went through the crowd at the tables, and I could see heads nod and lips smile. They had been waiting for this apparently, the gematriya, and they strained forward to listen. One of my teachers in school had told me about gematriya. Each letter of the Hebrew alphabet is also a number, so that every Hebrew word has a numerical value. The words for "this world" in Hebrew is "olam hazeh," and by adding the numerical value of each letter, the total numerical value of the word becomes one hundred and sixty-three. I had heard others do this before, and I enjoyed listening because sometimes they were quite clever and ingenious. I was beginning to feel relaxed again, and I listened carefully.

"Hear me now. Listen. How can we make our lives full? How can we fill our lives so that we are eighteen, chai, and not nine, not half chai? Rabbi Joshua son of Levi teaches us, 'Whoever does not labor in the Torah is said to be under the divine censure.' He is a nozuf, a person whom the Master of the Universe hates! A righteous man, a tzaddik, studies Torah, for it is written, 'For his delight is in the Torah of God, and over His Torah doth he meditate day and night.' In gematriya, 'nozuf' comes out one hundred forty-three, and 'tzaddik' comes out two hundred and four. What is the difference between 'nozuf' and 'tzaddik'? Sixty-one. To whom does a tzaddik dedicate his life? To the Master of the Universe! La-el, to God! The word 'La-el' in gematriya is sixty-one! It is a life dedicated to God that makes the difference between the nozuf and the tzaddik!"

Another murmur of approval went through the crowd. Reb Saunders was very good at gematriya, I thought. I was really enjoying myself now.

"And now listen to me further. In gematriya, the letter of the word 'traklin,' hall, the hall that refers to the world-to-come, comes out three hundred ninety-nine, and 'prozdor,' the vestibule, the vestibule that is this world, comes out five hundred thirteen. Take 'prozdor' from 'traklin,' and we have one hundred fourteen. Now listen to me. A righteous man, we said, is two hundred four. A righteous man lives by Torah. Torah is mayim, water; the great and holy rabbis always compare Torah to water. The word 'mayim' in gematriya is ninety. Take 'mayim' from 'tzaddik' and we also have one hundred fourteen. From this we learn that the righteous man who removes himself from Torah also removes himself from the world-to-come!"

The whisper of delight was loud this time, and men nodded their heads and smiled. Some of them were even poking each other with their elbows to indicate their pleasure. That one had really been clever. I started to go over it again in my mind.

"We see that without Torah there is only half a life. We see that without Torah we are dust. We see that without Torah we are abominations." He was saying this quietly, almost as if it were a litany. His eyes were still open, and he was looking directly at Danny now. "When we study Torah, *then* the Master of the Universe listens. *Then* he hears our words. *Then* He will fulfill our wishes. For the Master of the Universe promises strength to those who preoccupy themselves in Torah, as it is written, 'So ye may be strong,' and He promises length of days, as it is written. 'So that your days may be lengthened.' May Torah be a fountain of waters to all who drink from it, and may it bring to us the Messiah speedily and in our day. Amen!"

A chorus of loud and scattered amens answered.

I sat in my seat and saw Reb Saunders looking at Danny, then at me. I felt completely at ease, and I somewhat brazenly smiled and nodded, as if to indicate that I had enjoyed his words, or at least the gematriya part of his words. I didn't agree at all with his notions of the world as being contaminated. Albert Einstein is part of the world, I told myself. President Roosevelt is part of the world. The millions of soldiers fighting Hitler are part of the world.

I thought that the meal was ended now and we would start the Evening Service, and I almost began to get out of my seat when I realized that another silence had settled upon the men at the tables. I sat still and looked around. They seemed all to be staring at Danny. He was sitting quietly, smiling a little, his fingers playing with the edge of his paper plate.

Reb Saunders sat back in his leather chair and folded his arms across his chest. The little boy was poking at the tomato again and glancing at Danny from the tops of his dark eyes. He twirled a side curl around one of his fingers, and I saw his tongue dart out of his mouth, run over his lips, then dart back in. I wondered what was going on.

Reb Saunders sighed loudly and nodded at Danny. "Nu, Daniel, you have something to say?" His voice was quiet, almost gentle.

I saw Danny nod his head.

"Nu, what is it?"

"It is written in the name of Rabbi Yaakov, not Rabbi Meir," Danny said quietly, in Yiddish.

A whisper of approval came from the crowd. I glanced around quickly. Everyone sat staring at Danny.

Reb Saunders almost smiled. He nodded, and the long black beard went back and forth against his chest. Then I saw the thick black eyebrows arch upward and the lids go about halfway down across the eyes. He leaned forward slightly, his arms still folded across his chest.

"And nothing more?" he asked very quietly.

Danny shook his head—a little hesitantly, I thought.

"So," Reb Saunders said, sitting back in the leather chair, "there is nothing more."

I looked at the two of them, wondering what was happening. What was this about Rabbi Yaakov and Rabbi Meir?

"The words were said by Rabbi Yaakov, not by Rabbi Meir," Danny repeated. "Rabbi Yaakov, not Rabbi Meir, said, 'He who is walking by the way and studying, and breaks off his study and—'"

"Good," Reb Saunders broke in quietly. "The words were said by Rav Yaakov. Good. You saw it. Very good. And where is it found?"

"In *Pirkei Avos*," Danny said. He was giving the Talmudic source for the quote. Many of the quotes Reb Saunders had used had been from *Pirkei Avos*—or *Avot*, as my father had taught me to pronounce it, with the Sephardic rather than the Ashkenazic rendering of the Hebrew letter "tof." I had recognized the quotes easily. *Pirkei Avot* is a collection of Rabbinic maxims, and a chapter of it is studied by many Jews every Shabbat between Passover and the Jewish New Year.

"Nu," Reb Saunders said, smiling, "how should you not know that? Of course. Good. Very good. Now, tell me—"

As I sat there listening to what then took place between Danny and his father, I slowly realized what I was witnessing. In many Jewish homes, especially homes where there are yeshiva students and where the father is learned, there is a tradition which takes place on Shabbat afternoon: The father quizzes the son on what he has learned in school during the past week. I was witnessing a kind of public quiz, but a strange, almost bizarre quiz, more a contest than a quiz, because Reb Saunders was not confining his questions only to what Danny had learned during the week but was ranging over most of the major tractates of the Talmud and Danny was obviously required to provide the answers. Reb Saunders asked where else there was a statement about one who interrupts his studies, and Danny coolly, quietly answered. He asked what a certain medieval commentator had remarked about that statement, and Danny answered. He chose a minute aspect of the answer and asked who had dealt with it in an altogether different way, and Danny answered. He asked whether Danny agreed with this interpretation, and

Danny said he did not, he agreed with another medieval commentator, who had given another interpretation. His father asked how could the commentator have offered such an interpretation when in another passage in the Talmud he had said exactly the opposite, and Danny, very quietly, calmly, his fingers still playing with the rim of the paper plate, found a difference between the contradictory statements by quoting two other sources where one of the statements appeared in a somewhat different context, thereby nullifying the contradiction. One of the two sources Danny had quoted contained a Biblical verse, and his father asked him who else had based a law upon this verse. Danny repeated a short passage from the tractate *Sanhedrin*, and then his father quoted another passage from *Yoma* which contradicted the passage in *Sanhedrin*, and Danny answered with a passage from *Gittin* which dissolved the contradiction. His father questioned the validity of his interpretation of the passage in *Gittin* by citing a commentary on the passage that disagreed with his interpretation, and Danny said it was difficult to understand this commentary—he did not say the commentary was wrong, he said it was difficult to understand it—because a parallel passage in *Nedarim* clearly confirmed his own interpretation.

This went on and on, until I lost track of the thread that held it all together and sat and listened in amazement to the feat of memory I was witnessing. Both Danny and his father spoke quietly, his father nodding his approval each time Danny responded. Danny's brother sat staring at them with his mouth open, finally lost interest, and began to eat some of the food that was still on his plate. Once he started picking his nose, but stopped immediately. The men around the tables were watching as if in ecstasy, their faces glowing with pride. This was almost like the pilpul my father had told me about, except that it wasn't really pilpul, they weren't twisting the texts out of shape, they seemed more interested in b'kiut, in straightforward knowledge and simple explanations of the Talmudic passages and commentaries they were discussing. It went on like that for a long time. Then Reb Saunders sat back and was silent.

The contest, or quiz, had apparently ended, and Reb Saunders was smiling at his son. He said, very quietly, "Good. Very good. There is no contradiction. But tell me, you have nothing more to say about what I said earlier?"

Danny was suddenly sitting very straight.

"Nothing more?" Reb Saunders asked again. "You have nothing more to say?"

Danny shook his head, hesitantly.

"Absolutely nothing more to say?" Reb Saunders insisted, his voice flat, cold, distant. He was no longer smiling.

I saw Danny's body go rigid again, as it had done before his father began to speak. The ease and certainty he had worn during the Talmud quiz had disappeared.

"So," Reb Saunders said. "There is nothing more. Nu, what should I say?"

"I did not hear—"

"You did not hear, you did not hear. You heard the first mistake, and you stopped listening. Of course you did not hear. How could you hear when you were not listening?" He said it quietly and without anger.

Danny's face was rigid. The crowd sat silent. I looked at Danny. For a long moment he sat very still—and then I saw his lips part, move, curve slowly upward, and freeze into a grin. I felt the skin on the back of my neck begin to crawl, and I almost cried out. I stared at him, then looked quickly away.

Reb Saunders sat looking at his son. Then he turned his eyes upon me. I felt his eyes looking at me. There was a long, dark silence, during which Danny sat very still, staring fixedly at his plate and grinning. Reb Saunders began to play with the earlock along the right side of his face. He caressed it with the fingers of his right hand, wound it around the index finger, released it, then caressed it again, all the time looking at me. Finally, he sighed loudly, shook his head, and put his hands on the table.

"Nu," he said, "it is possible I am not right. After all, my son is not a mathematician. He has a good head on him, but it is not a head for mathematics. But we have a mathematician with us. The son of David Malter is with us. He is a mathematician." He was looking straight at me, and I felt my heart pound and the blood drain from my face. "Reuven," Reb Saunders was saying, looking straight at me, "you have nothing to say?"

I found I couldn't open my mouth. Say about what? I hadn't the faintest idea what he and Danny had been talking about.

"You heard my little talk?" Reb Saunders asked me quietly. I felt my head nod.

"And you have nothing to say?"

I felt his eyes on me and found myself staring down at the table. The eyes were like flames on my face.

"Reuven, you liked the gematriya?" Reb Saunders asked softly.

I looked up and nodded. Danny hadn't moved at all. He just sat there, grinning. His little brother was playing with the tomato again. And the men at the tables were silent, staring at *me* now.

"I am very happy," Reb Saunders said gently. "You liked the gematriya. Which gematriya did you like?"

I heard myself say, lamely and hoarsely, "They were all very good."

Reb Saunders's eyebrows went up. "All?" he said. "A very nice thing. They were all very good. Reuven, were they *all* very good?"

I felt Danny stir and saw him turn his head, the grin gone now from his lips. He glanced at me quickly, then looked down again at his paper plate.

I looked at Reb Saunders. "No," I heard myself say hoarsely. "They were not all good."

There was a stir from the men at the tables. Reb Saunders sat back in his leather chair.

"Nu, Reuven," he said quietly, "tell me, which one was not good?"

"One of the gematriyot was wrong," I said. I thought the world would fall in on me after I said that. I was a fifteen-year-old boy, and there I was, telling Reb Saunders he had been wrong! But nothing happened. There was another stir from the crowd, but nothing happened. Instead, Reb Saunders broke into a warm, broad smile.

"And which one was it?" he asked me quietly.

"The gematriya for 'prozdor' is five hundred and three, not five hundred and thirteen," I answered.

"Good. Very good," Reb Saunders said, smiling and nodding his head, the black beard going back and forth against his chest, the earlocks swaying. "Very good, Reuven. The gematriya for 'prozdor' comes out five hundred three. Very good." He looked at me, smiling broadly, his teeth showing white through the beard, and I almost thought I saw his eyes mist over. There was a loud murmur from the crowd, and Danny's body sagged as the tension went out of him. He glanced at me, his face a mixture of surprise and relief, and I realized with astonishment that I, too, had just passed some kind of test.

"Nu," Reb Saunders said loudly to the men around the tables, "say Kaddish!"

An old man stood up and recited the Scholar's Kaddish. Then the congregants broke to go back to the front section of the synagogue for the Evening Service.

Danny and I said nothing to each other throughout the service, and though I prayed the words, I did not know what I was saying. I kept going over what had happened at the table. I couldn't believe it. I just couldn't get it through my head that Danny had to go through something like that every week, and that I myself had gone through it tonight.

The followers of Reb Saunders obviously had been pleased with my performance, because I could see they were no longer staring questions at me but were glancing at me admiringly. One of them, an old man with a white beard who was sitting in my row, even nodded at me and smiled, the corners of his eyes crinkling. I had clearly passed the test. What a ridiculous way to gain admiration and friendship!

The Evening Service was over very quickly, and afterward one of the younger men chanted the Havdalah, the brief service that marks the end of the Shabbat. Danny's brother held the braided candle, his hand trembling a little as the molten wax spilled onto his fingers. Then the congregants wished one another and Reb Saunders a good week and began to leave the synagogue. It was late, and I thought my father would probably be worried about me by now, but I stood there and waited until the last congregant was gone and the synagogue was empty—except for me, Danny, Reb Saunders, and the little boy. The synagogue seemed to me suddenly very small without its throng of black-hatted, black-bearded, black-caftaned men.

Reb Saunders was stroking his beard and looking at Danny and me. He leaned an elbow upon the large podium, and then the hand that was stroking the beard began to play with an earlock. I heard him sigh and saw him shake his head slowly, his dark eyes moist and brooding.

"Reuven, you have a good head on you," he said quietly in Yiddish. "I am happy my Daniel has chosen you for a friend. My son has many friends. But he does not talk about them the way he talks about you."

I listened and said nothing. His voice was gentle, almost a caress. He seemed so altogether different now from the way he had been at the table. I glanced at Danny. He was looking at his father, and the rigid lines were gone from his face.

Reb Saunders clasped his hands behind his back.

"I know of your father," he said to me quietly. "I am not surprised you have such a head. Your father is a great scholar. But what he writes, ah, what he writes!" He shook his head. "I worry myself about my son's friends, especially if such a friend is the son of David Malter. Ah, what your father writes! Criticism. Scientific criticism. Ah! So when he tells me you are now his friend, I worry myself. The son of David Malter should be my Daniel's friend? But your father is an observer of the Commandments, and you have his head, and so I am happy you are friends. It is good my Daniel has a friend. I have many responsibilities, I am not always able to talk to him." I saw Danny stare down at the floor, his face hardening. "It is good he has acquired a friend. Just so his friend does not teach him scientific criticism." Reb Saunders looked at me, his eyes dark and brooding. "You think a friend is an easy thing to be? If you are truly his friend, you will discover otherwise. We will see. Nu, it is late and your father is certainly worried that you are away so long. Have a good week, Reuven. And come pray with us again. There will be no more mistakes in gematriya."

He was smiling broadly and warmly now, his eyes wrinkling at the corners, the hard lines of his face almost gone. And then he offered me his hand, his entire hand this time, not only the fingers, and I took it, and he held my hand a long time. I almost had the feeling he wanted to embrace me. Then our hands separated, and he went slowly up the aisle, his hands clasped behind his back, tall, a little stooped, and, I thought, a little majestic. His young son trailed behind him, holding on to the caftan.

Danny and I remained alone in the synagogue. It occurred to me suddenly that not a single word had passed between him and his father all evening, except for the Talmud contest.

"I'll walk you part of the way home," Danny offered, and we went out of the brownstone and down the stone stairway to the street. I could hear the caps of his shoes clearly against the stone of the stairway, and then against the cement pavement of the sidewalk.

It was night now, and cool, and a breeze blew against the sycamores and moved softly through the leaves. We walked in silence until Lee Avenue, then turned left. I was walking quickly, and Danny kept pace with my steps.

Walking along Lee Avenue, Danny said quietly, "I know what you're thinking. You think he's a tyrant."

I shook my head. "I don't know what to think. One minute he's a tyrant, the next minute he's kind and gentle. I don't know what to think."

"He's got a lot on his mind," Danny said. "He's a pretty complicated person."

"Do you always go through that routine at the table?"

"Oh, sure. I don't mind it. I even enjoy it a little."

"I've never seen anything like it in my life."

"It's a family tradition," Danny explained. "My father's father used to do it with him. It goes all the way back."

"It would scare me sick."

"It's not that bad. The bad part is waiting until he makes the mistake. After that it's all right. But the mistakes aren't really very hard to find. He makes ones that he knows I can find. It's a kind of game almost."

"Some game!"

"The second mistake tonight caught me off guard. But he made that one for you, really. That was very good, the way you caught it. He knew I wouldn't catch it. He just wanted to catch me, so he could tell me I wasn't listening. He was right. I wasn't listening. But I wouldn't have caught it even if I had listened. I'm no good in math. I've got a photographic memory for everything except math. You can't memorize math. You have to have a certain kind of head for it."

"I hate to tell you what I think about that game," I said, a little heatedly. "What happens if you miss the mistake?"

"I haven't missed in years."

"What happens when you *do* miss?"

He was silent a moment. "It's uncomfortable for a while," he said quietly. "But he makes a joke or something, and we go into a Talmud discussion."

"What a game!" I said. "In front of all those people!"

"They love it," Danny said. "They're very proud to see us like that. They love to hear the Talmud discussed like that. Did you see their faces?"

"I saw them," I said. "How could I not see them? Does your father always use gematriya when he talks?"

"Not always. Very rarely, as a matter of fact. The people love it and always hope for it. But he does it rarely. I think he did it tonight only because you were there."

"He's good at it, I'll say that much."

"He wasn't too good tonight. Some of it was a little forced. He was fantastic a few months ago. He did it with Talmudic laws then. He was really great."

"I thought it wasn't bad tonight."

"Well, it wasn't too good. He hasn't been feeling too well. He's worried about my brother."

"What's wrong with your brother?"

"I don't know. They don't talk about it. Something about his blood. He's been sick for a few years now."

"I'm sorry to hear that, Danny."

"He'll be all right. There's a pretty big doctor taking care of him now. He'll be all right." His voice had the same strange quality it had had when he had talked about his brother on our way over to the synagogue earlier in the day—hope, wistfulness, almost an eagerness for something to take place. I thought Danny must love his little brother very much, though I didn't remember his saying a word to him all the time they had been together. "Anyway," Danny said, "these contests, as you call them, are going to end as soon as I start studying with Rav Gershenson."

"Who?"

"Rav Gershenson. He's a great scholar. He's at Hirsch College. He teaches Talmud there. My father says that when I'm old enough to study with Rav Gershenson, I'll be old enough for him not to worry whether I can catch him at mistakes or not. Then we'll just have the Talmud discussions. I'll like that."

I was restraining my delight with considerable difficulty. The Samson Raphael Hirsch Seminary and College was the only yeshiva in the United States that offered a secular college education. It was located on Bedford Avenue, a few blocks from Eastern Parkway. My father had told me once that it had been built in the early twenties by a group of Orthodox Jews who wanted their sons to have both a Jewish and a secular education. Its college faculty was supposed to be excellent, and its rabbinic faculty consisted of some of the greatest Talmudists in the United States. A rabbinic ordination from its Talmud faculty was looked upon as the highest of Orthodox Jewish honors. It had been a foregone conclusion on my father's part and on mine that I would go on to there after high school for my bachelor's degree. When I told Danny that, his face burst into a smile.

"Well, that's wonderful!" he said. "I'm happy to hear that. That's really wonderful!"

"So we'll be going to the same college," I said. "Will you be going for a B.A.?"

"Sure. You have to. They don't let you study just Talmud in that college. I'll be majoring in psychology."

We had come to the corner of the synagogue in which my father and I prayed. Danny stopped.

"I have to go back," he said. "I've got schoolwork to do."

"I'll call you at your house tomorrow afternoon."

"I'll probably be in the library tomorrow afternoon, doing some reading in psychology. Why don't you come over there?"

"I won't be able to read anything."

"That's right." Danny smiled. "I forgot. You didn't duck."

"I'll come over anyway. I'll sit and think while you read."

"Wonderful. I'd like to watch you sit and think."

"Mitnagdim can think, too, you know," I said.

Danny laughed. "I'll see you tomorrow."

"Right," I said, and watched him walk away, tall and lean in his black caftan and black hat.

I hurried home and came into the apartment just as my father was beginning to dial the phone. He put the phone down and looked at me.

"Do you know what time it is?" he asked.

"Is it very late?" I glanced at my watch. It was almost ten-thirty. "I'm sorry, abba. I couldn't just walk out."

"You were at Reb Saunders's synagogue all this time?"

"Yes."

"Next time you are out so late you will call, yes? I was ready to telephone Reb Saunders to find out what happened. Come into the kitchen and sit down. What are you looking so excited about? Sit down. I'll make some tea. Did you eat? What happened that you were away so long?"

I sat at the kitchen table and slowly told my father everything that had taken place in Reb Saunders's synagogue. He sipped his tea and listened quietly. I saw him grimace when I began to go over the gematriyot. My father did not particularly care for gematriya. He had once referred to it as nonsense numerology and had said that anything could be proved that way, all that had to be done was to shift letters around adroitly so as to make the values come out any way you wanted. So he sat there, sipping his tea and grimacing, as I reviewed Reb Saunders's gematriyot. When I started to tell him what had happened afterward, the grimace left his face, and he listened intently, nodding his head from time to time and sipping his tea. And when I got to the part where Reb Saunders had asked me about the wrong gematriya, his face took on a look of astonishment, and he put the glass down on the table. Then I told him what Reb Saunders had said to me after Havdalah and what Danny and I had talked about on the way home, and he smiled proudly and nodded to indicate his happiness.

"Well," my father said, sipping his tea again, "you had some day, Reuven."

"It was an experience, abba. The way Danny had to answer his father's questions like that in front of everybody. I thought that was terrible."

My father shook his head. "It is not terrible, Reuven. Not for Danny, not for his father, and not for the people who listened. It is an old tradition, this kind of Talmudic discussion. I have seen it many times, between great rabbis. But it does not only take place between rabbis. When Kant became a professor, he had to follow an old tradition and argue in public on a philosophical subject. One day when you are a professor in a university and read a paper before your colleagues, you will also have to answer questions. It is part of Danny's training."

"But in public like that, abba!"

"Yes, Reuven. In public like that. How else would Reb Saunders's people know that Danny has a head for Talmud?"

"It just seemed so cruel to me."

My father nodded. "It is a little cruel, Reuven. But that is the way the world is. If a person has a contribution to make, he must make it in public. If learning is not made public, it is a waste. But the business about the mistakes I never heard before. That is something new. That is Reb Saunders's innovation. It is clever, but I am not sure I like it very much. No, I do not think I like it at all."

"Danny said the mistakes are always easy to find."

"Perhaps," my father said. "A man can do whatever he wishes to test his son's knowledge. But there are other ways than the way of Reb Saunders. At any rate, Reuven, it is good training for Danny. He will be involved in such things all his life."

"Reb Saunders is a very complicated man, abba. I can't make him out. One minute he's hard and angry, the next minute he's soft and gentle. I don't understand him."

"Reb Saunders is a great man, Reuven. Great men are always difficult to understand. He carries the burden of many people on his shoulders. I do not care for his Hasidism very much, but it is not a simple task to be a leader of people. Reb Saunders is not a fraud. He would be a great man even if he had not inherited his post from his father. It is a pity he occupies his mind only with Talmud. If he were not a tzaddik he could make a great contribution to the world. But he lives only in his own world. It is a great pity. Danny will be the same way when he takes his father's place. It is a shame that a mind such as Danny's will be shut off from the world."

My father sipped his tea again, and we sat quietly for a while.

"I am very proud of the way you handled yourself today," my father said, looking at me over the rim of the glass. "I am glad Reb Saunders will let you be Danny's friend. I was worried about Reb Saunders."

"I'm awfully sorry I came back so late, abba."

My father nodded. "I am not angry," he said. "But next time you will be so late, you will call, yes?"

"Yes, abba."

My father glanced at the clock on the shelf over the refrigerator. "Reuven, it is late, and tomorrow you are going to school. You should go to sleep now."

"Yes, abba."

"Remember, you must not read. I will read to you in the evenings and we will see if we can study that way. But you must not read by yourself."

"Yes, abba. Good night."

"Good night, Reuven."

I left him sitting at the kitchen table over his glass of tea and went to bed. I lay awake a long time before I was able to sleep.

EIGHT

WHEN I GOT BACK to school the next morning, I found I had become a hero, and during the fifteen-minute morning recess my friends, and even some boys I did not know, all crowded around me, wanting to know how I was and telling me what a great game I had played. Near the end of the recess, I went over to the pitcher's position and stood on the exact spot where I had been hit by the ball. I looked—tried to look; the yard was crowded with students—at home plate and imagined Danny standing there, grinning at me. I remembered his grinning that way again yesterday, and I closed my eyes for a moment, then went over and stood near the wire fence behind the plate. The bench on which the young rabbi had sat was still there, and I stared at it for a moment. It seemed impossible to me that the ball game had taken place only a week ago. So many things had happened, and everything looked so different.

Sidney Goldberg came over to me and started talking about the game, and then Davey Cantor joined us and added his opinion about "those murderers." I nodded at what they were saying without really listening. It seemed silly to me, the way they kept talking about the game. They both sounded so childish, and I got a little angry when Davey Cantor started talking about "that snooty Danny Saunders," but I didn't say anything.

I got out of school at two o'clock and took a trolley car over to the public library, where I was supposed to meet Danny. The library was a huge, three-story, gray stone building, with thick Ionic columns, and with the words BEAUTY IS TRUTH, TRUTH BEAUTY, THAT IS ALL YE KNOW ON EARTH, AND ALL YE NEED TO KNOW—JOHN KEATS engraved in the stone over its four glass entrance doors. It stood on a wide boulevard and there were tall trees in front of it and a grassy lawn bordered by flowers. On the right-hand wall of the vestibule, just inside the doors, there was a mural of the history of great ideas, beginning with a drawing of Moses holding the Ten Commandments, going on to Jesus, Mohammed, Galileo, Luther, Copernicus, Kepler, Newton, and ending with Einstein gazing at the formula $E = mc^2$. On the other wall there was a mural showing Homer, Dante, Tolstoi, Balzac, and Shakespeare engaged in conversation. They were beautiful murals, done in bright colors, and the great men in them looked alive. Probably because I had become so sensitive about eyes the past week, I noticed for the first time that Homer's eyes seemed glazed, almost without pupils, as if the artist had been trying to show that he had been blind. I had never noticed that before, and it frightened me a little to see it now.

I went quickly through the first floor, with its marble floors, its marble pillars, its tall bookcases, its long reference tables, its huge windows through which the sun streamed, and its glass-topped desks at which the librarians sat. I found Danny on the third floor against the far wall, partly hidden by a bookcase, wearing a black suit, a tieless shirt, and a skullcap. He was sitting at a small table, bent over a book, his long earlocks dangling down the sides of his face and almost reaching to the top of the table.

There were not many people on this floor; its stacks were filled mostly with bound volumes of scholarly journals and pamphlets. It was a large floor, and the closely set stacks gave it a mazelike appearance. They went from floor to ceiling, and they seemed to me to contain everything of importance that had ever been written on any subject in the world. There were journals in English, French, German, Russian, Italian, and even one collection in Chinese. Some of the English journals had names I couldn't pronounce. This was the one floor of the three-floored library I did not know well. I had been up here once to find an article in the *Journal of Symbolic Logic* which had been recommended to me by my mathematics teacher, an article which I had only dimly understood, and once to meet my father. Now was the third time in all the years I had belonged to this library that I was on its third floor.

I stood near a bookcase a few feet away from the table at which Danny was sitting, and I watched him read. His elbows were on the table, and he held his head in the palms of his hands, the fingers covering his ears completely, his eyes staring down at the book. Occasionally, the fingers of his right hand would play with his earlock, and once they stroked the tufts of sand-colored hair on his chin for a few seconds, then went back to the side of his face. His mouth was slightly open, and I could not see his eyes; they were

hidden by the lids. He seemed impatient each time he came to the foot of a
page, and he flipped the page with a quick gesture of his right hand, wetting
the forefinger with his tongue and turning the page by pushing upward with
the finger against the lower right-hand corner, the way one does a page of
Talmud—except that with a Talmud the left forefinger usually pushes against
the lower left-hand corner because it is read from right to left. He was reading
with phenomenal speed. I could almost *see* him read. He would start at the
head of a page, his head tilted slightly upward, and then his head would move
downward in a straight line until he got to the foot of the page. Then it would
tilt upward again and either move sideways to the right page or remain fixed
in its upward position until the page was turned, and then start downward
again. He did not seem to be reading from side to side but up and down, and,
watching him, I had the distinct impression that he was reading the middle of
the page only and was somehow able to ignore, or absorb without actually
reading, what was written on the sides.

I decided not to disturb him, and I sat down at another table a few feet
away and continued to watch him read. It was frustrating to be sitting there
surrounded by all those journals and not be able to read a thing myself, and I
decided after a while to review by heart some of the symbolic logic I had been
studying. I closed my eyes and went over the propositional calculus, trying to
visualize the truth tables for conjunction, disjunction, equivalence, and material implication. They were fairly simple, and I had no difficulty. I tried to do
some problems, but after a while it became complicated, I couldn't remember
all the deductive steps, and I stopped. I was about to begin going over the
steps of indirect proof when I heard Danny say, "You're always sleeping!
What a sleepyhead you are!" and I opened my eyes. Danny was sitting up in
his chair and looking at me.

"I was reviewing my logic," I told him. "I wasn't sleeping."

"Of course," he said, smiling. But his voice sounded sad.

"I was just going into the indirect proof. Do you want to hear it?"

"No. I can't stand that stuff. Why didn't you tell me you were here?"

"I didn't want to disturb you."

"You're nice. For a Misnaged." He gave the Hebrew letter "tof" its Ashkenazic pronunciation. "Come over here. I want you to see something."

I went over to his table and sat down next to him. "I'm not allowed to
read, you know."

"I want you to hear this. I'll read it to you."

"What is it?"

"It's from Graetz's *History of the Jews*." He sounded unhappy, and there was a somber look on his face. "It's about Hasidim. Listen. Graetz is talking about Dov Baer, who was the follower of the Besht. He just finished saying that Dov Baer invented the idea of the tzaddik." He looked down at the book on the table and began to read aloud. " 'Baer's idea, however, was not meant to remain idle and unfruitful, but to bring him honor and revenue. While the tzaddik cared for the conduct of the world, for the obtaining of heavenly grace, and especially for Israel's preservation and glorification, his adherents had to cultivate three kinds of virtues. It was their duty to draw nigh to him, to enjoy the sight of him, and from time to time to make pilgrimages to him. Further, they were to confess their sins to him. By these means alone could they hope for pardon from their iniquities.' That means sins," he told me.

"I know what it means," I said.

He went on. " 'Finally, they had to bring him presents, rich gifts, which he knew how to employ to the best advantage. It was also incumbent upon them to attend to his personal wants. It seems like a return to the days of the priests of Baal, so vulgar and disgusting do these perversities appear.' "

He looked up from the book. "That's pretty strong language, 'vulgar and disgusting.' " His eyes were dark and brooding. "It feels terrible to have a great scholar like Graetz call Hasidism vulgar and disgusting. I never thought of my father as a priest of Baal."

I didn't say anything.

"Listen to what else he says about Dov Baer." He turned a page. "He says here that Dov Baer used to crack vulgar jokes to make his people happy, and that he used to encourage his followers to drink alcohol, so they would pray fervently. He says that Rabbi Elijah of Vilna was a great opponent of the Hasidim, and that when he died—let me read it to you." He shuffled pages. "Here it is. Listen. 'After his death, the Hasidim took vengeance upon him by dancing upon his grave, and celebrating the day of his decease as a holiday, with shouting and drunkenness.' " He looked at me. "I never knew about any of these things. You were in our shul yesterday. Did anyone look drunk to you during the service?"

"No," I said.

"My father isn't like that at all." His voice was sad, and it trembled a little. "He really worries about his people. He worries about them so much he doesn't even have time to talk to me."

"Maybe Graetz is only talking about the Hasidim of his own day," I offered.

"Maybe," he said, not convinced. "It's awful to have someone give you an image like that of yourself. He says that Dov Baer had expert spies worthy of serving in the secret service. Those are his words, 'worthy of serving in the secret service.' He says they would go around discovering people's secrets and tell them to Dov Baer. People who came to see him about their personal problems would have to wait around until the Saturday after they came, and in the meantime these spies would investigate them and report back to him, so that when the person finally got to see him, Dov Baer would know everything, and the person would be impressed and think that Dov Baer had some sort of magical ability to look into his heart." He shuffled some more pages. "Listen to this. 'In the first interview Baer, in a seemingly casual manner, was able, in a skillfully arranged discourse, to bring in allusions to these strangers, whereby they would be convinced that he had looked into their hearts and knew their past.'" He shook his head sadly. "I never knew about anything like that. When my father talks about Dov Baer, he almost makes him out to be a saint."

"Did my father give you that book to read?"

"Your father said I should read Jewish history. He said the first important step in anyone's education is to know your own people. So I found this work by Graetz. It's a lot of volumes. I'm almost done with it. This is the last volume." He shook his head again, and the earlocks danced and brushed against the ridge of his jaw and the hollows of his cheeks. "What an image it gives me of myself."

"You ought to discuss it with my father first," I told him, "before you go believing any of that. He told me a lot about Hasidism on Friday night. He wasn't very complimentary, but he didn't say anything about drunkenness."

Danny nodded slowly. "I'll talk to him," he said. "But Graetz was a great scholar. I read up on him before I started reading his history. He was one of the greatest Jewish scholars of the last century."

"You ought to discuss it with my father," I repeated.

Danny nodded again, then slowly closed the book. His fingers played idly with the spine of the binding.

"You know," he brooded, "I read a psychology book last week in which the author said that the most mysterious thing in the universe to man is man himself. We're blind about the most important thing in our lives, our own selves. How could a man like Dov Baer have the gall to fool other people into thinking that he could look into their hearts and tell them what they were really like inside?"

"You don't know that he did. You only know Graetz's version of it."

He ignored me. I had the feeling he was talking more to himself than to me.

"We're so complicated inside," he went on quietly. "There's something in us called the unconscious that we're completely unaware of. It practically dominates our lives, and we don't even know it." He paused, hesitating, his hand moving from the book and playing now with an earlock. I was reminded of the evening in the hospital when he had stared out the window at the people on the street below and had talked of God and ants and the reading he did in this library. "There's so much to read," he said. "I've only really been reading for a few months. Did you know about the subconscious?" he asked me, and when I somewhat hesitantly nodded, he said, "You see? You're not even interested in psychology, and you know about it. I have so much catching up to do." He was suddenly conscious of the way his fingers were playing with the earlock, and he let his hand drop to the table. "Did you know that very often the subconscious expresses itself in dreams? 'The dream is the product of a transaction between conscious and unconscious wishes,'" he quoted, "'and the results during sleep are naturally very different from those during waking hours.'"

"What's this about dreams?" I asked.

"It's true," he said. "Dreams are full of unexpressed fears and hopes, things that we never even think of consciously. We think of them unconsciously deep down inside ourselves, and they come out in dreams. They don't always come out straight, though. Sometimes they come out in symbols. You have to learn to interpret the symbols."

"Where did you find out about that?"

"In my reading. There's a lot of work been done on dreams. It's one of the ways they have of getting to a person's unconscious."

I must have had a strange expression on my face, because he asked me what was the matter.

"I dream all the time," I told him.

"Everyone does," he said. "We just don't remember a lot of them. We repress them. We sort of push them away and forget them, because sometimes they're too painful."

"I'm trying to remember mine," I said. "Some of them weren't very pleasant."

"A lot of times they're not pleasant. Our unconscious isn't a nice place—I call it a place; it isn't a place, really; the book I read says it's more like a process—it isn't a nice place at all. It's full of repressed fears and hatreds, things that we're afraid to bring out into the open."

"And these things rule our lives?"

"According to some psychologists they do."

"You mean these things go on and we don't know anything about them?"

"That's right. That's what I said before. What's inside us is the greatest mystery of all."

"That's a pretty sad thing to think about. To be doing things without really knowing why you're doing them."

Danny nodded. "You can find out about it, though. About your unconscious, I mean. That's what psychoanalysis is all about. I haven't read too much about it yet, but it's a long process. Freud started it. You've heard about Freud. He started psychoanalysis. I'm teaching myself German, so I can read him in the original. He discovered the unconscious, too."

I stared at him and felt a shock of coldness move inside me. "You're studying German?"

He seemed surprised at my reaction. "What's wrong with studying German? Freud wrote in German. What are you looking at me like that for?"

"Aren't his writings translated into English?"

"Not all of them. Besides, I want to read a lot of other things in German that haven't been translated yet. What's the matter with you? You've got the funniest look on your face."

I didn't say anything.

"Just because Hitler speaks German doesn't mean that the language is corrupt. It's the most important scientific language in the world. What are you looking at me like that for?"

"I'm sorry," I said. "It just seems strange to me, your studying German."

"What's so strange about it?"

"Nothing. How are you teaching it to yourself?"

"There's a grammar book in the reference library. I'm almost done memorizing it. It's an interesting language. Very technical and precise. It's amazing the way they put nouns together. Do you know what the word for 'mysterious' is in German?"

"I don't know any German."

"It's *'geheimnisvoll.'* It means 'full of secret.' That's what the subconscious is, *'geheimnisvoll.'* The word for 'sympathetic' is *'teilnahmsvoll'*—literally 'full of part-taking.' The word for charity is *'Nächstenliebe'*—literally, it means—"

"All right," I said. "I'm impressed."

"It's quite a language. Yiddish is a lot like it. Yiddish was originally Middle German. When the German Jews came into Poland, they brought it with them."

"You mean in the thirteenth century, when Poland encouraged the Jews to come in?"

"That's right. You know about that."

"I didn't know about Yiddish being German."

"My father doesn't, either. At least, I don't think he does. He thinks Yiddish is almost holy. But it's really from Middle German."

I was going to ask him what the "Middle" meant in "Middle German," but I decided not to push the conversation any further. I was upset enough as it was about his learning German. And it had nothing to do with Hitler, either. I kept remembering what my father had told me about Solomon Maimon. It all sounded so weird. I almost had the feeling I was talking to Maimon's ghost.

We talked some more about Graetz's version of Hasidism, and then somehow we got onto the subject of Danny's brother. He had been examined by a big doctor that morning, and the doctor had said he would be all right, but that he would have to be careful, no strenuous studying or exercising. He had gone with his father, and Danny said his father was now very upset. But at least his brother would be all right. It had something to do with his blood chemistry, Danny said, and the doctor had prescribed three different pills for him to take. He hadn't been very optimistic about the condition clearing up, either. He said he would have to take the pills as long as it persisted. "It might persist his whole life," Danny said sadly. Again, I got the impression that he loved his brother very much, and I wondered why he hadn't said a word to him during all the time I had seen them together yesterday in the synagogue.

Finally, we decided it was getting late, and we started down the wide marble staircase. When we were about halfway down the staircase to the second floor, Danny stopped and looked carefully around. He did the same when we were going down to the main floor. He replaced the Graetz book, and we went outside.

It was cloudy and seemed ready to rain, so we decided to take a trolley car back rather than walk. Danny got off at his block, and I rode the rest of the way alone, my head full of what we had talked about, especially his teaching himself German.

I told my father about it over the supper table.

"What does Danny want to read in German?" he asked me.

"He wants to read Freud."

My father's eyes went wide behind their spectacles.

"He was very excited about it," I said. "He was talking about the unconscious and dreams. He was also reading Graetz on Hasidism."

"The unconscious and dreams," my father muttered. "And Freud. At the age of fifteen." He shook his head gloomily. "But it will not be possible to stop him."

"Abba, was Graetz right in what he said about Hasidism?"

"Graetz was biased, and his sources were not accurate. If I remember correctly, he calls the Hasidim vulgar drunkards, and he calls the tzaddikim priests of Baal. There is enough to dislike about Hasidism without exaggerating its faults."

I met Danny again in the library later that week, but he wasn't too enthusiastic when I told him what my father had said about Graetz. He told me he had read another book on Hasidism, and while the author hadn't accused the tzaddikim of encouraging drinking, he had accused them of almost everything else. I asked him how he was coming along with his German, and he said he had finished memorizing the grammar text and was reading a book he had borrowed from the German section of the library. He said he hoped to start reading Freud in a few weeks. I didn't tell him what my father had said about that. He looked upset and tense, and he kept playing with an earlock all the time we talked.

My father told me that night that there had been a serious question in his mind about how ethical it was for him to give Danny books to read behind his father's back.

"How would I feel if someone gave you books to read which I believed might be harmful to you?"

I asked him why he had done it.

"Because Danny would have continued to read anyway on his own. At least this way he has some direction from an adult. It was a fortunate accident that he stumbled upon me. But it is not a comfortable feeling, Reuven. I dislike doing this to Reb Saunders. He is certain to find out one day. It will be an uncomfortable situation when he does. But he will not be able to stop Danny from reading. What will he do when his son goes to college?"

I pointed out to my father that Danny was anyway reading on his own now, without direction from an adult. My father certainly hadn't told him to read Freud.

My father nodded his agreement. "But he will come to me to discuss what he reads," he said. "At least there will be a balance. I will give him other books to read, and he will see that Freud is not God in psychology. Freud yet. At fifteen." And he shook his head gloomily.

Danny and I arranged to spend Shabbat afternoon together with his father, studying *Pirkei Avot*. When I turned off Lee Avenue that Shabbat and started up the sunless street on which Danny lived, the feeling of having crossed into a twilight world was only a little less strong than it had been the week before. It was just after three o'clock, and there were no bearded, caftaned men or kerchief-wearing women on the street, but the children were outside, playing, shouting, running. Except for the children, the sidewalk in front of the three-story brownstone at the end of the block was deserted. I remembered how the black-caftaned men had parted for Danny and me the week before, and I remembered, too, the tapping of Danny's capped shoes on the pavement as we had gone through the crowd and up the wide stone staircase. The door in the hallway that led into the synagogue was open, but the synagogue was empty — except for the echoes it contained. I stood just inside the synagogue. The tables were covered with white cloths, but the food had not yet been put out. I stared at the table where I had sat, and I could still hear the gematriyot tumbling out of Reb Saunders's mouth and then his question to Danny, "Nothing more? You have nothing more to say?" I saw the idiot grin spread itself slowly across Danny's lips. I turned quickly and went back out into the hall.

I stood at the foot of the inside stairway and called up, "Hello! Anybody home?" After a moment, Danny appeared at the head of the stairs, wearing his black caftan, black pants, and a black skullcap, and told me to come on up.

He introduced me to his mother and sister. His sister was almost as tall as I, with dark, vivacious eyes and a face almost exactly like Danny's, except that the sculptured lines were a good deal softer. She wore a long-sleeved dress, and her dark hair was combed back severely and dangled in a thick braid behind her. She smiled at me and said, "I know all about you, Reuven Malter. Danny never stops talking about you." His mother was short, with blue eyes and a roundish body. Her head was covered with a kerchief, and there were faint tufts of sand-colored hair on her upper lip. They were both sitting in the living room and had apparently been reading or studying what looked to me to be a Yiddish book when we had interrupted them. I told them politely that it was nice to meet them and was rewarded with another smile from Danny's sister.

We left them and started up the stairway to the third floor. Danny explained that the third floor contained his room, his father's study, and a conference room. The second and third floors were completely separated, just as they were in any three-story brownstone. They had thought once of moving the family to the third floor, Danny said, so as to avoid the noise made by the people who were constantly climbing the stairs to see his father. But his mother wasn't well, and a three-floor climb would be too much for her.

I asked him how his brother was feeling.

"All right, I guess," he told me. "He's asleep now."

Danny took me through the third-floor rooms. They were identical with the ones in which my father and I lived. Danny's bedroom was located exactly where my father's bedroom was, the kitchen had been left intact—to serve the visiting dignitaries tea, Danny said with a grin—the bathroom was next to the kitchen, the study was where my father's study was—except that one of its walls had been knocked out so that it also included what in our apartment was my room—and the living room contained a long glass-topped conference table and leather chairs. Danny took me into the conference room first—we went through the outside hallway door—then into his room, which had a narrow bed, a bookcase full of old Hebrew and Yiddish books, and a desk cluttered with papers. A Talmud lay open on top of the papers. The walls were white and bare. All the walls were white and bare. I saw no photographs or paintings anywhere, neither on the floor where his family lived, nor here on the floor where he lived and his father worked.

We stood outside his father's study, and Danny knocked softly on the door. "He doesn't like me to barge in on him when he's in there," he whispered with a grin. His father said to come in, and we went in.

Reb Saunders sat behind a massive, black wood, glass-topped desk, wearing a black caftan and a tall, round, black skullcap. He was sitting in a straight-

backed red leather chair with intricately carved wooden arms. A single light
bulb glowed white behind its ceiling fixture. The study, with its additional
room, seemed enormous. A thick red carpet covered its floor, and its walls
were lined with glass-enclosed wooden bookcases jammed tight with books.
There were books everywhere—on the two wooden chairs near the desk,
on the desk itself, on the wooden file cabinet that stood near the door, on
cardboard boxes piled in a corner, on the small wooden stepladder, on the
black leather easy chair that stood in another corner, even on the window seat.
Many of the books were bound in black, red, and brown leather. One book
had been bound in white, and it stood out prominently on a shelf among the
black-bound books around it. Danny told me later that it contained the say-
ings of the Ba'al Shem Tov and had been presented to his father as a gift on his
fiftieth birthday by the members of his congregation. All the books seemed
to be in Hebrew or Yiddish, and many of them were very old and in their
original bindings. There was a musty odor in the room, the odor of old books
with yellow leaves and ancient bindings.

Reb Saunders told us to clear the books off the two chairs near the desk.
The desk stood in almost the exact spot where my father had his desk. Danny
sat at his father's right, I at his left.

Reb Saunders wanted to know about my eye. I told him it wasn't bothering me at all and that I was supposed to see the doctor this Monday morning.
He understood I was not permitted to read. I nodded. "So you will listen,"
he told me, playing with an earlock. "You are a good mathematician. Now
we will see what you know about more important things." He said it with a
smile on his lips, and I did not feel it as a challenge. I knew I could not match
him and Danny in the breadth of their knowledge, but I wondered if I might
not be able to keep up with them in terms of depth. Rabbinic literature can
be studied in two different ways, in two directions, one might say. It can be
studied quantitatively or qualitatively—or, as my father once put it, horizon-
tally or vertically. The former involves covering as much material as possible,
without attempting to wrest from it all its implications and intricacies; the
latter involves confining oneself to one single area until it is exhaustively covered, and then going on to new material. My father, in his classes and when he
studied with me at home, always used the latter method. The ideal, of course,
was to be able to do both, but none of the students in my school had that kind
of time available to him because of the school's heavy emphasis on English
studies.

Reb Saunders had a text of *Pirkei Avot* open in front of him. He began to read from it, stopping at the end of each passage. Danny and I took turns explaining each alternating passage. I realized soon enough that the *Pirkei Avot* text was merely being used as a sort of jumping-off point for them, because they were soon ranging through most of the major tractates of the Talmud again. And it wasn't a quiz or a quiet contest this time, either. It was a pitched battle. With no congregants around, and with me an accepted member of the family, Danny and his father fought through their points with loud voices and wild gestures of their hands almost to where I thought they might come to blows. Danny caught his father in a misquote, ran to get a Talmud from a shelf, and triumphantly showed his father where he had been wrong. His father checked the margin of the page for the textual corrections of Rabbi Elijah—the same Rabbi Elijah who had persecuted Hasidim!—and showed Danny that he had been quoting from the corrected text. Then they went on to another tractate, fought over another passage, and this time Reb Saunders agreed, his face glowing, that his son was correct. I sat quietly for a long time, watching them battle. There was an ease about them, an intimacy, which had been totally lacking from the show they had put on before the congregants last week. There was no tension here at all but a battle between equals, with Reb Saunders losing only a little less frequently than his son. And I soon realized something else: Reb Saunders was far happier when he lost to Danny than when he won. His face glowed with fierce pride and his head nodded wildly—the nod beginning from the waist and including the entire upper portion of his body, with the beard moving back and forth against his chest—each time he was forced to acquiesce to Danny's rendition of a passage or to Danny's incisive counter-questioning. The battle went on for a long time, and I slowly became aware of the fact that both Danny and his father, during a point they might be making or listening to, would cast inquisitive glances at me, as if to ask what I was doing just sitting there while all this excitement was going on: Why in the world wasn't I joining in the battle? I listened to them for a few minutes longer, and then I realized that though they knew so much more material than I did, once a passage was quoted and briefly explained, I was on almost equal footing with them. I had this time been able to retain hold of the chain of the argument—probably because there was no tension now—and so when Reb Saunders cited and explained a passage that seemed to contradict a point that had just been made by Danny, I suddenly found myself on the field of combat, offering an interpretation of the passage in support of Danny. Neither of them seemed at all surprised to hear my voice—I had the feeling they were surprised they hadn't heard it sooner—and from that point on the three of us seesawed back and forth through the infinite intricacies of the Talmud. I discovered that my father's method of teaching me Talmud and his patient insistence that I learn Talmudic grammar—I had painfully memorized an Aramaic grammar book—was now standing me in good stead. I saw allusions in passages that Danny and his father overlooked, and I resolved a contradiction with an appeal to grammar. "Grammar!" Reb Saunders threw up his hands. "Grammar we need yet!" But I insisted, explained, cajoled, raised my voice, gestured with my hands, quoted whatever proof texts I could remember from the grammar book, and finally he accepted my explanations. I found I was enjoying it all immensely, and once I even caught myself reading aloud from a Talmud—it was the grammatical discussion of the gender of "derech," road, in the tractate *Kiddushin*—before Reb Saunders realized what I was doing and told me to stop, I wasn't allowed to use my eye yet, Danny would read the passage. Danny didn't need to read the passage—he quoted it by heart with mechanical swiftness. It became clear quickly enough that though I was unequal to Danny in breadth, I was easily equal to him in depth, and this seemed to please Reb Saunders enormously. Danny and I were soon involved in a heated discussion concerning two contradictory commentaries on the same passage, and Reb Saunders sat back quietly and listened. Our argument ended in a draw; we agreed that the passage was obscure and that as it stood it could be explained either way.

There was a pause.

Reb Saunders suggested quietly that Danny might go down and bring us some tea.

Danny left.

The silence that now replaced our loud voices was almost uncomfortable. Reb Saunders sat quietly, stroking his beard with his right hand. I heard Danny's capped shoes in the apartment hallway outside the study. Then the door opened and closed. Reb Saunders stirred and looked at me.

"You have a good head," he said softly. The Yiddish phrase he used was, literally translated, "an iron head." He nodded, seemed to listen for a moment to the silence in the study, then folded his arms across his chest. He sighed loudly, his eyes suddenly sad. "Now we will see about your soul," he said softly. "Reuven, my son will return soon. We have little time to talk. I want you to listen to me. I know that my Daniel spends hours almost every day in the public library. No, do not say anything. Just listen. I know you are surprised that I know. It is not important how I found it out. The neighborhood is not so big that he could hide this from me forever. When my son does not come home in the afternoons week after week, I want to know where he is. Nu, now I know. I also know that he is sometimes with you in the library and sometimes with your father. I want you to tell me what he reads. I could ask my son, but it is difficult for me to speak to him. I know you do not understand that. But it is true. I cannot ask my son. One day perhaps I will tell you the reason. I know the mind he has, and I know I can no longer tell him what yes to read and what not to read. I am asking you to tell me what he reads."

I sat frozen and felt a long moment of blind panic. What my father had anticipated was now actually happening. But he hadn't anticipated it happening to *me*. He had thought Reb Saunders would confront *him*, not me. My father and I had acted behind Reb Saunders's back; now Reb Saunders was asking me to act behind Danny's back. I didn't know what to say.

Reb Saunders looked at me and sighed again. "Reuven," he said very quietly, "I want you to hear me out. No one lives forever. My father led his people before me, and my grandfather before him, and my great-grandfather before him. For six generations now we have led our people. I will not live forever. Daniel will one day take my place—" His voice broke, and he stopped. He put a finger to one of his eyes. Then he went on, his voice a little hoarse now. "My son is my most precious possession. I have nothing in the world compared to my son. I must know what he is reading. And I cannot ask him." He stopped and looked down at an open Talmud on his desk. "How did he come to meet your father in the library?" he asked, looking down at the Talmud.

I sat very still and said nothing. I realized I was sitting on top of a possible explosion between Danny and his father. How long would Reb Saunders remain silent about his son's visits to the library? And I didn't like the way my father seemed to appear in all of this—as if he were conspiring behind Reb Saunders's back to contaminate his son. I took a deep breath and began to talk slowly, choosing my words with care. I told Reb Saunders everything, how Danny had met my father, why my father was suggesting books for him to read, what he was reading, how my father was helping him—omitting that Danny was studying German, that he planned to read Freud, and that he had read some books on Hasidism.

When I finished, Reb Saunders just sat there and stared at me. I could see he was controlling himself with great effort. He covered his eyes and nose with his right hand and leaned forward, his elbow on the open Talmud, the upper portion of his body swaying slowly back and forth. I saw his lips move beneath the hand, and I heard the words "Psychology. Master of the Universe, psychology. And Darwin." They came out as a soft, whispered moan. He took the hand away from his face and let it drop to the Talmud. "What can I do?" he asked himself softly. "I can no longer speak to my own son. The Master of the Universe gave me a brilliant son, a phenomenon. And I cannot speak to him." He looked at me and seemed suddenly aware again of my presence. "The pain of raising children," he said quietly. "So many troubles. So many troubles. Reuven, you and your father will be a good influence on my son, yes?"

I nodded slowly, afraid now to speak.

"You will not make a goy out of my son?"

I shook my head, feeling numb at what I was hearing. His voice was an ache, a plea. I saw him stare up at the ceiling.

"Master of the Universe," he almost chanted. "You gave me a brilliant son, and I have thanked you for him a million times. But you had to make him *so* brilliant?"

I listened to his voice and felt myself go cold. There was so much pain in it, so much bewildered pain.

The apartment door opened and closed. Reb Saunders sat up in his chair, his face quickly regaining its composure. Clearly, almost like an echo in a cave, I heard the tap-tap-tap of Danny's metal-capped shoes against the linoleum hallway floor. Then he was in the study, carrying a tray with three glasses of tea, sugar, spoons, and some of his mother's cookies. I pushed some books aside on the desk, and he put the tray down.

From the moment he entered the room and saw my face, I knew he was aware that something had happened during his absence. We sipped our tea in silence, and I saw him glance at me from over the rim of his glass. He knew, all right. He knew something had happened between his father and me. What was I supposed to tell him? That his father now knew he was reading forbidden books and was not going to try to stop him? Reb Saunders hadn't said anything about not telling Danny what had gone on between us. I looked at him for a clue, but he was sipping his tea calmly. I hoped Danny wouldn't ask me today. I wanted to talk to my father first.

Reb Saunders put his glass down and folded his arms across his chest. He was acting as though nothing at all had happened.

"Tell me more about grammar in the Talmud, Reuven," he said to me, with a gentle hint of mockery in his voice. "All my life I have studied Talmud and paid no attention to grammar. Now you tell me a person must know grammar to know Talmud. You see what happens when you have a father who is a Misnaged? Grammar yet. Mathematics—nu, all right. Mathematics I can understand. But grammar!"

The three of us sat there and talked until it was time for the Afternoon Service. Danny found his father's deliberate mistake easily, and I was able to follow the ensuing Talmudic discussion without too much difficulty, though I did not join in.

After the Evening Service, Danny said he would walk me part of the way home, and as we turned into Lee Avenue he asked me what had happened between me and his father that afternoon.

I told him everything. He listened in silence, not seeming at all surprised that his father somehow had learned of his secret visits to the library.

"I knew he would find out about it sooner or later," he said softly, looking very sad.

"I hope you don't mind my telling him, Danny. I had to."

He shrugged. His eyes were moist and gloomy. "I almost wish he had asked *me* instead," he said quietly. "But we don't talk anymore, except when we study Talmud."

"I don't understand that."

"It's what I told you in the hospital. My father believes in silence. When I was ten or eleven years old, I complained to him about something, and he told me to close my mouth and look into my soul. He told me to stop running to him every time I had a problem. I should look into my own soul for the answer, he said. We just don't talk, Reuven."

"I don't understand that at all."

"I'm not so sure I understand it myself," he said gloomily. "But that's the way he is. I don't know how he found out I was reading behind his back, but I'm glad he knows about it. At least I won't have to walk around in that library scared to death. I just feel bad having had to fool my father like that. But what else could I have done?"

I agreed with him that he couldn't have done anything else, but I told him I wished he could somehow get around to talking about it with his father.

"I can't," he said, shaking his head. "I just can't. You don't know what torture it was talking to him about organizing a ball team. We just don't talk, Reuven. Maybe it sounds a little crazy to you. But it's true."

"I think you ought to at least try."

"I *can't!*" he said, a little angry now. "Don't you listen to what I'm saying? I just can't!"

"I don't understand it," I told him.

"Well, I can't explain it to you any better than I have," he said angrily.

When we stopped in front of the synagogue where my father and I prayed, he muttered his "Good night," turned, and walked slowly away.

My father seemed astonished when I told him what Danny had said to me.

"Silence? What do you mean, Danny is being brought up in silence?" His eyes were wide.

"They never talk, abba. Except when they study Talmud. That's what Danny told me."

He stared at me for a long time. Then he seemed to remember something, and his eyes narrowed suddenly.

"Once in Russia I heard something," he murmured softly, speaking to himself. "But I did not believe it."

"Heard what, abba?"

He looked at me, his eyes somber, and shook his head. "I am happy Reb Saunders knows now about his son's reading," he said quietly, evading my question. "I was concerned about all this subterfuge."

"But why can't he talk to Danny about it?"

"Reuven, he has already talked to Danny about it. He has talked to Danny through you."

I stared at him.

He sighed softly.

"It is never pleasant to be a buffer, Reuven," he told me quietly. And he would say nothing more about the strange silence between Reb Saunders and his son.

NINE

I WENT STRAIGHT HOME from school the next day and spent the afternoon and evening listening to my father read to me from my textbooks. At nine o'clock on Monday morning, my father took me to Dr. Snydman's office on Eastern Parkway. We were both nervous and silent on the way over. I had taken my school books with me, because we planned to go straight from Dr. Snydman's office to the school. Dr. Snydman looked at my eye and told me I was fine, it had healed perfectly, I could read now, play ball, swim, do whatever I wanted, just so long as I didn't try to stop a fast ball anymore with my head. My father's eyes were misty when we left the office, and I cried a little during the trolley ride to school. We stood outside the school, my father kissed my forehead and said thank God that it had all ended well, and now he had to go to his class, he had already missed one class today because of the doctor's appointment and the students were probably making the substitute teacher's life miserable. I grinned, then nodded when he told me to go to my class. He went off. As I climbed the stairs to the second floor, I realized I had forgotten to ask Dr. Snydman about Billy. I decided I would call Billy later in the week after my exams, and go over to see him.

That was a busy week. The final exams began that Monday afternoon. It was wonderful to be able to read and write again, and I didn't mind it at all that my first reading and writing in fifteen days was being done over final examinations. It was a kind of wild, soaring experience to be able to hold a pen again and look into a book or at a piece of paper with writing on it. I took my exams and enjoyed them immensely.

I didn't see Danny that entire week. He called me on Wednesday night, sounding sad, and we talked for a while. I asked him what he would be doing that summer, and he told me he always stayed home in the summer, studying Talmud. He added that he would probably also be reading Freud this summer. I said I would come over to his house that Shabbat and we could talk some more then, I was busy now studying for finals, and I hung up. His voice had been quiet, subdued, and I wondered if he had been reading any more books on Hasidism.

I took the last exam on Friday morning, and then the year was over; I was free until September. I wasn't worried about my grades. I knew I had done well.

When I came home from school early Friday afternoon, Manya asked me if I was hungry, and I said yes, I could eat a horse, a kosher horse, of course, and she quickly put a lunch on the table. My father came in a few minutes later and joined me. There had been a terrible storm in Europe that entire week, he told me, and it had hurt the invasion, but it was over now, thank God. I hadn't heard anything about it, I had been so busy with my exams.

My father left right after lunch, and I went over to the telephone to call Billy. I found his father's name in the phone book and dialed the number.

"Hello," a man's voice said.

"Mr. Merrit?"

"That's right."

"This is Reuven Malter, sir."

"Who?"

"Reuv—Bobby Malter. I had the bed next to Billy in the hospital."

"Oh, yes. Yes. Bobby Malter."

"Do you remember me, sir?"

"Of course. Of course I remember you."

"How is Billy, sir?"

There was a pause.

"Sir?"

"Yes?"

"Is Billy all right?"

"I'm afraid not. The surgery was not successful."

I felt myself break out into a cold sweat. The hand holding the phone began to tremble and I had to push the phone against my face to keep it steady.

"Hello?"

"Yes, sir."

"How is *your* eye, Bobby?"

"It's fine, sir. It's all healed."

"I'm happy to hear that. No, Billy's surgery was not successful."

"I'm awfully sorry to hear that, sir."

There was another pause. I thought I could hear Mr. Merrit breathing into the phone.

"Sir?"

"Yes?"

"May I come over to visit Billy?"

"Billy is in Albany with friends of mine. My company has transferred me to Albany. We're being moved out today."

I didn't say anything.

"Goodbye, Bobby. I'm glad your eye is all right. Be careful with your eyes."

"Yes, sir. Goodbye."

I hung up the phone and stood still for a minute, trying to calm myself. It didn't do any good. I went into my room and sat by the window for a while. I opened a book, stared at it blankly, then closed it. I kept hearing Mr. Savo saying, "Crazy world. Cockeyed." I began to wander aimlessly through the rooms of the apartment. My hands were freezing. I went out onto the porch, sat in the lounge chair, and stared across the yard at the ailanthus. Its leaves were bathed in sunlight, and its musky odor reached me faintly in the breeze that blew against the back of the house. Something moved faintly across the edge of the field of vision of my left eye, but I ignored it and kept staring at the sunlight on the ailanthus leaves. It moved again, and I heard a faint buzzing sound. I turned my head and looked at the wooden rail of the porch. A spider had spun a web across the corner of the upper rail, and there was a housefly trapped in it now, its wings spread-eagled, glued to the strands of the web, its legs flaying the air frantically. I saw its black body arching wildly, and then it managed to get its wings free, and there was the buzzing sound again as the wings struggled to free the body to which they were attached. Then the wings were trapped again by the filmy, almost invisible strands of the web, and the black legs kicked at the air. I saw the spider, a small, gray, furry-looking spider, with long, wispy legs and black eyes, move across the web toward the fly. I rose from the chair and went over to the web. The fly's tiny black legs flayed the air fiercely, then its wings were free again, buzzing noisily, but its body remained glued fast. I bent and blew hard against the web. It swayed, but remained intact. I blew again, harder now, and the strands seemed suddenly to melt. The fly fell on its back to the wooden floor of the porch, righted itself, then flew off, buzzing loudly. The spider tumbled from the broken web, hung by a single strand a few inches above the floor, then swiftly climbed the strand, scrambled across the top front rail of the porch, and disappeared. I went back to the lounge chair, sat down, and continued to stare at the sunlight on the ailanthus.

TEN

DANNY AND I were together almost every day during the first month of that summer. It was a hot, humid month, with a fierce summer sun that left a heat shimmer over the streets and softened the asphalt. Manya was forever muttering about the streaks of black tar that clung to my shoes and sneakers and rubbed off on the floor of the apartment.

Danny spent his mornings studying Talmud, either alone or with his father, while I spent Monday, Wednesday, and Friday mornings playing ball with my yeshiva friends, none of whom seemed to be bothered by my friendship with Danny—they accepted it and just didn't talk about it—and Sunday, Tuesday, and Thursday mornings studying Talmud with my father, either on our back porch when it was a nice day or in his study when it was not. My father and I were studying *Sanhedrin*—slowly, patiently, intensively, not leaving a passage until my father was satisfied that, at least for the present, we understood it fully. Often, we were only able to do about ten lines at a time. Danny, on the other hand, had his daily Talmud goal increased to three blatt by his father. It didn't seem to affect him very much; he was still able to spend all his afternoons on the third floor of the library, reading. I joined him there every afternoon, and frequently my father came with me. He was writing another article, on a passage in *Avodah Zarah*, which, he said, he was only now beginning to understand, and he needed one of the journal collections. So the three of us sat there in the afternoons, reading or talking quietly, until it was time for supper. Once I invited Danny to come home and eat with us, but he refused the invitation with a lame excuse, looking a little embarrassed. On our way home, my father told me that Danny probably didn't eat anywhere except in his own home, or in the home of one of his father's followers, because of kashruth, and that it would be wise for me not to embarrass him again with another invitation.

On Shabbat afternoons I would walk to Danny's house. Danny would take me up to his father's study, and we would all do battle again over the Talmud. Then would come the glass of tea, the Afternoon Service, the ritual of the contest—Danny didn't once miss finding his father's deliberate errors—the Evening Service, and the Havdalah. Reb Saunders didn't talk to me again about Danny's reading, but I knew he was bothered by it terribly. I could tell from the occasional silence that filled the study while Danny would be downstairs getting the tea. And Danny didn't talk about it, either. He just went on reading.

Only the evenings were unscheduled. We sort of played them by ear, as Mr. Galanter might have said, deciding during the afternoon whether we would spend the evening walking, or in my house or his, or alone. Often, I went to the movies either with my father or with some of my school friends. Danny never went to the movies. They were forbidden by his father, he said.

My father and I followed the war news very carefully, and there were now many more *New York Times* maps on the wall of my room. From the fourth to the tenth of July there was a violent battle in the La-Haye-du-Puits area. A panzer counterattack west of the Vire was smashed on the eleventh of July, but the American drive toward St.-Lô was stopped by a German parachute corps. Caen was finally captured, and then on the eighteenth of July St.-Lô fell. A war correspondent triumphantly announced that the lodgment area from which the Allied Armies would soon launch their major offensive into the heart of occupied France was now adequate and secure.

My father and I listened to the news broadcasts, read the *Times*, and studied the maps. It seemed to us that, despite the many announcements of victories, the war was going very slowly. My father looked grim as he studied the war maps that showed the Allied advance between D-day and the third week of July. Then the weather in France changed, and the war seemed to have come to a complete halt, swallowed by endless rain.

In the beginning of the third week of July, my father's research for the article he was writing made it necessary for him to travel to the library of the Jewish Theological Seminary in Manhattan. There were manuscripts there which he needed for the purpose of checking variant readings of the Talmudic passage on which he was working. So every day that week right after lunch he took the subway to Manhattan, and I went alone to the library to be with Danny. That was the week Danny began to read Freud in German.

It was difficult for him at first, and he admitted it openly. Not only was the language still a problem but also the terminology and ideas he encountered were strange and bewildering to him. This wasn't Graetz on Jewish history, he told me, or Minkin on Hasidism, or Hemingway, Fitzgerald, Dreiser, and Dickens. It wasn't even the Ogden and Flügel psychology books he had been reading. This was primary source material, research papers based on direct experimental data, involved theoretical constructions utilizing a complex vocabulary and containing a wealth of original ideas—and he was breaking his head on it.

I listened to him talk and felt a little awed by it all. Five or so weeks ago, he had talked of the unconscious and of dreams almost as a child talks about his first tricycle. Now he was talking about direct experimental data and involved theoretical constructions.

He spent the first part of that third week in July leafing through a collection of Freud's writings—to get a taste of the material, he said—while I sat opposite him, trying to make my way through the first volume of *Principia Mathematica* and finally giving it up as too difficult and settling for a rereading of the article my math teacher had recommended in the *Journal of Symbolic Logic*—it was called "Conditions Affecting the Application of Symbolic Logic," and I understood it a lot better this time—and for a book on logic by Susanne K. Langer. The first sections of the book were a little too easy for me, but the final chapter on logistics, in which she showed how *Principia Mathematica* provides a basis from which the concepts, operations, and relations of arithmetic and other branches of mathematics may be derived, I found to be very exciting.

By Thursday, Danny's side of the table was piled high with books, and he was looking thoroughly unhappy. He was sitting there, twisting an earlock and biting his lower lip, his face a mask of frustration. It was impossible, he said finally. The whole thing was ridiculous and impossible; he wasn't getting anywhere. It wasn't so much the German itself anymore as the technical terminology. He wasn't making any headway at all. Not only that, but he had begun to use English translations of the German works he had been reading, and they did nothing but confuse him even more. He showed me where in one translation the German word "*Unlust*" had been translated as "pain," in quotation marks, and the word "*Schmerz*" had been translated as "pain," without quotation marks.

How was he supposed to know what the translator had had in mind when he had used "pain" with and "pain" without quotation marks? And look at the word "*Besetzung*," he said angrily. What did it mean to translate it as "investment" or "charge"? And what good did it do to translate it as "cathexis"? What did "cathexis" mean? "*Angst*" was "anxiety," "*Furcht*" was "fear," "*Schreck*" was "fright." How was he supposed to know what the difference between "fear" and "fright" was? He wasn't getting anywhere, he would probably have to drop the whole thing; who did he think he was anyway trying to read Freud at the age of fifteen? He went home angry and disgusted, his face a picture of bewildered frustration.

When I got to Danny's house that Shabbat afternoon, I found him in an ugly mood. He was waiting for me outside. He greeted me with a curt nod of his head and muttered something about not really being in the mood for Talmud now but we had to go up anyway. He was very quiet during the first few minutes of the Talmud battle, and though I tried to make up for his silence by increasing the volume of my own enthusiasm, I could see that Reb Saunders was becoming more and more annoyed by his son's lack of participation. Danny was tense and edgy, his face still masked by frustration, his mind obviously not on what we were discussing. He's probably eating himself up alive over Freud, I thought, hoping his father wouldn't lose his temper. But Reb Saunders remained patient and left his son alone.

In the middle of a heated debate over an impossible passage in *Kiddushin* I heard Danny take a sudden loud breath, as if he had been punched in the stomach. Reb Saunders and I broke off our discussion and looked at him. He was staring down at the Talmud, and smiling. His face had come to life, and there was a light in his eyes. He jumped up from his chair, circled the room, then sat down again, and Reb Saunders and I just sat there, staring at him. Something is the matter? Reb Saunders wanted to know. There is a joke in the Talmud we did not see? What was so funny? Danny shook his head, still smiling, bent over the Talmud, and began to give his version of the passage. His voice trembled a little. There was a pause when he finished, and I thought for a moment that Reb Saunders would again ask his son what had been so funny. Instead, I heard him sigh a little, then offer a passage from the *Baba Bathra* that contradicted Danny's explanation. We returned to the battle, and Danny more than made up for his previous silence.

He was quiet as he walked me part of the way home that night, and when we got to the synagogue where my father and I prayed he muttered something about seeing me in the library the next day, then turned and went quickly back.

When I got to the library the next afternoon, I found him seated at his table. There were three books open in front of him. He smiled broadly and waved me to a chair. He had worked out a method of doing Freud, he said, and it seemed to be going all right, so far. He pointed to the three books. One was a volume of Freud's early papers, he told me. Some of them Freud had written together with Josef Breuer, a Viennese physician; others he had written alone. Another was the *Cassell's German-English Dictionary*. The third was a dictionary of psychological terms edited by someone called Warren. The Freud volume was open to a paper entitled "*Ein Fall Von Hypnotischer Heilung*." "*Fall*" meant "case," he said. The rest of the title I could figure out for myself from my Yiddish, he told me.

"I forgot what it was like to study Talmud," he said excitedly. "Talmud is so easy for me now, I didn't remember what I used to go through when I first started it as a kid. Can you study Talmud without the commentaries? Imagine Talmud without Rashi. How far would you get?"

I agreed with him that I wouldn't get very far at all.

He had been going at it all wrong, he said, his eyes bright with excitement. He had wanted to *read* Freud. That had been his mistake. Freud had to be *studied*, not read. He had to be studied like a page of Talmud. And he had to be studied with a commentary.

But Danny didn't know of any commentaries on Freud, so he had settled for the next best thing. He had needed something that would explain Freud's technical terminology, that would clarify the various shades of meaning the German words had—and he had found this dictionary of psychological terms. He was reading Freud now sentence by sentence. He didn't go on to the next sentence until the prior sentence was perfectly clear in his mind. If he came across a German word he did not know, he looked up its English meaning in the *Cassell's*. If the *Cassell's* gave him a translation he didn't understand, one that wouldn't fit the meaning of the sentence, he looked the English word up in the psychology dictionary. That psychological dictionary was his commentary. It had, for example, already explained to him the technical difference between "fear" and "fright." It had also explained the term "cathexis." It was working. He had already studied two and a half pages that afternoon.

Was Freud worth all that effort? I wanted to know.

Freud was a genius, Danny told me. Of course he was worth all that effort. Was symbolic logic worth all my effort?

I had nothing to say to that, except admit that he was probably right.

So I continued reading the Langer book, while Danny bent over the table studying Freud. He shuffled pages impatiently whenever he had to look something up in one of his dictionaries. The sounds of the shuffling pages were loud in the silence of the library.

On Thursday, I told him that my father and I would be leaving next Tuesday morning for the cottage near Peekskill where we always stayed in August, and I gave him two books I thought he might like to read. One was *The Making of the Modern Jew* by Milton Steinberg, the other was *The Thirteen Letters of Ben Uzziel* by Samson Raphael Hirsch. He thanked me and said he would read them. When my father and I left for Peekskill on Tuesday morning, Danny had completed the first paper and was started on the second, entitled *"Die Abwehr-Neuropsychosen."* We had agreed not to write to each other—probably out of an unspoken feeling that two boys our age writing one another when we were only going to be separated for a month was a little childish—and I didn't see him again until after Labor Day.

My father and I returned home the day after Labor Day, and I called Danny immediately. His mother answered and told me she was delighted I had had a good vacation but she was sorry, Danny wasn't home, he had gone with his father to visit a family friend in Lakewood. Danny called me later that evening, happy to hear I was back. He had missed me, he said. How was the trip to Lakewood? I wanted to know. Miserable, he said. Had I ever sat in a bus with my father for hours and not exchanged a single word of conversation, except for a short discussion about a passage of Talmud? No, I told him quietly, I had never had that kind of experience. I always talked to my father. I was lucky, he said. I didn't know how really lucky I was, he added, a little bitterly.

We chatted for a while, and agreed to meet in the library the following afternoon. I found him at his table, looking a little pale, but happy. His tufts of beard had grown a bit thicker, he blinked his eyes a little too often, as if weary from all his reading, but otherwise he was the same, everything was the same, and it was as though we had not seen each other for, at most, a single night of dream-filled sleep. Yes, he had read the two books I had given him. They had been very good, and he had learned a lot from them about the problems of contemporary Judaism. His father had thrown some poisonous looks at him when he had taken them into the house, but the looks had disappeared when Danny had somehow gotten up the courage to tell him that the books had come from Reuven Malter. He would give them back to me tomorrow. He had also read a great deal of Freud, he said. He had finished almost all of the first volume, and he wanted to talk to me about a paper of Freud's called "*Die Sexualität in der Ätiologie der Neurosen.*" It had been something of a shock to him to read that, he said, and he had no one else to talk to about it except me, he didn't want to discuss it with my father. I said fine, we could talk about it on Shabbat when I came over to his house.

But somehow we never got around to talking about it that Shabbat, and on Sunday morning we were both back in school again. The year—the real year of a person going to school—began, and for a long while I had no time at all to think about, let alone discuss, the writings of Sigmund Freud.

ELEVEN

FOR THE FIRST TWO MONTHS of that school year, Danny and I were able to get together regularly only on Shabbat afternoons. Only once did we manage to see each other during the week. I had been elected president of my class, and I found myself suddenly involved in student politics. The evenings that I might have spent with Danny I spent instead at student council or committee meetings. We talked frequently by phone, though, and neither of us felt our friendship was suffering any. But we never got around to discussing what he was reading in Freud.

During November, I managed to go over to his house one evening in the middle of the week. I brought him half a dozen books on Jewish subjects that my father had suggested he read, and he thanked me for them gratefully. He looked a little weary, but otherwise he was fine—except for his eyes, which tired easily, he said. He had been to a doctor, but he didn't need glasses, so everything was really all right. I asked him how he was coming along with Freud, and he said, looking uncomfortable, that he was rarely in the library these days, there was too much schoolwork, but he did manage to read a little of Freud now and then, and it had become very upsetting.

"One of these days I want to have a long talk with you about it," he told me, blinking his eyes.

But we had no real opportunity for any long talk. The Shabbat day grew shorter and shorter, my schoolwork seemed endless, and student politics took up every moment of my spare time.

And then, in the middle of December, just when it seemed that the war would be over very soon, the Germans launched a major offensive in the

Ardennes region, and the Battle of the Bulge began. There were reports of frightful American casualties—some newspaper said that two thousand American soldiers were being killed and wounded every day.

It was a cold, bitter winter in New York, bleak with the news of the fighting in the Ardennes, and at night, as I sat working at my desk, I could hear the radio in the kitchen where my father would be sitting with his war maps, following the news.

The Battle of the Bulge ended about the middle of January, with the newspapers reporting seventy-seven thousand Allied casualties and one hundred twenty thousand German casualties.

Throughout the entire month of that battle—from the middle of December to the middle of January—I did not see Danny once. We spoke on the phone a few times; he told me his brother was sick again and might have to spend some time in a hospital. But the next time I called him his brother was all right—the doctor had changed his pills, Danny said, and that seemed to work. He sounded tired and sad, and once or twice I could barely hear his voice over the phone. The Battle of the Bulge? Yes, he said vaguely, a terrible business. When was I coming over to see him? As soon as I could breathe a little, I said. He said not to wait too long, he needed to talk to me. Was it very important? I wanted to know. No, it could wait, it wasn't *very* important, he said, sounding sad.

So it waited. It waited through my midyear exams and through the first two weeks of February, when I managed to get to Danny's house twice and we fought our customary Talmud battles together with his father but didn't get a chance to be alone long enough for us to talk. And then the news of the war in Europe suddenly reached a peak of feverish excitement. The Russians captured Königsberg and Breslau and came within thirty miles of Berlin, and at the end of the first week in March American troops reached the Rhine River at Remagen and discovered, to their astonishment, that the Ludendorff Bridge had, for some reason, not been destroyed by the Germans. My father almost wept with joy when we heard the news. There had been talk of bloody battles and high casualties in crossing the Rhine. Instead, American troops poured across the bridge, the Remagen beachhead was quickly enlarged and held against German counterattacks—and everyone began to talk of the war ending in two months.

My father and I were overjoyed, and even Danny, whom I saw again in the middle of March and who generally took little interest in the details of the war, began to sound excited.

"It is the end of Hitler, may his name and memory be erased," Reb Saunders said to me that Shabbat afternoon. "Master of the Universe, it has taken so long, but now the end is here."

And he trembled as he said it and was almost in tears.

Danny caught the flu in the last week of March and was in bed for more than a week. During that time, the Saar and Silesia were taken, the Ruhr was encircled by American troops, and another bridgehead was formed across the Rhine by soldiers of General Patton's army. Almost every day now there were rumors that the war had ended. But each rumor proved to be false and did nothing but add to the already intolerable anxiety and suspense my father and I were feeling as we read the papers and listened to the radio.

Danny returned to school at the end of the first week in April, apparently too soon, for he was back in bed two days later with bronchitis. I called his mother to ask if I could visit him, but she said no, he was too sick, and besides what he had was contagious, even his brother and sister weren't permitted into his room. I asked if I could speak to him, but she told me he was running a high fever and could not leave his bed to come to the phone. She sounded worried. He was coughing a great deal, she told me, and was exhausted from the sulfa he was taking. Yes, she would give him my wishes for his speedy recovery.

On the Thursday afternoon of the second week in April, I was sitting at a meeting of the student council. The meeting had started pleasantly enough with the usual reading of the minutes and committee reports, when Davey Cantor burst into the room, looking as though he was crying, and shouted breathlessly that someone had just told him President Roosevelt was dead.

He was standing by the open door of the classroom, and there was a sudden movement of heads as everyone turned and gaped at him in total astonishment. I had been in the middle of a sentence, and I turned, too, remaining on my feet next to my desk, and I heard myself saying angrily that he had a hell of a nerve barging in here like that, he wasn't being one bit funny.

"It's true!" he shouted, crying. "Mr. Weinberg just told me! He heard it on the radio in the faculty room!"

I stared at him and felt myself slide slowly back onto my desk. Mr. Weinberg taught English. He was a short, bald man, with no sense of humor, and his motto was "Believe nothing of what you hear and only half of what you see." If Mr. Weinberg had told Davey Cantor that President Roosevelt was dead . . .

I found myself in a sudden cold sweat. Someone in the room giggled, someone else moaned, "Oh, no!" and our faculty advisor stood up and suggested that the meeting be adjourned.

We left the building and came out onto the street. All the way down the three flights of stairs I wouldn't believe it. I couldn't believe it. It was like God dying. Davey Cantor had said something about a cerebral hemorrhage. I didn't believe it. Until I got to the street.

It was a little after five o'clock, and there was still sunlight. The late afternoon traffic was heavy. Trucks, cars, and a trolley choked the street, waiting for the corner light to change. I crossed quickly, ran for the trolley, and made it just as the light changed. I found a seat next to a middle-aged lady who sat staring straight ahead, weeping silently. I looked around. No one in the trolley was talking. It was crowded, and it became more crowded as it went along, but there was only the silence inside. I saw one man put his hands over his eyes and just sit there like that for a while. I stared out the window. People stood around in small groups on the sidewalks. They didn't seem to be talking. They just stood there, together, like an animal herd bunching up for protection. An old gray-haired woman, walking with a child, held a handkerchief to her mouth. I saw the child look up at her and say something, but I couldn't hear it. I found myself crying, too, and felt a gnawing emptiness, as though I had been scraped clean inside and there was nothing in me now but a terrible darkness. I was feeling as though it had been my father who had died.

The whole ride home was like that: silence in the trolley car, weeping men and women, groups of people standing about dazedly in the streets, little children looking bewildered and wondering what had happened.

Manya and my father were home. I heard the radio in the kitchen as I opened the door, quickly put my books in my room, and joined them. Manya was cooking supper, and sobbing. My father was sitting at the table, his face ashen, his cheeks hollow, his eyes red, looking as he had when he had visited me in the hospital. I sat at the table and listened to the news announcer. He was talking in a hushed voice and giving details of President Roosevelt's death. Harry S Truman was now President of the United States. I sat there and listened and couldn't believe it. How could President Roosevelt die? I had never even thought of him as being mortal. And to die now, especially now, when the war was almost over, when there was to be a meeting soon of the new United Nations. How could a man like that die?

We ate our supper listening to the radio—something we had never done before; my father never liked to have the radio on during a meal. But it was on during that meal and every other meal we ate that entire weekend—except for the Shabbat—and it stayed on every moment either my father or Manya or I was home.

I tried calling Danny on Friday afternoon, but he was still too sick to come to the phone. My father and I spent Shabbat morning in the synagogue, where the pain of death showed itself clearly on every face, and where my friends and I just stood around aimlessly after the service, not knowing what to say. My father began to cough again, the deep, dry, racking cough that shook his frail body and frightened me terribly. On Shabbat afternoon, he talked of President Roosevelt, of the hope he had brought to the country during the Depression.

"You do not remember the Depression, Reuven," he told me. "Those were terrible days, black days. It is impossible to believe he is gone. It is like when—" His voice broke, and he was suddenly sobbing. I stared at him, feeling helpless and terrified. He went into his bedroom and stayed there the rest of the afternoon, and I lay on my bed, staring up at the ceiling, my hands clasped behind my head, trying to grasp what had happened. I couldn't. I saw only emptiness and fear and a kind of sudden, total end to things that I had never experienced before. I lay on my bed and thought about it a long time. It was senseless, as—I held my breath, feeling myself shiver with fear—as Billy's blindness was senseless. That was it. It was as senseless, as empty of meaning, as Billy's blindness. I lay there and thought of Roosevelt being dead and Billy being blind, and finally I turned over and lay with my face on the pillow and felt myself crying. I cried a long time. Then I slept, fitfully. When I woke, the room was dark, and I heard the radio going again in the kitchen. I lay on the bed awhile, then joined my father. We sat together in the kitchen. It was after midnight when we went to sleep.

The next day, President Roosevelt was buried. Our school was closed for the funeral, and my father and I sat in the kitchen all that day and listened to the radio.

Danny called me a few hours after the funeral. He sounded tired, and he coughed a good deal. But his temperature was down to normal, he said, and had been normal for twenty-four hours now. Yes, Roosevelt's death was a terrible thing, he said. His parents were all right. His brother was sick, though. He was running a high fever, and coughing. Could I come over during the week? he asked me. I didn't think so. Could I come over on Saturday, then? Yes, I could. I would see him on Shabbat, I said. He sounded relieved when we hung up, and I wondered what was happening.

But on Wednesday I came home from school with a fever, and by Thursday afternoon I was running 103.6. The doctor called it the flu and warned my father to keep me in bed or there might be complications. I asked my father to call Danny and tell him. I was in bed for ten days, and when I finally got back to school I found I had missed so much work that for two weeks I dropped all my student council activities and spent every moment I had catching up. I used Shabbat afternoons for reading, and by the first week of May I had caught up enough to be able to begin attending student council meetings again. Then Reb Saunders became ill, and at the same time my father also took to his bed with the flu, a severe case that bordered on pneumonia for a while and frightened me terribly. Both Reb Saunders and my father were quite ill on the day in May when word finally came that the war in Europe was over.

I was with my father when we heard the news over the radio in his bedroom.

"Thank God!" my father said, his eyes wet with joy. "What a price to have paid for Hitler and his madmen!" And he lay back on the pillow and closed his eyes.

And then, together with the official report of the signing of the unconditional surrender on May 7, there came the news, at first somewhat guarded, then, a few days later, clear and outspoken, of the German concentration camps. My father, recuperating slowly and looking worn and weary, sat in his bed propped on pillows, and read the newspaper stories of the horrors that had occurred in those camps. His face was grim and ashen. He seemed unable to believe what he was reading.

It was while my father read to me an account of what had happened at Teresienstadt, where the Germans had imprisoned and incinerated European Jews of culture and learning, that I saw him break down and weep like a child.

I didn't know what to say. I saw him lie back on his pillows and cover his face with his hands. Then he asked me to leave him alone, and I walked out and left him there, crying, and went to my room.

I just couldn't grasp it. The numbers of Jews slaughtered had gone from one million to three million to four million, and almost every article we read said that the last count was still incomplete, the final number would probably reach six million. I couldn't begin to imagine six million of my people murdered. I lay in my bed and asked myself what sense it made. It didn't make any sense at all. My mind couldn't hold on to it, to the death of six million people.

Danny called me a few days later, and I went over to his house the next Shabbat afternoon. We did not study Talmud. Instead, his father talked of the Jewish world in Europe, of the people he had known who were now probably dead, of the brutality of the world, of his years in Russia with the Cossack bands looting and plundering.

"The world kills us," he said quietly. "Ah, how the world kills us."

We were sitting in his study, and he was in his straight-backed chair. His face was lined with suffering. His body swayed slowly back and forth, and he talked in a quiet singsong, calling up the memories of his youth in Russia and telling us of the Jewish communities of Poland, Lithuania, Russia, Germany, and Hungary—all gone now into heaps of bones and ashes. Danny and I sat silent and listened to him talk. Danny was pale and seemed tense and distraught. He tugged constantly at an earlock, his eyes blinking nervously.

"How the world drinks our blood," Reb Saunders said. "How the world makes us suffer. It is the will of God. We must accept the will of God." He was silent for a long moment. Then he raised his eyes and said softly, "Master of the Universe, how do you permit such a thing to happen?"

The question hung in the air like a sigh of pain.

Danny could not walk me back that night, he had too much schoolwork to do, so I went home alone and found my father in his bedroom, listening to the radio. He was in pajamas, and he wore his small black skullcap. The announcer was talking about the United Nations. I sat in a chair and listened, and when the news program was over my father turned off the radio and looked at me.

"How is Reb Saunders?" he asked quietly.

I told him what Reb Saunders had talked about that afternoon.

My father nodded slowly. He was pale and gaunt, and his skin had a yellowish tint to it and was parchmentlike on his face and hands.

"Reb Saunders wanted to know how God could let something like this happen," I told him quietly.

My father looked at me, his eyes somber.

"And did God answer him?" he asked. His voice had a strange quality of bitterness to it.

I didn't say anything.

"Did God answer him, Reuven?" my father asked again, that same bitterness in his voice.

"Reb Saunders said it was God's will. We have to accept God's will, he said."

My father blinked his eyes. "Reb Saunders said it was God's will," he echoed softly.

I nodded.

"You are satisfied with that answer, Reuven?"

"No."

He blinked his eyes again, and when he spoke his voice was soft, the bitterness gone. "I am not satisfied with it, either, Reuven. We cannot wait for God. If there is an answer, we must make it ourselves."

I was quiet.

"Six million of our people have been slaughtered," he went on quietly. "It is inconceivable. It will have meaning only if we give it meaning. We cannot wait for God." He lay back on the pillows. "There is only one Jewry left now in the world," he said softly, staring up at the ceiling. "It is here, in America. We have a terrible responsibility. We must replace the treasures we have lost." His voice was hoarse, and he coughed. Then he was quiet for a long time. I saw him close his eyes, and I heard him say, "Now we will need teachers and rabbis to lead our people." He opened his eyes and looked at me. "The Jewish world is changed," he said, almost in a whisper. "A madman has destroyed our treasures. If we do not rebuild Jewry in America, we will die as a people." Then he closed his eyes again and was silent.

My father recovered slowly, and it was only at the end of May that he was able to return to his teaching.

Two days after I took my final examination, he suffered a heart attack. He was rushed by ambulance to the Brooklyn Memorial Hospital and put into a semiprivate room one floor below the eye ward. Manya took care of me during the first nightmarish days of blind panic when my mind collapsed and would not function. Then Reb Saunders called me one night and invited me to live in his house while my father recovered. How could I live alone with only a housekeeper to care for me? he wanted to know. Why should I stay alone in the apartment at night? Who knew, God forbid, what could happen?

It was terrible for a boy my age to be left alone. They could put another bed in Danny's room, and I could sleep there. When I told my father, he said it would be wise for me to accept the offer. And he told me to tell Reb Saunders how grateful he was to him for his kindness.

On the first day of July, I packed a bag and took a cab to Reb Saunders's house. I moved into Danny's room.

TWELVE

FROM THE DAY I entered Reb Saunders's house to the day I left to go with my father to our cottage near Peekskill where he was to convalesce, I was a warmly accepted member of Danny's family. Danny's mother, who had some kind of heart condition and needed to rest frequently, was forever adding food to my plate. Danny's sister, I noticed for the first time, was a very pretty girl, with dark eyes and long dark hair combed back into a single braid, and vivacious hands that seemed always in motion when she spoke. She was forever teasing Danny and me and referring to us as David and Jonathan. Danny's brother, Levi, was forever poking at his food when he sat at the kitchen table, or walking ghostlike around the house, picking his nose. And Danny's father was forever silent, withdrawn, his dark eyes turned inward, brooding, as if witnessing a sea of suffering he alone could see. He walked bent forward, as though there were some kind of enormous burden on his shoulders. Dark circles had formed around his eyes, and sometimes at the kitchen table I would see him begin to cry suddenly, and he would get up and walk out of the room, then return a few minutes later and resume eating. No one in the family talked about these sudden moments of weeping. And I didn't, either, though they frightened and bewildered me.

Danny and I did everything together that month. We would rise a little before seven, go down to the synagogue to pray the Morning Service with the congregation, have breakfast with the family, then go out onto his porch if the day was nice, or stay in his room if it wasn't, and spend the morning studying Talmud. After lunch, we would go together to the library, where we would spend the early hours of the afternoon. Danny was reading Freud, and I was doing symbolic logic. It was in the library that we did all the talking we had been unable to do during the year. Then, at about four o'clock, we would take the trolley together to the Brooklyn Memorial Hospital and visit my father. We would have supper together with Danny's family, then spend the evening either chatting with his sister and mother in the living room or reading quietly—Danny used the evenings to read the books on Jewish subjects I kept giving him—or, if his father was free, we would go up to the study and do battle over the Talmud. But Reb Saunders was rarely free. There seemed to be an endless number of people coming into the house and walking up the three flights of stairs to see him, and by the time we were ready for supper he was always visibly fatigued, and he would sit lost in thought, his eyes dark and brooding. And once, during a supper meal, I saw tears come slowly from his eyes and disappear into the tangle of his dark beard. He did not leave the table this time. He sat there, weeping in silence, and no one said anything. And then he dried his eyes with a handkerchief, took a deep, trembling breath, and went back to his food.

During the entire month I spent in Reb Saunders's house, the only time I ever saw him talk to Danny was when we argued over the Talmud. There was never any simple, intimate, human kind of conversation between him and his son. I almost had the impression that they were physically incapable of communicating with each other about ordinary things. It troubled me, but I said nothing about it.

Danny and I talked often about his reading of Freud. We sat at our table in the third floor of the library, surrounded by the mazelike stacks, and he told me what he had read during the past year and what he was reading now. Freud had clearly upset him in a fundamental kind of way—had thrown him off balance, as he once put it. But he couldn't stop reading him, he said, because it had become increasingly obvious to him that Freud had possessed an almost uncanny insight into the nature of man. And that was what Danny found upsetting. Freud's picture of man's nature was anything but complimentary, it was anything but religious. It tore man from God, as Danny put it, and married him off to Satan.

Danny knew enough about Freud now—his method of study had been so thoroughly successful—that he was able to use Freud's technical terminology with the same kind of natural ease that characterized our use of the technical terminology of the Talmud. For the first two weeks of July, Danny spent part of our reading time in the library patiently explaining to me some of Freud's basic concepts. We sat at our table, Danny in his dark suit—he wore a dark suit no matter how hot it was—his tieless shirt, his fringes, his skullcap, his long earlocks, and his beard, which was thick and full now, almost an adult beard, and me in my sport shirt, summer trousers, and skullcap, and we talked about Sigmund Freud. What I heard was new, so new that I couldn't grasp it at first. But Danny was patient, as patient as my father, and slowly I began to understand the system of psychological thought Freud had constructed. And I, too, became upset. Freud contradicted everything I had ever learned. What I found particularly upsetting was the fact that Danny didn't seem to have rejected what Freud taught. I began to wonder how it was possible for the ideas of the Talmud and the thinking of Freud to live side by side within one person. It seemed to me that one or the other would have to give way. When I told this to Danny, he shrugged, said nothing, and went back to his reading.

Had my father been well at that time, I would have talked to him about it, but he was in the hospital, recuperating slowly, and I didn't want to upset him with an account of Danny's reading. He was upset enough as it was with his own reading. Whenever Danny and I came to visit him, we found newspapers strewn all over his bed. He was reading everything he could find that told of the destruction of European Jewry. He talked of nothing else but European Jewry and the responsibility American Jews now carried. Occasionally he spoke of the importance of Palestine as a Jewish homeland, but mostly he was concerned about American Jewry and the need for teachers and rabbis. Once he asked Danny and me what we were reading these days, and Danny answered honestly that he was going through Freud. My father sat in his hospital bed, propped up on pillows, looked at him, and blinked. He had grown very thin—I hadn't thought he could ever get any thinner than he had been before his heart attack, but it seemed to me he had lost at least ten pounds—and he seemed to become easily upset by little things. I was frightened for a moment, because I didn't want him to get involved in an argument with Danny about Freud. But he only shook his head and sighed. He was very tired, he said; he would talk to Danny about Freud another time. Danny shouldn't think that Freud was the final word in psychoanalysis; many great thinkers disagreed with him. He let it go at that, and went back to talking about the destruction of European Jewry. Did we know, he asked us, that on December 17, 1942, Mr. Eden got up in the House of Commons and gave the complete details of the Nazi plan, already in full operation, to massacre the entire Jewish population of Europe? Did we know that Mr. Eden, though he had threatened the Nazis with retribution, hadn't said a word about practical measures to save as many Jews as possible from what he knew would be their inevitable fate? There had been public meetings in England, protests, petitions, letters—the whole machinery of democratic expression had been set in motion to impress upon the British Government the need for action—and not a thing was done. Everyone was sympathetic, but no one was sympathetic enough. The British let some few Jews in, and then closed their doors. America hadn't cared enough, either. No one had cared enough. The world closed its doors, and six million Jews were slaughtered. What a world! What an insane world! "What do we have left to us now, if not American Jewry?" he said. "Some Jews say we should wait for God to send the Messiah. We cannot wait for God! We must make our own Messiah! We must rebuild American Jewry! And Palestine must become a Jewish homeland! We have suffered enough! How long must we wait for the Messiah?"

It was bad for my father to get excited that way, but there was nothing I could do to stop him. He could talk of nothing else but the destruction of European Jewry.

One morning at breakfast Reb Saunders came out of a brooding silence, sighed, and for no apparent reason began telling us, in a soft, singsong chant, the story of an old, pious Hasid who had set out on a journey to Palestine— Eretz Yisroel, Reb Saunders called it, giving the land its traditional name and accenting the "E" and the "ro"—so as to be able to spend the last years of his life in the Holy Land. Finally, he reached the Wailing Wall in Jerusalem, and three days later he died while praying at the Wall for the Messiah to come and redeem his people. Reb Saunders swayed slowly back and forth as he told the story, and when he was done I said quietly, not mentioning my father's name, that a lot of people were now saying that it was time for Palestine to become a Jewish homeland and not only a place where pious Jews went to die. The reaction on the part of the entire family was instantaneous; it was as though someone had thrown a match onto a pile of straw. I could almost feel the heat that replaced the family warmth around the table. Danny went rigid and stared down at the plate in front of him. His brother let out a little whimper, and his sister and mother seemed frozen to their chairs. Reb Saunders stared at me, his eyes suddenly wild with rage, his beard trembling. And he pointed a finger at me that looked like a weapon.

"Who are these people? Who are these people?" he shouted in Yiddish, and the words went through me like knives. "Apikorsim! Goyim! Ben Gurion and his goyim will build Eretz Yisroel? They will build for us a Jewish land? They will bring Torah into this land? Goyishkeit they will bring into the land, not Torah! God will build the land, not Ben Gurion and his goyim! When the Messiah comes, we will have Eretz Yisroel, a Holy Land, not a land contaminated by Jewish goyim!"

I sat there stunned and terrified, engulfed by his rage. His reaction had caught me so completely by surprise that I had quite literally stopped breathing, and now I found myself gasping for breath. I felt as if I were being consumed by flames. The silence that followed his outburst had a fungus quality to it, as though it were breeding malignancies, and I had the uncanny feeling that I had somehow been stripped naked and violated. I didn't know what to do or say. I just sat there and gaped at him.

"The land of Abraham, Isaac, and Jacob should be built by Jewish goyim, by contaminated men?" Reb Saunders shouted again. "Never! Not while I live! Who says these things? Who says *we* should now build Eretz Yisroel? And where is the Messiah? Tell me, we should forget completely about the Messiah? For this six million of our people were slaughtered? That we should forget completely about the Messiah, that we should forget completely about the Master of the Universe? Why do you think I brought my people from Russia to America and not to Eretz Yisroel? Because it is better to live in a land of true goyim than to live in a land of Jewish goyim! Who says *we* should build Eretz Yisroel, ah? I'll tell you who says it! Apikorsim say it! Jewish goyim say it! True Jews do not say such a thing!"

There was a long silence. Reb Saunders sat in his chair, breathing hard and trembling with rage.

"Please, you should not get so angry," Danny's sister pleaded softly. "It is bad for you."

"I'm sorry," I said lamely, not knowing what else to say.

"Reuven was not talking for himself," Danny's sister said quietly to her father. "He was only — "

But Reb Saunders cut her off with an angry wave of his hand. He went rigidly through the Grace, then left the kitchen, wearing his rage visibly.

Danny's sister stared down at the table, her eyes dark and sad.

Later, when Danny and I were alone in his room, Danny told me to think ten thousand times the next time I wanted to mention anything like that again to his father. His father was fine, he said, until he was confronted by any idea that he felt came from the contaminated world.

"How was I supposed to know that Zionism is a contaminated idea?" I said. "My God, I feel as if I've just been through the seven gates of Hell."

"Herzl didn't wear a caftan and side curls," Danny said. "Neither does Ben Gurion."

"You can't be serious."

"I'm not talking about myself. I'm talking about my father. Just don't talk about a Jewish state anymore. My father takes God and Torah very seriously, Reuven. He would die for them both quite gladly. A secular Jewish state in my father's eyes is a sacrilege, a violation of the Torah. You touched a raw nerve. Please don't do it again."

"I'm glad I didn't mention it was my father who said it. He might have thrown me out of the house."

"He *would* have thrown you out of the house," Danny said grimly.

"Is he—is he feeling all right?"

"How do you mean?"

"The way he cries all the time like that. Is he—is something wrong?"

Danny's hand went slowly to an earlock, and I watched him tug at it nervously. "Six million Jews have died," he said. "He's—I think he's thinking of them. He's suffering for them."

I looked at him. "I thought he might be sick. I thought your sister said—"

"He's not sick," Danny broke in. He lowered his hand. "I—I really don't want to talk about it."

"All right," I said quietly. "But I don't think I want to study any Talmud this morning. I'm going to take a long walk."

He didn't say anything. But his face was sad and brooding as I went out of his room.

When I saw Reb Saunders again at lunch, he seemed to have forgotten the incident completely. But I found myself thinking carefully now before I said anything to him. And I was constantly on my guard with him from that time on.

During an afternoon in the last week of July, Danny began talking about his brother. We were sitting in the library, reading, when he suddenly looked up, rested his head in the palm of his right hand, the elbow on the table, and said his eyes were bothering him again and that he wouldn't be at all surprised if he ended up wearing glasses soon, his brother was having glasses made and he was only nine. I told him his brother didn't seem to be doing much reading, what did he need glasses for?

"It has nothing to do with reading," Danny said. "His eyes are just plain bad, that's all."

"Your eyes look bloodshot," I told him.

"They are bloodshot," he said.

"Your eyes look as if you've been reading Freud."

"Ha-ha," Danny said.

"What does Freud say about an ordinary thing like bloodshot eyes?"

"He says to rest them."

"A genius," I said.

"You know, my brother's a good kid," Danny said. "His sickness is quite a handicap, but everything considered he's a good kid."

"He's quiet, I'll say that for him. Does he study at all?"

"Oh, sure. He's bright, too. But he has to be careful. My father can't pressure him."

"Lucky boy."

"I don't know. I wouldn't want to be sick all my life. I'd much rather be pressured. He's a nice kid, though."

"Your sister's pretty nice, too," I said.

Danny didn't seem to have heard me—or if he had, he chose to ignore my words completely. He went on talking about his brother. "It must really be hell to walk around sick all the time and have to depend upon pills. He's really a sweet kid. And bright, too." He seemed to be rambling, and I wasn't quite sure I knew what he was trying to say. His next words jarred me. "He'd probably make a fine tzaddik," he said.

I looked at him. "How's that again?"

"I said my brother would probably make a fine tzaddik," Danny said quietly. "It occurred to me recently that if I didn't take my father's place I wouldn't be breaking the dynasty after all. My brother could take over. I had talked myself into believing that if I didn't take his place I would break the dynasty. I think I had to justify to myself having to become a tzaddik."

I was frightened and said tightly, "Your home hasn't blown up recently, so I take it you haven't told your father."

"No, I haven't. And I'm not going to, either. Not yet."

"When will you tell him? Because I'm going to be out of town that day."

"No," he said quietly. "I'm going to need you around that day."

"I was only kidding," I told him, feeling sick with dread.

"It also occurred to me recently that all my concern about my brother's health was a fake. I don't have much of a relationship with him at all. He's such a kid. I pity him a little, that's all. I was really concerned about his health because all along I've wanted him to be able to take my father's place. That was something, all right, when I realized that. How am I doing? Are you bored yet?"

"I'm bored stiff," I said. "I can't wait until the day you tell your father."

"You'll wait," Danny said tightly, blinking his eyes. "You'll wait, and you'll be around, too, because I'm going to need you."

"Let's talk about your sister for a change," I said.

"I heard you the first time. Let's not talk about my sister, if you don't mind. Let's talk about my father. You want to know how I feel about my father? I admire him. I don't know what he's trying to do to me with this weird silence that he's established between us, but I admire him. I think he's a great man. I respect him and trust him completely, which is why I think I can live with his silence. I don't know why I trust him, but I do. And I pity him, too. Intellectually, he's trapped. He was born trapped. I don't ever want to be trapped the way he's trapped. I want to be able to breathe, to think what I want to think, to say the things I want to say. I'm trapped now, too. Do you know what it's like to be trapped?"

I shook my head slowly.

"How could you possibly know?" Danny said. "It's the most hellish, choking, constricting feeling in the world. I scream with every bone in my body to get out of it. My mind cries to get out of it. But I can't. Not now. One day I will, though. I'll want you around on that day, friend. I'll *need* you around on that day."

I didn't say anything. We sat in silence a long time. Then Danny slowly closed the Freud book he had been reading.

"My sister's been promised," he told me quietly.

"What?"

"My father promised my sister to the son of one of his followers when she was two years old. It's an old Hasidic custom to promise children away. She'll be married when she reaches eighteen. I think we ought to go over and visit your father now."

That was the only time Danny and I ever talked about his sister.

A week later. I went up with my father to our cottage near Peekskill. While we were there, America destroyed Hiroshima and Nagasaki with atomic bombs, and the war with Japan came to an end.

I didn't tell my father about that last conversation I had with Danny, and I had many nightmares that year in which Reb Saunders screamed at me that I had poisoned his son's mind.

That September Danny and I entered Hirsch College. I had grown to five feet nine inches, an inch shorter than Danny, and I was shaving. Danny hadn't changed much physically during his last year in high school. The only thing different about him was that he was now wearing glasses.

BOOK THREE

A word is worth one coin;
silence is worth two.

—The Talmud

THIRTEEN

By THE END of our first week in college, Danny was feeling thoroughly miserable. He had discovered that psychology in the Samson Raphael Hirsch Seminary and College meant experimental psychology only, and that the chairman of the department, Professor Nathan Appleman, had an intense distaste for psychoanalysis in general and for Freud in particular.

Danny was quite vocal about his feelings toward Professor Appleman and experimental psychology. We would meet in the mornings in front of my synagogue and walk from there to the trolley, and for two months he did nothing during those morning trolley rides except talk about the psychology textbook he was reading—he didn't say "studying," he said "reading"—and the rats and mazes in the psychology laboratory. "The next thing you know they'll stick me with a behaviorist," he lamented. "What do rats and mazes have to do with the *mind*?"

I wasn't sure I knew what a behaviorist was, and I didn't want to make him more miserable by asking him. I felt a little sorry for him, mostly because I had found college to be exciting and was thoroughly enjoying my books and my teachers, while he seemed to be going deeper and deeper into misery.

The building that housed the college stood on Bedford Avenue. It was a six-story white stone building, and it occupied half a block of a busy store-filled street. The noise of the traffic on the street came clearly through the windows and into our classrooms. Behind the college was a massive brownstone armory, and a block away, across the street, was a Catholic church with a huge cross on its lawn upon which was the crucified figure of Jesus. In the evenings, a green spotlight shone upon the cross, and we could see it clearly from the stone stairs in front of the college.

The street floor of the building consisted of administrative offices, an auditorium, and a large synagogue, a section of which contained chairs and long tables. The entire second floor was a library, a beautiful library, with mazelike stacks that reminded me of the third floor of the library in which Danny and I had spent so much time together. It had bright fluorescent lights—that didn't flicker or change color, I noticed immediately the first time I walked in—and a trained, professional library staff. It also contained a large reading room, with long tables, chairs, a superb collection of reference books, and an oil painting of Samson Raphael Hirsch which was prominently displayed on a white wall—Hirsch had been a well-known Orthodox rabbi in Germany during the last century and had fought intelligently through his writings and preachings against the Jewish Reform movement of his day. The third and fourth floors had white-painted, modern classrooms and large, well-equipped chemistry, physics, and biology laboratories. There were also classrooms on the fifth floor, as well as a psychology laboratory, which contained rats, mazes, screens, and a variety of instruments for the measuring of auditory and visual responses. The sixth floor consisted of dormitory rooms for the out-of-town students.

It was a rigidly Orthodox school, with services three times a day and with European-trained rabbis, many of them in long, dark coats, all of them bearded. For the first part of the day, from nine in the morning to three in the afternoon, we studied only Talmud. From three-fifteen to six-fifteen or seven-fifteen, depending on the schedule of classes we had chosen for ourselves, we went through a normal college curriculum. On Fridays from nine to one, we attended the college; on Sundays, during that same time span, we studied Talmud.

I found that I liked this class arrangement very much; it divided my work neatly and made it easy for me to concentrate separately upon Talmud and college subjects. The length of the school day, though, was something else; I was frequently awake until one in the morning, doing homework. Once my father came into my room at ten minutes to one, found me memorizing the section on river flukes from my biology textbook, asked me if I was trying to do four years of college all at once, and told me to go to bed right away. I went to bed—half an hour later, when I had finished the memorizing.

Danny's gloom and frustration grew worse day by day, despite the fact that the students in his Talmud class looked upon him with open-mouthed awe. He had been placed in Rav Gershenson's class, the highest in the school, and I had been placed one class below. He was the talk of the Talmud Department by the end of two weeks and the accepted referee of all Talmudic arguments among the students. He was also learning a great deal from Rav Gershenson, who, as Danny put it, loved to spend at least three days on every two lines he taught. He had quickly become the leader of the few Hasidic students in the school, the ones who walked around wearing dark suits, tieless shirts, beards, fringes, and earlocks. About half of my high school class had entered the college, and I became friendly enough with many of the other non-Hasidic students. I didn't mix much with the Hasidim, but the extent to which they revered Danny was obvious to everyone. They clung to him as though he were the reincarnation of the Besht, as though he were their student tzaddik, so to speak. But none of this made him too happy; none of it was able to offset his frustration over Professor Appleman, who, by the time the first semester ended, had him so thoroughly upset that he began to talk about majoring in some other subject. He just couldn't see himself spending four years running rats through mazes and checking human responses to blinking lights and buzzing sounds, he told me. He had received a B for his semester's work in psychology because he had messed up some math equations on the final examination. He was disgusted. What did experimental psychology have to do with the human mind? he wanted to know.

We were in the week between semesters at the time. Danny was sitting on my bed and I was at my desk, wishing I could help him, he looked so thoroughly sad. But I didn't know a thing about experimental psychology, so there was little I could offer by way of help, except to urge him to stick out the year, something might come of it, he might even get to like the subject.

"Did you ever get to like my father and his planned mistakes?" he asked testily.

I shook my head slowly. Reb Saunders had stopped inserting deliberate errors into his Shabbat evening talks the week we had entered college, but the memory of it still rankled. I told Danny that I had disliked the mistake business and had never really gotten used to it, despite my having witnessed it many times.

"So what makes you think sitting long enough through something you hate will get you to like it?"

I had nothing to say to that, except to urge him again to stick out the year with Professor Appleman. "Why don't you talk to him about it?" I asked.

"About what? About Freud? The one time I mentioned a Freudian theory in class, all I got out of Appleman was that dogmatic psychoanalysis was related to psychology as magic was related to science. 'Dogmatic Freudians,'" Danny was imitating Professor Appleman—or so I assumed; I didn't know Professor Appleman, but Danny's voice had taken on a somewhat professorial quality—"'Dogmatic Freudians are generally to be regarded as akin to the medieval physicists who preceded the era of Galileo. They are interested solely in confirming highly dubious theoretical hypotheses by the logic of analogy and induction, and make no attempt at refutation or intersubjective testing.' That was my introduction to experimental psych. I've been running rats through mazes ever since."

"Was he right?" I asked.

"Was who right?"

"Professor Appleman."

"Was he right about what?"

"About Freudians being dogmatic?"

"What followers of a genius *aren't* dogmatic, for heaven's sake? The Freudians have plenty to be dogmatic about. Freud was a genius."

"What do they do, make a tzaddik out of him?"

"Very funny," Danny said bitterly. "I'm getting a lot of sympathy from *you* tonight."

"I think you ought to have a heart-to-heart talk with Appleman."

"And tell him what? That Freud was a genius? That I hate experimental psychology? You know what he once said in class?" He assumed the professorial air again. "'Gentlemen, psychology may be regarded as a science only to the degree to which its hypotheses are subjected to laboratory testing and to subsequent mathematization.' Mathematization yet! What should I tell him, that I hate mathematics? I'm taking the wrong course. *You* should be taking that course, not me!"

"He's right, you know," I said quietly.

"Who?"

"Appleman. If the Freudians aren't willing to try testing their theories under laboratory conditions, then they *are* being dogmatic."

Danny looked at me, his face rigid. "What makes you so wise about Freudians all of a sudden?" he asked angrily.

"I don't know a thing about the Freudians," I told him quietly. "But I know a lot about inductive logic. One of these days remind me to give you a lecture on inductive logic. If the Freudians—"

"Damn it!" Danny exploded. "I never even mentioned the followers of Freud in class! I was talking about Freud himself! Freud was a scientist. Psychoanalysis is a scientific tool for exploring the mind. What do rats have to do with the human mind?"

"Why don't you ask Appleman?" I said quietly.

"I think I will," Danny said. "I think I'll do just that. Why not? What have I got to lose? It can't make me any more miserable than I am now."

"That's right," I said.

There was a brief silence, during which Danny sat on my bed and stared gloomily down at the floor.

"How are your eyes these days?" I asked quietly.

He sat back on the bed, leaning against the wall. "They still bother me. These glasses don't help much."

"Have you seen a doctor?"

He shrugged. "He said the glasses should do it. I just have to get used to them. I don't know. Anyway, I'll talk to Appleman next week. The worst that could happen is I drop the course." He shook his head grimly. "What a miserable business. Two years of reading Freud, and I have to end up doing experimental psychology."

"You never know," I said. "Experimental psychology might come in handy some day."

"Oh, sure. All I need to do is get to love mathematics and rats. Are you coming over this Saturday?"

"I'm studying with my father Shabbat afternoon," I told him.

"*Every* Saturday afternoon?"

"Yes."

"My father asked me last week if you were still my friend. He hasn't seen you in two months."

"I'm studying Talmud with my father," I said.

"You review?"

"No. He's teaching me scientific method."

Danny looked at me in surprise, then grinned. "You're planning to try scientific method on Rav Schwartz?"

"No," I said. Rav Schwartz was my Talmud teacher. He was an old man with a long, gray beard who wore a black coat and was constantly smoking cigarettes. He was a great Talmudist, but he had been trained in a European yeshiva, and I didn't think he would take kindly to the scientific method of studying Talmud. I had once suggested a textual emendation in class, and he had given me a queer look. I didn't think he even understood what I had said.

"Well, good luck with your scientific method," Danny told me, getting to his feet. "Just don't try it on Rav Gershenson. He knows all about it and hates it. When will my father get to see you?"

"I don't know," I said.

"I've got to go home. What's your father doing in there?" The sound of my father's typewriter had been clearly heard throughout the time we had been talking.

"He's finishing another article."

"Tell him my father sends his regards."

"Thanks. Are you and your father talking to each other these days?"

Danny hesitated a moment before answering. "Not really. Only now and then. It's not really talking."

I didn't say anything.

"I think I had really better go home," Danny said. "It's late. I'll meet you in front of your shul Sunday morning."

"Okay."

I walked him to the door, then stood there listening to the tapping of his metal-capped shoes on the hallway floor. He went out the double door and was gone.

I came back to my room and found my father standing in the doorway that led to his study. He had a bad cold and was wearing a woolen sweater and a scarf around his throat. This was his third cold in five months. It was also the first time in weeks that he had been home at night. He had become involved in Zionist activities and was always attending meetings where he spoke about the importance of Palestine as a Jewish homeland and raised money for the Jewish National Fund. He was also teaching an adult studies course in the history of political Zionism at our synagogue on Monday nights and another adult course in the history of American Jewry at his yeshiva on Wednesday nights. He rarely got home before eleven. I would always hear his tired steps in the hallway as he came in the door. He would have a glass of tea, come into my room and chat with me for a few minutes, telling me where he had been and what he had done that night, then he would remind me I didn't have to do four years of college all at once, I should go to bed soon, and he would go into his study to prepare for the classes he would be teaching the next day. He had begun taking his teaching with almost ominous seriousness these past months. He had always prepared for his classes, but there was a kind of heaviness to the way he went about preparing now, writing everything down, rehearsing his notes aloud—as if he were trying to make certain that nothing of significance would remain unsaid, as if he felt the future hung on every idea he taught. I never knew when he went to sleep; no matter what time I got to bed he was still in his study. He had never regained the weight he had lost during the weeks he had spent in the hospital after his heart attack, and he was always tired, his face pale and gaunt, his eyes watery.

He stood now in the doorway to his study, wearing the woolen sweater, the scarf, and the round, black skullcap. His feet were in bedroom slippers and his trousers were creased from all the sitting over the typewriter. He was visibly tired, and his voice cracked a few times as he asked me what Danny had been so excited about. He had heard him through the door, he said.

I told him about Danny's misery over Professor Appleman and experimental psychology.

He listened intently, then came into my room and sat down on my bed with a sigh. "So," he said, "Danny is discovering that Freud is not God."

"I told him at least to talk it over with Professor Appleman."

"And?"

"He'll talk to him next week."

"Experimental psychology," my father mused. "I know nothing about it."

"He said there was a lot of math in it."

"Ah. And Danny does not like mathematics."

"He hates it, he says. He's feeling pretty low. He feels he wasted two years reading Freud."

My father smiled and shook his head but remained silent.

"Professor Appleman sounds a lot like Professor Flesser," I said. Professor Abraham Flesser was my logic teacher, an avowed empiricist and an enemy of what he called "obscurantist Continental philosophies," which, he explained, included everything that had happened in German philosophy from Fichte to Heidegger, with the exception of Vaihinger and one or two others.

My father wanted to know what it was the two professors had in common, and I told him what Professor Appleman had said about psychology being a science only to the extent to which its hypotheses can be mathematized. "Professor Flesser made the same remark once about biology," I said.

"You talk about biology in a symbolic logic class?" my father asked.

"We were discussing inductive logic."

"Ah. Of course. The point about mathematizing hypotheses was made by Kant. It is one of the programs of the Vienna Circle logical positivists."

"Who?"

"Not now, Reuven. It is too late, and I am tired. You should go to sleep soon. Take advantage of the nights when you have no schoolwork."

"You'll be working late tonight, abba?"

"Yes."

"You're not taking care of yourself, you know. Your voice sounds awful."

He sighed again. "It is a bad cold," he said.

"Does Dr. Grossman know you're working so hard?"

"Dr. Grossman worries a little bit too much about me," he said, smiling.

"Are you going for another checkup soon?"

"Soon," he said. "I am feeling fine, Reuven. You worry like Dr. Grossman. Worry better about your schoolwork. I am fine."

"How many fathers do I have?" I asked.

He didn't say anything, but he blinked his eyes a few times.

"I wish you'd take it a little easy," I said.

"This is not a time to take things easy, Reuven. You read what is happening in Palestine."

I nodded slowly.

"This is a time to take things easy?" my father asked, his hoarse voice rising. "The Haganah and Irgun boys who die are taking it easy?"

He was talking about what was now going on in Palestine. Two Englishmen, an army major and a judge, had been kidnaped recently by the Irgun, the Jewish terrorist group in Palestine, and were being held as hostages. A captured member of the Irgun, Dov Gruner, had been sentenced to hanging by the British, and the Irgun had announced instant retaliation against these hostages should the sentence be carried out. This was the latest of a growing list of terrorist activities against the British Army in Palestine. While the Irgun engaged in terror—blowing up trains, attacking police stations, cutting communications lines—the Haganah continued smuggling Jews through the British naval blockade in defiance of the British Colonial Office, which had

sealed Palestine off to further Jewish immigration. Rarely did a week go by
now without a new act of terror against the British. My father would read
the newspaper accounts of these activities, and I could see the anguish in his
eyes. He hated violence and bloodshed and had an intense distaste for the
terrorist policy of the Irgun, but he hated the British nonimmigration policy
even more. Irgun blood was being shed for the sake of a future Jewish state,
and he found it difficult to give voice to his feelings of opposition to the acts
of terror that were regularly making front-page headlines now. Invariably,
the headlines spurred him on to new bursts of Zionist activity and to loud,
excited justification of the way he was driving himself in his fund-raising and
speechmaking efforts in behalf of a Jewish state.

I could see he was beginning to get excited now, too, so to change the
subject quickly, I told him Reb Saunders had sent his regards. "He wonders
why he doesn't see me," I said.

But my father didn't seem to have heard me. He sat on the bed, lost in
thought. We were quiet for a long time. Then he stirred and said softly, "Reuven, do you know what the rabbis tell us God said to Moses when he was
about to die?"

I stared at him. "No," I heard myself say.

"He said to Moses, 'You have toiled and labored, now you are worthy of
rest.'"

I stared at him and didn't say anything.

"You are no longer a child, Reuven," my father went on. "It is almost
possible to see the way your mind is growing. And your heart, too. Inductive
logic, Freud, experimental psychology, mathematizing hypotheses, scientific
study of the Talmud. Three years ago, you were still a child. You have become
a small giant since the day Danny's ball struck your eye. You do not see it.
But I see it. And it is a beautiful thing to see. So listen to what I am going to
tell you." He paused for a moment, as if considering his next words carefully,
then continued. "Human beings do not live forever, Reuven. We live less than
the time it takes to blink an eye, if we measure our lives against eternity. So it
may be asked what value is there to a human life. There is so much pain in the
world. What does it mean to have to suffer so much if our lives are nothing
more than the blink of an eye?" He paused again, his eyes misty now, then
went on. "I learned a long time ago, Reuven, that a blink of an eye in itself
is nothing. But the eye that blinks, *that* is something. A span of life is nothing. But the man who lives that span, *he* is something. He can fill that tiny

span with meaning, so its quality is immeasurable though its quantity may be insignificant. Do you understand what I am saying? A man must fill his life with meaning, meaning is not automatically given to life. It is hard work to fill one's life with meaning. *That* I do not think you understand yet. A life filled with meaning is worthy of rest. I want to be worthy of rest when I am no longer here. Do you understand what I am saying?"

I nodded, feeling myself cold with dread. That was the first time my father had ever talked to me of his death, and his words seemed to have filled the room with a gray mist that blurred my vision and stung as I breathed.

My father looked at me, then sighed quietly. "I was a little too blunt," he said. "I am sorry. I did not mean to hurt you."

I couldn't say anything.

"I will live for many more years, with God's help," my father said, trying a smile. "Between my son and my doctor, I will probably live to be a very old man."

The gray mist seemed to part. I took a deep breath. I could feel cold sweat running down my back.

"Are you angry at me, Reuven?"

I shook my head.

"I did not want to sound morbid. I only wanted to tell you that I am doing things I consider very important now. If I could not do these things, my life would have no value. Merely to live, merely to exist—what sense is there to it? A fly also lives."

I didn't say anything. The mist was gone now. I found the palms of my hands were cold with sweat.

"I am sorry," my father said quietly. "I can see I upset you."

"You frightened me," I heard myself say.

"I am sorry."

"Will you please go for that checkup?"

"Yes," my father said.

"You really frightened me, talking that way. Are you sure you're all right?"

"I have a bad cold," my father said. "But I am fine otherwise."

"You'll go for that checkup?"

"I will call Dr. Grossman tomorrow and make an appointment for next week. All right?"

"Yes."

"Fine. My young logician is satisfied. Good. Let us talk of happier things. I did not tell you that I saw Jack Rose yesterday. He gave me a thousand-dollar check for the Jewish National Fund."

"Another thousand dollars?" Jack Rose and my father had been boyhood friends in Russia and had come to America on the same boat. He was now a wealthy furrier and a thoroughly nonobservant Jew. Yet, six months ago, he had given my father a thousand-dollar contribution to our synagogue.

"It is strange what is happening," my father said. "And it is exciting. Jack is on the Building Committee of his synagogue. Yes, he joined a synagogue. Not for himself, he told me. For his grandchildren. He is helping them put up a new building so his grandchildren can go to a modern synagogue and have a good Jewish education. It is beginning to happen everywhere in America. A religious renaissance, some call it."

"I can't see Jack Rose in a synagogue," I said. On the few occasions when he had been over to our apartment, I had found his open disregard for Jewish tradition distasteful. He was a short man, with round, pink features, always immaculately dressed, always smoking long, expensive cigars. Once I asked my father why they had remained friends, their views about almost everything of importance were so different. He replied by expressing dismay at my question. Honest differences of opinion should never be permitted to destroy a friendship, he told me. "Haven't you learned that yet, Reuven?" Now I was tempted to tell my father that Jack Rose was probably using his money to salve a bad conscience. But I didn't. Instead, I said, a little scornfully, "I don't envy his rabbi."

My father shook his head soberly. "Why not? You should envy him, Reuven. American Jews have begun to return to the synagogue."

"God help us if synagogues fill up with Jack Roses."

"They will fill up with Jack Roses, and it will be the task of rabbis to educate them. It will be your task if you become a rabbi."

I looked at him.

"*If* you become a rabbi," my father said, smiling at me warmly.

"*When* I become a rabbi, you mean."

My father nodded, still smiling. "You would have been a fine university professor," he said. "I would have liked you to become a university professor. But I think you have already decided. Am I right?"

"Yes," I said.

"Even with a synagogue full of Jack Roses?"

"Even with a synagogue full of Jack Roses," I said. "God help me."

"America needs rabbis," my father said.

"Well, it's better than being a boxer," I told him.

My father looked puzzled.

"A bad joke," I said.

"Will you have some tea with me?"

I said I would.

"Come. Let us have some tea and continue to talk about happy things."

So we drank tea and talked some more. My father told me about the Zionist activities he was engaged in, the speeches he was making, the funds he was raising. He said that in a year or two the crisis in Palestine would come to a head. There would be terrible bloodshed, he predicted, unless the British would give over the problem to the United Nations. Many American Jews were not yet aware of what was going on, he said. The English papers did not tell the entire story. A Jew had to read the Yiddish press now if he wished to know everything that was happening in Palestine. American Jews had to be awakened to the problem of a Jewish state. His Zionist group was planning a mass rally in Madison Square Garden, he told me. The publicity would be going out this week, and there would be a large ad soon in the *New York Times*, announcing the rally. It was scheduled for late February.

"I wonder how Reb Saunders will feel when he finds out that Danny is the friend of the son of a Zionist," I mused. I had told my father about Reb Saunders's explosion.

My father sighed. "Reb Saunders sits and waits for the Messiah," he said. "I am tired of waiting. Now is the time to bring the Messiah, not to wait for him."

We finished our tea. My father returned to his study, and I went to bed. I had some terrible dreams that night, but I could remember none of them when I woke in the morning.

It was Friday, and I had nothing planned. Danny always spent his mornings studying Talmud, so I decided that rather than waste the day I would go over to the college library and see if I could find something on experimental psychology. It was a little before ten o'clock when I woke, and my father had already left to teach, so Manya served me breakfast alone, calling me a lazy sleepyhead and a few other things in Russian which I didn't understand, and then I took the trolley over to the college.

The library had a large section devoted to psychology. I found some books on experimental psychology and leafed through them slowly, then checked the indexes and bibliographies. What I discovered made it very clear why Danny was feeling so miserable.

I had chosen the books at random, but even a quick glance at them made it apparent that they were all structured along similar lines. They dealt only with experimental data and were filled with graphs, charts, tables, photographs of devices for the measuring of auditory, visual, and tactile responses, and with mathematical translations of laboratory findings. Most of the books didn't even cite Freud in their bibliographies. In one book, Freud was referred to only once, and the passage was far from complimentary.

I checked the indexes under "unconscious." Some of the books didn't even have it listed. One book had this to say:

It is impossible here to discuss the "new psychology of the unconscious," but exaggerated as are many of the statements made as to the revolution in psychology caused by psychoanalysis there is little doubt that it has influenced psychology permanently. And it is well that the teacher should study something of it, partly because of its suggestiveness in many parts of his work, and partly to be on guard against the exaggerated statements of extremists, and the uncritical advocacy of freedom from all discipline, based upon them.

That "uncritical advocacy of freedom from all discipline" sounded a lot like Professor Appleman. Then I found something that really sounded like Professor Appleman:

Magic depends on tradition and belief. It does not welcome observation, nor does it profit by experiment. On the other hand, science is based on experience; it is open to correction by observation and experiment.

The book in which I found that passage was full of tables and graphs showing the results of experiments on frogs, salamanders, rats, apes, and human beings. It didn't mention Freud or the unconscious anywhere.

I felt sorry for Danny. He had spent two years studying about the mind from the point of view of Freudian analysis. Now he was studying about the mind from the point of view of physiology. I understood what he had meant when he said that experimental psychology had nothing to do with the human mind. In terms of psychoanalytic theory, it had very little to do with the human mind. But psychoanalysis aside, I thought the books were very valuable. How else could a science of psychology be built except by laboratory findings? And what else could you do in a laboratory except experiment with the physiology of animals and men? How could you experiment with their *minds*? How could anyone subject Freud's concept of the unconscious to a laboratory test?

Poor Danny, I thought. Professor Appleman, with his experimental psychology, is torturing your mind. And your father, with his bizarre silence—which I still couldn't understand, no matter how often I thought about it—is torturing your soul.

I went home, feeling sad and a little helpless. Danny would have to work out his own problem. I couldn't help him much with psychology.

The second semester of college began the following Monday, and during lunch Danny told me he planned to speak to Professor Appleman that afternoon. He looked tense and nervous. I suggested that he be polite but honest, and that he listen to what Appleman might have to say. I was a little nervous myself, but I told him I had done some reading in experimental psychology on Friday and that I thought it had a lot to contribute. How could you have a science without experimentation? I wanted to know. And how could anyone experiment on the unconscious, which, by definition, seemed to defy laboratory techniques of testing?

I saw Danny become tight-lipped with anger. "Thanks a lot," he said bitterly. "That's just what I need now. A kick in the pants from my best friend."

"I'm telling you how I feel," I said.

"And I'm telling you how *I* feel!" he almost shouted. "Thanks a million!"

He stormed angrily out of the lunchroom, leaving me to finish the meal alone.

We usually met outside the building after our final class and went home together, but that evening he didn't show up. I waited about half an hour, then went home alone. The next morning, as I walked up Lee Avenue, I saw him waiting for me in front of the synagogue where my father and I prayed.

"Where were you last night?" he asked.

"I waited half an hour," I said. "What time did you get out?"

"A quarter after seven."

"You were with him an *hour*?"

"We had a long talk. Listen, I'm sorry I blew up like that yesterday at lunch."

I told him I had a pretty thick skin and, besides, what was a friend for if not to be blown up at every now and then.

We were walking toward the trolley station. It was a bitter cold morning. Danny's earlocks lifted and fell in the stiff wind that blew through the streets.

"What happened?" I asked.

"It's a long story," Danny said, looking at me sideways and grinning. "We had a long talk about Freud, Freudians, psychology, psychoanalysis, and God."

"And?"

"He's a very fine person. He said he's been waiting all term for me to talk to him."

I didn't say anything. But now *I* was grinning.

"Anyway, he knows Freud forwards and backwards. He told me that he wasn't objecting to Freud's conclusions as much as to his methodology. He said Freud's approach was based on his own limited experiences. He generalized on the basis of a few instances, a few private patients."

"That's the problem of induction in a nutshell," I said. "How do you justify jumping from a few instances to a generalization?"

"I don't know anything about the problem of induction," Danny said. "That's your department. Appleman said something else, though, that made a lot of sense to me. He admitted that Freud was a genius and a cautious scientist, but he said that Freud evolved a theory of behavior based only on the study of *abnormal* cases. He said that experimental psychology was interested in applying the methodology of the natural sciences to discover how *all* human beings behaved. It doesn't generalize about personality behavior only on the basis of a certain segment of people. That makes a lot of sense."

"Well, well," I said, grinning broadly.

"He also said his quarrel was mainly with the Freudians, not so much with Freud himself. He said they were happy to earn their fat fees as analysts and refused to let anyone challenge their hypotheses."

"There's our trolley," I said. "Come on!"

The trolley was waiting for a light, and we made it just in time. Some of the people inside stared curiously at Danny as we went up the aisle looking for seats. I had grown accustomed to people staring at Danny, at his beard and side curls. But Danny had become increasingly self-conscious about his appearance ever since the time he had read Graetz on Hasidism. He looked straight ahead, trying to ignore the stares. We found seats in the rear of the trolley and sat down.

"So he said analysts don't let anyone challenge their hypotheses," I said. "What happened then?"

"Well, we talked a lot about experimental psychology. He told me that it was almost impossible to study human subjects because it was too difficult to control the experiments. He said we use rats because we can vary the conditions. He repeated a lot of things he'd already said in class, but he made a lot more sense this time. At least, I think he made a lot more sense. Maybe after what he said about Freud being a genius I was just more willing to listen to him. He said he admired my knowledge of Freud but that in science no one was God, not even Einstein. He said even in religion people differed about what God was, so why shouldn't scientists take issue with other scientists? I couldn't argue with that. He said experimental psychology would be a healthy balance to my knowledge of Freud. Maybe. I still don't think it has anything to do with the human mind. It's more physiology than anything else, I think. Anyway, Appleman told me that if I had any problem with math he was willing to help me as much as he could. But his time is limited, he said, so he suggested I get a friend to help me on a regular basis."

I didn't say anything.

He looked at me and grinned.

"Okay," I said. "I don't charge very much."

"It won't make me love running rats through mazes," Danny said. "But at least he's sympathetic. He's really a fine person."

I smiled at him but didn't say anything. Then I noticed the psychology textbook he was carrying. It was one of the books I had seen on Friday that didn't mention Freud once. I asked him what he thought of it, and he said it was a grind. "If I ever get to love experimental psychology after this book I'll assume the Messiah has come," he said.

"Well, just call on your friendly tzaddik for help," I told him.

He looked at me queerly.

"I meant me," I said.

He looked away and didn't say anything. We rode the rest of the way to school in silence.

• • •

So I began coaching Danny in math. He caught on very quickly, mostly by memorizing steps and procedures. He wasn't really interested in the *why* of a mathematical problem but in the *how.* I enjoyed coaching him and learned a lot of experimental psychology. I found it fascinating, a lot more substantial and scientific than Freud had been, and a lot more fruitful in terms of expanding testable knowledge on how human beings thought and learned.

Throughout the early weeks of February, Danny and I met in the lunchroom, sat at a table by ourselves, and discussed the difficulties he was having with his mathematical translations of psychological experiments. I showed him how to set up his graphs, how to utilize the tables in his textbook, and how to reduce experimental findings to mathematical formulas. I also kept arguing for the value of experimentation. Danny remained convinced of his original argument that experimental psychology had nothing to do with the human mind, though he began to see its value as an aid to learning theory and intelligence testing. His frustration over it went up and down like a barometer, the climate being the extent to which he was able to comprehend and resolve whatever mathematical problem preoccupied him at any given moment.

I saw very little of my father during those early weeks of February. Except for breakfast, supper, and Shabbat, he was never home. Sometime between eleven and twelve every night, he would return from wherever he had been, have a glass of tea, spend a few minutes with me in my room, then go into his study. I never knew what time he went to bed, though his tired, stooped body and his haggard face made it clear that he was sleeping very little. He had gone for his checkup, and Dr. Grossman had been satisfied with his health, though he had suggested that he get more rest. My father took a vitamin pill every morning now with his orange juice, but they didn't seem to be doing much good. He completely ignored Dr. Grossman's suggestion that he rest more, and every time I brought up the subject he either waved it away or talked about the violence now going on in Palestine. It was impossible to talk to him about his health. There was nothing more important to him now than the two ideas around which his life revolved: the education of American Jewry and a Jewish state in Palestine. So he continued teaching his adult classes and planning for the Madison Square Garden rally due to take place in the last week of February.

Not only had my home life been affected by Palestine but my school life as well. Every shade of Zionist thought was represented in Hirsch College, from the Revisionists, who supported the Irgun, to the Neturai Karta, the Guardians of the City, the city being Jerusalem. This latter group was composed of severely Orthodox Jews, who, like Reb Saunders, despised all efforts aimed at the establishment of a Jewish state prior to the advent of the Messiah. A recent influx of Hungarian Jews into our neighborhood had swelled their ranks, and they formed a small but highly vocal element of the school's student population. Even the rabbinic faculty was split, most of the rabbis voicing their hope for a Jewish state, some of them opposing it, while all of the college faculty seemed to be for it. There were endless discussions during the afternoon college hours about the problem of dual loyalty—what sort of allegiance could an American Jew have toward a foreign Jewish state?— and invariably these arguments revolved around this hypothetical question: On what side would an American Jew fight should America ever declare war against a Jewish state? I always answered that the question was silly, America would never send Jews to fight against a Jewish state; during the Second World War she had sent Japanese Americans to fight the Germans, not the Japanese. But my answer never seemed to satisfy anyone. What if America *did* want to send Jews to fight against a Jewish state? the theorists countered. What then? The discussions were quite heated at times, but they went on only among those students and teachers who favored a Jewish state. Many of the Hasidim ignored the question completely. Despising as they did all efforts in behalf of a Jewish state, they despised as well all discussions that had to do with even its possible existence. They called such discussions bitul Torah, time taken away from the study of Torah, and looked upon all the disputants with icy disgust.

Toward the middle of February, the various factions began to firm up their ranks as the entire spectrum of Zionist youth movements moved into the school in a drive for membership, the second such drive since I had entered the college. From that time on—the recruitment drive lasted a few days—every student's position was clearly defined by the Zionist philosophy of the group he had joined. Most of the pro-Zionist students, myself included, joined a religious Zionist youth group; a few joined the youth arm of the Revisionists. The anti-Zionist students remained aloof, bitter, disdainful of our Zionism.

In the lunchroom one day, one of the Hasidim accused a member of the Revisionist youth group of being worse than Hitler. Hitler had only succeeded in destroying the Jewish body, he shouted in Yiddish, but the Revisionists were trying to destroy the Jewish soul. There was almost a fistfight, and the two students were kept apart with difficulty by members of their respective sides. The incident left a bitter taste in everyone's mouth and succeeded only in increasing the tension between the pro-Zionist and anti-Zionist students.

As I expected, Danny did not join any of the Zionist groups. Privately, he told me he wanted to join my group. But he couldn't. Did I remember his father's explosion over Zionism? he wanted to know. I told him I had had nightmares about that explosion. How would I like an explosion like that with every meal? Danny asked me. I didn't think the question required an answer and told him so. Danny nodded grimly. Besides, he added, the anti-Zionists among the Hasidic students looked upon him as their leader. How would it be if he joined a Zionist group? It would do nothing but add to the already existing bitterness. He was trapped by his beard and earlocks, he said, and there was nothing he could do. But one day . . . He did not finish the sentence. He remained aloof, however, never participating in the quarrels between the pro-Zionist and anti-Zionist groups. And during the near fistfight in the lunchroom, his face went rigid as stone, and I saw him look with hatred at the Hasidic student who had started the quarrel. But he said nothing, and after the disputants had been half carried, half dragged, from the lunchroom he returned immediately to the math problem we had been discussing.

In the third week of February, the newspapers reported that British Foreign Minister Bevin had announced his intention to bring the Palestine issue to the United Nations in September. My father was delighted, despite the fact that the news cost him some extra nights of work rewriting the speech he was to give at the rally.

He read the speech to me the Shabbat afternoon before the rally. In it he described the two-thousand-year-old Jewish dream of a return to Zion, the Jewish blood that had been shed through the centuries, the indifference of the world to the problem of a Jewish homeland, the desperate need to arouse the world to the realization of how vital it was that such a homeland be established immediately on the soil of Palestine. Where else could the remnant of Jewry that had escaped Hitler's ovens go? The slaughter of six million Jews would have meaning only on the day a Jewish state was established. Only then would their sacrifice begin to make some sense; only then would the songs of faith they had sung on their way to the gas chambers take on meaning; only then would Jewry again become a light to the world, as Ahad Ha'am had foreseen.

I was deeply moved by the speech, and I was very proud of my father. It was wonderful to know that he would soon be standing in front of thousands of people, reading the same words he read to me that Shabbat.

The day before the scheduled date of the Madison Square Garden rally there was a violent snowstorm, and my father walked like a ghost through our apartment, staring white-faced out the window at the swirling snow. It fell the entire day, then stopped. The city struggled to free itself of its white burden, but the streets remained choked all the next day, and my father left in the evening for the rally, wearing a look of doom, his face ashen. I couldn't go with him because I had a logic exam the next day and had to remain home to study. I forced myself to concentrate on the logic problems, but somehow they seemed inconsequential to me. I kept seeing my father standing at the rostrum in front of a vast, empty hall, speaking to seats made vacant by the snow. I dreaded the moment I would hear his key in the lock of our apartment door.

I did as much studying as I could, hating Professor Flesser for springing the exam on us the way he had done; then I wandered aimlessly through the apartment, thinking how stupid it was to have all my father's work ruined by something like a snowstorm.

Shortly before one in the morning, I heard him open the door. I was in the kitchen, drinking milk, and I ran out into the hallway. His face was flushed with excitement. The rally had been a wild success. The Garden had been packed, and two thousand people had stood on the street outside, listening to the speeches over loudspeakers. He was elated. We sat at the kitchen table, and he told me all about it. The police had blocked off the street; the crowd's response to the speeches urging an end to the British mandate and the establishment of a Jewish state had been overwhelming. My father's talk had been wildly cheered. A senator who had spoken earlier had come up to him after the rally and had enthusiastically shaken his hand, promising him his complete support. There was no question that the rally had been a success. It had been a stunning success — despite the snow-choked streets.

It was after three in the morning when we finally went to bed.

The rally made the front pages of all the New York papers the next day. The English papers carried excerpts of the senator's speech and briefly mentioned my father. But all the Yiddish papers quoted him extensively. I was the center of considerable attention on the part of the Zionist students and the target of icy hatred from the ranks of the anti-Zionists. I paid no attention to the fact that Danny did not meet me in the lunchroom. Between my fatigue over lack of sleep and my excitement over the rally, I did quite poorly in the logic exam. But I didn't care. Logic didn't seem at all important now. I kept seeing my father's excited face and heard his voice telling me over and over again about the rally.

That evening I waited for Danny more than half an hour just inside the double door of the school before I decided to go home alone. The next morning he wasn't in front of the synagogue. I waited as long as I could, then took the trolley to school. I was sitting at a table preparing for the Talmud session, when I saw him pass me and nod his head in the direction of the door. He looked white-faced and grim, and he was blinking his eyes nervously. He went out, and a moment later I followed. I saw him go into the bathroom, and I went in after him. The bathroom was empty. Danny was urinating into one of the urinals. I stood next to him and assumed the urinating position. Was he all right? I wanted to know. He wasn't all right, he told me bitterly. His father had read the account of the rally in the Yiddish press. There had been an explosion yesterday at breakfast, last night at supper, and this morning again at breakfast. Danny was not to see me, talk to me, listen to me, be found within four feet of me. My father and I had been excommunicated from the Saunders family. If Reb Saunders even once heard of Danny being anywhere in my presence, he would remove him immediately from the college and send him to an out-of-town yeshiva for his rabbinic ordination. There would be no college education, no bachelor's degree, nothing, just a rabbinic ordination. If we tried meeting in secret, Reb Saunders would find out about it. My father's speech had done it. Reb Saunders didn't mind his son reading forbidden books, but *never* would he let his son be the friend of the son of a man who was advocating the establishment of a secular Jewish state run by Jewish goyim. It was even dangerous for Danny to meet me in the bathroom, but he had to tell me. As if to emphasize how dangerous it was, a Hasidic student came into the bathroom just then, took one look at me, and chose the urinal farthest away from me. A moment later, Danny walked out. When I came into the hallway, he was gone.

I had expected it, but now that it had happened I couldn't believe it. Reb Saunders had drawn the line not at secular literature, not at Freud—assuming he knew somehow that Danny had been reading Freud—but at Zionism. I

found it impossible to believe. My father and I had been excommunicated—
not only from the Saunders family, apparently, but also from the anti-Zionist
element of the Hasidic student body. They avoided all contact with me, and
even stepped out of my way so I would not brush against them in the halls.
Occasionally I overheard them talking about the Malter goyim. During lunch
I sat at a table with some of my non-Hasidic classmates and stared at the
section of the room the Hasidic students always took for themselves. They
sat together in the lunchroom, and my eyes moved slowly over them, over
their dark clothes, fringes, beards, and earlocks—and it seemed to me that
every word they were saying was directed against me and my father. Danny
sat among them, silent, his face tight. His eyes caught mine, held, then looked
slowly away. I felt cold with the look of helpless pleading I saw in them. It
seemed so incredible to me, so outrageously absurd. Not Freud but Zionism had finally shattered our friendship. I went through the rest of the day
alternating between violent rage at Reb Saunders's blindness and anguished
frustration at Danny's helplessness.

When I told my father about it that night, he listened in silence. He was
quiet for a long time afterward; then he sighed and shook his head, his eyes
misty. He had known it would happen, he said sadly. How could it not happen?

"I don't understand it, abba." I was almost in tears. "In a million years I'll
never understand it. He let Danny read all the books I gave him, he let us be
friends all these years even though he knew I was your son. Now he breaks us
up over this. I just don't understand it."

"Reuven, what went on between you and Danny all these years was private. Who really knew? It was probably not difficult for Reb Saunders to answer questions from his followers, assuming there were any questions, which
I doubt, simply by saying that I was at least an observer of the Commandments. But he has no answer anymore to my Zionism. What can he tell his
people now? Nothing. He had to do what he did. How could he let you continue to be friends? I am sorry I was the cause of it. I brought you together,
and now I am the cause of your separation. I am deeply sorry."

"He's such a—a fanatic!" I almost shouted.

"Reuven," my father said quietly, "the fanaticism of men like Reb Saunders kept us alive for two thousand years of exile. If the Jews of Palestine have
an ounce of that same fanaticism and use it wisely, we will soon have a Jewish
state."

I couldn't say anything else. I was afraid my anger would bring me to say the wrong words.

I went to bed early that night but lay awake a long time, trying to remember all the things Danny and I had done together since the Sunday afternoon his ball had struck me in the eye.

FOURTEEN

FOR THE REST of that semester, Danny and I ate in the same lunchroom, attended the same classes, studied in the same school synagogue, and often rode in the same trolley car—and never said a single word to each other. Our eyes met frequently, but our lips exchanged nothing. I lost all direct contact with him. It was an agony to sit in the same class with him, to pass him in the hallway, to see him in a trolley, to come in and out of the school building with him—and not say a word. I grew to hate Reb Saunders with a venomous passion that frightened me at times, and I consoled myself with wild fantasies of what I would do to him if he ever fell into my hands.

It was an ugly time and it began to affect my schoolwork to a point where some of my college teachers called me into their offices and wanted to know what was happening—they expected better from me than they were receiving. I made vague allusions to personal problems and went away from them cold with despair. I talked about it with my father as often as I could, but there seemed to be little he could do to help me. He would listen somberly, sigh, and repeat that he had no intention of quarreling with Reb Saunders, he respected his position in spite of its fanaticism.

I wondered often during those months whether Danny was also going through these same dreadful experiences. I saw him frequently. He seemed to be losing weight, and I noticed he was wearing different eyeglasses. But he was very carefully avoiding me, and I knew enough to stay away from him. I didn't want word to get back to his father that we had been seen together.

I hated the silence between us and thought it unimaginable that Danny and his father never really talked. Silence was ugly, it was black, it leered, it was cancerous, it was death. I hated it, and I hated Reb Saunders for forcing it upon me and his son.

I never knew myself capable of the kind of hatred I felt toward Reb Saunders all through that semester. It became, finally, a blind, raging fury, and I would find myself trembling with it at odd moments of the day—waiting to get into a trolley car, walking into a bathroom, sitting in the lunchroom, or reading in the library. And my father only added to it, for whenever I began to talk to him of my feelings toward Reb Saunders he invariably countered by defending him and by asserting that the faith of Jews like Reb Saunders had kept us alive through two thousand years of violent persecution. He disagreed with Reb Saunders, yes, but he would countenance no slander against his name or his position. Ideas should be fought with ideas, my father said, not with blind passion. If Reb Saunders was fighting him with passion, that did not mean that my father had to fight Reb Saunders with passion.

And Reb Saunders was fighting with passion. He had organized some of the Hasidic rebbes in the neighborhood into a group called The League for a Religious Eretz Yisroel. The work of this organization had begun mildly enough in early March with the handing out of leaflets. Its aims were clear: no Jewish homeland without the Torah at its center; therefore, no Jewish homeland until the coming of the Messiah. A Jewish homeland created by Jewish goyim was to be considered contaminated and an open desecration of the name of God. By the end of March, however, the leaflets had become inflammatory in tone, threatening excommunication to all in the neighborhood who displayed allegiance to Zionism, even at one point threatening to boycott neighborhood stores owned by Jews who contributed to, participated in, or were sympathetic with Zionist activities. A mass anti-Zionist rally was announced for a date a few days before Passover. It was poorly attended, but it made some of the English papers, and the reports of what had been said were ugly.

The student body of the college was tense with suppressed violence. An angry fistfight broke out in a classroom one afternoon, and it was only because the Dean threatened immediate expulsion to any future participants in such quarrels that more fistfights were avoided. But the tension was felt everywhere; it spilled over into our studies, and arguments over Milton, Talleyrand, or deductive procedures in logic were often clear substitutes for the outlawed fistfights over Zionism.

I took the finals in the middle of June and came away from them sick with despair. I had botched my midterms badly, and I didn't do too much better on my finals. My father didn't say a word when he saw my report card at the end of June. Both of us were by that time looking forward very eagerly to the quiet month of August when we would be together in the cottage near Peekskill. It had been a terrible time, these past four months, and we wanted to get away from the city.

But the cottage proved to be not far enough away. We took to it the horrifying news that the Irgun had hanged two innocent British sergeants in retaliation for the three Irgunists who were hanged on the twenty-ninth of July. My father was outraged by the Irgun act, but said nothing more about it after his first burst of anger. Two weeks after we left for the cottage we were back in the city. Urgent Zionist meetings had been called to plan for the coming United Nations session that was to discuss the Palestine problem. My father was on the Executive Committee of his Zionist group and had to attend the meetings.

For the rest of August, I saw my father only on Shabbat. He was gone in the mornings when I woke and he returned at night when I was asleep. He was filled with fiery excitement, but it was clear that he was wearing himself out. I couldn't talk to him at all about his health. He refused to listen. Our Shabbat afternoon Talmud sessions had stopped; my father spent all of Shabbat resting so as to be prepared for each coming week of furious activity. I haunted the apartment, wandered the streets, barked at Manya, and thought of Danny. I remembered him telling me how much he admired and trusted his father, and I couldn't understand it. How could he admire and trust someone who wouldn't talk to him, even if that someone was his father? I hated his father. Once I even went up to the third floor of the public library, hoping I might find Danny there. Instead, I found an old man sitting in the chair Danny had once occupied, staring nearsightedly at the pages of a scholarly journal. I went away from there and walked the streets blindly until it was time to go home to a lonely supper.

In the second week of September, I returned to school for the preregistration student assembly and found myself sitting in the auditorium a few seats away from Danny. He looked thin and pale, and constantly blinked his eyes. During the registrar's brief words of instruction concerning registration procedure, I saw Danny turn his head, stare at me for a moment, then turn slowly away. His face had remained expressionless; he hadn't even nodded a greeting. I sat very still, listening to the registrar, and felt myself get angry. To hell with you, Danny Saunders, I thought. You could at least show you know I'm alive. To hell with you and your fanatic father. I became so completely absorbed in my anger that I stopped listening to the instructions. I had to ask one of my classmates to repeat them to me after the assembly. To hell with you, Danny Saunders, I kept saying to myself all that day. I can live without your beard and earlocks with no trouble at all. You're not the center of the world, friend. To hell with you and your damn silence.

By the time the fall semester officially began two days later, I had promised myself to forget Danny as quickly as possible. I wasn't going to let him ruin another semester's work. One more report card like the one I had shown my father at the end of June and I wouldn't even be graduated *cum laude*. To hell with you, Danny Saunders, I kept saying to myself. You could at least have nodded your head.

But it proved to be a good deal more difficult to forget him than I had anticipated, mostly because I had been moved up into Rav Gershenson's Talmud class, where Danny's presence was always felt.

Rav Gershenson was a tall, heavy-shouldered man in his late sixties, with a long, pointed gray beard and thin, tapered fingers that seemed always to be dancing in the air. He used his hands constantly as he talked, and when he did not talk his fingers drummed on his desk or on the open Talmud in front of him. He was a gentle, kindly person, with brown eyes, an oval face, and a soft voice, which at times was almost inaudible. He was an exciting teacher, though, and he taught Talmud the way my father did, in depth, concentrating for days on a few lines and moving on only when he was satisfied that we understood everything thoroughly. He laid heavy emphasis on the early and late medieval Talmudic commentators, and we were always expected to come to class knowing the Talmud text and these commentators in advance. Then he would call on one of us to read and explain the text—and the questions would begin. "What does the Ramban say about Rabbi Akiva's question?" he might ask of a particular passage, speaking in Yiddish. The rabbis spoke only Yiddish in the Talmud classes, but the students could speak Yiddish or English. I spoke English. "Everyone agrees with the Ramban's explanation?" Rav Gershenson might go on to ask. "The Me'iri does not. Very good. What does the Me'iri say? And the Rashba? How does the Rashba explain Abaye's answer?" And on and on. There was almost always a point at which the student who was reading the text would become bogged down by the cumulative intricacies of the questions and would stare down at his Talmud, drowning in the shame produced by his inability to answer. There would be a long, dreaded silence, during which Rav Gershenson's fingers would begin to drum upon his desk or his Talmud. "Nu?" he would ask quietly. "You do not know? How is it you do not know? Did you review beforehand? Yes? And you still do not know?" There would be another long silence, and then Rav Gershenson would look around the room and say quietly, "Who does know?" and, of course, Danny's hand would immediately go up, and he would offer the answer. Rav Gershenson would listen, nod, and his fingers would cease their drumming and take to the air as they accompanied his detailed review of Danny's answer. There were times, however, when Rav Gershenson did not nod at Danny's answer but questioned him on it instead, and there would then ensue a lengthy dialogue between the two of them, with the class sitting by and listening in silence. Most often these dialogues took only a few minutes, but by the end of September there had already been two occasions when they had lasted more than three quarters of an hour. I was constantly being reminded by these dialogues of the way Danny argued Talmud with his father. It made it not only difficult to forget him but quite impossible. And now it was also I and not only Reb Saunders who was able to listen to Danny's voice only through a Talmudic disputation.

The hours of the Talmud classes in the school were arranged in such a way that we were able to spend from nine in the morning to noon preparing the material to be studied with Rav Gershenson. We would then eat lunch. And from one to three we would have the actual Talmud session itself, the shiur, with Rav Gershenson. No one in the class knew who would be called on to read and explain, so all of us worked feverishly to prepare. But it never really helped, because no matter how hard we worked there would always be that dreaded moment of silence when the questions could no longer be answered and Rav Gershenson's fingers would begin their drumming.

There were fourteen students in the class, and each one of us, with the exception of Danny, sooner or later tasted that silence personally. I was called on in the first week of October and tasted the silence briefly before I managed to struggle through with an answer to an almost impossible question. The answer was accepted and amplified by Rav Gershenson, thereby forestalling Danny's poised hand. I saw him look at me briefly afterward, while Rav Gershenson dealt with my answer. Then he looked away, and a warm smile played on his lips. My anger at him melted away at the sight of that smile, and the agony of not being able to communicate with him returned. But it was a subdued agony now, a sore I was somehow able to control and keep within limits. It was no longer affecting my schoolwork.

By the middle of October everyone in the class, except me, had been called on at least twice. I prepared feverishly, expecting to hear my name called any day. But it wasn't. By the end of October, I began to feel uneasy. By the middle of November I still hadn't been called on again. I took part in the class discussions, asked questions, argued, raised my hand almost as frequently as Danny raised his in response to Rav Gershenson's "Who does know?"—but I was not called on to read. I couldn't understand it, and it began to upset me. I wondered if this was his way of participating in Reb Saunders's ban against me and my father.

There were other things, too, that were upsetting me at the time. My father had begun to look almost skeletal as a result of his activities, and I dreaded the nights he came wearily home, drank his glass of tea, spent some minutes with me in my room, looking hollow-eyed and not really listening to what I told him, and then went into his study. Instead of studying Talmud with him on the Shabbat, I studied alone while he slept. The Palestine issue was being debated now by the United Nations, and the Partition Plan would soon be voted upon. Every day there were headlines announcing new acts of terror and bloodshed; every week, it seemed, there was another massive rally in Madison Square Garden. I was able to attend two of those rallies. The second time I went I made sure to arrive early enough to get a seat inside. The speeches were electrifying, and I joined in the applause and the cheering until my hands were sore and my voice was hoarse. My father spoke at that rally, his voice booming out clearly through the public address system. He seemed so huge behind the microphones, his voice giving his body the stature of a giant. When he was done, I sat and listened to the wild applause of the crowd, and my eyes filled with tears of pride.

In the midst of all this, Reb Saunders's League for a Religious Eretz Yisroel continued putting out its anti-Zionist leaflets. Everywhere I went I found those leaflets—on the streets, in the trolley cars, in my classroom desks, on my lunch table, even in the school bathrooms.

It became clear as November went by that the United Nations vote on the Partition Plan would take place sometime at the end of the month. My father was at a meeting on Sunday evening, November 29, when the vote was finally held, and I listened to it over the kitchen radio. I cried like a baby when the result was announced, and later, when my father came home, we embraced and wept and kissed, and our tears mingled on our cheeks. He was almost incoherent with joy. The death of the six million Jews had finally been given meaning, he kept saying over and over again. It had happened. After two thousand years, it had finally happened. We were a people again, with our own land. We were a blessed generation. We had been given the opportunity to see the creation of the Jewish state. "Thank God!" he said. "Thank God! Thank God!" We alternately wept and talked until after three in the morning when we finally went to bed.

I woke groggy from lack of sleep but still feeling the sense of exhilaration, and was eager to get to school to share the joy with my friends. My exhilaration was dampened somewhat during breakfast when my father and I heard over the radio that a few hours after the United Nations vote a bus on its way from Tel Aviv to Jerusalem had been attacked by Arabs and seven Jews had been killed. And my exhilaration was snuffed out and transformed into an almost uncontrollable rage when I got to school and found it strewn with the leaflets of Reb Saunders's anti-Zionist league.

The leaflets denounced the United Nations vote, ordered Jews to ignore it, called the state a desecration of the name of God, and announced that the league planned to fight its recognition by the government of the United States.

Only the Dean's threat of immediate expulsion prevented me from engaging in a fistfight that day. I was tempted more than once to scream at the groups of anti-Zionist students huddling together in the halls and classrooms that they ought to go join the Arabs and the British if they were so opposed to the Jewish state. But I managed somehow to control myself and remain silent.

In subsequent weeks, I was grateful for that silence. For as Arab forces began to attack the Jewish communities of Palestine, as an Arab mob surged through Princess Mary Avenue in Jerusalem, wrecking and gutting shops and leaving the old Jewish commercial center looted and burned, and as the toll of Jewish dead increased daily, Reb Saunders's league grew strangely silent. The faces of the anti-Zionist Hasidic students in the school became tense and pained, and all anti-Zionist talk ceased. I watched them every day at lunch as they read to each other the accounts of the bloodshed reported in the Jewish press and then talked about it among themselves. I could hear sighs, see heads shaking and eyes filling with sadness. "Again Jewish blood is being spilled," they whispered to one another. "Hitler wasn't enough. Now more Jewish blood, more slaughter. What does the world want from us? Six million isn't enough? More Jews have to die?" Their pain over this new outbreak of violence against the Jews of Palestine outweighed their hatred of Zionism. They did not become Zionists; they merely became silent. I was glad during those weeks that I had restrained my anger.

I received straight A's in my college courses at the end of that semester. I also received an A in Talmud, despite the fact that Rav Gershenson had only called on me once during the entire four-month period I had spent in his class. I planned to talk to him about it during the inter-semester break, but my father suffered a second heart attack on the first day of that break.

He collapsed at a Jewish National Fund meeting and was rushed to the Brooklyn Memorial Hospital by ambulance. He hovered tenuously between life and death for three days. I lived in a nightmare of hallucinatory dread, and if it hadn't been for Manya constantly reminding me with gentle kindness that I had to eat or I would get sick, I might well have starved.

My father was beginning to recover when the second semester began, but he was a shell of a man. Dr. Grossman told me that he would be in the hospital at least six weeks, and that it would take from four to six more months of complete rest before he would be able to return to his work.

My classmates had all heard the news by the time the semester began, but their words of consolation didn't help very much. The look on Danny's face, though, when I saw him for the first time, helped a little. He passed me in the hallway, his face a suffering mask of pain and compassion. I thought for a moment he would speak to me, but he didn't. Instead, he brushed against me and managed to touch my hand for a second. His touch and his eyes spoke the words that his lips couldn't. I told myself it was bitter and ironic that my father needed to have a heart attack in order for some contact to be established once again between myself and Danny.

I lived alone. Manya came in the mornings and left after supper, and during the long winter nights of January and February I was all alone in the house. I had been alone before, but the knowledge that my father would return from his meetings and spend a few minutes with me had made the loneliness endurable. Now he wasn't attending meetings and wasn't coming into my room, and for the first few days the total silence inside the apartment was impossible for me to take, and I would go out of the house and take long walks in the bitter, cold winter nights. But my schoolwork began to suffer, and I finally took hold of myself. I spent as much of the early parts of every evening as I could visiting my father in the hospital. He was weak and could barely talk and kept asking me if I was taking care of myself. Dr. Grossman had warned me not to tire him, so I left as soon as I could, went home, ate, then spent the night studying.

By the time my father had been in the hospital three weeks, the evenings had become almost an automatic routine. The dread of his possible death was gone. It was now a matter of waiting out the silence until he came home. And I waited out the silence by studying.

I began especially to study Talmud. In the past, I had done all my Talmud studying on Shabbat and during the morning preparation periods. Now I began to study Talmud in the evenings as well. I tried to finish my college work as quickly as I could, then I would turn to the passage of Talmud we were studying with Rav Gershenson. I would study it carefully, memorize it, find the various commentaries—those which were not printed in the Talmud itself could always be found in my father's library—and memorize them. I tried to anticipate Rav Gershenson's tangled questions. And then I began to do something I had never done before with the Talmud I studied in school. After I was done memorizing the text and the commentaries, I began to go over the text again critically. I checked the Talmudic cross-references for parallel texts and memorized whatever differences I found. I took the huge volumes of the Palestinian Talmud from my father's library—the text we studied in school was the Babylonian Talmud—and checked its parallel discussions just to see how it differed from the discussions in the Babylonian Talmud. I worked carefully and methodically, using everything my father had taught me and a lot of things I now was able to teach myself. I was able to do all of this in real depth because of Rav Gershenson's slow-paced method of teaching. And by doing all of this, I was able to anticipate most of Rav Gershenson's questions. I also became more and more certain of when he would call on me again.

He had never called on me since that day in October. And it was now the middle of February. As a result of my night sessions with Talmud, I had pulled ahead of the class by at least five or six days and was tangled in one of the most complicated discussions I had ever encountered. The complication was caused not only by the Talmud text itself, which seemed filled with gaps, but by the commentaries that struggled to explain it. The text consisted of nine lines. One of the commentaries on the text ran to two and a half pages, another ran to four pages. Neither was very clear. A third commentary, however, explained the text in six lines. The explanation was terse, clipped, and simple. The only thing wrong with it was that it seemed not to be based on the text it was explaining. A later commentary tried to reconcile the three commentaries by the method of pilpul, the result being a happy one for someone who enjoyed pilpul but quite strained as far as I was concerned. It looked to be a hopeless situation.

As we came closer and closer to this text, I became more and more convinced that Rav Gershenson was going to call on me to read and explain it. I didn't quite know *why* I was convinced of that; I just knew that I was.

I began painfully to unravel the puzzle. I did it in two ways. First, in the traditional way, by memorizing the text and the commentaries, and then inventing all sorts of questions that Rav Gershenson might ask me. I would ride the trolley, walk the streets, or lie in bed—and ask myself questions. Second, in the way my father had taught me, by attempting to find or reconstruct the correct text, the text the commentator who had offered the simple explanation must have had before him. The first way was relatively simple; it was a matter of brute memorization. The second way was tortuous. I searched endlessly through all the cross-references and all the parallel passages in the Palestinian Talmud. When I was done, I had four different versions of the text on my hands. I now had to reconstruct the text upon which the simple commentary had been based. I did it by working backward, using the commentary as a base, then asking myself what passage among the four versions the commentator could have had before him as he wrote the commentary. It was painstaking work, but I finally thought I had it down right. It had taken hours and hours of precious time, but I was satisfied I had the correct text, the only text that really made sense. I had done it this way only to satisfy myself. When Rav Gershenson called on me, I would, of course, only use the first method of explanation. When my father returned from the hospital, I would show him what I had done with the second method. I felt very proud of my accomplishment.

Three days later, we came to that passage in our Talmud class, and for the second time that year Rav Gershenson called out my name and asked me to read and explain.

The class was deathly silent. Some of my friends had told me earlier that they dreaded being called on for that passage; they hadn't been able to make any sense at all out of it and the commentaries were impossible. I was a little frightened, too, but very eager to show off what I had learned. When I heard my name called, I felt myself tingle with a mixture of fear and excitement, as if a tiny electric shock had gone through my body. Most of the students had been waiting apprehensively to hear who would be asked to read. They had sat staring down at their texts, afraid to meet Rav Gershenson's eyes. Now they were all looking at me, even Danny was looking at me, and from one of the students at my right came a barely audible sigh of relief. I bent over my Talmud, put the index finger of my right hand below the first word of the passage, and began to read.

Every Talmudic passage is composed of what, for the sake of convenience, might best be called thought units. Each thought unit is a separate stage of the total discussion that makes up the passage. It might consist of a terse state-ment of law, or a question on the statement, an answer to the question, a brief or lengthy commentary on a Biblical verse, and so on. The Talmud con-tains no punctuation marks, and it is not always a simple matter to determine where a thought unit begins and ends; occasionally, a passage will have a tight, organic flow to it which makes breaking it up into thought units difficult and somewhat arbitrary. In most instances, however, the thought units are clearly discernible, and the decision on how to break up a passage into such units is a matter of common sense and a feel for the rhythm of the argument. The need to break up a passage into its thought units is simple enough. One has to decide when to stop reading and start explaining, as well as when to appeal to the commentaries for further explanation.

I had broken up the passage into its thought units as I had studied it, so I knew precisely at what points I would stop reading and begin my ex-planations. I read aloud a thought unit that consisted of a citation from the Mishnah—the Mishnah is the written text of rabbinic oral law; in form and content it is for the most part terse and clipped, a vast collection of laws upon which are based almost all the rabbinic discussions which, together with the Mishnah, compose the Talmud. When I came to the end of the Mishnaic thought unit, I stopped, and reviewed it briefly, together with the commen-taries of Rashi and the Tosafists. I tried to be as clear as I could, and acted as if I myself were teaching the class rather than merely acting as a springboard for Rav Gershenson's comments. I finished the explanation of the Mishnaic text and read the next thought unit, which consisted of another Mishnah found in a different tractate from the one we were now studying. This sec-ond Mishnah flatly contradicted the first. I explained the Mishnah carefully, showed why there was a contradiction, then read from the commentaries of

Rashi and the Tosafists, both of which are printed on the same page as the Talmud text. I expected to be stopped at any moment by Rav Gershenson, but nothing happened. I continued reading and explaining, my eyes fixed on the text as I read and looking at Rav Gershenson as I explained. He let me continue without interruption. By the time I was four lines into the passage, the discussion had become so involved that I had already begun to appeal to one of the medieval commentaries that were not printed on the same page as the text but were rather placed separately at the end of the tractate. I kept a finger of my right hand on the appropriate place in the text, flipped the Talmud to where the commentary had been printed, and read from it. I then indicated that other commentaries had offered different explanations, and I cited them by heart because they were not found in the Talmud edition the class used. Having said that, I returned to the passage and continued to read. When I raised my eyes to explain the thought unit I had just read, I saw that Rav Gershenson had sat down—the first time since I had come into the class that he was sitting during a shiur. He was holding his head in the palms of his hands, the elbows on the open Talmud in front of him, and listening intently. As I continued with my explanation of the thought unit I had just read, I glanced at my wristwatch and discovered to my amazement that I had been talking for almost an hour and a half without interruption. I had to utilize all the commentaries this time and was able to finish explaining the thought unit a moment before the three o'clock bell sounded. Rav Gershenson said nothing. He just sat there and dismissed the class with a wave of his hand.

The next day he called on me again, and I continued to read and explain. I spent two hours on seven words, and again sometime during the session he sat down, with his head in the palms of his hands. He said not a single word. The bell caught me in the middle of a lengthy explanation of the four-page commentary, and when he called on me again the third day I read the seven words quickly, briefly went through my explanations of the day before, then continued where I had stopped.

Between the third and fourth day, my mood jumped back and forth erratically from wild exhilaration to gloomy apprehension. I knew I was doing well, otherwise Rav Gershenson would have stopped me, but I kept wishing he would say something and not just stand or sit in complete silence.

Some of the Hasidic students in the class were giving me mixed looks of awe and jealousy, as if they couldn't restrain their feelings of admiration over how well I was doing but at the same time were asking themselves how someone like me, a Zionist and the son of a man who wrote apikorsische articles, could possibly know Talmud so well. Danny, though, seemed absolutely delighted over what was happening. He never looked at me while I read and explained, but I could see him nodding his head and smiling as I went through my explanations. And Rav Gershenson remained silent and impassive, listening intently, his face expressionless, except for an occasional upward curving along the corners of his lips whenever I clarified a particularly difficult point. By the end of the third day, it began to be something of a frustrating experience. I wished he would at least say or do something, nod his head, smile, even catch me at a mistake—anything but that awful silence.

I was prepared for Rav Gershenson to call on me again the fourth day, and he did. There was by now only one more thought unit left in the passage, and I had decided in advance that when I was done explaining it I would quickly review the entire passage and all the commentaries, outlining the difficulties they had found in the text and showing the different ways they had explained these difficulties. Then I would go into the attempt of the late medieval commentary to reconcile the diverse explanations of the commentaries. All of that took me just under an hour, and when I was satisfied that I had done the best I could, I stopped talking. Rav Gershenson was sitting behind his desk, looking at me intently. It felt strange to me for a moment not to be hearing my own voice anymore. But I had nothing more to say.

There was a brief silence, during which I saw one of the Hasidic students grin and lean over to whisper something into another Hasidic student's ear. Then Rav Gershenson got to his feet and folded his arms across his chest. He was smiling a little now, and the upper part of his body was swaying slowly back and forth.

He asked me to repeat a point I had made two days earlier, and I did. He asked me to make myself a little clearer on a passage in one of the commentaries, and I repeated the passage by heart and explained it again as best I could. He asked me to go over the difficulties I had found in the various commentaries, and I repeated them carefully. Then he asked me to show how the late medieval commentary had attempted to reconcile these difficulties, and I went over that, too.

Again, there was a brief silence. I glanced at my watch and saw it was two-thirty. I wondered if he would start on the next passage with only half an hour left to the shiur. He usually preferred to start a new passage—or inyan, as it is called—at the beginning of a shiur, so as to give the class time to get into it. I was feeling very satisfied with the way I had explained the passage and answered his questions. I promised myself that I would tell my father all about it when I visited him in the hospital that evening.

Then I heard Rav Gershenson ask me whether I was satisfied with the late medieval commentary's attempt at reconciliation.

It was a question I hadn't expected. I had regarded the effort at reconciliation as the rock bottom of the entire discussion on the passage and had never thought that Rav Gershenson would question it. For a long moment, I felt myself wallowing in that dreaded silence that always followed a question of his that a student couldn't answer, and I waited for the drumming of his fingers to begin. But his arms remained folded across his chest, and he stood there, swaying slowly back and forth, and looking at me intently.

"Nu," he said again, "there are no questions about what he says?"

I waited for Danny's hand to go up, but it didn't. I glanced at him and saw his mouth had fallen slightly open. The question had caught him by surprise, too.

Rav Gershenson stroked his pointed beard with his right hand, then asked me for the third time if I was satisfied with what the commentary said.

I heard myself tell him that I wasn't.

"Ah," he said, smiling faintly. "Good. And why not?"

"Because it's pilpul," I heard myself say.

There was a stir from the class. I saw Danny stiffen in his seat, throw me a quick, almost fearful glance, then look away.

I was suddenly a little frightened at the disparaging way I had uttered the word "pilpul." The tone of disapproval in my voice hung in the air of the classroom like a threat.

Rav Gershenson slowly stroked his pointed gray beard. "So," he said softly, "it is pilpul. I see you do not like pilpul. . . . Nu, the great Vilna Gaon also did not like pilpul." He was talking about Rabbi Elijah of Vilna, the eighteenth-century opponent of Hasidism. "Tell me, Reuven"—that was the first time he had ever called me by my first name—"why is it pilpul? What is wrong with his explanation?"

I answered that it was strained, that it attributed nuances to the various conflicting commentaries that were not there, and that, therefore, it really was not a reconciliation at all.

He nodded his head slowly. "Nu," he said, not speaking only to me but to the entire class now, "it is a very difficult inyan. And the commentaries"—

he used the term "Rishonim," which indicates the early medieval Talmudic commentators—"do not help us." Then he looked at me. "Tell me, Reuven," he said quietly, "how do *you* explain the inyan?"

I sat there and stared at him in stunned silence. If the commentators hadn't been able to explain it, how could I? But he didn't let the silence continue this time. Instead, he repeated his question, his voice soft, gentle. "You cannot explain it, Reuven?"

"No," I heard myself say.

"So," Rav Gershenson said. "You cannot explain it. You are sure you cannot explain it?"

For a moment I was almost tempted to tell him the text was wrong and to give him the text I had reconstructed. But I didn't. I was afraid. I remembered Danny telling me that Rav Gershenson knew all about the critical method of studying Talmud, and hated it. So I kept silent.

Rav Gershenson turned to the class. "Can anyone explain the inyan?" he asked quietly.

He was answered by silence.

He sighed loudly. "Nu," he said, "no one can explain it. . . . The truth is, I cannot explain it myself. It is a difficult inyan. A very difficult inyan." He was silent for a moment, then he shook his head and smiled. "A teacher can also sometimes not know," he said softly.

That was the first time in my life I had ever heard a rabbi admit that he didn't understand a passage of Talmud.

We sat there in an uncomfortable silence. Rav Gershenson stared down at the open Talmud on his desk. Then he closed it slowly and dismissed the class.

As I was gathering up my books, I heard him call my name. Danny heard him, too, and looked at him. "I want to talk with you a minute," Rav Gershenson said. I went up to his desk.

Standing near him, I could see how wrinkled his face and brow were. The skin on his hands looked dry, parchmentlike, and his lips formed a thin line beneath the heavy tangle of gray beard. His eyes were brown and gentle, and deep wrinkles spread from their outside corners like tiny furrows.

He waited until all the students were out of the classroom. Then he asked me quietly, "You studied the inyan by yourself, Reuven?"

"Yes," I said.

"Your father did not help you?"

"My father is in the hospital."

He looked shocked.

"He's better now. He had a heart attack."

"I did not know," he said softly. "I am sorry to hear that." He paused for a moment, looking at me intently. "So," he said. "You studied the inyan alone."

I nodded.

"Tell me, Reuven," he said gently, "do you study Talmud with your father?"

"Yes," I said.

"Your father is a great scholar," he said quietly, almost wistfully. "A very great scholar." His brown eyes seemed misty. "Reuven, tell me, how would your father have answered my question?"

I stared at him and didn't know what to say.

He smiled faintly, apologetically. "You do not know how your father would have explained the inyan?"

The class was gone, we were alone, and somehow I felt an intimacy between us that made it not too difficult for me to say what I then said. I didn't say it without feeling a little frightened, though. "I think I know what he would have said."

"Nu," Rav Gershenson prodded me gently. "What?"

"I think he would have said the text is wrong."

I saw him blink his eyes a few times, his face expressionless. "Explain what you mean," he said quietly.

I explained how I had reconstructed the text, then quoted the reconstructed text from memory, showing him how it fitted perfectly to the explanation offered by the simplest of all the commentaries. I ended by saying I felt certain that was the text of the Talmud manuscript the commentator had had before him when he had written his commentary.

Rav Gershenson was silent for a long moment, his face impassive. Then he said slowly, "You did this by yourself, Reuven?"

"Yes."

"Your father is a good teacher," he told me quietly. "You are blessed to have such a father."

His voice was soft, reverent.

"Reuven?"

"Yes?"

"I must ask you never to use such a method of explanation in my class." He was speaking gently, almost apologetically. "I am myself not opposed to such a method. But I must ask you never to use it in my class. Do you understand me?"

"Yes."

"I will call on you often now," he said, smiling warmly. "Now that you understand, I will call on you very often. I have been waiting all year to see how good a teacher your father is. He is a great teacher and a great scholar. It is a joy to listen to you. But you must not use this method in my class. You understand?"

"Yes," I said again.

And he dismissed me with a quiet smile and a gentle nod of his head.

That evening after my last class, I went to the school library and looked for Rav Gershenson's name in the Hebrew and English catalogues. His name wasn't listed anywhere. It was then that I understood why my father was not teaching in this school.

FIFTEEN

MY FATHER RETURNED from the hospital in the middle of March. He was weak and gaunt, confined to his bed and almost completely incapable of any kind of physical activity. Manya cared for him as though he were a child, and Dr. Grossman visited him twice a week, on Mondays and Thursdays, until the end of April, when the visits were reduced to once a week. He was satisfied with my father's progress, he kept telling me. There was nothing to worry about anymore, except to make sure that he had complete rest. During the first four weeks my father was home a night nurse came in every evening, stayed awake through the night in my father's room, then left in the morning. Talking tired him quickly; even listening seemed to tire him. We weren't able to spend too much time together the first six weeks he was home. But it was wonderful to have him there, to know he was back in his room again and out of the hospital, and to know that the dark silence was finally gone from the apartment.

I had told him about my experience with Rav Gershenson while he had still been in the hospital. He had listened quietly, nodded, and had said that he was very proud of me. He hadn't said anything at all about Rav Gershenson. I was being called on regularly now in the Talmud class, and there were no silences when I read and explained a passage.

I saw Danny all the time in school, but the silence between us continued. I had finally come to accept it. We had begun to communicate with our eyes, with nods of our heads, with gestures of our hands. But we did not speak to each other. I had no idea how he was getting along in psychology, or how his family was. But I heard no bad news, so I assumed things were more or less all right.

The grim faces of the teachers and students in school reflected the newspaper headlines that told of Arab riots and attacks against the Jews of Palestine, Jewish defense measures, many of which were being hampered by the British, and continued Irgun activities. The Arabs were attacking Jewish settlements in the Upper Galilee, the Negev, and around Jerusalem, and were incessantly harassing supply convoys. Arabs were killing Jews, Jews were killing Arabs, and the British, caught uncomfortably in the middle, seemed unable and at times even unwilling to stop the rising tide of slaughter.

The Zionist youth groups in the school became increasingly active, and on one occasion some of the members of my group were asked to cut our afternoon classes and go down to a warehouse in Brooklyn to help load uniforms, helmets, and canteens onto huge ten-ton trucks that were waiting outside. We were told that the supplies would soon be on a ship heading for Palestine and would be used by the Haganah. We worked long and hard, and somehow loading those trucks made me feel intimately bound up with the news bulletins that I kept hearing on the radio and seeing in the papers.

In April, Tiberias, Haifa, and Safed were occupied by the Haganah, and the Irgun, with the help of the Haganah, captured Jaffa.

My father was a good deal stronger now and had begun walking around a bit inside the house. We were able to talk at length, and we talked of little else but Palestine. He told me that before his heart attack he had been asked to go as a delegate to the Zionist General Council that was to meet in Palestine during the coming summer. "Now I will be glad if I can go to the cottage this summer," he said, and there was a wry smile on his lips.

"Why didn't you tell me?" I asked him.

"I did not want to upset you. But I could not keep it to myself any longer. So I am telling you now."

"Why didn't you tell me when they asked you?"

"They asked me the night I had the attack," he said.

We never talked about it again. But if I was around, I always knew when he thought about it. His eyes would become dreamy, and he would sigh and shake his head. He had worked so hard for a Jewish state, and that very work now kept him from seeing it. I wondered often during the coming months what meaning he could possibly give to that. I didn't know, and I didn't ask him.

We wept quite openly that Friday in the second week of May when Israel was born. And on my way to the synagogue the next morning, I saw the newspaper headlines announcing the birth of the Jewish state. They also announced that the Arab armies had begun their threatened invasion.

The next few weeks were black and ugly. The Etzion area in the Hebron Mountains fell, the Jordanian Army attacked Jerusalem, the Iraqi Army invaded the Jordan Valley, the Egyptian Army invaded the Negev, and the battle for Latrun, the decisive point along the road to Jerusalem, turned into a bloodbath. My father became grim and silent, and I began to worry again about his health.

In early June, a rumor swept through the school that a recent graduate had been killed in the fighting around Jerusalem. The rumor ran wild for a few days, and was finally confirmed. I hadn't known him at all, he had been graduated before I had entered, but apparently most of the present members of the senior class remembered him well. He had been a brilliant mathematics student, and very popular. He had gone to the Hebrew University in Jerusalem to get his doctorate, had joined the Haganah, and had been killed trying to get a convoy through to Jerusalem. We were stunned. We had never thought the war would come so close.

On a day in the second week of June, the same week the United Nations truce went into effect and the fighting in Israel ceased, the entire school attended an assembly in memory of the student. Everyone was there, every rabbi, student, and college teacher. One of his Talmud teachers described his devoutness and dedication to Judaism, his mathematics professor talked about his brilliance as a student, and one of the members of the senior class told of the way he had always spoken of going to Israel. Then we all stood as a prayer was chanted and the Kaddish was said.

Reb Saunders's anti-Zionist league died that day as far as the students in Hirsch College were concerned. It remained alive outside the school, but I never again saw an anti-Zionist leaflet inside the school building.

The final examinations were not too much of a problem to me that semester, and I made all A's. July came and brought sweltering heat, and the happy announcement from Dr. Grossman that my father was now well enough to be able to go to the cottage in August and resume teaching in September. But he was to rest in the cottage, not work. Yes, he could write—since when was writing work? My father laughed at that, the first time he had laughed in months.

In September, my father resumed his teaching, and I entered my third year of college. Since symbolic logic was part of philosophy, I had chosen philosophy as my major subject, and I was finding it very exciting. The weeks passed quickly. My father was doing nothing but teaching for the first few months; then, with the approval of Dr. Grossman, he went back to some of his Zionist activities and to teaching an adult class one night a week.

The war in Israel continued sporadically, especially in the Negev. But the initiative had passed to the Israelis, and the tension was gone from it by now.

Reb Saunders's anti-Zionist league seemed to have gone out of existence. I heard nothing about it, even in my own neighborhood. And one day in the late spring of that year, while I was eating lunch, Danny came over to my table, smiled hesitantly, sat down, and asked me to give him a hand with his experimental psychology; he was having difficulty setting up a graph for a formula involving variables.

SIXTEEN

I FELT A LITTLE SHIVER hearing his voice.

"Welcome back to the land of the living," I said, staring up at him and feeling my heart turn over. It had been over two years now that we hadn't talked to each other.

He smiled faintly and rubbed his beard, which was quite thick. He was wearing his usual dark suit, tieless shirt, fringes, and skullcap. His earlocks hung down along the sides of his sculptured face, and his eyes were bright and very blue.

"The ban has been lifted," he said simply.

"It feels good to be kosher again," I told him, not without some bitterness in my voice.

He blinked his eyes and tried another smile. "I'm sorry," he said quietly.

"I'm sorry, too. I needed you around for a while. Especially when my father was sick."

He nodded, and his eyes were sad.

"How do you do it?" I asked.

He blinked again. "Do what?"

"How do you take the silence?"

He didn't say anything. But his face tightened.

"I hated it," I told him. "How do you take it?"

He pulled nervously at an earlock, his eyes dark and brooding.

"I think I would lose my mind," I said.

"No you wouldn't," he said softly. "You'd learn to live with it."

"Why does he do it?"

The hand pulling at the earlock dropped down to the table. He shook his head slowly. "I don't know. We still don't talk."

"Except when you study Talmud or he explodes."

He nodded soberly.

"I hate to tell you what I think of your father."

"He's a great man," Danny said evenly. "He must have a reason."

"I think it's crazy and sadistic," I said bitterly. "And I don't like your father at all."

"You're entitled to your opinion," Danny said softly. "And I'm entitled to mine."

We were silent for a moment.

"You've lost weight," I told him.

He nodded but remained silent. He sat there slumped over, looking small and uncomfortable, like a bird in pain.

"How are your eyes?" I asked.

He shrugged. "They bother me sometimes. The doctor says it's nervous tension."

There was another silence.

"It's good to have you back," I said. And I grinned.

He smiled hesitantly, his blue eyes bright and shining.

"You and your crazy way of hitting a baseball," I said. "You and your father with his crazy silences and explosions."

He smiled again, deeply now, and straightened up in the chair. "Will you help me with this graph?" he asked.

I told him it was about time he helped himself with graphs, and then showed him what to do.

When I told my father about it that night, he nodded soberly. He had expected it, he said. The Jewish state was not an issue anymore but a fact. How long would Reb Saunders have continued his ban over a dead issue?

"How is Danny feeling?" he wanted to know.

I told him Danny didn't look well and had lost a lot of weight.

He was thoughtful for a moment. Then he said, "Reuven, the silence between Danny and Reb Saunders. It is continuing?"

"Yes."

His face was sad. "A father can bring up a child any way he wishes," he said softly. "What a price to pay for a soul."

When I asked him what he meant, he wouldn't say anything more about it. But his eyes were dark.

So Danny and I resumed our old habits of meeting in front of my synagogue, of riding to school together, eating lunch together, and going home together. Rav Gershenson's class became a particular joy, because the ease between Danny and myself now permitted us to engage in a constant flow of competitive discussion that virtually monopolized the hours of the shiur. We dominated the class to such an extent that one day, after a particularly heated Talmudic battle between Danny and me that had gone on uninterrupted for almost a quarter of an hour, Rav Gershenson stopped us and pointed out that this wasn't a private lesson he was giving; there were twelve other students in the class—didn't anyone else have something to say? But he said it with a warm smile, and Danny and I were delighted by his oblique compliment.

A few days after we had resumed talking, Danny told me that he had resigned himself to experimental psychology and was even beginning to enjoy it. When he talked about psychology now, he invariably used the technical language of the experimentalist: variables, constants, manipulation, observation, recording of data, testing hypotheses, and the advantages of attempting to refute hypotheses as against confirming them. Mathematics no longer seemed to be much of a problem to him. Only rarely now did he need my help.

We were sitting in the lunchroom one day when he told me of a conversation he had had with Professor Appleman. "He said if I ever wanted to make any kind of valuable contribution to psychology I would have to use the scientific method. The Freudian approach doesn't really provide a method of accepting or rejecting hypotheses, and that's no way to acquire knowledge."

"Well, well." I grinned. "Goodbye Freud."

He shook his head. "No. It's not goodbye Freud. Freud was a genius. But he was too circumspect in his findings. I want to know a lot more than just the things Freud dealt with. Freud never really did anything with perception, for example. Or with learning. How people see, hear, touch, smell, taste, and learn is a fascinating subject. Freud never went into any of that. But he was a genius, all right, in what he did go into."

"You're going to become an experimentalist?"

"I don't think so. I want to work with people, not with rats and mazes. I talked to Appleman about it. He suggested I go into clinical psychology."

"What's that?"

"Well, it's the same as the difference between theoretical and applied physics, say. The experimental psychologist is more or less the theoretician; the clinical psychologist applies what the experimentalist learns. He gets to work with people. He examines them, tests them, diagnoses them, even treats them."

"What do you mean, treats them?"

"He does therapy."

"You're going to become an analyst?"

"Maybe. But psychoanalysis is only one form of therapy. There are many other kinds."

"What kinds?"

"Oh, many kinds," he said vaguely. "A lot of it is still very experimental."

"You're planning to experiment on people?"

"I don't know. Maybe. I really don't know too much about it yet."

"Are you going on for a doctorate?"

"Sure. You can't move in this field without a doctorate."

"Where are you planning to go?"

"I don't know yet. Appleman suggested Columbia. That's where he got his doctorate."

"Does your father know yet?"

Danny gave me a tight, strained look. "No," he said quietly.

"When will you tell him?"

"The day I receive my smicha." "Smicha" is the Hebrew term for rabbinic ordination.

"That's next year," I said.

Danny nodded grimly. Then he looked at his watch. "We'd better move or we'll be late for the shiur," he said.

We raced up the stairs to Rav Gershenson's class and made it just a moment before he called on someone to read and explain.

During another one of our lunchroom conversations, Danny asked me what good symbolic logic was going to be for me when I entered the rabbinate. I told him I didn't know, but I was doing a lot of reading in philosophy and theology, and some good might come of that.

"I always thought that logic and theology were like David and Saul," Danny said.

"They are. But I might help them get better acquainted."

He shook his head. "I can't get over your becoming a rabbi."

"I can't get over your becoming a psychologist."

And we looked at each other in quiet wonder.

In June, Danny's sister was married. I was invited to the wedding and was the only one there who wasn't a Hasid. It was a traditionally Hasidic wedding, with the men and women sitting separately and with a lot of dancing and singing. I was shocked when I saw Reb Saunders. His black beard had begun to go gray, and he seemed to have aged a great deal since I had seen him last. I went over to congratulate him, and he shook my hand warmly, his eyes dark and piercing. He was surrounded by people, and we didn't have a chance to talk. I didn't care. I wasn't particularly eager to talk to him. Levi had grown up a little, but he still looked white-skinned, and his eyes seemed large behind his shell-rimmed glasses. Danny's sister had become a beautiful girl. The boy she married was a Hasid, with a black beard, long earlocks, and dark eyes. He looked rather severe, and I quickly decided that I didn't like him. When I congratulated him after the wedding and shook his hand, his fingers were limp and moist.

When the school year ended and July came around, I went over to Danny's house one morning. Except for the wedding, I hadn't seen Reb Saunders at all since Danny and I had begun talking again, because my father was teaching me Talmud on Shabbat afternoons. So I decided it would be the polite thing to do to go over one morning after the school year. Danny took me up to his father's study. The third-floor hallway was crowded with dark-caftaned men, waiting around in silence to see his father. They nodded and murmured respectful greetings to Danny, and one of them, an incredibly old man with a white beard and a bent body, reached out and touched his arm as we passed. I found the gesture distasteful. I was beginning to find everything connected with Reb Saunders and Hasidism distasteful. We waited until the person who was with his father came out, then we went in.

Reb Saunders sat in his straight-backed red leather chair surrounded by books and the musty odor of old bindings. His face seemed lined with pain, but his voice was soft when he greeted me. He was, he said quietly, very happy to see me. He hesitated, looked at me, then at Danny. His eyes were dark and brooding. Where was I keeping myself, he asked, and why wasn't I coming over anymore on Shabbos afternoons? I told him my father and I were studying Talmud together on Shabbat. His eyes brooded, and he sighed. He nodded vaguely. He wished he could spend more time talking to me now, he said, but there were so many people who needed to see him. Couldn't I come over some Shabbos afternoon? I told him I would try, and Danny and I went out.

That was all he said. Not a word about Zionism. Not a word about the silence he had imposed upon Danny and me. Nothing. I found I disliked him more when I left than when I had entered. I did not see him again that July.

SEVENTEEN

OUR LAST YEAR of college began that September. Over lunch one day I told Danny a mild anti-Hasidic story I had heard, and he laughed loudly. Then, without thinking, I mentioned a remark one of the students had made a few days back: "The tzaddik sits in absolute silence, saying nothing, and all his followers listen attentively," and the laughter left his lips as suddenly as if he had been slapped, and his face froze.

I realized immediately what I had said, and felt myself go cold. I muttered a helpless apology.

For a long moment, he said nothing. His eyes seemed glazed, turned inward. Then his face slowly relaxed. He smiled faintly. "There's more truth to that than you realize," he murmured. "You can listen to silence, Reuven. I've begun to realize that you can listen to silence and learn from it. It has a quality and a dimension all its own. It talks to me sometimes. I feel myself alive in it. It talks. And I can hear it."

The words came out in a soft singsong. He sounded exactly like his father.

"You don't understand that, do you?" he asked.

"No."

He nodded. "I didn't think you would."

"What do you mean, it talks to you?"

"You have to want to listen to it, and then you can hear it. It has a strange, beautiful texture. It doesn't always talk. Sometimes—sometimes it cries, and you can hear the pain of the world in it. It hurts to listen to it then. But you have to."

I felt myself go cold again, hearing him talk that way. "I don't understand that at all."

He smiled faintly.

"Are you and your father talking these days?"

He shook his head.

I didn't understand any of it, but he seemed so somber and strange that I didn't want to talk about it anymore. I changed the subject. "You ought to get yourself a girl," I told him. I was dating regularly now on Saturday nights. "It's a wonderful tonic for a suffering soul."

He looked at me, his eyes sad. "My wife has been chosen for me," he said quietly.

I gaped at him.

"It's an old Hasidic custom, remember?"

"It never occurred to me," I said, shocked.

He nodded soberly. "That's another reason it won't be so easy to break out of the trap. It doesn't only involve my own family."

I didn't know what to say. There was a long, uncomfortable silence. And we walked together in that silence to Rav Gershenson's shiur.

Danny's brother's bar mitzvah celebration, which I attended on a Monday morning during the third week in October, was a simple and unpretentious affair. The Morning Service began at seven-thirty—early enough to enable Danny and me to attend and not come late to school—and Levi was called to recite the blessing over the Torah. After the service there was a kiddush, consisting of schnapps and some cakes and cookies. Everyone drank *l'chaim*, to life, then left. Reb Saunders asked me quietly why I wasn't coming over to see him anymore, and I explained that my father and I were studying Talmud together on Shabbat afternoons. He nodded vaguely and walked slowly away, his tall frame somewhat stooped.

Levi Saunders was now tall and thin. He seemed a ghostly imitation of Danny, except that his hair was black and his eyes were dark. The skin on his hands and face was milky white, almost translucent, showing the branching veins. There was something helplessly fragile about him; he looked as if a wind would blow him down. Yet at the same time his dark eyes burned with a kind of inner fire that told of the tenacity with which he clung to life and of his growing awareness of the truth that for the rest of his days his every breath would depend upon the pills he put into his mouth at regular intervals. The eyes told you that he had every intention of holding on to his life, no matter what the pain.

As if to emphasize the tenuousness of Levi Saunders's existence, he became violently ill the day following his bar mitzvah and was taken by ambulance to the Brooklyn Memorial Hospital. Danny called me during supper as soon as the ambulance pulled away from in front of his house, and I could tell from his voice that he was in a panic. There wasn't much I could say to him over the phone, and when I asked him if he wanted me to come over, he said no, his mother was almost hysterical, he would have to stay with her, he had only wanted to let me know. And he hung up.

My father apparently had heard my troubled voice, because he was standing now outside the kitchen, asking me what was wrong.

I told him.

We resumed our supper. I wasn't very hungry now, but I ate anyway to keep Manya happy. My father noticed how disturbed I was, but he said nothing. After the meal, he followed me into my room, sat on my bed while I sat at my desk, and asked me what was wrong, why was I so upset by Levi Saunders's illness, he had been ill before.

It was at that point that I told my father of Danny's plans to go on for a doctorate in psychology and abandon the position of tzaddik he was to inherit one day from Reb Saunders. I also added, feeling that I ought to be completely honest about it now, that Danny was in a panic over his brother's illness because without his brother it might not be possible for him to break away from his father; he did not really want to destroy the dynasty.

My father's face became more and more grim as he listened. When I was done, he sat for a long time in silence, his eyes grave.

"When did Danny tell you this?" he asked finally.

"The summer I lived in their house."

"That long ago? He knew already that long ago?"

"Yes."

"And all this time you did not tell me?"

"It was a secret between us, abba."

He looked at me grimly. "Does Danny know what pain this will cause his father?"

"He dreads the day he'll have to tell him. He dreads it for both of them."

"I knew it would happen," my father said. "How could it not happen?" Then he looked at me sharply. "Reuven, let me understand this. Exactly what is Danny planning to tell Reb Saunders?"

"That he's going on for a doctorate in psychology and doesn't intend to take his place."

"Is Danny thinking to abandon his Judaism?"

I stared at him. "I never thought to ask him," I said faintly.

"His beard, his earlocks, his clothes, his fringes—all this he will retain in graduate school?"

"I don't know, abba. We never talked about it."

"Reuven, how will Danny become a psychologist while looking like a Hasid?"

I didn't know what to say.

"It is important that Danny know exactly what he will tell his father. He must anticipate what questions will be on Reb Saunders's mind. Talk to Danny. Let him think through exactly what he will tell his father."

"All this time I never thought to ask him."

"Danny is now like a person waiting to be let out of jail. He has only one desire. To leave the jail. Despite what may be waiting for him outside. Danny cannot think one minute beyond the moment he will have to tell his father he does not wish to take his place. Do you understand me?"

"Yes."

"You will talk to him?"

"Of course."

My father nodded grimly, his face troubled. "I have not talked to Danny in so long," he said quietly. He was silent for a moment. Then he smiled faintly. "It is not so easy to be a friend, is it, Reuven?"

"No," I said.

"Tell me, Danny and Reb Saunders still do not talk?"

I shook my head. Then I told him what Danny had said about silence. "What does it mean to hear silence, abba?"

That seemed to upset him more than the news about Danny's not becoming a tzaddik. He sat up straight on the bed, his body quivering. "Hasidim!" I heard him mutter, almost contemptuously. "Why must they feel the burden of the world is only on their shoulders?"

I looked at him, puzzled. I had never heard that tone of contempt in his voice before.

"It is a way of bringing up children," he said.

"What is?"

"Silence."

"I don't understand—"

"I cannot explain it. I do not understand it completely myself. But what I know of it, I dislike. It was practiced in Europe by some few Hasidic families." Then his voice went hard. "There are better ways to teach a child compassion."

"I don't—"

He cut me short. "Reuven, I cannot explain what I do not understand. Danny is being raised by Reb Saunders in a certain way. I do not want to talk about it anymore. It upsets me. You will speak to Danny, yes?"

I nodded.

"Now I have work I must do." And he went from the room, leaving me as bewildered as I had been before.

I had planned to talk to Danny the next day, but when I saw him he was in such a state of panic over his brother that I didn't dare mention what my father had said. The doctors had diagnosed his brother's illness as some kind of imbalance in the blood chemistry caused by something he had eaten, Danny told me over lunch, looking pale and grim, and blinking his eyes repeatedly. They were trying out some new pills, and his brother would remain in the hospital until they were certain the pills worked. And he would have to be very careful from now on with his diet. Danny was tense and miserable all that day and throughout the week.

Levi Saunders was discharged from the Brooklyn Memorial Hospital the following Wednesday afternoon. I saw Danny in school the next day. We sat in the lunchroom and ate for a while in silence. His brother was fine, he said finally, and everything seemed to have settled down. His mother was in bed with high blood pressure, though. But the doctor said it was caused by her excitement over Levi's illness and all she needed now was to rest. She would be better soon.

He told me quietly that he was planning to write to three universities that day—Harvard, Berkeley, and Columbia—and apply for a fellowship in psychology. I asked him how long he thought he would be able to keep his applications a secret.

"I don't know," he said, his voice a little tight.

"Why don't you tell your father now and get it over with?"

He looked at me, his face grim. "I don't want explosions with every meal," he said tightly. "All I get are either explosions or silence. I've had enough of his explosions."

Then I told him what my father had said. As I spoke, I could see him become more and more uncomfortable.

"I didn't want you to tell your father," he muttered angrily.

"My father kept your library visits a secret from me," I reminded him. "Don't worry about my father."

"I don't want you to tell anyone else."

"I won't. What about what my father said? Are you going to remain an Orthodox Jew?"

"Whatever gave you the notion that I had any intention of not remaining an Orthodox Jew?"

"What if your father asks about the beard, the caftan, the—"

"He won't ask me."

"What if he does?"

He pulled nervously at an earlock. "Can you see me practicing psychology and looking like a Hasid?" he asked tightly.

I hadn't really expected any other answer. Then something occurred to me. "Won't your father see the mail you get from the graduate schools you've applied to?"

He stared at me. "I never thought of that," he said slowly. "I'll have to intercept the mail." He hesitated, his face rigid. "I can't. It comes after I leave for school." And his eyes filled with fear.

"I think you ought to have a talk with my father," I said.

Danny came over to our apartment that night, and I took him into my father's study. My father came quickly around from behind his desk and shook Danny's hand.

"I have not seen you in such a long time," he said, smiling warmly. "It is good to see you again, Danny. Please sit down."

My father did not sit behind his desk. He sat next to us on the kitchen chair he had asked me earlier to bring into the study.

"Do not be angry at Reuven for telling me," he said quietly to Danny. "I have had practice with keeping secrets."

Danny smiled nervously.

"You will tell your father on the day of your ordination?"

Danny nodded.

"There is a girl involved?"

Danny nodded again, giving me a momentary glance.

"You will refuse to marry this girl?"

"Yes."

"And your father will have to explain to her parents and to his followers."

Danny was silent, his face tight.

My father sighed softly. "It will be a very uncomfortable situation. For you and for your father. You are determined not to take your father's place?"

"Yes," Danny said.

"Then you must know exactly what you will tell him. Think carefully of what you will say. Think what your father's questions will be. Think what he will be most concerned about after he hears of your decision. Do you understand me, Danny?"

Danny nodded slowly.

There was a long silence.

Then my father leaned forward in his chair. "Danny," he said softly, "you can hear silence?"

Danny looked at him, startled. His blue eyes were wide, frightened. He glanced at me. Then he looked again at my father. And, slowly, he nodded his head.

"You are not angry at your father?"

Danny shook his head.

"Do you understand what he is doing?"

Danny hesitated. Then he shook his head again. His eyes were wide and moist.

My father sighed again. "It will be explained to you," he said softly. "Your father will explain it to you. Because he will want you to carry it on with your own children one day."

Danny blinked his eyes nervously.

"No one can help you with this, Danny. It is between you and your father. But think carefully of what you will say to him and of what his questions will be."

My father came with us to the door of our apartment. I could hear Danny's capped shoes tapping against the outside hallway floor. Then he was gone.

"What is this again about hearing silence, abba?" I asked.

But my father would say nothing. He went into his study and closed the door.

Danny received letters of acceptance from each of the three universities to which he had applied. The letters came in the mail to his home and lay untouched on the vestibule table until he returned from school. He told me about it in early January, a day after the third letter had come. I asked him who usually picked up the mail.

"My father," he said, looking tense and bewildered. "Levi's in school when it comes, and my mother doesn't like climbing stairs."

"Were there return addresses on the envelopes?"

"Of course."

"Then how can't he know?" I asked him.

"I don't understand it," he said, his voice edged with panic. "What is he waiting for? Why doesn't he say something?"

I felt sick with his fear and said nothing.

Danny told me a few days later that his sister was pregnant. She and her husband had been over to the house and had informed his parents. His father had smiled for the first time since Levi's bar mitzvah, Danny said, and his mother had wept with joy. I asked him if his father gave any indication at all of knowing what his plans were.

"No," he said.

"No indication at all?"

"No, I get nothing from him but silence."

"Is he silent with Levi, too?"

"No."

"Was he silent with your sister?"

"No."

"I don't like your father," I told him. "I don't like him at all."

Danny said nothing. But his eyes blinked his fear.

A few days later, he told me, "My father asked me why you're not coming over anymore on Shabbat."

"He talked to you?"

"He didn't talk. That isn't talking."

"I study Talmud on Shabbat."

"I know."

"I'm not too eager to see him."

He nodded unhappily.

"Have you decided which university you're going to?"

"Columbia."

"Why don't you tell him and get it over with?"

"I'm afraid."

"What difference does it make? If he's going to throw you out of the house, he'll do it no matter when you tell him."

"I'll have my degree in June. I'll be ordained."

"You can live with us. No, you can't. You won't eat at our house."

"I could live with my sister."

"Yes."

"I'm afraid. I'm afraid of the explosion. I'm afraid of anytime I'll have to tell him. God, I'm afraid."

My father would say nothing when I talked to him about it. "It is for Reb Saunders to explain," he told me quietly. "I cannot explain what I do not completely understand. I cannot do it with my students, and I cannot do it with my son."

A few days later, Danny told me that his father had asked again why I wasn't coming over to their house anymore.

"I'll try to get over," I said.

But I didn't try very hard. I didn't want to see Reb Saunders. I hated him as much now as I had when he had forced his silence between me and Danny.

The weeks passed and winter melted slowly into spring. Danny was working on an experimental psychology project that had to do with the relationship between reinforcement and rapidity of learning, and I was doing a long paper on the logic of ought statements. Danny pushed himself relentlessly in his work. He grew thin and gaunt, and the angles and bones of his face and hands jutted like sharp peaks from beneath his skin. He stopped talking about the silence between him and his father. He seemed to be shouting down the silence with his work. Only his constantly blinking eyes gave any indication of his mounting terror.

The day before the start of the Passover school vacation period, he told me that his father had asked him once again why I wasn't coming over to their house anymore. Could I possibly come over on Passover? he had wanted to know. He especially wanted to see me the first or second day of Passover.

"I'll try," I said halfheartedly, without the slightest intention of trying at all.

But when I talked to my father that night, he said, with a strange sharpness in his voice, "You did not tell me Reb Saunders has been asking to see you."

"He's been asking all along."

"Reuven, when someone asks to speak to you, you must let him speak to you. You still have not learned that? You did not learn that from what happened between you and Danny?"

"He wants to study Talmud, abba."

"You are sure?"

"That's all we've ever done when I go over there."

"You only study Talmud? You have forgotten so quickly?"

I stared at him. "He wants to talk to me about Danny," I said, and felt myself turn cold.

"You will go over the first day of the holiday. On Sunday."

"Why didn't he tell me?"

"Reuven, he did tell you. You have not been listening."

"All these weeks—"

"Listen next time. Listen when someone speaks to you."

"Maybe I should go over tonight."

"No. They will be busy preparing for the holiday."

"I'll go over on Shabbat."

"Reb Saunders asked you to come on Passover."

"I told him we study Talmud on Shabbat."

"You will go on Passover. He has a reason if he asked you to come especially on Passover. And listen next time when someone speaks to you, Reuven."

He was angry, as angry as he had been in the hospital years ago when I had refused to talk to Danny.

I called Danny and told him I would be over on Sunday.

He sensed something in my voice. "What's wrong?"

"Nothing's wrong. I'll see you on Sunday."

"Nothing's wrong?" His voice was tight, apprehensive.

"No."

"Come over around four," he said. "My father needs to rest in the early afternoons."

"Four."

"Nothing's wrong?"

"I'll see you on Sunday," I told him.

EIGHTEEN

ON THE AFTERNOON of the first day of Passover, I walked beneath the early spring sycamores on my street, then turned into Lee Avenue. The sun was warm and bright, and I went along slowly, past the houses and the shops and the synagogue where my father and I prayed. I met one of my classmates and we stopped to talk for a few minutes; then I went on alone, turning finally into Danny's street. The sycamores formed a tangled bower through which the sun shone brightly, speckling the ground. There were tiny buds on these sycamores now and on some I could see the green shoots of infant leaves. In a month, those leaves would shut out the sky, but now the sun came through and brushed streaks of gold across the sidewalks, the street, the talking women, and the playing children. I walked along slowly, remembering the first time I had gone up this street years ago. Those years were coming to an end now. In three months, in a time when the leaves would be fat and full, our lives would separate like the branches overhead that made their own way into the sunlight.

I went slowly up the wide stone staircase of Danny's house and through the wooden double door of the entrance. The hallway was dim and cold. The synagogue door stood open. I peered inside. Its emptiness whispered echoes at me: mistakes, gematriya, Talmud quizzes, and Reb Saunders staring at my left eye. You do not know yet what it is to be a friend. Scientific criticism, ah! Your father is an observer of the Commandments. It is not easy to be a true friend. Soft, silent echoes. It seemed tiny to me now, the synagogue, so much less neat than when I had seen it for the first time. The stands were scarred, the walls needed paint, the naked light bulbs seemed ugly, their bare, black wires like the dead branches of a stunted tree. What echoes will Reb Saunders's study have? I thought. And I felt myself go tight with apprehension.

I stood at the foot of the inner stairway and called Danny's name. My voice moved heavily through the silent house. I waited a moment, then called his name again. I heard the tapping of metal-capped shoes upon the third-floor stairway, then in the hallway over my head; and then Danny was standing at the head of the stairs, tall, gaunt, an almost spectral figure with his beard and earlocks and black satin caftan.

I climbed the stairs slowly, and he greeted me. He looked tired. His mother was resting, he said, and his brother was out somewhere. He and his father were studying Talmud. His voice was dull, flat, only faintly edged with fear. But his eyes mirrored clearly what his voice concealed.

We went up to the third floor. Danny seemed to hesitate before the door to his father's study, almost as if he was wishing not to have to go back in there again. Then he opened the door, and we stepped inside.

It had been almost a year since I had last been inside Reb Saunders's study, but nothing about it had changed. There was the same massive, black wood, glass-topped desk, the same red carpet, the same glass-enclosed wooden bookcases jammed tight with books, the same musty old-book odor in the air, the same single light bulb glowing white behind its ceiling fixture. Nothing had really changed—nothing, except Reb Saunders himself.

He sat in his straight-backed, red leather chair and looked at me from behind the desk. His beard had gone almost completely gray, and he sat stooped forward, bent, as though he were carrying something on his shoulders. His brow was crisscrossed with wrinkles, his dark eyes brooded and burned with some kind of invisible suffering, and the fingers of his right hand played aimlessly with a long, gray earlock.

He greeted me quietly, but did not offer me his hand. I had the feeling that a handshake was a physical effort he wanted to avoid.

Danny and I sat in the chairs by his desk, Danny to his right, I to his left. Danny's face was expressionless, closed. He tugged nervously at an earlock.

Reb Saunders moved forward slightly in the chair and put his hands on the desk. Slowly, he closed the Talmud from which he and Danny had been studying. Then he sighed, a deep, trembling sigh that filled the silence of the room like a wind.

"Nu, Reuven," he said quietly, "finally, finally you come to see me." He spoke in Yiddish, his voice quavering a little as the words came out.

"I apologize," I said hesitantly, in English.

He nodded his head, and his right hand went up and stroked his gray beard. "You have become a man," he said quietly. "The first day you sat here, you were only a boy. Now you are a man."

Danny seemed suddenly to become conscious of the way he was twisting his earlock. He put his hand on his lap, clasped both hands tightly together, and sat very still, staring at his father.

Reb Saunders looked at me and smiled feebly, nodding his head. "My son, my Daniel, has also become a man. It is a great joy for a father to see his son suddenly a man."

Danny stirred faintly in his chair, then was still.

"What will you do after your graduation?" Reb Saunders asked quietly.

"I have another year to study for smicha."

"And then what?"

"I'm going into the rabbinate."

He looked at me and blinked his eyes. I thought I saw him stiffen for a moment, as though in sudden pain. "You are going to become a rabbi," he murmured, speaking more to himself than to me. He was silent for a moment. "Yes. I remember. . . . Yes. . . ." He sighed again and shook his head slowly, the gray beard moving back and forth. "My Daniel will receive his smicha in June," he said quietly. Then he added, "In June. . . . Yes. . . . His smicha. . . . Yes. . . ." The words trailed off, aimless, disconnected, and hung in the air for a long moment of tight silence.

Then, slowly, he moved his right hand across the closed Talmud, and his fingers caressed the Hebrew title of the tractate that was stamped into the spine of the binding. Then he clasped both hands together and rested them on top of the Talmud. His body followed the movements of his hands, and his gray earlocks moved along the sides of his aged face.

"Nu," he said, speaking softly, so softly I could barely hear him, "in June my Daniel and his good friend begin to go different ways. They are men, not children, and men go different ways. You will go one way, Reuven. And my son, my Daniel, he will—he will go another way."

I saw Danny's mouth fall open. His body gave a single convulsive shudder. Different ways, I thought. *Different* ways. Then he—

"I know," Reb Saunders murmured, as if he were reading my mind. "I have known it for a long time."

Danny let out a soft, half-choked, trembling moan. Reb Saunders did not look at him. He had not once looked at him. He was talking to Danny through me.

"Reuven, I want you to listen carefully to what I will tell you now." He had said: Reuven. His eyes had said: Danny. "You will not understand it. You may never understand it. And you may never stop hating me for what I have done. I know how you feel. I do not see it in your eyes? But I want you to listen.

"A man is born into this world with only a tiny spark of goodness in him. The spark is God, it is the soul; the rest is ugliness and evil, a shell. The spark must be guarded like a treasure, it must be nurtured, it must be fanned into flame. It must learn to seek out other sparks, it must dominate the shell. Anything can be a shell, Reuven. Anything. Indifference, laziness, brutality, and genius. Yes, even a great mind can be a shell and choke the spark.

"Reuven, the Master of the Universe blessed me with a brilliant son. And he cursed me with all the problems of raising him. Ah, what it is to have a brilliant son! Not a smart son, Reuven, but a brilliant son, a Daniel, a boy with a mind like a jewel. Ah, what a curse it is, what an anguish it is, to have a Daniel, whose mind is like a pearl, like a sun. Reuven, when my Daniel was four years old, I saw him reading a story from a book. And I was frightened. He did not read the story, he swallowed it, as one swallows food or water. There was no soul in my four-year-old Daniel, there was only his mind. He was a mind in a body without a soul. It was a story in a Yiddish book about a poor Jew and his struggles to get to Eretz Yisroel before he died. Ah, how that man suffered! And my Daniel *enjoyed* the story, he *enjoyed* the last terrible page, because when he finished it he realized for the first time what a memory he had. He looked at me proudly and told me back the story from memory, and I cried inside my heart. I went away and cried to the Master of the Universe, 'What have you done to me? A mind like this I need for a son? A *heart* I need for a son, a *soul* I need for a son, *compassion* I want from my son, righteousness, mercy, strength to suffer and carry pain, *that* I want from my son, not a mind without a soul!'"

Reb Saunders paused and took a deep, trembling breath. I tried to swallow; my mouth was sand-dry. Danny sat with his right hand over his eyes, his glasses pushed up on his forehead. He was crying silently, his shoulders quivering. Reb Saunders did not look at him.

"My brother was like my Daniel," he went on quietly. "What a mind he had. What a mind. But he was also not like my Daniel. My Daniel, thank God, is healthy. But for many, many years my brother was ill. His mind burned with hunger for knowledge. But for many years his body was wasted with disease. And so my father did not raise him as he raised me. When he was well enough to go off to a yeshiva to study, it was too late.

"I was only a child when he left to study in Odessa, but I still remember what he was able to do with his mind. But it was a cold mind, Reuven, almost cruel, untouched by his soul. It was proud, haughty, impatient with less brilliant minds, grasping in its search for knowledge the way a conqueror grasps for power. It could not understand pain, it was indifferent to and impatient with suffering. It was even impatient with the illness of its own body. I never saw my brother again after he left for the yeshiva. He came under the influence of a Maskil in Odessa and went away to France where he became a great mathematician and taught in a university. He died in a gas chamber in Auschwitz. I learned of it four years ago. He was a Jew when he died, not an observer of the Commandments, but not a convert, thank God. I would like to believe that before he died he learned how much suffering there is in this world. I hope so. It will have redeemed his soul.

"Reuven, listen to what I am going to tell you now and remember it. You are a man, but it will be years before you understand my words. Perhaps you will never understand them. But hear me out, and have patience.

"When I was very young, my father, may he rest in peace, began to wake me in the middle of the night, just so I would cry. I was a child, but he would wake me and tell me stories of the destruction of Jerusalem and the sufferings of the people of Israel, and I would cry. For years he did this. Once he took me to visit a hospital—ah, what an experience that was!—and often he took me to visit the poor, the beggars, to listen to them talk. My father himself never talked to me, except when we studied together. He taught me with silence. He taught me to look into myself, to find my own strength, to walk around inside myself in company with my soul. When his people would ask him why he was so silent with his son, he would say to them that he did not like to talk, words are cruel, words play tricks, they distort what is in the heart, they conceal the heart, the heart speaks through silence. One learns of the pain of others by suffering one's own pain, he would say, by turning inside oneself, by finding one's own soul. And it is important to know of pain, he said. It destroys our self-pride, our arrogance, our indifference toward others. It makes us aware of how frail and tiny we are and of how much we must depend upon the Master of the Universe. Only slowly, very slowly, did I begin to understand what he was saying. For years his silence bewildered and frightened me, though I always trusted him, I never hated him. And when I was old enough to understand, he told me that of all people a tzaddik especially must know of pain. A tzaddik must know how to suffer for his people, he said. He must take their pain from them and carry it on his own shoulders. He must carry it always. He must grow old before his years. He must cry, in his heart he must always cry. Even when he dances and sings, he must cry for the sufferings of his people.

"You do not understand this, Reuven. I see from your eyes that you do not understand this. But my Daniel understands it now. He understands it well.

"Reuven, I did not want my Daniel to become like my brother, may he rest in peace. Better I should have had no son at all than to have a brilliant son who had no soul. I looked at my Daniel when he was four years old, and I said to myself, How will I teach this mind what it is to have a soul? How will I teach this mind to understand pain? How will I teach it to *want* to take on another person's suffering? How will I do this and not lose my son, my precious son whom I love as I love the Master of the Universe Himself? How will I do this and not cause my son, God forbid, to abandon the Master of the Universe and His Commandments? How could I teach my son the way I was taught by my father and not drive him away from Torah? Because this is America, Reuven. This is not Europe. It is an open world here. Here there are libraries and books and schools. Here there are great universities that do not concern themselves with how many Jewish students they have. I did not want to drive my son away from God, but I did not want him to grow up a mind without a soul. I knew already when he was a boy that I could not prevent his mind from going to the world for knowledge. I knew in my heart that it might prevent him from taking my place. But I had to prevent it from driving him away completely from the Master of the Universe. And I had to make certain his soul would be the soul of a tzaddik no matter what he did with his life."

He closed his eyes and seemed to shrink into himself. His hands trembled. He was silent for a long time. Tears rolled slowly down alongside the bridge of his nose and disappeared into his beard. A shuddering sigh filled the room. Then he opened his eyes and stared down at the closed Talmud on the desk. "Ah, what a price to pay. . . . The years when he was a child and I loved him and talked with him and held him under my tallis when I prayed. . . . 'Why do you cry, Father?' he asked me once under the tallis. 'Because people are suffering,' I told him. He could not understand. Ah, what it is to be a mind without a soul, what ugliness it is. . . . Those were the years he learned to trust me and love me. . . . And when he was older, the years I drew myself away from him. . . . 'Why have you stopped answering my questions, Father?' he asked me once. 'You are old enough to look into your own soul for the answers,' I told him. He laughed once and said, 'That man is such an ignoramus, Father.' I was angry. 'Look into his soul,' I said. 'Stand inside his soul and see the world through his eyes. You will know the pain he feels because of his ignorance, and you will not laugh.' He was bewildered and hurt. The nightmares he began to have. . . . But he learned to find answers for himself. He suffered and learned to listen to the suffering of others. In the silence between us, he began to hear the world crying."

He stopped. A sigh came from his lips, a long, trembling sigh like a moan. Then he looked at me, his eyes moist with his own suffering. "Reuven, you and your father were a blessing to me. The Master of the Universe sent you to my son. He sent you when my son was ready to rebel. He sent you to listen to my son's words. He sent you to be my closed eyes and my sealed ears. I looked at your soul, Reuven, not your mind. In your father's writings I looked at his soul, not his mind. If you had not found the gematriya mistake, Reuven, it would have made a difference? No. The gematriya mistake only told me you had a good mind. But your soul I knew already. I knew it when my Daniel came home and told me he wanted to be your friend. Ah, you should have seen his eyes that day. You should have heard his voice. What an effort it was for him to talk to me. But he talked. I knew your soul, Reuven, before I knew your mind or your face. A thousand times I have thanked the Master of the Universe that He sent you and your father to my son.

"You think I was cruel? Yes, I see from your eyes that you think I was cruel to my Daniel. Perhaps. But he has learned. Let my Daniel become a psychologist. I know he wishes to become a psychologist. I do not see his books? I did not see the letters from the universities? I do not see his eyes? I do not hear his soul crying? Of course I know. For a long time I have known. Let my Daniel become a psychologist. I have no more fear now. All his life he will be a tzaddik. He will be a tzaddik for the world. And the world needs a tzaddik."

Reb Saunders stopped and looked slowly over at his son. Danny still sat with his hand over his eyes, his shoulders trembling. Reb Saunders looked at his son a long time. I had the feeling he was preparing himself for some gigantic effort, one that would completely drain what little strength he had left.

Then he spoke his son's name.

There was silence.

Reb Saunders spoke his son's name again. Danny took his hand away from his eyes and looked at his father.

"Daniel," Reb Saunders said, speaking almost in a whisper, "when you go away to study, you will shave off your beard and earlocks?"

Danny stared at his father. His eyes were wet. He nodded his head slowly.

Reb Saunders looked at him. "You will remain an observer of the Commandments?" he asked softly.

Danny nodded again.

Reb Saunders sat back slowly in his chair. And from his lips came a soft, tremulous sigh. He was silent for a moment, his eyes wide, dark, brooding, gazing upon his son. He nodded his head once, as if in final acknowledgment of his tortured victory.

Then he looked back at me, and his voice was gentle as he spoke. "Reuven, I—I ask you to forgive me . . . my anger . . . at your father's Zionism. I read his speech. . . . I—I found my own meaning for my . . . brother's death . . . for the death of the six million. I found it in God's will . . . which I did not presume to understand. I did not—I did not find it in a Jewish state that does not follow God and His Torah. My brother . . . the others . . . they could not— they could not have died for such a state. Forgive me . . . your father . . . it was too much . . . too much—"

His voice broke. He held himself tightly. His beard moved faintly with the trembling of his lips.

"Daniel," he said brokenly. "Forgive me . . . for everything . . . I have done. A—a wiser father . . . may have done differently. I am not . . . wise."

He rose slowly, painfully, to his feet. "Today is the—the Festival of Freedom." There was a soft hint of bitterness in his voice. "Today my Daniel is free. . . . I must go. . . . I am very tired. . . . I must lie down."

He walked heavily out of the room, his shoulders stooped, his face old and torn with pain.

The door closed with a soft click.

Then I sat and listened to Danny cry. He held his face in his hands, and his sobs tore apart the silence of the room and racked his body. I went over to him and put my hand on his shoulder and felt him trembling and crying. And then

I was crying, too, crying with Danny, silently, for his pain and for the years of his suffering, knowing that I loved him, and not knowing whether I hated or loved the long, anguished years of his life. He cried for a long time, and I left him in the chair and went to the window and listened to his sobs. The sun was low over the brownstones on the other side of the yard, and an ailanthus stood silhouetted against its golden rim, its budding branches forming a lace curtain through which a wind moved softly. I watched the sun set. The evening spread itself slowly across the sky.

Later, we walked through the streets. We walked for hours, saying nothing, and occasionally I saw him rub his eyes and heard him sigh. We walked past our synagogue, past the shops and houses, past the library where we had sat and read, walking in silence and saying more with that silence than with a lifetime of words. Late, late that night I left Danny at his home and returned alone to the apartment.

My father was in the kitchen and there was a strange brooding sadness on his face. I sat down and he looked at me, his eyes somber behind their steel-rimmed spectacles. And I told him everything.

When I was done, he was quiet for a very long time. Then he said softly, "A father has a right to raise his son in his own way, Reuven."

"In *that* way, abba?"

"Yes. Though I do not care for it at all."

"What kind of way is that to raise a son?"

"It is, perhaps, the only way to raise a tzaddik."

"I'm glad I wasn't raised that way."

"Reuven," my father said softly, "I did not have to raise you that way. I am not a tzaddik."

During the Morning Service on the first Shabbat in June, Reb Saunders announced to the congregation his son's intention to study psychology. The announcement was greeted with shocked dismay. Danny was in the synagogue at the time, and all eyes turned to stare at him in astonishment. Whereupon Reb Saunders further stated that this was his son's wish, that he, as a father, respected his son's soul and mind—in that order, according to what Danny later told me—that his son had every intention of remaining an observer of the Commandments, and that, therefore, he felt compelled to give his son his blessing. The turmoil among Reb Saunders's followers that was caused by this announcement was considerable. But no one dared to challenge

Reb Saunders's tacit transference of power to his younger son. After all, the tzaddikate was inherited, and the charisma went automatically from father to son—all sons.

Two days later, Reb Saunders withdrew his promise to the family of the girl Danny was supposed to marry. There had been some fuss over that, Danny told me afterward. But it had quieted down after a while.

The reaction at Hirsch College, once the news of Reb Saunders's announcement was out, lasted all of about two or three days. The non-Hasidic students talked about it for a day or so, and then forgot it. The Hasidic students sulked, scowled, glowered, and then forgot it, too. Everyone was busy with final examinations.

That June Danny and I were among the seventy-eight students who were graduated from Hirsch College, to the accompaniment of numerous speeches, applause, honorary degrees, and family congratulations. Both of us had earned our degrees *summa cum laude*.

Danny came over to our apartment one evening in September. He was moving into a room he had rented near Columbia, he said, and he wanted to say goodbye. His beard and earlocks were gone, and his face looked pale. But there was a light in his eyes that was almost blinding.

My father smiled at him warmly. "Columbia is not so far," he said. "We will see you on Shabbat."

Danny nodded, his eyes glowing, luminous.

I asked him how his father had reacted when he had seen him without the beard and earlocks.

He smiled sadly. "He's not happy about it. He said he almost doesn't recognize me."

"He talked to you?"

"Yes," Danny said quietly. "We talk now."

There was a long, gentle silence. A cool breeze moved soundlessly through the open windows of the living room.

Then my father leaned forward in his chair. "Danny," he said softly, "when you have a son of your own, you will raise him in silence?"

Danny said nothing for a long time. Then his right hand rose slowly to the side of his face and with his thumb and forefinger he gently caressed an imaginary earlock.

"Yes," he said. "If I can't find another way."

My father nodded, his eyes calm.

Later, I went down with Danny to the street.

"You'll come over sometimes on a Saturday and we'll study Talmud with my father?" he asked.

"Of course," I said.

We shook hands and I watched him walk quickly away, tall, lean, bent forward with eagerness and hungry for the future, his metal-capped shoes tapping against the sidewalk. Then he turned into Lee Avenue and was gone.

HISTORY, CONTEXT, AND CRITICISM

Edited by Rena Potok

CONTENTS

PART ONE

THE STORY OF *THE CHOSEN*

THE BIRTH OF *THE CHOSEN*

Robert Gottlieb

Chaim Potok's acclaimed and beloved novel of 1967 is the story of two Jewish boys growing up in the Williamsburg area of Brooklyn during and immediately after World War II. It's a story of deep-rooted friendship, of traumatic divisions between fathers and sons, of the clash between modern Orthodox Judaism and Hasidism and the clash between religion in general and secularism. And one of its driving metaphors is baseball. An unlikely prescription for a major bestseller.

Its start with us at Simon and Schuster had been rocky. An agent I had never before worked with sent over the manuscript, which was seriously dog-eared—a sign, in those pre-Xerox days, that this was a single copy that had already been turned down by a series of publishers. Ordinarily I would have read it that night, but I wasn't free to and so asked my astute assistant, Toinette Rees, to do a first reading. Toinette was a young Englishwoman of very firm opinions, and my interest was piqued when the next morning I read her long report that said, in essence, that it was utterly wonderful but a highly unlikely publishing venture. Toinette ambivalent? When I rushed through the manuscript that night after work I saw how right she was: It *was* wonderful, but it was certainly unpublishable—as it stood. The next morning I called the agent and told her I would publish it in a flash if Mr. Potok could agree with me that his very long novel actually ended midway through his manuscript, at which point he had added a whole second novel. Mr. Potok agreed, we met to discuss it, and a partnership was launched that flourished for thirty-five affectionate and unclouded years.

Chaim was a dedicated writer, his literary idol Hemingway, whose work, fortunately, his own didn't closely resemble. He was an ordained rabbi, a student of religions with a PhD in philosophy, the editor in chief of the Jewish Publication Society of America, and—key to his success—a happy family man, whose warm but formidable wife, Adena, a psychiatric social worker, effortlessly managed their three children, their large house in Philadelphia, and Chaim.

After the two novels he had written were reduced to one and the usual editorial work had been accomplished, there remained a major problem: the title. I can't remember what the original one was, but it was hopelessly fancy. Some books arrive with perfect titles, others don't, and this was a severe example of the latter kind. No one could come up with anything plausible: the book had so many aspects that it seemed impossible to find something that reflected the whole. Very late in the day we still had no title, and a jacket had to be designed and the book announced. What happened was one of the very few miracles I've ever stumbled into—maybe the only one. I was brooding on the problem as I was walking down the hall from my office to the men's room when I ran into a man named Arthur Sheekman, to whom I had given an office when Groucho Marx, his closest friend, asked him to come east and lend a hand in putting together *The Groucho Letters*, which I was overseeing at the time. Arthur was a screenwriter—he had written a bunch of Marx Brothers movies, starting with *Monkey Business*, as well as movies for Eddie Cantor, Danny Kaye, and others—and he possessed a friendly elegance and refinement that made him a favorite on our floor. "You look worried," he said to me as we passed each other in the hall. "What's the problem?" So I told him I was going nuts trying to find a title for a book about boys in wartime Brooklyn, Hasidism, and baseball. "Call it *The Chosen*," he said casually, and walked on. Literary history was made because I had to take a leak.

The book took off like a missile after the *Chicago Tribune Book World* plastered the kind of review on its cover that we all dream about: "Let there be dancing in the streets," it began, and in essence, "Run, do not walk, to your nearest bookstore." Toinette and I—and my dearest friend and colleague, Nina Bourne, who was in charge of advertising, and much more—*were* dancing in the streets, or at least in our office hallways. *The Chosen* made its way to the top of the fiction bestseller list—that, I suppose, was the *true* miracle, and the kind that makes publishing so fulfilling. It was impossible that a novel by a complete unknown, on so obscure and parochial a subject, should win such a large audience. But it happened. And *The Chosen* is still selling and—as you see—is still being celebrated fifty years later.

How did it happen? First and foremost, naturally, through its large merits. And the fact that it revealed to readers an unfamiliar and fascinating world they didn't know—something I've seen happen again and again. Other examples: Maxine Hong Kingston's *The Woman Warrior*, and in a very different way, John le Carré's *The Spy Who Came in from the Cold*. But there was also our unanimous belief that Potok's novel was not only first-rate but *could* achieve a popular success. When I lecture about publishing and the personal conviction that motors it, I tell this story: When the manuscript was completely ready, I gave it to Nina—I hadn't wanted her to see it before I was one hundred percent satisfied. The next morning she rushed into my office, saying, "When I finished it last night I loved it so much that I needed to tell someone about it, but it was too late to call you. So I made myself a cup of tea, sat down, and told myself!"

The Chosen opened up the worlds of Orthodox Judaism and Hasidism not only to gentiles but to nonpracticing Jews like myself who had no religious upbringing whatsoever.

Even so, its continuing popularity over half a century suggests that it's not only its exotic (to most of us) setting and specific religious conflicts that roused our interest but that Chaim Potok touched on universal issues and feelings that continue to resonate. Fathers and sons still clash; teenagers still undergo emotional turbulence; close friendship is still crucial and complicated for young people; growing up isn't easy, whether in Williamsburg or Detroit or El Paso; rejecting tradition in order to pursue one's own path remains both imperative and frightening. *The Chosen* will almost surely go on illuminating these verities for readers both young and old through the *next* fifty years.

Original book jacket.

FOREWORD TO 25TH ANNIVERSARY EDITION OF *THE CHOSEN*

Chaim Potok

The twenty-fifth anniversary edition of *The Chosen*! This seemingly fragile raft of a novel; this rarefied weave of signs, symbols, and metaphors; this odd tale of two boys from different backgrounds spinning out their adolescent lives in an arcane realm of Brooklyn homes, streets, playgrounds, libraries, houses of worship, and academies of learning around the closing years of the Second World War—still in print so many years after it first saw light.

That it saw light at all is miracle enough. But that it has been read by millions over the decades and is now required reading in schools from America to Europe to Australia—how did this happen?

Authors, beleaguered and bewildered and intuition-driven creatures, are probably the last to whom such queries about their books should be directed. But an account of the way this particular book was born might be of some interest to those curious enough about what the book has become.

I wrote the first draft in Jerusalem during the fall and winter of 1963–64. My wife and baby daughter and I were there quite by chance: two of the leading scholars in post-Kantian epistemology—the subject of the doctoral dissertation I was at work on for the University of Pennsylvania—were then teaching at the Hebrew University.

Unheated stone Jerusalem apartments are often mountain-cold in the fall and winter, the air dry and relentlessly penetrating. I would sit at an old desk in the small bedroom of our rented apartment, enveloped by a narrow circle of warmth thrown off by an aged kerosene heater. To step out of that circle was to enter a zone of frigid air that cut swiftly through clothes and flesh to bone and marrow. Fingers stiffened, teeth chattered, breath vaporized. The cold served to reduce my visits to the refrigerator and the bathroom, and wonderfully focused the mind on the manuscript.

Mornings in the apartment I worked on the novel; afternoons in the Hebrew University library I worked on the dissertation. A city bus would take me from one writing fit to the other. Baseball, Talmud, Bible, scientific textual criticism, Hasidism, Zionism, Freud, psychology—in the bedroom during the mornings; Kant, Hume, Maimon, Fichte, Hegel, Vaihinger, idealism, fictionism, positivism, skepticism, dialectics—in the library during the afternoons.

Unforgettable, like a granite bedrock in memory, was the intimacy with poverty. I grew up in the Great Depression; for a while in the thirties we were on welfare. But there was an immense difference between the poor child in New York and the poor husband and father in Jerusalem. Three lucrative jobs had been offered me the summer before, and with my wife's concurrence I had turned all of them down: I wanted to write, on my own terms. Letters from concerned relatives arrived in Jerusalem—what was I doing with my life? wasn't it time I settled down?—and added weight to the dismal poverty in which we lived. There is nothing noble or redemptive about poverty, nothing; I've lived in it long enough to be able to say that with certainty. Mostly it enervates; sometimes one can turn it into anger. And the anger, if wisely and carefully managed, may help stoke the furnaces of the imagination.

Mornings that year I lived in a left-behind world I was reimagining.

It had seemed to me once a coherent world and, in spite of the horrors of the Second World War and the Holocaust, I had retained a fairly intact view of my place in it. Then, in 1956, I left it for the Far East, where I spent sixteen months as a chaplain with front-line army units in Korea. There my neat world came undone in a cacophony of dilemmas and ambiguities. Farther from home than I had ever been, from that comforting world of childhood and community, I began to wonder who I was and what my culture and heritage meant to me.

Seven years later, in Jerusalem, buried memories of Korea began to return. All around me that year were Holocaust survivors, and stark reminders of Israel's War of Independence: barbed wire, pitted houses, burnt-out vehicles on the road to Jerusalem; and people with endless tales of siege, adversity, horror. I felt resurfacing in me a long-repressed dread and rage in the face of blind divisiveness, for Jerusalem was divided then, as was Korea, and some were killed that year, as others had been during my months in Korea; indeed, I had lost a close friend there.

Cold Jerusalem, six thousand miles away from New York, returned me in memory to the warmer world of my beginnings, and I began to see those early years through a new map of meaning. Sentence by sentence I constructed that map, sensing it intuitively, not fully aware of what I was doing, feeling my way.

I remember what seemed at the time an insurmountable struggle for an encompassing metaphor. How to make a unity of such disparate entities—the war in Europe, a childhood eye injury, the mesmerizing quality and dark menace of certain books, Freud, religion, psychology, mathematical logic, sacred texts, scientific text criticism, Zionism, the Holocaust?

And then, one particularly gray November morning, a memory glided into consciousness from the reservoir in which we store the daily detritus of our lives. I remembered watching Hasidic youngsters in a Brooklyn park playing the game called running bases: two stand on bases tossing a baseball back and forth while a third runs between them trying to get to one or the other base without being tagged. Black skullcaps on their short-cropped heads, earlocks flicking against their pale faces, white shirts hanging loose from dark trousers, ritual fringes flying.

And within a day or two, I knew I had my metaphor—the game of baseball, combat in a playing field in Brooklyn, in synagogues and schools and homes, in Europe and Asia, in the Middle East, in the minds and hearts of adolescents and their families; combat cool and hot; combat controlled and violent; combat physical and cultural.

Very early in the writing I made a deliberate decision about the style of the work. I could not imagine the exotic story of Reuven Malter and Danny Saunders told in any mode other than a spare simplicity of language and structure. It seemed to me that ordinariness of style would serve as ironic counterpoint to the complexity and unfamiliarity of the subject. Semantic clarity and syntactic simplicity: that was to be the language in which Reuven Malter would tell his story—without Second-Avenue-theater kitsch, without Borscht Belt clowning and tummling, without the clichés, inept Yiddishisms, and gratuitous vulgarity that befog so much of modern Jewish writing in the English language. This was to be an American story—it is inconceivable in any other setting—and it would be told without apology. Reuven Malter has as much right to his map of meaning as Huckleberry Finn, Antonia Shimerda, Amory Blaine, Nick Adams, Studs Lonigan, Carol Kennicott, Holden Caulfield, and Augie March have to theirs.

I put into the book the bitter cold of relationships shattered on the battlefield of ideas, a cold reinforced by the winds of that Jerusalem winter. I put into it memories of my early love of libraries, a love given weight by my daily afternoon sojourns in the library of the Hebrew University. I put into it all my mind and heart in an attempt to create a map that would make meaningful to me the New York world I had experienced during my adolescence.

The Chosen was my first attempt to answer the question of who I had once been and what had happened to me in Korea, though Korea appears nowhere in the book.

The second draft was completed in the late spring of 1964, and I brought it back with me to New York. It was a huge manuscript, nearly one thousand pages long, a work still in progress; even as it was being shepherded through publishing houses by Arlene Friedman, my agent at William Morris, I was constantly rewriting. Several editors turned it down: too unwieldy, too unbelievable, too uncommercial. Then Toinette Rees, on Bob Gottlieb's staff at Simon and Schuster, read it. I've been told that she was intensely moved by it but was disconcerted by its structure and some of the characters. Bob had never known her to be ambivalent about anything before, and he decided to see for himself.

Reading the novel, he sensed, in his extraordinarily perceptive way, that it ended at a certain point, and I had simply continued writing.

Bob Gottlieb and I met in his office one afternoon, and we talked about the book. One of the ways a writer knows he or she is working with a great editor is when the editor voices the writer's own deepest doubts and gently suggests possible solutions. After listening to Bob, I took the manuscript home. I had already trimmed it down considerably on my own. Now I rewrote the ending. A week or so later I was back in Bob's office with the reworked manuscript. Bob read it again, and accepted it. Some additional cuts were made. And the book came to life in the spring of 1967, twenty-five years ago.

The title was suggested by Arthur Sheekman, who was at the time editing the Groucho Marx letters. I liked it because it seemed simultaneously ambiguous and ampliate: chosen people; making choices; choosing to see or ignore threatening truths; choosing teams in a baseball game, books in a library, friends in a neighborhood, sides in a culture war.

I saw no prospect of the novel's eliciting wide interest. Indeed, it seemed to me I had written a book only a few would want to read.

Then, to my astonishment, came the many reviews and the climb up the best-seller charts to the number one position and the deluge of letters. Letters from secularists; letters from Christians; letters from missionaries; letters from teachers in the outback of Australia; letters from children in Alaska and Mississippi and Alabama; letters from past and present New Yorkers; letters from nuns, parish priests, Jesuits, pastors, rabbis. And news drifted in that the book was being banned in certain rigidly Orthodox Jewish circles because of its entanglements with secularism, and was becoming required reading in less benighted regions of the planet. Astonishments!

It took some months before I realized what I had done. Reuven Malter and Danny Saunders grew up in the very center of their world: they went to its best schools, experienced fully its values, were aware of its expectations. Growing up, they encountered certain elements from the general culture in which we all live: textual criticism and Freudian psychoanalytic theory, both profound challenges to any religious view of the world, one because it casts doubt upon the validity of sacred texts, the other because it undermines our ordinary understanding of the nature of man and society. I had stumbled upon what I have subsequently come to refer to as core-to-core culture confrontation: individuals raised in the heart of one culture encountering alternate readings of the human experience that come to them from the heart of a possibly adversary culture. This experience, which, as an example, James Joyce describes in *A Portrait of the Artist as a Young Man* in terms of the conflict between Dublin Irish Catholicism and modern literature, is as deep a part of all contemporary Western civilization as are its many other kinds of culture confrontations. I thought I had described in *The Chosen* an experience unique to myself and my world; it turned out that, though the content was indeed unique, the form was universal.

It is enormously gratifying to be a witness to the continuing life of *The Chosen*. Having it reemerge as a Knopf title twenty-five years after publication brings a felt dimension of unity to all my books, for now they are all under the roof of a single house. My deepest thanks to Knopf and to my readers. And, with the wisdom of hindsight, an acknowledgment to the cold, the dread, the frenzy, and the disciplining fall and winter winds of that difficult distant year in Jerusalem.

Chaim Potok
Merion, Pennsylvania

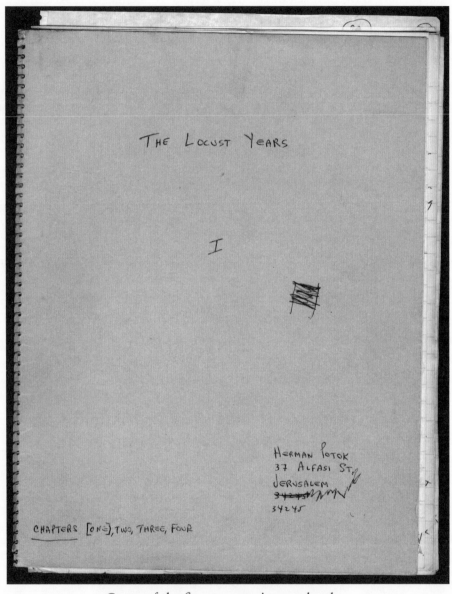

THE LOCUST YEARS

I

HERMAN POTOK
37 ALFASI ST.
JERUSALEM
34245

CHAPTERS [ONE], TWO, THREE, FOUR

Cover of the first manuscript notebook.

CULTURE CONFRONTATION IN URBAN AMERICA: A WRITER'S BEGINNINGS

Chaim Potok

The Bronx of the Thirties and Forties was my Mississippi River Valley. Yes, I saw poverty and despair, and I remember to this day the ashen pallor on my father's face that night in the late Thirties when he told us we would have to go on welfare. And, yes, the streets were on occasion dark with gang violence and with the hate that had made the sea journey from the anti-Semitic underbelly of Europe. But there were books and classes and teachers; there were friends with whom I invented street games limited only by the boundaries of the imagination. And alone, on a concrete and asphalt Mississippi, I journeyed repeatedly through the crowded sidewalks and paved-over backyards, the hallways of the brick apartment houses, the hushed public libraries, dark movie houses, candy stores, grocery stores, Chinese laundries, Italian shoe-repair shops, the neighborhoods of Irish, Italians, blacks, Poles—journeys impelled by eager curiosity and a hunger to discover my sense of self, my place in the tumult of the world. I was an urban sailor on the raft of my own two feet.

I had little quarrel with my Jewish world. I was deep inside it, with a child's slowly increasing awareness of his own culture's richness and shortcomings. But beyond the tiny Hannibal of our apartment, there was an echoing world that I longed to embrace; it streamed in upon me, its books, movies, music, appealing not only to the mind but also to the senses. Faintly redolent of potential corruptions of the flesh, dark with the specter of conquest by assimilation, it seemed to hold out at the same time the promise of wordly wisdom, of tolerance, of reward for merit and achievement, and—the most precious promise of all—the creations of the great minds of man.

I was one of millions, millions, making that concrete Mississippi journey. We were the children and grandchildren of the last great tribal migration of our species on this planet, the east-west wandering of the frightened, the persecuted, the hungry, the poor, the seekers after new wealth and power—the movement around the turn of the century from Europe that inundated this land. The immigrant generation crashed into urban America. Often I think that our parents and grandparents, watching the world of urban America work its beguiling charms upon us, must have wondered if they had acted wisely in leaving their land, desolate and oppressive as it no doubt had been. To lose a child to an alien culture is to suffer a lifetime of anguish and pain.

Wandering through the urban world of my early years, I encountered almost everywhere the umbrella civilization in which all of us live today, the culture we call western secular humanism. It is western because it functions pretty much only on this side of our planet; the eastern side is off on a tack all its own. It is secular because it makes no fundamental appeal to the supernatural; it is committed to the notion that man will either make it alone or he will not make it at all. No gods, no God, no comforting Truths and Absolutes; only stumbling, fumbling man, provisional truths, and an indifferent cosmos in which man, though a trifling speck in the totality of things, commits himself to life and dreams and to pumping meaning into the universe. It is humanist because of its concept of the individual, the self, not as a member of a community, but as a separate entity hungering to fulfill his or her own potentialities the one time around each of us has on this planet.

I encountered many of the cultures embedded beneath this umbrella civilization, varieties of Judaism and Christianity, ethnic groups, interest groups. I saw how each of these sub-cultures rubs up against the other and also against the umbrella civilization. In the world of urban America these rub-ups are intense, grating, relentless. Ideally, the umbrella acts as a protective cover that keeps all the sub-groups in check and prevents any of them from becoming so powerful that it can threaten the existence of the others. The umbrella is tenuous, fragile. When it fails—and it fails too often—there are riots in the streets, as there were in my teens when the city grew dark with the rage of one of its suffering people.

In the libraries of urban America I learned that a culture is the still mysterious creation on the part of members of our species who have somehow clustered together—whether for reasons of geography, tribal loyalty, cataclysm, and the like—and have worked out their own unique responses to the questions we normally conceal from ourselves during the busy day, the four-o'clock-in-the-morning questions that sometimes snap us awake in the night. We lie in the darkness and listen to the questions swarm around us. What is all this really about? Does anything that I do mean anything? How can I ever hope to comprehend this awesome universe in which I live? I barely understand myself, how can I ever understand another human being? What is this narrow river of light I wander upon between the darkness from which I came and the darkness toward which I am inexorably headed? Cultures work out hard responses to these questions, responses which adherents are at times asked to defend with their lives. Often different sets of responses collide—as a result of armies in the field, merchants at fairs, scholars in libraries, or a youngster's urban wanderings. The collision generates questions and tension: Why are my answers better than those of another culture? Sometimes the tension gets out of hand, and there is bloodshed. Sometimes it results in creativity— books, music, art—and gold is given us to mine forever. Sumerians and Akkadians, Israelites and Canaanites, Judaism and Hellenism, Christianity and Rome, Islam and ancient Greek thought, Christianity and Judaism—and ancient Greek thought: these collisions of great thought systems and styles of life were culture confrontations.

I learned as I grew up that culture confrontation has been one of the ongoing dynamics of our species for the five thousand years that we can track ourselves through writing. Today, in the western world, the dynamic is umbrella and sub-culture in confrontation. The rhythm of confrontation has accelerated in this century. The culture highways are wide open. The traffic is dense, especially in cities. The word "civilization"—it cannot hurt to remind ourselves—comes from the Latin *civitas*, which means city or city-state.

Those who made that urban journey confronted other cultures in a variety of ways. Let me briefly describe one such confrontation—my own.

In the Jewish tradition, writing stories occupies no point of any significance in the hierarchy of values by which one measures achievement. Scholarship—especially Talmudic scholarship—is the measure of an individual. Fiction, even serious fiction—as far as the religious Jewish tradition is concerned—is at best a frivolity, at worst a menace.

When I was about fourteen or fifteen years old, I read *Brideshead Revisited* by Evelyn Waugh. That was the first serious adult novel I ever read. In high school English classes in those days you read works like *Treasure Island* and *Ivanhoe*. I was overwhelmed by that book. Somehow Evelyn Waugh reached across the chasm that separated my tight New York Jewish world from that of the upper-class British Catholics in his book. I remember finishing the book and marveling at the power of this kind of creativity. We each have our own beginnings with the hot madness called writing fiction.

From that time on, I not only read works of literature for enjoyment but also studied them with Talmudic intensity in order to teach myself how to create worlds out of words on paper. During the mornings in my school I studied the sacred subjects of my religious tradition; during the afternoons I studied the secular subjects of our umbrella civilization; at night and during weekends I read and wrote fiction. The great writers who created modern literature became my teachers.

The years went by.

In time I discovered that I had entered a tradition—modern literature. Fundamental to that tradition was a certain way of thinking the world; and basic to that was the binocular vision of the iconoclast, the individual who grows up inside inherited systems of value and, while growing, begins to recoil from the games, masks, and hypocrisies he sees all around him. About three hundred years ago, on this side of the planet, certain writers began to use one of the oldest instrumentalities of communication known to our species—story-telling—as a means of exploring the taut lines of relationship between individuals on the one hand and societies on the other, the small or large coherent worlds with which those individuals had entered into tension. Individual and society in polarization—that is one of the mighty rivers in the geography of modern literature. Sometimes the world of that individual is tiny and benign, as in Jane Austen; sometimes it is cruel and sentimental, as in Dickens; sometimes it is stagnant and decadent, as in James Joyce and Thomas Mann; sometimes it is icy and brutal, as in the early Hemingway. That is what I saw in the novels I read during my high school and college years in the teeming urban world of New York.

It was not difficult for me to realize that nothing was sacred to the serious novelist; nothing was so sacrosanct an inheritance from the past that it could not be opened up and poked into by the pen of the novelist. Someone born into an ancient tradition enters the world with baggage on his shoulders. If, in your growing up, no one messed up your particular world in an irreversible way—parents and teachers brought patience and love to your problems—

you might come out of your sub-culture appreciating its richness, its echoing history, and eager to cope with its shortcomings. And if, at the same time, you have stumbled upon modern literature during the years of your growing loyalty to your private past, you find by the time you are nineteen or twenty years old that you have become a battleground for a culture confrontation of a certain kind. I call it a core-to-core culture confrontation. From the heart of your sub-culture, trained in its best schools, able to maneuver through its system of thought, its language, its way of structuring the world, you have come upon literature, an element from the core of the umbrella civilization in which all of us live today. Literature is a core endeavor of western secular man; it is one of the ways western secular man gives configuration to his experience — through the faculty of the imagination and a certain aesthetic form. In the history of our species, core-to-core culture confrontations have often resulted in explosions of creativity. An encounter with soaring alien ideas often sets us soaring toward new ideas of our own; or we enter into a process of selective affinity, finding in the alien thought system elements with which we feel the need to fuse. Few experiences are more extraordinary in the history of our species than that sort of culture confrontation in which one culture will spark another into seminal creativity.

I do not intend to write a novel about my encounter with the novel. But some who grew up with me might have encountered other elements from the core of western secular humanism. And that is what my work has been about so far. In *The Chosen*, Danny Saunders encounters Freudian psychoanalytic theory; in *The Promise*, Reuven Malter encounters text criticism; in *My Name Is Asher Lev*, a young man encounters western art; in *In the Beginning*, David Lurie encounters modern Bible scholarship. All these disciplines are located in the core of western culture. And all my people are located in the core of their sub-culture.

You can grow up along the periphery of your sub-culture and enter the rich heart of western secular humanism — say, by going to a university, the generating plant of western secular civilization. You will experience a periphery-to-core culture confrontation. Saul Bellow's *Herzog* is about such a culture confrontation: Herzog at the heart of western secular humanism experiencing the crises of our world and his life through his peripheral emotive connection to his sub-culture, his memories of an ethnic past.

You can grow up along the periphery of your sub-culture and experience only the periphery of western civilization. That is a periphery-to-periphery culture confrontation. The early stories of Philip Roth are accounts of that kind of collision of cultures. Almost always, that sort of culture confrontation gives rise to cultural aberrations, awkward misunderstandings, bizarre fusions.

At the core of a culture is its world view, its literature, art, and music, its special ways of thinking the world. The more difficult it becomes to move inside an alien culture, the closer you are to its core. Peripheries of culture—street language, foods, clothes, fad music, superstitions—are almost always the easiest elements to understand, imitate, absorb.

I am writing about a particular sub-culture, about people and events that were of special concern to me as I grew up and began my own Mississippi journey into this world. The compression of urban existence, the living mix of peoples and cultures in my Bronx world, made possible for me a rich variety of culture confrontations. I chose to write about core-to-core confrontation because that is the world I know best.

What happens when two ultimate commitments—one from your sub-culture, the other from the umbrella culture—meet in you and you love them both and they are antithetical one to the other? There is a dimension of Greek tragedy in this collision of two equally valid systems of values. How do you maneuver? How do you talk on the phone, go to school, ride a train, cross a street, attend class, relate to others, talk to your parents and friends, go out on a date, read texts? What are your dreams? What are your loves, your hates? I am writing about the feelings involved in the experience of core-to-core culture confrontation.

Urban wanderings that result in core-culture confrontations often shape a certain kind of individual. I call that individual a *Zwischenmensch*, a between-person. Such an individual will cross the boundaries of his or her own culture and embrace life-enhancing elements from alien worlds. I remember the pink-faced, bald-headed Italian shoemaker who sang in his tenor voice as he pounded away at my torn shoes. He taught me the word "opera." That was the birth of that passion for me. I always listened carefully from then on to the classical radio station. Can you conceive of how distant the tumultuous world of opera is from the mind-centered ambience of Talmudic disputation?

Late one spring day a seedy-looking man wandered into my parochial school. He was an artist, he said, and was willing to teach a summer course in art for a pittance. It would keep the children off the street, he said; give them something to do. He was in his late forties, a tired man reeking of tobacco, his eyes watery, the cuffs of his shirtsleeves frayed, his jacket and trousers creased. He looked weary, worn. Inexplicably, he was taken on. There were sixteen of us in that class. I was about ten years old. He watched me move colors across a canvas board one day and took me aside. "How old are you, kid?" he asked. "Who've you studied with?" That was my first step into the world of western art. In my childhood, what Joyce was to Jesuits, painting was to Talmud.

To be a *Zwischenmensch* is to feel at home everywhere and nowhere simultaneously, to be regarded with suspicion by those along the banks as they watch you float by on your raft.

My Mississippi has no Delta ending. It runs on and on. We are most human when we communicate creatively across the Hannibals we make for ourselves. Yes, the raft is frail. Anything made and experienced by man seems frail—anything. Each new day of sun and sky is frail, frail. Still we remember the journeys begun a long time ago on the cement rivers of urban America. Different cities boil within each of us. There is so much we hate—the dirt, the poverty, the prejudice; there is so much we love—the one or two friendships that somehow crossed boundaries, the libraries where we joined ourselves to the dreams of others, the places where we composed dreams of our own, the museums where we learned how to defeat time, certain streets, alleys, staircases, apartment-house roofs, certain radio stations we would listen to deep into the night, certain newspapers we read as if they were a testament to the ages. We remember the terrors and joys of our early urban wanderings. We write, and continue the journey.

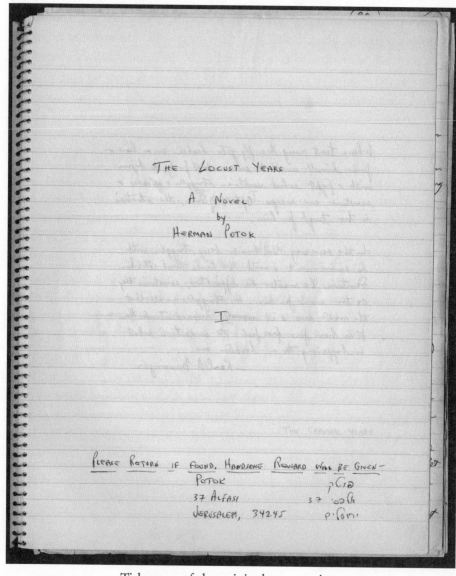

THE LOCUST YEARS

A NOVEL

by

HERMAN POTOK

I

PLEASE RETURN IF FOUND. HANDSOME REWARD WILL BE GIVEN—
POTOK
37 ALFASI
JERUSALEM, 34245

Title page of the original manuscript.

THE CULTURE HIGHWAYS WE TRAVEL

Chaim Potok

Early in February of 1957, I stood in Hiroshima on the blast site of the atomic bomb. I had been in Korea for a year as a chaplain, first with a front line medical battalion and then with a combat engineer battalion. All through my months in Korea I had felt myself drawn to that site. To this day I don't quite understand why. Standing there, I remembered how I had felt as a teenager when I had first heard about the dropping of the bomb. My initial response was an enormous sense of joy: the war would soon be over. And then there came a slowly-dawning sense of horror, a feeling that somehow our species had turned a corner in its history and nothing would ever be the same again. I returned to my unit in Korea, spent four more months there, and came home.

But the encounter with Hiroshima lingered. I began to ask myself, what did it mean to me, that moment when I stood at the site of that explosion? What did it mean to me as a member of western civilization? What did it mean to me as a Jew? And I began to explore that moment through my fiction.

Slowly, through the writing, a model began to develop, a model describing the various ways that cultures confront one another. I would like to deal here with one of the components of that model: the confrontation that occurs when ideas from the heart of one culture confront the central elements of another culture.

This article was originally presented at The University of Notre Dame, in November 1986, as one in a series of lectures given under the auspices of the Abrams Chair of Jewish Thought and Culture. © Chaim Potok, 1986.

All of us live inside the general civilization we call western secular human-ism. It is about three hundred years old, and has come to us in the wake of the Enlightenment. Its founding fathers were Voltaire, Diderot, Rousseau, Kant, Hume, and so many others. It replaced the previous general civilization on the western side of our planet, the civilization known as Christendom, which replaced Rome, which replaced Greece. We call it "western" because it only pertains to our side of the planet and our cultural colonies—Australia, New Zealand, Israel, to a very great extent South Africa, and so on. It is "secular" because it makes no appeal to the supernatural. We will do it alone. Absolutes are provisional. Truths are with small t's. It is an ongoing self-correcting civ-ilization whose goal is intersubjective knowledge, that is to say, statements about reality that can be tested under laboratory conditions. It is "humanist" because of its emphasis on the individual *qua* individual, not as a member of a tribe but as a person, as a self riddled with problems.

All of us are that civilization. We are its scientists, its entrepreneurs, its artists. If we are clergymen, we service those who are its artists, its entrepre-neurs, its scientists. We give it our best creative energies. Most of us, no matter what religion we may belong to, do our best creating inside the various occu-pations and disciplines of that civilization—mathematics, literature, art, busi-ness, sociology, philosophy, chemistry, physics, psychology, law, medicine.

This civilization is to a great degree anxiety-ridden, nihilistic, hedonistic; often its members are filled with a sense of alienation, a feeling that they be-long nowhere. Absence of community is one of the central problems of this civilization; it has been unable to form within itself deep communal roots. Indeed this civilization may well be in a post-cultural phase, as George Steiner and others have pointed out. But it is still rife with seminal creativity.

Inside this civilization, as part of its ongoing dynamic, is a vast array of past cultures and civilizations that are constantly rubbing up against one an-other. Sometimes that rubbing-up gets out of hand and we have blood in the streets, as we had here in the Sixties and early Seventies.

Sometimes out of that rubbing-up come tension and creativity. I had a problem with becoming a writer of fiction. It was a problem of how to bring together antagonistic and conflicting passions: my love for my own tradition on the one hand, and my love for modern literature on the other—a literature that glories in its image-breaking stance, its nihilism, its cool ironic suspicion of human emotions, and its basic skepticism regarding all givens from the past. From the heart of my own world, I learned about the richness at the heart of another world: literature is a central endeavor of western secular man. I am writing about core-to-core cultural confrontations, some experienced by me and some by others. I am writing about the *thoughts* and *feelings* of individuals who are trying to come to terms with two universes of discourse that they love passionately—and that are at times in absolute conflict.

Three of my novels are deliberately arranged in an ascending order of confrontation, each more difficult than the previous one to resolve: Danny Saunders in Brooklyn [*The Chosen*], Asher Lev in Paris [*My Name Is Asher Lev*], and Gershon Loran in Asia [*The Book of Lights*].

Danny Saunders was born into the heart of the Jewish tradition, into one of the great pietist sects of contemporary Jewish life. Growing up, he encounters an element from the heart of western secular humanism: Freud.

Freud is antithetical to any western religion's view of man. Freud's secularism contains no appeal to the supernatural: no sin, no guilt, no priest, no rabbi. You find the source of the pathology; you try to understand it as best you can; you learn to live with it somehow. It is, in its most essential nature, a system that is utterly alien to any western religion's attempt to structure the human experience.

Danny Saunders, the son of a Hasidic rabbi, learns from his father the religious value of sharing another individual's suffering. But at the same time, he encounters a secular system that deals with suffering, that attempts to explore the dimensions of a certain kind of human pathology and alleviate its pain. What do you do with a system which you feel has certain truths but which at the same time contains components that are antagonistic to your own sense of values, your system of ideas?

Repeatedly the narrator in *The Chosen* asks Danny how he can come to terms with Freud's anti-religious view of the nature of man. And Danny Saunders does not respond. For him, psychoanalysis is a tool for research and healing. He will not use the Freudian system as a statement about the nature of man. For that, he will go to his native world, the culture of Hasidic Judaism. This method of handling an antagonistic system of thought is *culture compartmentalization*.

Here is another example of culture compartmentalization. Reuven Malter, in *The Chosen* and in *The Promise*, is being taught how to handle one of the most radical instrumentalities that has come to us as a gift from western secular humanism: text criticism. Text criticism uses the powerful tools of philology, archaeology, and the new discoveries about ancient cultures and literatures in which the biblical world was embedded. Reuven uses these tools in order to acquire a contemporary, enlightened awareness of the central sacred texts of the western tradition, the Bible. No fundamentalism can countenance these tools. To this day we don't quite know how to live with instruments that rip apart and re-establish biblical texts. In coming to terms with these tools, Reuven decides to use them only on the Talmud. He will not use them on the Bible. This is another form of culture compartmentalization.

Culture compartmentalization enables you to take on an antagonistic system of values and to use that part of it with which you feel most comfortable, while letting you ignore those elements toward which you feel the greatest measure of antagonism. There is no ongoing crossover of the two cultures. You can be a great physicist and do seminal work in the world of material reality—and then leave that all behind as you enter your church or your synagogue and live inside the world of the spirit. There are no permanently wide-open doors through which you smoothly pass from culture to culture.

The fact that you approached an alien culture in the first place is a result of an interesting process. If that culture is entirely alien, if it says nothing to you at all, you would walk away from it. An individual approaches an alien culture because some element in it speaks to him or to her. Danny Saunders enters the world of Freud precisely (and ironically) because his father is trying to sensitize him to human suffering. It is through that portal that he enters the Freudian system and begins to poke around in ever-widening circles.

Now you might very legitimately ask: You pick, you choose, you throw out what you want, you keep what you want—Is this an honest way of handling another system of thought? The answer is that that is indeed one of the ways. It was precisely what the founding fathers of western humanism did. They skipped backwards across the vast civilization we call Christendom into the classical Greek and Roman world, and very carefully chose those elements of that world toward which they felt the greatest degree of affinity: its rationalism, its cool skepticism, its literature, its philosophy, its drama. They ignored totally its orgiastic elements, its lust for power, its indifference toward suffering, its grotesque and irrational mystery religions.

We do this instinctively when we lock with another system of ideas. We select out of another culture those elements toward which we feel the closest, for whatever reasons. And we merge with those elements, our hope being that out of that merging will come something of significance, a challenge, something that will elicit creativity. You learn to live with, to use, to create within a system of ideas alien to your own. You can work very seriously inside that system—and leave it at will as you move back into your own particular world, the world that taught you its value system first. New system here, old system here, with little if any significant communication between the two.

When you deal with the sciences, compartmentalization seems to work: material realm, spiritual realm. But when it comes to the humanities, a serious problem presents itself, because the humanities consistently cut across all dimensions and make statements that pertain to all components of the human experience. . . .

I had been taught all through my young life that Jewish suffering made sense in a strange way. I remember my parents and my teachers telling me this. We are different from the rest of the world. We are the teacher of morality to the rest of humanity. Well, you want to stick your neck out all the time? You want to be the eternal Other? You will get your head chopped off now and then. People don't like Others. My father spent three and a half years in the trenches in the First World War, with a Polish unit of the Austrian army. He used to talk to me in military terms. He would describe the Jews as the reconnaissance troops of mankind. He would say to me over and over again that reconnaissance troops take the highest casualties. When I was in Korea I learned what he meant.

I saw suffering in Korea that made no sense whatsoever: blind suffering of people caught in the paths of empires. I felt the absurdity and meaninglessness of that suffering, the suffering of peasants who were part of a pagan universe. (I say "pagan" not in any derogatory way, but descriptively.) *That* suffering, not my own people's suffering, opened up for me the question of evil in this world. That was one of the questions that I came away with from my fifteen and a half months in the Far East. It is one of the questions that Gershon Loran asks himself—and finds no answer.

One afternoon, walking through a marketplace in Tokyo, I came to a Shinto temple. In that temple, before an idol, stood an old man—gray fedora hat, bearded, tattered coat and suit, with a prayer book in his hands, swaying back and forth before that idol. Looking at that old man, I remembered the old Jews in the little synagogue that I grew up in, swaying before the sacred Ark. What intensity of devotion I saw in that old man as he stood before that idol, praying! Standing there, I asked myself, "What am I looking at? Is the God I pray to listening to this old man's prayers? If He isn't listening, why not? Where can there ever be a greater act of devotion in a moment of prayer than the act that I am now witnessing? And if the God that I pray to *is* listening to that pagan pray to that idol, then what are Judaism and Christianity all about?"

Once, wandering through the streets of Kyoto, I experienced an overwhelming sense of freedom, a lightness of being. I realized that for the first time in my life I was in a world where there was no anti-Semitism. I cannot describe to you what it is to be a Jew and suddenly to find oneself in a world where the concept of anti-Semitism doesn't exist and where it is certainly not practiced—or wasn't when I was there. What a feeling of freedom that is! And I was in a *pagan* world, a world that I had been taught all my life to treat with contempt. Here was another question for which I had no answer.

I had been taught over and over again that paganism was a system of thought and a way of life which western religions rightfully condemned; that one had to be wary of the allure of paganism. But I saw beauty in the world of Japan, indeed in certain parts of Korea, that I had never known possible before. I saw not only natural beauty, but beauty created by members of our species—loveliness in the worship of pagan gods. I learned to appreciate the beauty of God's world not on the streets of New York, not in the American countryside that I would live in from time to time in the summers on vacation, but in a pagan land. Again, a question for which there is no answer.

I had been taught by teachers, by my parents, that western civilization is inconceivable without its Jewish component; and that indeed is quite true. Think of western civilization without the Jewish element in it! It is literally not thinkable. For fifteen and a half months I found myself inside a world in which the terms "Jew" and "Judaism" were simply the emptiest of words. No Jews; no Judaism. And they seemed to get along without Jews and Judaism with no difficulty whatsoever. Another question for which there is no easy answer.

All the neat coherence of my world . . . came undone. Everything was rendered ambiguous. . . .

And for us too—all the dreams with which this century began haven't quite worked out for us. There was such a high feeling of optimism as we turned the corner into the Twentieth Century: we really can do it by ourselves; we can solve the basic problems of mankind. Then, the First World War, the Second World War, the Holocaust, Hiroshima, Nagasaki. The fundamental ideas with which our century began seem to have run down. We seem indeed to be in a post-cultural situation, with a probable fifty-fifty chance of survival. . . .

The confrontations that I am trying to explore are collisions from the very hearts of rich and diverse cultures. Danny Saunders from the heart of his Judaism encounters Freud, a gift to us from the heart of secularism. Asher Lev from the heart of Judaism encounters art, one of the glories of western civilization. Gershon Loran from the center of the Jewish tradition encounters the heart of a rich, alluring, often magnificent and at times quite horrifying pagan world and its juncture point with the West at Hiroshima.

I am not advocating such confrontations. As a novelist, I am only describing them.

It has been for me a long journey from Hiroshima. There is much that I still need to clear up and think through for myself. I hope to continue to take Danny Saunders, Reuven Malter, Asher Lev, and Gershon Loran—as well as a number of women—along this journey that so many of us are on today. We are, I think, many of us, in one way or another, Danny Saunders and Asher Lev and Reuven Malter and Gershon Loran. We endlessly travel culture highways crowded with ideas. And we continue to encounter new visions of the human experience.

ONE

Danny was the son of a rabbi, & I was the son of a teacher. His grandfather had been a well-known Hassidic rabbi in a small town in southern Russia, & his father had been the second of two sons. The first-born son had been in line to inherit his father's rabbinic position, an office which had been dynastic for some generations in that particular Jewish community, but during a period of study in a distant house of learning in Odessa, he suddenly vanished. Some said he had been murdered by Cossacks; for a time there was even a rumor that he had converted to Christianity & had gone to live in France. The second son, who was reputed to be only a little less brilliant than his older brother, was ordained at the age of seventeen, & by the time he was twenty had achieved an awesome reputation as a Talmudist. When his father died, he automatically inherited the position of rabbinic leadership. He was twenty-one years old at this time.

He remained the rabbi of his community throughout the years of Russia's participation in the First World War. One week before the Bolshevist Revolution, in the autumn of 1917, his young wife bore him a second child, a son. Two months later, his wife, his son, & his eighteen month old daughter were shot to death by a band of marauding Cossacks, one of the many bandit gangs that roamed through Russia during the period of chaos that followed the revolution. He himself was left for dead, with a pistol bullet in his chest & a saber wound in his pelvis. He lay unconscious for half a day near the bodies of his wife & children, & then the Russian peasant who tended the stove in the synagogue & swept

A page from the early manuscript, with revisions by the author—
original first page of chapter one.

TWO

For the first fifteen years of our lives, Donny & I lived within five blocks of each other & neither of us knew of the other's existence. Our friendship came out of a long two hours of intense, competition-born hatred that ended up causing me a serious, almost crippling injury.

Though we lived only five blocks apart, we were separated by about half a dozen different worlds.

Donny's block was heavily populated by the followers of his father, Russian Hassidic Jews in somber garb, whose habits & frames of reference were born on the soil of the land they had abandoned. They drank tea from samovars, sipping it slowly through cubes of sugar held between their teeth; they ate the food of their homeland, drank soup or borsht directly from the bowl, talked loudly, occasionally in Russian, most often in a Russian Yiddish, were fierce in their loyalty to their rabbi, Donny's father, proud of his piety, & endlessly grateful for that Shabbat morning when he had ordered them all to America.

A block away lived another Hassidic sect, Jews from southern Poland & Hungary, who walked the streets like specters, with their black hats, long, black coats, black beards, & sidecurls. These Jews had their own rabbi, their own dynastic rules, who could trace his family's position of rabbinic leadership back to the time of the Ba'al Shem Tov, the eighteenth century founder of Hassidism whom they all regarded as a God-invested personality.

A page from the early manuscript, with revisions by the author—original first page of chapter two.

THE INVISIBLE MAP OF MEANING: A WRITER'S CONFRONTATIONS

Chaim Potok

A writer's scaffolding ought to remain below the surface of the work, pulsing distantly, sensed but unobtrusive, like the laws of physics that sustain the universe. This is about the invisible design that holds my stories together.

Long ago, in *The Chosen*, I set out to draw a map of the New York world through which I had once journeyed.

It was to be a map not only of broken streets, menacing alleys, concrete-surfaced backyards, neighborhood schools and stores; of gangs and bullies; of friends my age and adults desperate to bolster themselves and their families during the fearful years of the Great Depression and the Second World War; a map not only of the *physical* elements of my early life, but of the *spiritual* ones as well: sacred and secular texts, clashing ideas and dreams, with the battle lines drawn in kitchens and dining rooms, in classrooms and libraries and playing fields—an interior world that had molded me at least as much if not more than had the tactile realities of the early years of my life.

I thought it a small and interesting world through which I and a few friends and acquaintances had pretty much been lone voyagers.

During the entire writing of *The Chosen*, from 1963 to 1965, I believed that only a few would show any interest in its story. But I was determined to write it anyway, because I needed to understand and come to terms with what and where I had once been, and the only way to do that was by trying to shape that past in words and images drawn from the kilns of the imagination.

In the wake of the astonishing reaction to the novel, I came to understand that I had stumbled upon an experience that had not been exclusively mine. Rather, it appeared that I had unknowingly shared it with millions of others. I had filled a universal experience with a particular content.

Soon after the publication of the book it became apparent to me that I had mapped a certain kind of confrontation, which I will name later. That awareness led me to consider a series of works that would further explore the various facets of that confrontation.

Each of the subsequent books became a section of a large map, which I have been drawing and redrawing for the past decades.

I've resisted writing about that map until now, because it seemed too large and unwieldy a creation, indeed at times a blur, a shifting, changing blueprint in constant need of modification. Also it appeared at first to be less about literature than the sociology of literature. But even the most adamant of deconstructionists will admit that there is some fabric of contextuality to literature. And I've talked about the map often before different kinds of audiences; it has served me well over the years as a sort of loran for my work. And so perhaps now is as good a time as any to present it—in order to determine whether it has any broad value or is merely an idiosyncratic and parochial reading of literature by one writer of stories.

Until the modern period most people on this planet grew up, lived, and died, and never seriously contended with a new idea during their entire lives. People lived the only lives they would have, never traveling more than twenty-five miles from their place of birth, never entering into a relationship with a stranger, never engaging an alien idea. Only a few aristocrats, philosophers, scientists, and clergymen ventured regularly beyond the walls of their world for an outside look at their culture's basic assumptions. Often they paid a high price for their effort.

If you lived in a village—as lord, priest, steward, bailiff, reeve, warden or serf—from where would a new idea come? Even in a town—city or suburb—people worked close to where they lived. And if you had to labor far away from home, rarely would you enter into any significant relationship with fellow workers. People lived and died inside a small, shared world of family, friends, neighbors, enemies, coreligionists.

All dwelt in a stable, vertical world of faith—even those in vaunted Elizabethan England, that purported secular hour between two ages of Protestantism. God, Scripture, and the eternal rewards of radiant Heaven above; Satan and the lengthy torments of mephitic Hellfire below; and errant humans moving up and down the verticality, now closer to Heaven, now to Hell, depending upon the measure of one's acquiescence at any given moment to the dictates of divine authority.

Today, as in the past, each of us is born into a small and particular world: a family of some kind, a small town, a big-city neighborhood. In various ways and with different degrees of intensity, we are taught by parents, relatives, teachers, and peers the values of our small and particular worlds. For most of us, signals of approval and disapproval begin to come our way even before we are out of diapers.

Now, however, early on there begin to impinge upon the periphery of our consciousness alternate values from outside our small and particular worlds.

Parents teach us to respond in certain ways to specific moral situations; we turn on the television set and witness those same situations dealt with altogether differently. Relatives, friends, and teachers prompt us toward this or that path out of a serious problem; a new family moves into our neighborhood, we befriend the children of that family, and discover that they resolve that same problem in an entirely different way. Newspapers, magazines, movies, radio, theater, pop music, telephones, computers, facsimile machines, summer camps, social clubs: we are bombarded with alternate ways of thinking the human experience.

There was a time when most of us heard a single melody, repeatedly played and quickly learned. Today, we register cacophonies.

Some take this to be normal, as if life has been this way since our beginnings on this planet. But this mass onslaught of alternatives isn't more than about two hundred and fifty years old.

As we grow up, many of us learn to absorb the repeated shocks of this relentless assault. By the time we're out of our teens, we've more or less formed a picture of the world, and only a jarring encounter with an unusually provocative and competing picture will tear us from our commitment to our own.

We experience the world in a kind of choreography of confrontation. Some of our best novelists have been tracking—in most cases, unknowingly, instinctively—the steps of this choreography as they explore and present to us their personal visions of their encounters with the world.

It is this choreography that I wish to explore. Here, then, is a model—

a mapping—of how we encounter, as a matter of course, values and cultures not our own, and of some of the ways writers of stories have been exploring those encounters.

In the small and particular world of my beginnings, a writer of stories is of no importance.

Scholarship is the highest achievement in the Orthodox Jewish tradition, especially talmudic scholarship—followed closely by medicine, law, and success in business. In the edifice of valued Orthodox Jewish accomplishment, writing stories is somewhere in the basement.

This may come as a surprise to those aware of the great tradition of narrative in the Bible and Talmud, and the power and presence of tales in Midrash, Kabbalah, and Hasidism.

But we must remember that, with very few exceptions, in the ancient, classical, and medieval worlds, the stuff of stories was born in the collective consciousness of the people. For the most part, stories were tribal tales told to transmit the word of God or gods and enhance the mores of the people. Even the angriest of Israelite writers and Greek tragedians—the author of Job and the astonishing and fearless Euripides—were fully integrated into their people's map of meaning. Until the modern period, those who created or disseminated tales—who shaped even the most startling of similes, metaphors and metonyms—were acting in behalf of their people.

The purpose of those tales was to amplify, embellish, find a unique interpretation of, quarrel with, or transmit a more or less commonly held view of the world.

Tales born out of the sequestered imagination; narratives conceived by a single sensibility from a landscape containing only a private cluster of experience; startling visions of the world and humankind's place in it, visions that strikingly differ from those commonly accepted—all of that is new in the history of storytelling.

The modern writer of serious stories, obligated only to his or her art and introspective vision of the world, is more often than not viewed as a threat by religious authority and is discouraged, opposed, fought, censored, persecuted.

How then did it come about that someone committed to his small and particular world took up with an instrumentality—serious story writing— that his world judged to be a menace?

• • •

This is a story about a culture confrontation of the kind that I've been trying to explore in my books.

I am sixteen. It is the dead of winter, the end of a school term. I am done with my final exams and know I will have free time the following week. In my school world a long stretch of free time means time to read.

I have never read a difficult contemporary novel before. In my school we read only classics. I decide to read a serious adult novel.

To this day I don't know why I decided to do that.

I walk in frigid winter air on a Friday afternoon to the neighborhood public library, where I always bring my most secret fantasies. Past the towering steel girders of the elevated train and the gagging hops stench of the brewery and on up the steep hill. There it is: white stone exterior; marble interior; imagined naiads beckoning from the head of the wide stairway. The temple of an alluring goddess.

In the adult fiction section dust motes dance lazily in the winter afternoon sunlight streaming in from tall windows. I browse for a long time through the silent rows of books.

I have always had this sense of books as lined up and waiting, patiently waiting, for people to find them; books anticipating with infinite forbearance the caressing hand and the wonder-filled eye of a reader.

I remove from a shelf a novel whose title intrigues me: *Brideshead Revisited* by Evelyn Waugh.

I attend at the time a Jewish parochial high school in New York City. I wake up at 6:30 every weekday morning, dress, pray the Morning Service, eat breakfast, catch a bus, and am in school about a quarter to nine. From nine in the morning to one in the afternoon, I and about twenty other boys in my class study the most important subject taught in that school: Talmud. From two to five or six, depending upon the day's schedule, we attend classes in the various secular subjects mandated by the State of New York. I arrive home, eat supper, do my homework, go to bed.

Once or twice a week I catch the radio program called *The Lone Ranger*. Sometimes I listen to classical music. On the infrequent occasions when I have time for *Gangbusters* and *The Green Hornet*, the day seems resonant with the miraculous.

I will never forget the experience of reading *Brideshead Revisited*.

The *world* of that book—how other than my own it was! And its prose; I had never read prose like that before. It took me about eighty pages of effort before I grew accustomed to the prose and began to feel somewhat at home in that world—an effort urged upon me by the librarian who'd checked the book out.

She knew I was making an intergalactic leap in my reading.

"This is not like any book you've read before," she had said. "You owe this sort of book an investment of sixty to eighty pages of time and effort *before* you make the decision whether or not to continue reading it."

I am forever grateful to her for that wise counsel.

Once I felt myself comfortable with the novel's prose and at home in its strange world, I began to sense its mesmerizing power. I read day after day, awed by the tenacious faith of the mother of that aristocratic English Catholic family, by the wavering faith of the daughter and the disintegrating being of the young man, and by the gradual advance into that faith of the one who was telling the story. I lived more deeply inside the world of that novel than I lived inside my own world for the length of time it took me to read it.

I remember finishing it—late one night in the living room of our New York apartment—looking down at it, and feeling suddenly bereaved: all its people were gone! The white expanse of page below the last orderly rows of prose seemed an open pit, a grave, into which the entire world of the novel had fallen.

And then came astonishment. What had he done to me, Evelyn Waugh? The whole thing had only been a story! How had he taken words and, together with his imagination, created a world on empty sheets of paper, a world that had become more real to me than the one in which I was actually living?

More important. I had read stories before; indeed, I can barely remember a time when I wasn't reading. But there had always been a sense of the reading experience; I *knew* that I was reading. The encounter with *Brideshead Revisited* marked the first time that I had read a lengthy work while hours went by when I was unaware of reading, when I felt myself inside the people I was reading about, experiencing their emotions, at times anticipating their thoughts. I had been a legitimate voyeur in a world I would otherwise never have come to know. What magic!

Most astonishing of all—I came to understand the role of language in the writing of a story.

Until the encounter with that novel, I had never wanted to deal with an author's words. A story's language was best when invisible, a clear stream through which I could gaze with ease at the pebbled bed of narrative. The task of language was to convey the tale so that I could read it effortlessly. An unfamiliar and cumbersome word; an odd locution; a rhetorical flourish; a deliberate ambiguity—such authorial sleights of hand would annoy me. Now, for the first time, I grew aware of how language could be made to carry a story: the texture and nuances of a phrase, a sentence; the intricate rhythms of a paragraph; the living style of a work that was as much a part of its presence as the story itself. Indeed, I began to sense that story alone might not be the most important element in a novel. A serious novel was a multifaceted animate entity, and not the least of the sparks that brought it to life was its language.

Very soon after reading *Brideshead Revisited* I read *A Portrait of the Artist as a Young Man* by James Joyce.

Yet another astonishment!

Here was someone trying to give shape to turmoil I myself was experiencing: a growing sense of a world outside my own; pulsing sexuality; questions about God and the nature of my own self. Here was an author shaping his deepest thoughts and feelings with language, exploring an interior human terrain I had never thought it possible to configure with words.

What awesome and mysterious power there was in this kind of creativity!

I began to read ravenously, and to write.

In my tight New York Orthodox Jewish world, it was not likely that a young person could become involved in anything of an extracurricular nature without sooner or later being traduced by a classmate or discovered by someone in authority.

And so, one afternoon, at the close of our Talmud class, an intense and wearying session of mental acrobatics that involved reconciling seemingly contradictory views attributed to a great sage, I am heading toward the door with classmates, when I hear my Talmud teacher call me over to him.

This teacher is a graduate of one of the great Eastern European academies of Jewish learning. He does not engage in small talk, is not given to intimacies and rarely hesitates to express his contempt for American culture. A stocky man of middle height, he wears a dark suit, a dark skullcap, has a dark beard and glittering dark eyes.

The two of us alone, my heart beating in my throat, he says to me, speaking in Yiddish, "What is this that I hear?"

Immediately on guard, I respond by answering his question with a question. "I don't understand, what do you mean, what is this that you hear?"

He says, "I hear you want to be a writer."

I say, "Yes."

He says, "What is it that you want to write?"

I say, "Stories."

His eyes burn. Why did I want to write stories?

I tell him I don't know, I have this need to write stories.

He says isn't it enough that the school has to waste every afternoon of each day on secular studies in order to be licensed by the government. I have to add to that, and instead of giving every spare moment to the study of sacred texts, I was writing *stories*!

He gives a special spin to the word "stories," making it sound alien, unclean, beyond the pale of the permitted. And vaguely demonic.

In the months that follow, he tries hard to deter me from this strange love affair I am experiencing with the goddess of literature.

My father, as truculent as he is devout, thinks it all childish nonsense tainted with secular menace, and loses no opportunity to let me know how he feels.

I receive a letter from an editor of the *Atlantic Monthly* to which I sent a short story. The editor wants to know: Am I writing a novel? If I am, she would like to see it. I am eighteen years old.

The letter enrages my father. The Gentile world has set out snares for his son! He wants me to be a teacher of Talmud in an academy of Jewish learning.

My mother, pious but educated in a gymnasium in Vienna during the First World War, quietly encourages me, though her voice is too frequently lost in the thunder from my father.

Father and Talmud teachers join in a warning threnody: writing stories is frivolous, writing stories is potentially calamitous, writing stories is a Gentile enterprise that will ultimately separate me from the sacred world of Torah.

They sense that I have come into contact with an element from the general civilization in which we now all live, the civilization we've inherited from the eighteenth-century European Enlightenment and which we now call by a variety of names: humanism, secularism, Western secular humanism, modernism, postmodernism. For my father and Talmud teachers, any significant contact with that civilization is a threat to what they understand to be Jewish civilization—especially contact with its literature.

• • •

As it turned out, they were right. They sensed something, those Eastern European Jews—my father, my Talmud teachers—they sensed something about the nature of literature that I, a driven teenager, could never have perceived.

I didn't want to be an entertainment writer. My religious world led me to a more sober view of the writing enterprise. I would not use words as slavish messengers of comfort and ease, but to explore seriously—I knew not what at that time in my life.

Early on I discovered that there are two kinds of serious writing: one makes use of previously tested forms; the other sets about inventing new forms; both probe into areas not yet explored by language. Dickens and Tolstoy are examples of the first kind; Joyce and Kafka, the second.

What do you do if you want to become a serious writer?

Granted that you possess basic talent, a focused will and crazed passion—there isn't much mystery about it. You read and you write. You make the masters of modern fiction your teachers. You take apart what they've written and put it back together to see if you can discover how they got it to work. You send stories out to magazines, and they come back with rejection slips or encouraging letters from editors—all of which means your apprenticeship isn't over. You read and you write. And the years go by.

You discover, as the years go by, that you've entered a tradition. It's a tradition we call Modern Literature. In the English language it pretty much has its beginnings with the work of Defoe, Richardson, Fielding, and Austen. And you discover, too, that fundamental to that tradition is a certain way of looking at the world, a unique set of eyes gazing with startling new vision upon the human experience.

They are, by and large, the eyes of the angry iconoclast, the breaker of inherited models of the world, the rebel who grows up inside a small and particular world, as most of us do, and who, during the growing up, begins to sense the games that people often play, the masks they often wear, the small and large hypocrisies that are too often used by us as mechanisms of defense that help us make our way through the very difficult business of living.

For some, the games, masks, and hypocrisies become intolerable.

Three possibilities open up to them. One: they can break with the world that gave them life, and never return to it—and be filled with all the guilt and self-doubt that attend such a relationship to one's beginnings. Two: they can break with their world, return to it, break with their world, return to it, live in constant tension with it—and be filled with all the guilt and self-doubt that shadow such a relationship to one's early world. Or, three: they can quit the struggle, join their world, marry and raise children in it, watch the children grow up, wonder what sorts of choices the children will make when they take their first solo flights in the real world—and be filled with guilt and self-doubt, thinking, What might my life have been had I made one of the other choices?

For the past two hundred fifty years or so, on our side of the planet—Western civilization and its culture colonies: Australia, New Zealand, South Africa, Israel, other pockets here and there—certain individuals have been using one of the oldest forms of communication known to our species, the story, in a most unique way. Employing it as an instrument for imaginative mapmaking, they have focused it upon the tense line of relationship that has come about in the modern period between people from small and particular worlds, and the systems of value—secular, religious, political—with which those people have entered into conflict, for any or all of the realities that have given rise to contemporary life: rapid industrialization and urbanization; the deterioration of rural life; the astonishing successes and dangers of science and technology; the easy availability of alternate models of the human experience; the growing awareness by workers of managerial exploitation; the general democratization of Western society; the ease of communication; the expansion of global trade; the new sobering visions of the clockwork of creation bequeathed us by Copernicus, Darwin, and Freud.

The story is one of the ways we give configuration to the dense waves of disorderly perceptions that incessantly impinge upon our consciousness; it is a form of model-making activity which we use to think and shape the world, to explore with words and images realms of experience heretofore sealed to us, to map those experiences by means of language charged and heightened by the imagination, and to transmit those models to one another, thereby adding them to the pool of accumulating knowledge about ourselves and our world.

Take *Huckleberry Finn*, as an example. A child can read *Huckleberry Finn*, but it is hardly a child's book. In its early pages the woman raising Huck turns out to be a bit of a hypocrite with her advice about not smoking. Soon afterward, Huck's father tries to kill him. Huck quickly lights out for the river.

Scholars have pointed out how the book is structured. Huck is traveling on a raft along the vast and rolling Mississippi, the river that drains and carries in its waters the heartland of America. On the banks of that river are towns. A town is a cluster of humans who have banded together for the purpose of acquiring, utilizing, expanding, and disseminating commerce and culture. It may be difficult for some of us to grasp this notion today, but we are at our most civilized in towns. Indeed, the word "civilization" comes from the Latin *civitas*, which means "city" or "city-state."

As Huck travels along the Mississippi, he stops at times in one or another of these centers of commerce and culture. People are tarred and feathered, one man is shot dead, there is brutality, violence, hypocrisy—almost every time he sets foot in civilization. But traveling on that raft, at first alone and then with the slave Jim, he finds himself on a voyage of moral self-discovery. He goes on the journey of modern Western humankind: the journey into the self.

The notion of the value of the self—individuality in and of itself, an identity entirely separate and distinct from community and embarked upon a quest for its own destiny—was virtually unknown until the modern period.

That journey leads Huck to the realization that his very conscience, which is telling him to return the slave Jim or he, Huck, will burn in Hell, is to be doubted. For Huck knows that it cannot be right to return Jim! Hence his conscience, formed in the world of Hannibal, is wrong, as is the value system of his early world.

The smoking incident; the clash with his father; the journey along the river: an ascending order of confrontations that ultimately lead Huck to break with the world that gave him life.

This polarization, this tension of opposites, between new self-engendered values and old communal ones, or between different value systems no matter how old or new—constitutes a fundamental motif of modern literature, from the cradle of the English novel, with the opening words in Richardson's *Pamela*—"Dear Father and Mother, I have great trouble, and some comfort, to acquaint you with"—to Fielding, Austen, Trollope, Dickens, Joyce; to Hawthorne, Melville, James, Cather, Fitzgerald, Hemingway, Faulkner, Bellow; to most working serious writers today. Clearly it is not the only motif—there is the different line that runs from Sterne to Nabokov to Gass, which I continue to enjoy. But it was the motif that affected me most as I was growing up and hungrily making my way through richly stocked stacks in public and private libraries.

As it turned out, my father and my Talmud teachers proved correct. Reading modern literature in a closed ancient world can turn out to be a dangerous business—especially if you accept with deadly seriousness what you read and are unaware that literary canonization simply means that a work is worth contending with and not that its vision of the world is to be regarded as absolute truth.

Reading steadily, I encountered an array of embattled individuals, in some instances the discord poignant yet cool, controlled, keeping to the bounds of civility; in others, hot, cruel, violent, all good form discarded, men and women reduced to bestiality.

I encountered a young English woman contending with the marriage mores of her society—Fanny in *Mansfield House* by Jane Austen; a French woman whose view of reality, shaped by her reading, led to disaster—Emma in *Madame Bovary* by Gustave Flaubert; individuals in contention with the bourgeois class of Germany during the decades preceding the First World War—in *Buddenbrooks* and *The Magic Mountain* by Thomas Mann; men and women caught up in static, stifling, turn-of-the-century Dublin—*Dubliners*, *A Portrait of the Artist as a Young Man*, and *Ulysses* by James Joyce; a woman trapped in the vacuousness of small-town Midwestern life in the United States during the early decades of this century—Carol Kennicott in *Main Street* by Sinclair Lewis; a man in confrontation with all of Western civilization and running from the horrors of a meaningless war in which tens upon tens of thousands of men were dying for words like king, kaiser, fatherland, motherland, glory, honor, sacrifice, courage, bravery, a civilization that seemed not to mind too much having its young men slaughtered in trench warfare but would throw up its arms in horror should a man fall in love with a woman, and they have a child out of wedlock. Which is the greater moral obscenity, Ernest Hemingway asks us in *A Farewell to Arms*, a civilization that slaughters its young men this way or this kind of love affair?

Those were among the many novels I read during that time. Mornings, Talmud. Evenings and weekends, literature. Year after year.

It seemed to me that nothing was sacred to the modern novelist, no value or inheritance so intrinsically sacrosanct that it could not be poked into, opened up, its parts removed, labeled, listed, and then reconstituted by the novelist's pen and imagination. The modern novel has been the stage for a steady march from drawing room and ballroom and dining room to bedroom and bathroom, from the niceties of church and social institutions to the vilest of brothels and factories and battlefields, from the pleasantries of casual conversation and polite society to unconscious psychological states and our most deeply repressed motives and passions.

Even the novel itself as an art form is not sacred to the novelist; it too has journeyed, through realism, naturalism, symbolism, minimalism to—what next? It has in the course of the journey attained a Huckleberry-Finn-like awareness of its own self, a self-consciousness which, like art in the hands of Picasso and music in the hands of Cage, has turned it upon its own inner clockwork and reason for being, and brought it to use its own forms, and unusual forms from other realms of expression, as subjects for art. Literature as the subject of literature, language writing about language rather than about the world—perhaps because it can no longer focus upon the chaotic brutality of our current existence and map the shifting complexities of contemporary values; it cannot deal with the primacy of possibilities, with a world that offers the self a panorama of endless promise from which there is absent a sense of rooted belonging. Promise without premise—a special sort of hell. So the artist makes his or her own art the premise of life. Myth died in this modern period of decreation, and the novel has done a long tracking shot of that death, while decreating itself in the process. For the modernist, the details of life were the center of attention: focus on the details, order them, understand them. An act of secular redemption. For the postmodernist, even the details no longer exist in stable form. Nothing is redeemable. All is flux. Now many look upon the artist as secular creator and prophet, as the only one capable of carving into some sort of significance the anarchic storms of contemporary experience, and perhaps finding new patterns and myths in the roiling and commonplace events of our present lives. Nothing is sacred to the serious novelist, save perhaps the act of writing.

That's what I learned about literature.

I entered the world of modern civilization by breaking through the walls of a small and particular culture that is more than three thousand years old.

I grew up with baggage on my shoulders: certain things *were* sacred. On streets and in schools, no one messed up my small world for me in an irreversible way. I had questions; teachers tried to answer them. I had problems; parents tried to cope with them.

More important, I had one teacher, a professor of English literature, who repeatedly was able to brighten my growing sense of the regions of benightedness in my small world. And most important of all, my parents lived what they taught me; they didn't teach me one standard of values, one pattern of behavior, and themselves live by another.

I entered my midteens and the world of literature while still appreciating my small world. Despite the parochialism around me, that appreciation grew over the years into an understanding of the unique way my world had come to construct the human experience. It grew during the same stretch of years and along a track that paralleled the one I was on in my journey through literature.

By the time I was in my late teens, it had become clear to me that my stable fundamentalist world could not long sustain the volatile voyeurism of modern literature, with its powerful lenses on alternate worlds, and that sooner or later the tracks would cease running parallel and would either start to cross one another, or run off in different directions.

The first meant possible collision; the second, certain separation. Yet I didn't want to leave my world entirely; there was much in it that seemed of intrinsic worth.

I began to realize that I had become like one of the characters in the novels I was reading: I was a battlefield for a confrontation of cultures. And after I published *The Chosen* I came to see it as a confrontation of a certain kind.

Raised in the very heart of a small and particular world, attending its best schools, learning how that world constructs the human adventure on this planet, I had come upon an element—literature—at the heart of the general secular world in which we all live. Literature is a major endeavor of Western humankind. It is one of the ways modern Western men and women think the world.

I have been calling this kind of encounter a *core-to-core culture confrontation.*

An individual growing up in the center of a small and particular world— for me, it was Orthodox Judaism, but it can be any world: Christian, Muslim, Native-American, African-American, Hispanic, secular, Australian aborigine, others—and encountering an element from the center of the umbrella civilization on the Western side of our planet. In my case, it was literature. But it can be any of the main elements of Western culture: science, philosophy, painting, sculpture, filmmaking, and so on. Core-to-core culture confrontation.

At the core of modern Western civilization reside, among many others, the following individuals: Rousseau, Diderot, Marx, Darwin, Freud, Einstein, Kafka, Joyce, Picasso, Stravinsky. It makes little difference whether we have or haven't studied Marx or Freud, read a word by Kafka or Joyce, seen a painting by Picasso, heard a bar of music by Stravinsky. The creations of those individuals pervade the air we breathe, light our world and serve us as maps for our own journeys.

At the core of my first culture—and here, substitute for yourselves others at the core of your early world if it differs from mine—reside, among others, an individual named Hillel, one of the greatest of the sages of the talmudic period; Akiba, a talmudic sage of heroic distinctiveness; Maimonides, the most innovative of the medieval rabbis; Ibn Ezra, for me the most daring of the medieval Spanish-Jewish commentators on the Bible; Rashi, by far the greatest of the Franco-German commentators on the Bible and Talmud; Isaac Luria, the most remarkable of the Jewish mystics; and the like.

Often the two cores are in harmony and generate little friction as they rub up against each other. At times, however, they see the world in very different ways. Someone caught up in and committed to both cultures simultaneously may suddenly find it necessary to navigate turbulent cultural waters. Commitments will have to be weighed, choices made. That is culture confrontation.

A culture is a very mysterious creation. We still do not fully understand how we go about originating cultures.

Those who know of such matters tell us that we've been around on this planet as a more or less recognizable species for about one hundred thousand years. When writing begins, about five or six thousand years ago, there are rich cultures already in place. In the history of culture, writing is not a creator of culture but a by-product.

Perhaps the beginnings of cultures were something like this. In the distant past, long before the start of writing, members of our species, located in various parts of the planet—an island, a desert, a river valley, a plateau, a chain of hills—felt the need to come up with collective responses to what I call the four-o'clock-in-the-morning questions. These are questions we don't like to ask ourselves too often during the day, and so we keep ourselves very busy instead. But sometimes they wake us in the early hours of the morning and hover over our heads in the darkness, and we lie there, listening to them:

What am I doing here?

Does anything that I do with my life really mean anything in any ultimate way?

What am I really ready to go to the barricades for?

What am I really teaching my children?

How can I ever hope to understand and communicate with another human being when I can barely understand and communicate with myself?

What is this thin ribbon of light I'm traversing between the darkness from which I came and the darkness toward which I am inevitably headed?

Four-o'clock-in-the-morning questions.

A culture is a series of hard responses to these ultimate questions—responses born of long-tested answers that are seen over time to be effective repressors of individual wants and life-enhancing for the group; responses that elicit loyalty, often to the death; responses unified by a recognizable style. We don't know how styles of culture developed, but we will recognize, say, an English style, a French, an Italian, a German style, a Japanese style. And when one set of these responses enters into confrontation with another, immense tension is often generated. And more often than not it is of little relevance where and when the confrontation occurs. It can take place in a library, a classroom, a sports field, a home, a street. Businessmen meeting at conventions; students encountering old manuscripts in a dusty library. You look at that other map of the human experience and say to yourself: Wait a minute, that way of looking at things seems to make an awful lot of sense. It's alluring, intriguing, compelling, convincing. Should I now start thinking of altering or discarding my own map of the world in order to take into account this new one?

Most people will turn away from such a confrontation: Who has the energy or the will to break apart one's established world and reshape its shards into a new vision?

In some cases, the confrontation might be so intense that one will not know how to react, and paralysis results. That's what happens to Michael, the boy in *The Promise*, the second of the novels.

Sometimes one culture will obliterate another culture. It depends upon where cultures are at in their development when the confrontation occurs: an old, doddering culture will be profoundly affected by a young, vigorous, seminal culture, as were Judaism and Christendom in their confrontations with the Enlightenment and modernism.

And sometimes, out of the tension of the confrontation, creativity ensues by way of response, ideas are born, music is composed, paintings are made, books are written—gold is given us, which we can mine for all the rest of our existence as a species.

Israelites enter a new land after a long wilderness wandering and encounter what we now know to have been the highly sophisticated, literate, feudal culture of ancient Canaan. Eight hundred years of culture war follow. Out of that war emerges a remarkable literature, elements of which consist of fusions of core elements of both cultures. Much of the Book of Psalms is a result of core-to-core culture confrontation: Canaanite literary forms and Israelite monotheistic content.

A medieval rabbi encounters the thought of a long-dead Greek pagan. The rabbi is awed by the mind of the pagan. It is inconceivable to him that his revealed religious tradition does not contain the thought of that pagan—how can the word of God be inferior in quality to the philosophy of a Greek?—or the ability to refute it. The rabbi writes one of the great works of medieval thought in which he subjects the tradition to radical reinterpretation. The tradition has never been the same since.

Decades later, a Catholic encounters the thought of that same Greek pagan. The Catholic is familiar with the work of the rabbi, and in response to the pagan creates some of the greatest works of medieval theology.

The rabbi—Maimonides. The Catholic—Aquinas. The Greek—Aristotle.

In our own time, one of the greatest painters who ever lived encountered what to him was a new—it was fairly old—way of depicting the human form. Out of the ensuing tension came a new way of seeing the world.

The painter—Picasso. The different way of depicting the human form—African art. The result—cubism and modern art.

Repeatedly in the history of our species, when cores of culture have entered into confrontation, out of the resulting tension—sometimes tumultuous, sometimes tranquil—has come creativity that has helped to move us that much farther away from the dark magic of our beginnings.

Any living culture will have at least two elements at its core: one fixed upon the past, the other facing the present and the future.

The Chosen is about two components of the small and particular world of Orthodox Judaism. The world of Danny Saunders, contemptuous of contemporary culture, gazes with intense and rigid faith upon a sacred past; the world of Reuven Malter, aware of the possibilities of new knowledge, opens itself to a resonating present; both are involved in a double confrontation with remarkable gifts or curses, depending upon one's point of view, given us by secularism: one, the window opened into our deepest selves by

Freudian psychoanalytic theory; the other, the political Zionism of Theo-
dore Herzl.

Danny Saunders is raised by his father in silence as an education in pain
and an antidote to his intellectual hubris. It is precisely this psychological
pain that brings Danny to Freud. And it is his pain that causes him to reach
out to Reuven and his nonfundamentalist reading of the tradition. Culture
irony!

What does one do with the truths one senses in an alien system of thought?
Is blindness to any possibility of new, threatening knowledge the price one
must pay for loyalty to one's small and particular world?

That's the dilemma that confronts Danny Saunders in *The Chosen*. . . .

The confrontations in the novels are quite deliberately arranged in an ascending order of complexity. Some are intellectual encounters, some are esthetic,
others are both.

Danny Saunders tries to resolve his problems with Freud through the
process of *culture compartmentalization*. He will carefully select those aspects of Freud's thought toward which he feels a measure of affinity: the use-
fulness of probing and charting the landscape of dreams; psychoanalysis as a
tool for exploring the human psyche, as an aid for the alleviation of suffering,
as a possible mapping of the origins of culture and the dark side of human
nature. With those Danny will come to terms, absorbing them and making the
necessary adjustments to his prior perception of the world.

But he can never accept Freud's anthropology, his view of instinct-driven
man, his assessment of the nature of religion, his bleak projection of human
destiny. Those, among others, he will discard as he goes about picking and
choosing his way through Freud, adopting this, dropping that, building walls
between himself and those aspects of Freudian thought with which he cannot
make peace — much as a contemporary physicist who is also a devout religion-
ist might claim that physics deals only with the material world and religion
deals with the world of the spirit, and the two are separate realms with different sets of premises.

One might ask: By what right does one go about picking, choosing, accepting, rejecting this or that element in another system of thought? Don't we
compromise intellectual honesty when we do that?

Well, perhaps. But we do it all the time. Indeed, the founding fathers of
modernism did precisely that when they skipped over Christendom, which

they abhorred, and entered into a cultural alliance with the more rational elements of Roman and Greek civilization, knowingly overlooking the cruelty, the greed, the hunger for power, the orgiastic mystery religions, and many of the other unpleasantries that were fairly commonplace features of those pagan cultures.

Danny Saunders relates to Freud as many of us do when we confront an intriguing, challenging, compelling, threatening body of ideas: we select out of those ideas those elements toward which we feel a measure of affinity; *those* we take into ourselves, the rest we ignore.

That's what Reuven Malter does in *The Promise.* He uses the methodology of text criticism on the Talmud, but not on the central text of Judaism, the Bible. To use it on the Bible would render the biblical text fluid. There would suddenly be no solid ground in Reuven's life, no core.

There is no logical way one can defend restricting the use of this method to the Talmud only, and refraining from using it on the Bible—other than to argue from the premise that the Bible was revealed to us by God and is therefore the bedrock of Jewish law, and once we start tampering with it— doubting this, emending that—all of Jewish law will begin to crumble. Hence, Reuven Malter walls away the Bible from this new methodology. . . .

Sixteen months as an officer with the American Army in Asia—the time I spent in Korea and Japan during the 1950's, after the end of the Korean War. Korea was a ravaged land; Japan, dense with culture and myth, still echoed with the war and the Bomb.

I found that the questions raised by my confrontations with those Asian cultures were profoundly disturbing, and in the end unanswerable.

Here are some of those questions:

I was taught by my parents and by teachers in the parochial schools I attended that Western civilization is inconceivable without its Jewish component; that Jews and Judaism are part of the weave of Western thought; that the world is richer for the presence of Jews. Yet I lived for sixteen months deep inside a world where "Jews" and "Judaism" were barely words in a dictionary—and that world seemed to find it not at all difficult to get along without Jews and Judaism; indeed, it seemed in certain matters a richer culture than the one into which I had been born. How was it possible for so vast a portion of the world to be so utterly unaffected by the absence of Jewish resonance?

I was always taught to be wary of the allure of pagan culture. Yet my sense of the beautiful was awakened in Asia. I saw there loveliness not only in the world of nature but also in the exquisite creations of human beings — creations dedicated to idols! I educated my eyes to the beauty in God's world by letting them feast upon the radiance I beheld in a pagan land. How was I to come to terms with such irony?

I remember walking one evening along the streets of Kyoto and suddenly feeling a sense of buoyancy, as if I had somehow been set free from my corporeal being and was now gliding slowly like some human bird above the shrines and temples of that ancient expanse of idolatrous sanctity. Walking along, I began to wonder about the source of that odd sensation, and it occurred to me that I was in a country that did not hate Jews. I don't know what Judaism means in Japan today — it can never mean what it meant in Europe, because there is in Japan no history of kinship with Christianity — but in my time there, few Japanese knew to distinguish between one white face and another. To feel myself in a land where I could never be hated simply for *being!* What a lightness that settled upon my soul! A world without anti-Semitism. Yet this was a *pagan* world, a world I had been taught to loathe, an idolatrous culture my ancestors had engaged in mortal conflict! How was I to make sense of that?

One winter afternoon, in a small Shinto temple in Tokyo, I saw an old man in a tattered brown coat and a gray fedora, praying before the figure of a goddess. His face covered by a long white beard; in his hands a prayer book. He swayed back and forth before the idol, an intensity of devotion on his aged features that reminded me immediately of the old people in the little synagogue where I would pray with my father as a child; the old men praying on the Day of Atonement, the most sacred of Jewish holy days, their bodies swaying, their voices murmurous, their faces luminous with the flame of passionate worship.

There I stood, watching an old man in an act of prayer, in a pagan temple.

I remember asking myself: What am I witnessing here? Is God, the God to whom I pray, listening to this old pagan's prayer? If God is *not* listening, why not? When can there ever be a more intense and more heartfelt expression of prayer than what I was then witnessing? And if the God to whom I pray *is* listening to this old pagan's prayer, then what are Judaism and Christianity all about?

I grew up in the years of the Depression, the Second World War and the Holocaust. All through my young life I had angry questions about the silence of God in the face of evil. Rarely would I think to utter them to parents or teachers. How repressed that rage was during my early years!

Once, during the Israel War of Independence, when the Old City of Jerusalem fell, I remember shouting to my father, "How could this happen? Where was God?"

It seemed to me that after the Holocaust, after the destruction of so many millions, after the loss of all—*all!*—the European branch of our family, God could at least have given us Jerusalem.

My father responded with a sudden flaring look of anger, but said nothing.

My father used to tell me that Jews suffered because we were the moral reconnaissance troops of the world—he had served nearly four years in the trenches in a Polish unit of the Austrian Army during the First World War, and he tended when excited to lapse into vivid military language—and reconnaissance troops, he would add, always took the highest casualties. There was in my mind some strange and terrible rationale for *Jewish* suffering.

In Korea I saw suffering I could not fathom, absurdly meaningless suffering endured by *pagans*, who had by chance been in the path of grinding empires. Why had *pagans* been subjected to such slaughter? What sense did *their* suffering make?

Gershon Loran grows up tremulous with uncertainty. His parents go off on a trip to Palestine, and are killed. His cousin joins the Air Force to fight in the Pacific, and is shot down, his body never recovered. He senses all around him the tenuousness of existence. It is in the suffering of pagans that he experiences the shredding of the veils of meaning he has built for himself. Mystic texts beckon to him, offer him strange solace in the mythic maps of meaning by which they chart the treacherousness of reality. And it is to those mystical texts that he repeatedly returns for navigational instructions—not for ultimate answers but for a way of holding on to the world as he lives his day-to-day life.

There were more questions, many more. To almost none of them have I come up with even remotely satisfying answers.

That core-to-core confrontation of cultures resulted not in compartmentalization or fusion but in *culture ambiguity*: Judaism simply one more culture among others, quite possibly no better and no worse than most. And no sense at all to human suffering. Gershon Loran keeps trying to navigate through a world in which satisfactory answers to the really hard questions — questions that bubble up to the surface of consciousness and then are quickly gone as the machinery of repression kicks in — may quite possibly be intrinsically unanswerable.

This invisible scaffolding — recondite, cerebral, perhaps bordering on pedantry — how does a writer of stories charge it with the drama of fictive life? How conceal it and yet make its presence known and felt? How bring to it the necessary passion that will enable it to penetrate varieties of culture envelopes?

That's the challenge that has faced me throughout my years as a writer of stories: to use that scaffolding as a structure for the stories and at the same time not only to make the reader an outside observer of a newly uncovered human experience but also to generate in him and her the powerful feeling of being vividly subjected to it, identified with it, overcome by it.

The sentences I write are steps in my search for the core of an intellectual-moral-emotional moment. That core has to consist of an idea-image or a series of idea-images that I can render in words. Idea and image constitute a single essence. I call that *essentialist writing*.

I look for images, ideas, feelings in which we can all participate, no matter who we are and what the small and particular worlds we came from; essentialist core images that will connect the reader to the scaffolding through conduits of ideas, small hairs rising on the back of the neck, unfamiliar sensations in the pit of the stomach.

Essentialist images: a baseball striking a player's eye; a caring father oddly silent in the presence of his son; a nosebleed on a roller coaster; a carnival game filled with promises made and broken; an old family photograph of a group of young men with weapons; a painting of a crucified woman; a crumpled sandcastle on a sandy beach; a man vanishing into the boiling chaos of the bombing of Guernica; the Hiroshima Peace Monument on a cold winter morning; a man carrying his little daughter to a hospital along dark rainswept cobblestone streets; a family hiding from the Germans in a sunless Paris apartment. Images thought and felt, images not overwhelmed by writing that repeatedly and dramatically calls attention to itself, essential elementary images, threaded to the invisible scaffolding.

• • •

Clearly we do not only confront the world from the unique perspective of core to core.

One can grow up in the core of a small and particular world and encounter only peripheral elements of the outside world. In Brooklyn one afternoon I take our tricolored Scotch collie out for a walk. Coming toward me along Eastern Parkway is a Hasidic boy, about five or six, walking with a dark-bearded man in his forties. The boy sees the dog, and pipes up to the man, in Yiddish, "Daddy, give a look, that's Lassie!"

I do not know how that boy, raised in a closed Hasidic home, knew about Lassie. Lassie is quite possibly one of those elements of a culture more caught than taught. But I don't think too many of us would be too hard put to admit that Lassie is not exactly a core element of Western civilization. Together with most of the pop culture that surrounds us, Lassie is essentially peripheral to Western culture. I like Lassie and enjoy much of pop culture. But I have no illusion as to where those elements are located in the spectrum of our civilization.

That little boy, located solidly in the heart of the Jewish tradition, at the moment of his encounter with my dog, experienced a *core-to-periphery culture confrontation*.

The baseball game in *The Chosen* is a core-to-periphery confrontation: Reuven, from the heart of his understanding of Judaism, encountering the angry periphery of Danny Saunders. And Reb Saunders, Danny's father, has a similar experience when he meets Reuven Malter: he regards the Malters and their modernist reading of the Jewish tradition as peripheral to Judaism. The book is an account of the two conflicting elements at the core of Jewish Orthodoxy and, at the same time, a record of Reuven's journey into the core of Danny's world.

In a core-to-periphery culture confrontation, the individual at the core of a tradition can, if he or she so wishes, meet with and, unless a threat is perceived, absorb whole elements from the periphery of another culture and not be changed to any significant degree. The French will watch all the American television we send them; it will not alter the essential nature of French civilization. Fundamentalists will use television, radio, comic strips, adventure stories—filling them with their core content, to advance their own causes. Generally, in a core-to-periphery confrontation, the core will hold firm.

And so we now have two ways that we encounter the world around us: core to core, and core to periphery.

Here is a third way. You can grow up along the periphery of a small and particular world; it was somehow never clearly taught by parents and teachers. Then you go off to a college or a university. The university is core in Western culture; it is the citadel of secularism. That's where the seminal ideas come from or go to for testing, packaging, transmission. Religious parents raise a son or daughter, don't transmit their values, send the offspring away to be educated. Six months or a year later the son or daughter is utterly transformed.

The reverse is true as well. Raise a child in a secular home, don't transmit a core of values, the child has no sense of self, of rootedness. Off goes the child, encounters the hot core of a religious cult, and is changed. It is difficult not to be swayed by an alluring core if you are only peripherally attached to your past, your beginnings, your self.

That is a *periphery-to-core culture confrontation.*

Saul Bellow's *Herzog*: a picture of periphery-to-core culture confrontation. Herzog along the periphery of his Jewish world and in the center of the university world.

Here is a fourth way we encounter the world around us. You can grow up along the periphery of your small world *and* along the periphery of the general culture. You know neither world well.

That is a *periphery-to-periphery culture confrontation*: a rub-up of ignorances that generates effluvia, aberrations, ugliness.

Much of modern literature—because of the democratization of the novel, and because many novelists have themselves only experienced periphery-to-periphery confrontation—makes this brittle aspect of contemporary life the focus of exploration. Alienated, bewildered, contentious individuals, belonging nowhere, tenuously connected to culture and community, many committed only to the hermeneutics of doubt: the Man from Underground, the shadows populating the world of Kafka, Jake Barnes, Lieutenant Henry, Catherine Barkley, Sister Carrie, Rabbit Angstrom, people in the work of Philip Roth.

For the texture of core-to-core confrontation, read James Joyce's *A Portrait of the Artist as a Young Man*. Stephen Dedalus, from the core of Irish Catholicism, in confrontation with the core of modern secularism: literature. And read *Buddenbrooks* and *The Magic Mountain* by Thomas Mann. And most of Ibsen. And *Brideshead Revisited* by Evelyn Waugh.

• • •

Clearly, this is not a spatial model. "Core" and "periphery" are meant to be abstract loci along a cultural plane. How can we know with certainty what is core and what periphery? Moses and Jesus are core. Plato and Aristotle are core. Jefferson and Lincoln are core. Marie Curie is core. Do things change position on the culture spectrum? Of course they do, especially in a living culture. Where do we put jazz in the spectrum of our culture? How do we evaluate the culture form known as the comic strip, now being used to deal with the Holocaust? Do we continue to reassess our core? Yes. And novelists will track and contribute to that reassessment. Only dead cultures, like dead volcanoes, have stable cores.

We live in a tumultuous world of culture, and are rarely fully engaged in only one form of confrontation all the time. The fact is that at one moment we might be core to core, at another core to periphery, at a third periphery to core, at a fourth periphery to periphery, and back again—depending upon how much we know and how we feel about our deepest selves at each different moment of confrontation. We live in a complex, distracting, often confounding tangle of ideas. Often we are different beings with each idea we encounter. We are the *relationships* between ourselves and the elements of the world around us. And those relationships by and large fall into one or another of the categories of the model I've presented here.

Some questions:

Is anti-Semitism core in Western civilization?

Is core necessarily elitist? Where do we locate the ongoing stream of folk culture transmitted from generation to generation that significantly shapes the way we see the world?

Is it not possible for periphery so to inundate a culture that it becomes core?

Is the demonic as much core as the saintly?

Does the contemporary blurring of reality and illusion affect the distinction between core and periphery?

What are core and periphery in deconstructed creation?

Those are not the only questions.

Not so long ago, around the turn of the last century, we thought that if we discovered the truth about ourselves and our world we might live in bliss.

"I wanted to be part of this new age that was dawning," says Rebecca in Ibsen's play *Rosmersholm*, "and in on all the new ideas."

As this century begins its turn, spinning us into the new millennium, we know that the truths we discovered have left us diminished and sundered.

We're told that a woman who has been raped reports the atrocity in incoherent bits and pieces. To questions, she will often respond with contradictory answers. Images vivid one moment dissolve the next. Reality, shattered by trauma, becomes fluid, prismatic, kaleidoscopic, chaotic.

When the bits and pieces begin to become coherent; when she starts shaping them into a story, any kind of story—the process of healing has begun.

It might be imagined that in the eighteenth and nineteenth centuries, the God of the religion of Sinai and Jerusalem began further to withdraw His being from our world in order to make room for a new creation: the revelation of unpleasant truths. For a while that revelation was radiant, and we seemed able to handle it. Then in our century it broke apart in two world wars, the Holocaust, disillusionment. Infinite shards of creative light spilled into the darkness of decreation.

In our time, sundered by truths about ourselves and our world that yield more trauma than comfort, we often look upon story-making as the beginning of healing. If stories merely entertain, if they serve only to anesthetize us, to paper over gritty truths, we will continue to be Emma Bovary to our new understanding of the world. And tales of self-pitying despair; and clever, titillating, morally evasive language games—is that the entire tomorrow of literature? I hope not, unless we want the novel to perish of anemia. To take those new hard truths, gaze deeply into their essential nature, come to terms with what they really tell us about ourselves; to turn those truths into the cores of stories about human beings, into vivid new visions of our selves, into mythologies that shape through language and idea-images new maps of our place on this fragile planet, in this violent universe, among the stars and gases and black holes that stud the mind-numbing expanses all around us—that's the essential task of a writer.

How we make those maps, what goes on in the head and the heart as we try in our daily lives to make structures out of incoherence, and how we might map the mapmaking itself—that is what has lately begun to interest me.

I've been writing about people and events that were of particular concern to me and to others like me as I grew up and began to make my way into this world. My hope has been that if I wrote about those people and events honestly, with simplicity of language and invisibility of structure, and with as much controlled focus as I could bring to bear upon them, that my world would open up, and others would be caught up in it just as I was once caught up in the small and particular worlds of *A Portrait of the Artist as a Young Man* and *Brideshead Revisited*. I've been writing about the dreams, thoughts, and passions of individuals caught up in core-to-core culture confrontation; how they relate to parents, friends, teachers, peers, to themselves, when their world is suddenly challenged by an alternate powerful map of meaning.

Someone asked James Joyce why he only wrote about Dublin. The response, found in Richard Ellmann's biography, is worth citing. It gives us some notion of Joyce's view of the nature and task of literature:

> For myself I always write about Dublin, because if I can get to the heart of Dublin, I can get to the heart of all the cities of the world. In the particular is contained the universal.

A novel is about particulars: the commonplace grittiness of life as reimagined by someone with a facility for setting down images with words on paper and making a map so rich in detail and resonance that it will become eyeglasses of sorts, worn by readers who will forever see the world of the writer through those lenses. No one who reads Tolstoy can ever see Russia the same way after finishing Tolstoy as he or she might have seen it before coming to Tolstoy. No one who reads Kafka and Joyce can ever see the inner world of humankind the same way after finishing Kafka and Joyce as he or she might have seen it before coming to Kafka and Joyce. The great writers create maps that affect our view of the world and help us to chart our outer and inner destinies on this planet.

A final word.

On occasion someone will ask me: Why do you write only about Jews? I now answer that I have used Jews much as Ibsen used Norwegians. People will come to understand that in time.

10c

By tradition & unvoiced unanimity to a single area of study: Talmud. Virtuosity in Talmud was the most sought after achievement by every student of a yeshiva, for it was the automatic guarantee of a reputation for brilliance.

Danny attended the small yeshiva established by his father. Williamsburg area, in town... away, I attended the yeshiva in which my father taught. This latter yeshiva was somewhat looked down upon by the students of the other Jewish parochial schools of the area; it offered more English subjects than the government required minimum, & it taught its Jewish subjects in Hebrew rather than Yiddish. Most of the students who attended this yeshiva were children of immigrant Jews who preferred to regard themselves as having been emancipated from the fervid ghetto mentality typical of the other Jewish parochial schools in the neighborhood.

Danny & I would probably never have met .... [Pg. 11 top]

I sat down on the asphalt flung the ball with both hands over my eye... I felt a flow of pain run through my head to the back of my neck.

New chapter: I woke a few minutes later in a terror on my way to... "where are we going?" — "what do we pray to a hospital?"

PLOT OUTLINE
- Belgian Bulge episode, they follow war together; Don & Bob, fathers
- The news of the holocaust comes out: Don, Bob, two fathers.
- End of war episode - May 1945: Death of Roosevelt first; Atom bomb. FACE OF OLD JEWS
- Sept. 1946 - College. Don goes there to study with a particular Rebbi...
- ISRAEL—DON, BOB, FATHERS, FRIENDS, ON VOTE ---- REACTION OF SOME HASIDIM...
- 1950 - Bob enters rabbinate & Dan/droppers; & go to P.A.; sent by yeshiva.
- Trip to Berkeley, meets Karen & Don. Then Dan vanishes again then Phila & Cantor & Dan
- Conversation between Bob & father during rabbinate period; solution ended up wanting to change himself alone. Conversation re. and I would be a surgeon; but Bob & Talmud teacher...
- But meets path in Phila or P.A. ....

Pages from the early manuscript, with author's notes and plot outline.

fumblers into the top team of our league. His name was Mr. Galanter, all of us wondered why he was not off somewhere fighting in the war.

During my two years with the team, I had become quite adept at second base & had also developed a swift, underhand pitch which I was frequently able to flatten into a drop that would tempt a batter into a swing but would cross into a curve at the last moment & slide just below the player, but for a strike. Mr. Galanter always began a ball game by putting me at second base & would use me as a pitcher only in very tight moments, because, as he put it once, "My baseball philosophy is grounded on the defensive solidarity of the infield."

That afternoon we were scheduled to play the winning team of the other neighborhood league, the Rabbi Abraham Joshua team, a team with an reputation for wild, offensive slugging and poor fielding. Mr. Galanter was counting upon our solid infield to act as a solid, defensive front against their slugging. Throughout the warm-up period, with only our team in the yard, he kept thumping his right fist into his left palm & shouting at us to be a solid defensive front.

"No holes," he shouted from near home plate. "No holes, you hear? A butterfly could get between you and Malter. That's it, Schwartz, what are you doing, looking for partridge? This is a ballgame. The enemy's on the ground. That throw was wide, Goldberg. Throw it like a shortstop. Give him the ball again. Throw it. Good. Like a shortstop. Very good. Keep the infield solid. No offensive holes in this war."

We batted & threw the ball around, & it was warm & sunny, & there was the smooth, happy feeling of the summer soon to come, & the tight excitement of the ballgame. We wanted very much to

PART TWO

OTHER VOICES

A ZWISCHENMENSCH ("BETWEEN PERSON") IN THE CULTURES

Daniel Walden

University of Pennsylvania
December 15, 2002

Born in 1929 in the Bronx, New York—his father, Benjamin Potok, a Belzer Hasid and his mother, Molly, a descendant of the Hasidic Ryzner dynasty—Chaim Tzvi grew up in an Orthodox Jewish family in an Orthodox Jewish neighborhood. Attending a cheder, a primary Jewish parochial school, his interest in and talent for painting came to the fore when one summer his yeshiva inexplicably hired an artist to give a course in painting to the children. That was his first step into the world of Western art. In his childhood, what Joyce was to Jesuits, painting was to Talmud. Deep into the study of Torah, and Talmud, he had begun that journey that would put his focus within the core of the Jewish tradition in confrontation with the world we all inhabit, the world of Western secular humanism. At the same time he was reading *Ivanhoe* and *Treasure Island* in his high school English subjects, he was browsing in the public library and came across Evelyn Waugh's *Brideshead Revisited*, an adult novel about upper-class British Catholics. He remembered asking himself, "What did he do to me? How do you do this kind of thing with words?" That's where his commitment to write began.

What Chaim Potok discovered as he was writing *The Chosen* (1967), his first published book, was a cultural dynamic, a "culture war." Within the overarching culture in which we all live is the culture we call Western humanism—what Peter Gay calls "modern paganism"—and within that culture is a whole spectrum of subcultures. What happens is that these subcultures clash in a variety of ways with the overarching culture. What he seems to have stumbled across was a kind of core-to-core cultural confrontation.

To that point he had been committed to study. After reading *Brideshead Revisited* and soon afterward Joyce's *A Portrait of the Artist as a Young Man*, a strange hunger arose to create worlds of his own out of words on paper, to tell stories. You have to understand, explained Potok, that Judaism is a text-oriented world; it is a word world. And to study is the central text of the tradition. It is a commandment. Not to study the text is a transgression. It was this that concerned the rabbi, the teacher of Talmud. He sensed that in some strange and unexpected fashion, Potok had made contact with a fundamental element from the general civilization in which we all live—with the world of Newton, Voltaire, Diderot, Rousseau, Nietzsche, and Freud. He had made contact with Western literature.

This powerful movement that the young Potok joined was part of a revolt of the modern contest against the grip of the emerging middle class, involving those individuals using the story in order to act as a mouthpiece against the ordinary, the callousness, the hypocrisy, the games they witnessed everywhere and felt they could no longer tolerate. He attempted to track one element of this confrontation; that is, ideas from the heart of one culture crashing up against ideas from the heart of another culture is what happens for individuals caught in what he called a core-to-core confrontation—in his case, the rigidity of his Hasidic upbringing and Freudian psychoanalytic theory. For example, Reuven Malter, in *The Promise*, was in confrontation with the Jewishness that he still loved. For *In the Beginning*'s David Lurie, given his father's very militant Jewishness, all was in confrontation with a radical new way of looking at the central text of all Western traditions—the Bible. *The Book of Lights*, the most difficult of Potok's novels to read and fully grasp, the novel about the atomic bomb, dealt with one individual's confrontation with that core element of Western civilization and its effect on the world of Asia. *Davita's Harp*, a book about a young woman's struggles, was based in part on his wife's experiences in an Orthodox world.

But Potok was also concerned with images and metaphors. The central metaphor of *The Chosen* is "combat of various kinds," the central metaphor of *The Promise* is "people gambling and winning or losing," and the central metaphor in *The Book of Lights* is "the mystery and the awe that some of us sense in the grittiness of reality." True, these metaphors are visual, which brings up the connection between metaphors, visualizing, and painting. Artists, to Potok, possessed the power to create metaphoric visions of reality, which is why Picasso's *Guernica* was a central element of his life. Picasso changed the way we look at the world; *Guernica* became the most significant achievement in this century of the redescriptive power of the artist. The fact is that an artist deals in images, and the Jewish tradition, embodied in the second commandment, was against image making, because image making was part of ancient worship. All through the Middle Ages and into the Renaissance, Jewish law saw Christianity as essentially an idolatrous civilization. As a result there were no Jewish motifs in Western art, except for a few introduced by Rembrandt and a few others. In the modern period, Christianity was replaced by secular humanism, all of the Christological elements became attenuated, and the Crucifixion, as a salvationist motif, became a motif for suffering and lost its salvationist tonality. But, he felt, in using this the artist was not violating Jewish law; what he was violating was an aesthetic line, for in the eyes of the Jews, the Orthodox Jew especially, the Crucifixion immediately triggers images of Jewish blood and the deicide charge.

Chaim Potok, a different kind, a new kind of Jewish writer, has written as a Jew and because he is a Jew. His version of the American Jew has never left the traditional Jewish community, although from age fourteen or so, growing up in the Bronx, New York, he began to understand that "the compression of urban existence, the living mix of peoples and cultures in my Bronx world, made possible for me a rich variety of cultural confrontations." This conflict between his traditional Jewish background and the echoing world he longed to embrace led to his perception of culture confrontation in urban America. As he put it in an interview, "In *The Chosen*, for example, the heart of the Jewish tradition, which is represented by the two boys, Danny and Reuven, that I write about, comes into contact with an element right from the heart of the umbrella civilization in which we all live today, with secular humanism." In short, having read Evelyn Waugh's *Brideshead Revisited* as a teenager and entered a new tradition, modern literature, he came to recognize that fundamental to that new tradition "was a certain way of thinking the world; and basic to that was the binocular vision of the iconoclast, the individual who grows up inside inherited systems of value and, while growing, begins to recoil from the games, masks, and hypocrisies he sees all around him."

By the time he was eighteen or nineteen, young Potok had begun to experience what would later be called a core-to-core culture confrontation. Significantly, all the disciplines he encountered that were alien, the exciting ideas, were from the core of Western culture; he and the people he came from were in the core of the subculture. In his case, having been formed by his very urban, very Jewish upbringing in the Bronx, but meeting with the umbrella culture, his urban and intellectual and literary wanderings produced a "Zwischenmensch," a "between person."

Basic to every Potok novel are two questions: (1) how to live as an observant Jew in a secular society, and (2) to what degree one can hold to the tradition of Orthodox separateness in a secular society. In *The Chosen* and *The Promise*, Danny Saunders and Reuven Malter symbolize the two poles within Orthodox Judaism, the Orthodox and Hasidic. At the same time, there is seen a confrontation between Western secular humanism and religious orthodoxy. In *My Name Is Asher Lev*, however, the realm of aesthetics is the subject of the book, a very different realm to navigate in the Jewish tradition. In *In the Beginning*, the confrontation is between the core of Judaism and modern Western anti-Semitism.

In *The Chosen*, set in the urban Crown Heights and Williamsburg sections of Brooklyn, a baseball game brings together Danny, son of the rebbe and thus heir to the Hasidic dynasty, and Reuven, son of a modern Orthodox Talmudic textual scholar. Reb Saunders, the tzaddik (the Hasidic sect's spiritual leader), believing that there is a danger that his gifted son's soul might be dominated by mind, communicates to him through silence; in this way he feels that he will foster the values of heart and soul. Mr. Malter, viewed by the Hasidim as one of the *mitnagdim* (a Jewish rational intellectual) who denies the basic Jewish religious tenets, and is thus one of the *apikorsim*, fuses the best of secular learning with the best in Talmudic scholarship. What cannot be predicted is that Danny will decide to become a psychologist while remaining an observant Jew, which means he is abdicating his role as the heir to his father's Hasidic leadership. Meanwhile, in a significant crossing pattern, Reuven decides to become a rabbi; from his point of view, such subjects as symbolic logic, math, and secular philosophy fuse the sacred and the secular. Each is combining two cultures. Each is reflecting his and Potok's own attempts as a "between person" to explicate the role of Judaism in a secular society.

In *The Chosen* and *The Promise*, Potok's emphasis is on Jewish scholarship and study in an Orthodox milieu in Brooklyn. Family, neighborhood, and synagogue are beautifully drawn; they are a necessary environment. True, physical poverty is present, but spiritually there is richness. Only from outside the ghetto do the influences impinge. Whether from the radio or the newspaper, or from friends or acquaintances, the news of World War II, the Holocaust, and the Senator Joseph McCarthy charges come through; from liberal and progressive Jews like Rachel Gordon (who learns to appreciate James Joyce at Brooklyn College), further cracks in Hasidism appear.

Probably as a direct result of his interest in the tensions of faith and scholarship in his first two books, Potok's third book, *My Name Is Asher Lev*, concentrates on the tensions between members of one Orthodox family and, in particular, on the possible aesthetic dimensions. Asher must become an artist, from within or without a society that doesn't recognize art for art's sake or its Western cultural (including Christian and pagan) antecedents. In his first-person identity as "the notorious and legendary Lev of the *Brooklyn Crucifixion*," as "a traitor, an apostate," he has to confront his father's duty and Jewish culture as a young man devoted to art, divorced from the history of his people. What reconciles him is suffering; he learns that his relatives, and millions of Jews, suffered because they were Jews. In this context, with signals coming from all sides, he uses the aesthetic model of the Crucifixion to depict his mother's suffering in the *Brooklyn Crucifixion* because he has no comparable aesthetic mold in his own religious tradition. The point, as Potok has explained, is that "for Asher Lev, the cross is the aesthetic motif for solitary, protracted torment." Potok believes that any artist functioning in the secular would who has used the cross "has emptied the cross of its Christological vicarious atonement content and uses it as a form only." Again, as in *The Chosen* and *The Promise*, a between person's concerns are demonstrated, except that this time the lessons of history are central.

In *In the Beginning*, Max Lurie, a Jew impressed into the Polish Army who realized he was not a full citizen, is the vehicle for David Lurie's story. At issue is anti-Semitism. Eddie Kulanski, for example, hates Jews with a "kind of mindless demonic rage"; "his hatred bore the breeding of a thousand years." At the end, having felt the suffering of the Holocaust, David, walking along the Hudson River, recognizes that the death camps have become a part of him. From the home and the yeshiva to Poland and the camps and back, from the isolated Orthodox and Hasidic ghettos of Williamsburg and Crown Heights, from Genesis's *berashith* ("in the beginning") to David's remembered prophetic bar mitzvah reading from Amos, Potok moves from despair to hope, to the restoration of the health of the people of Israel.

When he was a chaplain in Korea, Chaim Potok realized that his traditional Jewish education had not prepared him for a culture that did not know or care about Jews or Judaism, and it had not prepared him for a "confrontation with the beautiful and the horrible in the world of oriental human beings." In *Wanderings*, therefore, where the emphasis is on the influences of Egypt, Greece, Rome, Islam, Christianity, and modern secularism, he noted that the Jewish people were acculturated but not absorbed. As a witness to that process, as a part of that venture, Potok felt that "my people is now engaged in an attempt to create for itself a third civilization." What is needed is for Judaism "to rebuild its core from the treasures of our past, fuse it with the best in secularism, and create a new unity, and take seriously the meaning of the emancipation." As a rabbi, as a religious scholar, as a secular intellectual in the Western tradition, as an American, as a Zwischenmensch, and as a novelist, Chaim Potok was involved in the struggle to maintain the viability of Judaism as a living civilization.

In interview after interview, and especially in his books and articles, Chaim Potok tried to explain those events that transformed him and what resulted. When he read Waugh's *Brideshead Revisited*, he realized that challenging questions could be put down in words. When he served in Korea in 1956 for sixteen months, he understood that the world he had known was now relativized. When he saw Picasso's *Guernica*, he found a metaphor for life and suffering. In sum, he saw a continuing struggle between tradition and modernity, a struggle between Judaism for its own sake and Judaism in the wider world. What he as an individual was trying to achieve were his goals—that is, his sense of authenticity, his sense of self, vis-à-vis his place in community. The tension is what he was trying to explore in his books. As a writer, as a rabbi, as a teacher—in all three—he was trying to understand and explain the forces that exist and the culture confrontation that he saw as Judaism, traditional and modern, came into contact with the world we all know, the technologized, secular humanist, religiously driven societies of the second and now third millennium.

THE CHOSEN

by Chaim Potok

FOR THE FIRST FIFTEEN YEARS of our lives, Danny and I lived
within five blocks of each other and neither of us knew of
the other's existence.

Danny's block was heavily populated by the followers of
his father, Russian Hasidic Jews. They drank tea from samovars, sipping it through cubes of sugar held between their
teeth; they talked loudly, occasionally in Russian, most often in a Russian Yiddish, and were fierce in their loyalty to
Danny's father. Three or four such Hasidic sects populated
the Williamsburg area of Brooklyn during the Depression, each with
its own rabbi, its own little synagogue, its own fierce loyalties.

The sidewalks of Williamsburg were cracked squares of
cement, the streets paved with asphalt that softened in the
stifling summers and broke apart into potholes in the bitter
winters. Many of the houses were brownstones, set tightly together. In these houses lived Jews, Irish, Germans, and some
Spanish Civil War refugee families. Most of the stores were
run by Gentiles, but some were owned by Orthodox Jews, members

First page of typescript.

THE CHOSEN

The Hasidim and the Orthodox

Edward A. Abramson

Many non-Jews think that the Jewish community is a homogeneous one with each member having substantially the same beliefs as the other. While there is less sectarianism among Jews than Christians, there is a wide divergence in the interpretation of law and ritual among Liberal, Reform, Conservative, Orthodox, and Hasidic Jews. Hasidic Jews are the most extreme in their beliefs, feeling that they adhere to the only correct form of Judaism and by so doing are fulfilling God's will.

Hasidism arose in eighteenth-century Poland as a reaction against the formal learning and intellectuality stressed by the rabbinic Judaism of the time. This learning was largely restricted to discussion and study of the Talmud, a collection of sixty-three books usually set out in eighteen folio volumes. The Talmud consists of civil, religious, and ethical laws based upon Jewish teaching and biblical interpretation that was originally oral and was passed down over the ages from Israel's earliest history. Around 200 C.E., Rabbi Judah the Prince collated them into the *Mishnah*. Scholars studied the *Mishnah* closely, their discussions being printed as the *Gemara*. The Talmud is the *Mishnah* and *Gemara* together. There are two Talmuds, one produced in Palestine and one in Babylon at each of the two great academies. The Palestinian Talmud was never completed, so the one usually studied and considered more authoritative is the Babylonian Talmud, finished about 500 C.E. It is the greatest work of Jewish religious literature after the Bible itself and has had a profound effect upon Jewish life and thought.

The difficulty of the Talmud meant that it was accessible to only a very small number of individuals who would often keep themselves aloof from the mass of the people. It was in this situation that Israel Baal Shem began to preach that the way to serve God was not through scholarship, study, and learning but through piety, love, and prayer. The Baal Shem (literally "Master of the Name") also stressed joy and emotion in worship, even through the use of song and dance. He was a charismatic individual, and many who were skeptical of his practices were won over. Eventually this included almost half of the Jews in Eastern Europe, who referred to him as the "Baal Shem Tov," the "Master of the Good Name" in recognition of his saintly nature.

The established religious authorities counted themselves as *Mitnagdim* (opponents) and were determined to destroy the new movement which they saw as heretical. They did not succeed, but great bitterness grew between the two groups, which is reflected in Potok's first novel, *The Chosen*, where Reb Saunders, his son Danny, and the Hasidic sect to which they belong are compared in terms of their attitudes toward things religious and secular with David Malter, his son Reuven, and the Orthodox group that holds their loyalties. Unlike the Vilna Gaon, the eighteenth-century leader of the *Mitnagdim*, David Malter is somewhat more compassionate and understanding of Reb Saunders's position, since he appreciates that "the fanaticism of men like Reb Saunders kept us alive for two thousand years of exile. If the Jews of Palestine have an ounce of that same fanaticism and use it wisely, we will soon have a Jewish state."[1]

In spite of this understanding which David Malter shows, when he hears that Reb Saunders's is raising Danny in silence his reaction is closer to that of the eighteenth-century opponent: "He sat up straight on the bed, his body quivering. 'Hasidim!' I heard him mutter, almost contemptuously. 'Why must they feel the burden of the world is only on their shoulders?'" (266). This viewpoint is shared by the Orthodox Jews in the synagogue where he prays with his son.

This distaste with Hasidism is based upon their self-righteousness; the enclosed nature of their communities; what is often seen as the dry scholasticism of their methods of studying the Talmud, especially surprising since their beginnings were rooted in a rebellion against this very scholasticism; the anti-Zionism of the Williamsburg Hasidim; and, perhaps most importantly, the position and role of the *tzaddik* within their communities.

Louis Jacobs has written:

Hasidism is hardly intelligible without the doctrine of the *Zaddik*, the spiritual superman whose holy living not only provides his followers with inspiration for their lives but who raises them aloft with him through the spiritual powers that are his. . . .

The central idea in this connection is that the *Zaddik's* prayer on behalf of his followers can achieve results far beyond the scope of their own puny efforts at prayer. . . . God has delivered into his hands the means whereby the flow of divine grace can either be arrested or encouraged to flow. All depends on the *Zaddik*.[2]

The reaction of non-Hasids to this set of beliefs is that they border on idolatry and have no place in true Jewish belief. Jews are supposed to approach God directly, intermediaries not being required. A rabbi is someone who knows more about Jewish law than a layman, but a rabbi is not necessary in order for religious services to be held. Any Jew who can gather a *minyan* (ten Jewish males) may conduct a religious service. Indeed, a Jewish proverb states that "Nine rabbis do not make a minyan, but ten cobblers do." In other words, the overwhelming centrality which the Hasidim give to their rabbis is not shared by most non-Hasidic Jews.

Potok presents this conflict in *The Chosen*. Reuven Malter is astonished at the manner in which Reb Saunders is treated by his followers, particularly when Danny tells him that his entire community uprooted from Russia and traveled to America because Reb Saunders said that they should go. They followed him, Danny says, because "He's a *tzaddik*." To Reuven, however, this explanation is not sufficient:

> "I can't understand how Jews can follow another human being so blindly."
> "He's not just another human being."
> "Is he like God?"
> "Something like that. He's a kind of messenger of God, a bridge between his followers and God."
> "I don't understand it. It almost sounds like Catholicism." (122)

This virtual deification of Reb Saunders extends to Danny, who is expected to inherit his father's office and is assumed also to have taken on the mantle of his sanctity. Thus, an aged Hasid with a white beard touches Danny's arm reverently, a gesture that Reuven finds most distasteful. As an Orthodox Jew, Reuven believes that he is following the 613 commandments set out for Jews as best he can. Hasidism appears to be an anachronism, and one with some highly questionable features.

As with most fanatical religious groups, the Hasidim are firmly convinced that their way of approaching God is right and all other ways are wrong. There is, however, a further level of belief among Hasids. They believe that their rebbe is right, has the only entirely true way of performing the various rituals, and places proper emphasis upon different aspects of the faith. Each rebbe stresses slightly different aspects of Judaism: certain prayers may be stressed instead of others; different interpretations of Jewish law may occur; the length of various services may be different; the attitude toward other Jews and non-Jews will vary from one rebbe to another and, therefore, extend to his followers. The results of these Hasidic beliefs are depicted throughout *The Chosen*, particularly in relation to conflicts between Hasidic and Orthodox Jewish beliefs.

The dramatic beginning to the novel turns a baseball game into a holy war. Reuven states that his school is looked down upon because it is filled with pupils who are interested in getting away from the ghetto mentality that pervades other Brooklyn Jewish schools. The Hasidim consider observant Jews like Reuven little better than heathen, and Danny threatens to "kill you *apikorsim*":

> The word had meant, originally, a Jew educated in Judaism who de-
> nied basic tenets of his faith, like the existence of God, the revela-
> tion, the resurrection of the dead. To people like Reb Saunders, it also
> meant any educated Jew who might be reading, say, Darwin, and who
> was not wearing side curls and fringes outside his trousers. I was an
> *apikoros* to Danny Saunders, despite my belief in God and Torah, be-
> cause I did not have side curls and was attending a parochial school
> where too many English subjects were offered and where Jewish
> subjects were taught in Hebrew instead of Yiddish, both unheard-of-
> sins. . . . (30–31)

The Hasidim have suffered even more than other Jews because of their purposeful visibility; that is, they have throughout their history worn their Jewish identity before the world. During the Nazi era in Europe, they suffered savage persecution. After the war, those rebbes who survived gathered together those of their people who remained and took them to America or what was then Palestine to try to reestablish their communities. They tried to move their culture intact from one continent to another and to preserve it in the face of strong assimilatory pressures. Whereas many Orthodox and other Jews were concerned to blend as much as possible into American society, the Hasidim enclosed themselves in their own communities and did not suffer problems of whether or not it was desirable to become a part of the new country. Thus, in one sense, they had an easier time in America than less "enlightened" Jews: they knew precisely who they were and what values they wanted to retain. In their community in the Williamsburg section of Brooklyn, which is where *The Chosen* is set, Hasidim who originated largely from Hungary, but also from Poland, set up tightly organized groups. As Solomon Poll points out: "Thus among the Hasidim of Williamsburg are the most outspoken separatists. By isolating themselves, they try to (a) re-create a traditional society that they have transplanted from Europe, (b) divert threats of assimilation by the secular world outside, and (c) combat internal change."[3]

Hasidim outside Williamsburg are usually much more open to outsiders. Indeed, the Habad-Lubavitch, located in the Crown Heights section of Brooklyn; the Bostoner, located in Boston; and the Bratslaver Hasidim, located in various parts of New York City as well as in Jerusalem, all seek converts to their type of Hasidism from their fellow Jews. The Satmar Hasidim, who are the largest group in Williamsburg, are probably the ones on which Potok modeled Reb Saunders and his Hasidim. Their extremism provided Potok with a strong dramatic contrast to the more broad-minded Orthodoxy of David Malter although, as mentioned, members of his synagogue dislike the Hasidim almost as much as the Hasidim dislike them. As with Reb Saunders's group, the Satmar are anti-Zionist, and Potok uses the struggle to create a Jewish state as an important dramatic conflict in the novel.

Solomon Poll explains the basis of the conflict: "Whereas some Hasidim are strong Zionists and see in the State of Israel a sign of the coming of the Messiah, the Hasidim of Williamsburg are anti-Zionist. They reject everything and everyone that is associated with the new state. They conceive that the existence of the State of Israel is a threat to their traditional perception of the Messiah, because 'all of it must emerge through holiness.'"[4] This belief in the Messiah has been with the Jews throughout most of their long history. In the darkest days of persecution, the belief that redemption would surely come helped the people survive their tribulations. The Messiah was seen as a man of flesh and blood, not a supernatural being and certainly not divine. It is this individual whom the Hasidim of Williamsburg, and Reb Saunders in *The Chosen*, await to usher in an era of holiness and peace. In addition, the Messiah is to be responsible for gathering together the people of Israel from all the nations of their exile in order to bring them to a reconstituted Holy Land.

For many Orthodox Jews, like David Malter, a somewhat different but no less valid Messianic belief exists; that is, a belief in a Messianic Age. This belief existed alongside that of a Messianic individual in the writings of the prophets and certain Jewish sages and stressed not that a single man would hold the Messianic key but that through the work of good men the "Days of the Messiah" could be brought into existence. This concept stressed the efforts of individuals here and now to work in order to bring about, with God's help, a redeemed mankind on earth and a reborn Israel. Belief in a Messianic Individual or in a Messianic Age need not be exclusive. Both beliefs lead to the same ends for mankind and for Israel; both require divine guidance. The only difference lies in the number of individuals affected by the divine will and working toward the same Godly ends.

The response to Zionism in *The Chosen* is related to differing attitudes toward Messianism, God's will, and the Holocaust. Reb Saunders's response to the murder of six million Jews is to say that it is God's will; it is a seemingly passive acceptance of the catastrophe. David Malter's response is to say that American Jews, now constituting the largest Jewish community in the world, must work to give the tragedy meaning through preserving the Jewish people. His approach is an obviously active one that finds expression in Zionism: "Some Jews say we should wait for God to send the Messiah. We cannot wait for God! We must make our own Messiah! We must rebuild American Jewry! And Palestine must become a Jewish homeland!" (197).

Reb Saunders's "passive" approach is only apparently so in that he accepts what he believes to be God's will. He is, however, most active in his resistance to the efforts of people who believe as David Malter does, which belief he sees as antithetical to this will. When Reuven mentions to him that many people now believe that the time has come for a Jewish homeland to be established in Palestine, he explodes: "God will build the land, not Ben Gurion and his goyim! When the Messiah comes, we will have Eretz Yisroel, a Holy Land, not a land contaminated by Jewish goyim!" (198). Allen Guttman comments that "The thought that David Ben Gurion can be considered a Gentile may amuse some readers, but Reb Saunders speaks from the same tradition that burned the works of Moses Maimonides and excommunicated Baruch Spinoza."[5] Even Danny sees the wrongheadedness of his father's approach to this issue, when he disclaims the belief for himself (he would join a Zionist group if not for his father) but tells Reuven with a certain wryness: " 'Herzel didn't wear a caftan and side curls,' Danny said. 'Neither does Ben Gurion' " (199).

The result of this difference of opinion is that Reb Saunders almost destroys Reuven's and Danny's friendship by refusing to let Danny speak to Reuven, and ostracizing (Reuven uses the word "excommunicate") both Reuven and his father from the Saunders's family. Reb Saunders emerges from the novel as a fanatical patriarch who rules his family and flock with an iron hand. However, Potok clearly does not want the reader to detest Reb Saunders but to appreciate the immense pressures under which he labors. Even Danny holds him in great respect and awe, and at times he emerges as a wise, compassionate man who carries on his shoulders the weight of suffering of his Hasidim and of the world. When Reuven lashes out at his seeming heartlessness in raising Danny in silence, his father, who has borne the brunt of Reb Saunders's wrath over Israel, tells him, "I did not have to raise you that way. I am not a *tzaddik*" (282).

Notes

1. *The Chosen* (New York, 1967), 232; hereafter cited in the text.
2. Louis Jacobs, *Hasidic Prayer* (London: Routledge & Kegan Paul, 1972), 126–27.
3. Solomon Poll, *The Hasidic Community of Williamsburg* (New York, 1969), ix–x.
4. Ibid., ix.
5. Allen Guttman, *The Jewish Writer in America: Assimilation and the Crisis of Identity* (New York: 1971), 126.

On Novel   Change ch. sequence

- ✓ Cut down hosp. scene
- ✓ Cut down D-Day considerably   } keep it toned down to focus of novel
- ✓ Solinten thing toned down
- ✓ Get to rel. of 2 boys & concentrate on that
- ✓ Remove first ch. or insert Danny's father section in — Get well in one or two R.
- ✓ Thin out Servs somewhat
- ✓ Cut down on Danny's sculpt. fire & eakish tugging
- ✓ Four-cornered garment – find subst.
- ✓ Owlish glasses.
- ✓ P. 34 – cut out Danny descr. – & low 4-corn. garment descr.
- ✓ P. 59 ff. – cut dream sequence down — or out
- ✓ Billy – make him eleven; eliminate his foddce fire
- ✓ Billy is too beautiful; his somewhat etheral & overdone
- ✓ Portitch redhead – worthes?

Author's editorial notes.

✓ P 374 - too much as if he loved Denny — make the dream a
fantasy + set it down

✓ One too many requests from Pet Saunders for Reuven
to see him.... Omit one ----

✓ Call Dave Kimmelman re. eye open under bandage : (149
✓? Do we need Reuven's visit to the hosp. to see
Billy ? If not, eliminate reference to visit from
hosp. prev. stuff.

T ITLE
The ECHOES of SILENCE
THE SILENCE

Author's editorial notes.

THE CHOSEN BOROUGH: CHAIM POTOK'S BROOKLYN

Joan Zlotnick

UNLIKE MOST BROOKLYN AUTHORS, Chaim Potok grew up in the Bronx, which he would later call "my Mississippi River Valley."[1] It was here, in the urban north, that he, like his rural southern counterpart, Huck Finn, experienced the estrangement of being an outsider, his background and upbringing having placed him at odds with the dominant culture. In his urban Mississippi River Valley, the place of his education and enlightenment, he, like Huck, explored the physical and metaphysical terrain; yet while Huck eventually eschewed the dominant culture, the young Potok sought rapprochement with it and the mature author made this, the conflict between his traditional Jewish background and "the echoing world I longed to embrace,"[2] his most important fictional theme.

Like his protagonists Danny Saunders, Reuven Malter, Asher Lev, David Lurie, and Gershon Loran, the emerging author sought to embrace the traditions of Western culture, while bound by the values of a radically different subculture; like them, he met with disapprobation from family and community when at the age of fifteen, by writing fiction, he demonstrated his commitment to the secular world. As he was later to explain, writing fiction is an occupation considered frivolous by the Orthodox Jewish community; furthermore, it takes time away from the study of Talmud.[3]

Reflecting on his youth, Potok expressed the view that "the compression of urban existence, the living mix of peoples and cultures in my Bronx world, made possible for me a rich variety of culture confrontations."[4]

Yet it was Brooklyn, not the Bronx, that Potok chose as the dominant setting for most of his fiction, which might best be described as partly autobiographical.

The shift of locale is understandable, considering the fact that Brooklyn is the home of several well-known Hasidic sects. In dramatizing what he chooses to call the "core-to-core confrontation"[5] experienced by Orthodox Jews reaching out toward new intellectual or aesthetic horizons, Potok undoubtedly recognized that both the confrontation and the "local color" in his fiction would be enhanced by placing the protagonist in conflict not only with his family and his religious heritage, but also with a monolithic Hasidic community. Furthermore, Potok certainly must have felt a connectedness to his tradition since his mother was a direct descendent of one of the great Hasidic dynasties.

Potok's first two novels, *The Chosen* (1967) and *The Promise* (1969), are set in Williamsburg during the 1940's. There had, of course, been a significant Jewish community in Williamsburg prior to this time. Jews had begun to settle there in large numbers at about the time of World War I. Until then, the only Jewish residents had been wealthy German-Jewish families, but gradually there developed a community of less affluent Orthodox Eastern European Jews, many of them coming from the Lower East Side, Brownsville, and the Bronx. Soon they were joined by others, mostly Hasidim, fleeing from Nazi persecution and, some years later, by concentration camp survivors.

In *The Chosen*, Potok, chronicler of many of the changes that took place in post–World War II Williamsburg, describes the area during the Depression, when only a small proportion of the population was Hasidic. There were then three of four sects, among them

> Russian Hasidic Jews in somber garb, whose habits and frames of reference were born on the soil of the land they had abandoned. . . . A block away lived another Hasidic sect, Jews from southern Poland, who walked the Brooklyn streets like specters, with their black hats, long black coats, black beards, and earlocks. These Jews had their own rabbi, their own dynastic ruler, who could trace his family's position of rabbinic leadership back to the time of the Ba'al Shem Tov. . . .[6]

The population of Williamsburg however, was, mixed, and in the three- and four-story brownstone houses

> lived Jews, Irish, Germans, and some Spanish Civil War refugee fam- ilies that had fled the new Franco regime before the onset of the Sec- ond World War. Most of the stores were run by gentiles, but some were owned by Orthodox Jews, members of Hasidic sects in the area. They could be seen behind their counters, wearing black skullcaps, full beards, and long earlocks, eking out their meagre livelihoods and dreaming of Shabbat and festivals when they could close their stores and turn their attention to their prayers, their rabbi, their God.[7]

In *The Promise*, Potok explains that only a few years later, the Hasidic population had increased dramatically:

> They had come from the sulfurous chaos of the concentration camps, remnants, one from a hamlet, two from a village, three from a town, dark, somber figures in long black coats and black hats and long beards, earlocks hanging alongside gaunt faces, eyes brooding, like balls of black flame turned inward upon private visions of the demonic. Here, in Williamsburg, they set about rebuilding their burned-out world. Families had been destroyed; they remarried and created new families. Dynasties had been shattered; elders met and formed new dynasties. . . . And by the fifth year after the war, Lee Avenue, the main street of the neighborhood, was filled with their bookstores and bookbinderies, butcher shops and restaurants, bees- wax candle stores, dry-cleaning stores, grocery stores and vegetable stores, appliance stores and hardware stores—the signs in Yiddish and English, the storekeepers bearded and in skullcaps, the gen- tiles now gone from behind the counters, the Italians and Irish and Germans and the few Spanish Civil War refugee families all gone now too from the neighborhood. . . . [The newcomers] lived in a dimension of reality that made trees and grass and flowers irrele- vant to their needs. So the street[s] began to sag with neglect. The grassy back yards went slowly bald, the hydrangeas were left to fade and die, and the brownstones became old and worn. Soon even the musky odor of the ailanthus trees in the back yards was gone. . . .[8]

In *The Chosen* and *The Promise*, Potok's description of the area is not limited to street scenes. His depiction of Williamsburg interiors, particularly of *shtibblach* and other types of synagogues where Jews of varying degrees of observance prayed, and of religious ceremonies and customs and garb are powerful, as is his portrayal of the painful choices faced by a young Hasid struggling to find intellectual fulfillment without severing ties to family, community, and heritage.

Notes

1. Chaim Potok, "Culture Confrontation in Urban America: A Writer's Beginnings," in *Literature and the Urban Experience: Essays on the City and Literature*, eds. Michael C. Jaye and Ann Chalmers Watts (New Brunswick, Rutgers University Press, 1981), p. 161.
2. Ibid.
3. Articles providing insights into Potok's personal conflict as an Orthodox Jew and a novelist include those in the *Philadelphia Bulletin* (May 16, 1974), the *Philadelphia Inquirer* (April 27, 1976), the *Times-Picayune* (February 25, 1973), and the *Fort Lauderdale News* (March 22, 1976).
4. Potok, "Culture Confrontation in Urban America," p. 166.
5. Ibid.
6. Chaim Potok, *The Chosen* (New York: Simon and Schuster, 1967), p. 11.
7. Ibid., p. 12.
8. Chaim Potok, *The Promise* (New York: Alfred A. Knopf, 1969), pp. 3–4.

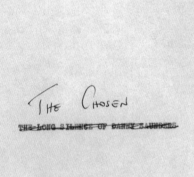

Chaim Potok
c/o Arlene Friedman
William Morris Agency
1740 Broadway
New York, N.Y. 10019

Title page from the early typescript, with revisions by the author.

THE HEAD, THE HEART, AND THE CONFLICT OF GENERATIONS IN CHAIM POTOK'S *THE CHOSEN*

Sam Bluefarb

Some Zaddikim serve the Lord in the old way: they walk on the state road. Others at times adopt a new way: they walk on the side road. Still others pursue a way of their own choosing: they walk on the path. The last reach their destination first.

—Hasidic saying

Jewish tradition contains many tensions.

—Irving Malin, *Jews and Americans*

The conflict in Chaim Potok's novel *The Chosen* functions at several levels. These are: the generational conflict; the temperamental; the conflict between head and heart; the opposition between a petrified fanaticism and a humane tolerance; and, finally, the split between two visions of God and man's relationship to Him. Of all of these, however, it is the opposition between the head and the heart which predominates.

The locale of the story is the Crown Heights section of Williamsburg in Brooklyn from the Depression years to the founding of the State of Israel. Although much of the story's direction is determined by the conflict between Hasidic and Misnagdic traditions in Judaism (as respectively represented by the Saunders and Malter families), it is the conflict between two generations and the Hawthornesque split between the obsessions of the head and the impulses of the heart that carry the major thrust of *The Chosen.*

The Hasidic view originated as a revolt against the arid intellectual concerns of 18th century scholastic (i.e., Misnagdic) Judaism with its tortuous explications in Talmudic *pilpul* and its aristocratic disdain for the poor and illiterate Jew. This resulted in the Hasidic heresy (according to the Vilna Gaon) toward the stress on joy and the intuitions. Yet in its turn (especially as portrayed in *The Chosen*) Hasidism itself evolved into the very thing it had attacked. The distance between the *Ba'al Shem Tov* (or the *Besht*, as he was affectionately called by his followers) and his latter-day followers is relatively short, as history goes: a mere two hundred years or so; but the distance between the gentle piety of the founder of Hasidism and the fanaticism of his later followers qualitatively spans a greater distance than time alone can account for. Indeed, Reb Saunders, the Hasidic leader in *The Chosen*, has really reverted to the earlier arid scholasticism which Hasidism in its own beginnings had set itself up in opposition to.

However, in *The Chosen*, the quarrel between the Hasidim and the Misnagdim (these days, roughly those practicing Jews who are not Hasidim) though decreasing in intensity and bitterness after the slaughter of six million in the Nazi Holocaust, still makes up a substantial aspect of this novel. It is this group—the Misnagdim (or, to acknowledge Potok's Sephardic dialectal usage, Mitnagdim)—to which Reuven Malter, the young protagonist, belongs. We must of course remember that many Hasidim consider most Jews beyond their own circle *apikorsim* (heretics). While it is true that the Misnagdim in *The Chosen* did not actively oppose the Hasidim, the baseball game between the Misnagdic and the Hasidic schools on which the novel opens not only triggers the conflict but determines the direction the novel will take. In a sense, *The Chosen* is a kind of exercise in the "Hegelian" dialectic which the Hasidim and the Misnagdim have engaged in for the last two and a half centuries; however, in doing so, they have articulated their respective visions toward life and God, and, in a sense, have managed to exert some beneficial influence on each other.

One of the central problems in *The Chosen* is communication—or lack of it. Part of this is deliberate and "chosen." Reb Saunders, in his oddly "Talmudic" way, believes that he can best teach his son the language and wisdom of the heart by forbidding, or discouraging, what he considers "frivolous" discourse—what most of us might think of as the minimal conversational civilities. Thus Reb Saunders denies Danny what Mr. Malter the yeshiva teacher freely gives to his son Reuven: warmth, communication, and understanding. On those rare occasions when Reb Saunders permits himself to address Danny, these exchanges take place during the periodic quizzes on Talmud, which the *rebbe* subjects Danny to—or when he blows up in exasperation at his son's passivity in the face of his own religious (near violent) commitments.

On the other hand, the relationship between Reuven and *his* father is a tender one, made all the more trusting by the easy and affectionate exchange of confidences that go on between them. They, at least, can do what Danny and his father seem unable to do: communicate. In the instance of Reb Saunders it is an admixture of pride and fanatic pietism that prevents any intimacy between himself and his son (rationalized by the elder Saunders's commitment to the Talmudic *A word is worth one coin; silence is worth two*). In Danny's case it is simply fear of his father that prevents any viable relationship between the two. Conceivably, Mr. Malter, the yeshiva teacher, and Reb Saunders, the Hasidic Talmudist, are of a common generation, if not of a common age; yet it is Reb Saunders's rigidity, and his stiff-necked pride, that give the illusion that he is much older than Mr. Malter—even as Hasidism itself *appears* to be rooted in an older tradition than its Misnagdic counterpart.

The difference between Mr. Malter and Reb Saunders expresses itself most forcefully in their respective visions toward the Holocaust: Reb Saunders can do little more than shed (very real) tears for the martyred Jews of Europe. "How the world drinks our blood. . . . [But] It is the will of God. We must accept the will of God." (Chaim Potok, *The Chosen*. Fawcett Crest Edition, p. 181. All further quotations are cited by page number within parentheses following them.) Reuven's more Westernized father, on the other hand, attempts to counter the existential nullity of the "world" by becoming ever more active in a resuscitated Zionist movement. Reb Saunders, to the contrary, in conformance with orthodox Hasidism, is bound by the Messianic belief—that only with the coming of the Messiah will Jews achieve the millennial dream, the ingathering of the exiles, the return to Eretz Yisroel.

What we find in *The Chosen* is a kind of *doppelgänger* effect—minus the *doppelgänger* itself. For Reuven and Danny are symbolically two halves of a single (perhaps ideal? Jewish?) personality, each half searching for its complement, which we already know can never be found in an imperfect world (*Siz a falsher velt!*—It's a hypocritical world! says a Yiddish Koheleth). In short, no perfection is to be attained, except in unity. But that is precisely the problem of the characters in *The Chosen*: Theirs is a search for that elusive (or illusory) goal. For neither of these two boys growing into manhood can really be said to exist at their fullest potential unless they retain some sort of relationship with each other, which on one occasion is suspended when Reb Saunders forbids Danny any association with Reuven for an interval of about a year, making the two boys doubly miserable.

Reuven, whose father allows his son forays into symbolic logic, the mathematics of Bertrand Russell, ends up a rabbi! Danny, who throughout the novel is coerced into following Hasidic tradition, and is expected to succeed Reb to the leadership of the sect on his father's death, ultimately breaks away. Danny, for want of a better word—the word has been overly used and abused, though it applies here—has been alienated—from his father, from Hasidism, and finally from the Hasidic community itself. In a sense Danny is recapitulating (suffering through) the transitions and adjustments so traumatically demanded by the exodus from the Old World to the New, adjustments required of his father and his followers, "pilgrims" who came to America from the East European *shtetle* one step ahead of Hitler's kill-squads.

The American Diaspora has also given Danny Freud and Behaviorist psychology (though initially he has mixed feelings about the latter); but after reading Graetz's *History of the Jews*, he has found that "Freud had clearly upset him in a fundamental way—had thrown him off-balance" (p. 148).

More significant than the conflict of belief in *The Chosen* is the conflict between the generations—each of which is so often collateral with the other. The novel itself could as easily, if not originally, have been called *Fathers and Sons*. For it is as much about the old split between the fathers and their offsprings as it is about the conflicts between religious views and personalities. The sons have been molded by the fathers, though in the case of Danny that influence is a negative one. For Reb Saunders is a fanatic, or at least has those propensities; he represents the archetypal, God-intoxicated Hasid. And it is he who has caused Danny to grow into a tense, coldly introverted personality. Reuven's father, on the other hand, is the tolerant (albeit religious) humanist, opposed both in mind and in heart to the cold scholasticism of the Saunderses.

In the growing estrangement between Danny and his father, the conflict of generations and of visions toward life surfaces. And it is America that is the catalyst: the old East European ambiance is gone (unless one accepts Williamsburg as a pale substitute milieu for the vanished *shtetle*); and in the second instance the old ghetto traditions have become influenced, perhaps eroded—the old acculturation-assimilation story—by the pressures of urbanism and secular intellectualism.

The relationship between Reuven Malter and his father is rooted organically, not in principle—self or externally imposed—but in tolerance and mutual respect. Mr. Malter is a yeshiva teacher, yet he can comfortably discuss the secular philosophers with Reuven as Danny's father, the Hasidic Reb Saunders, never can with him. Mr. Malter tells Reuven, "the point about mathematizing hypotheses was made by Kant. It is one of the programs of the Vienna Circle logical positivists" (p. 202). Yet with all his easy familiarity with philosophical schools and systems, his acumen in grasping them, Reuven's father allows his son to seek truth in his own way (possibly because of his own exposure to the rationalist winds of Western philosophy). Where Danny is coerced into the study of a specific mode of religious thought, Reuven is allowed by his father to roam free through the country of ideas. This seemingly minor approach to pedagogical technique—both fathers are teachers in their own ways—will determine the direction each of the boys will later take as young men.

Reuven's father hopes his son will become a rabbi—but would not coerce him into it. The elder Saunders not only expects Danny to take his place in the rabbinic dynasty when his own time comes (as Hasidic custom requires), but can hardly imagine an alternative. On the other hand fanaticism and intolerance go to form the iron bond that binds Danny to his father. What is important here, though, is that Danny becomes an object, manipulated by his father, rather than a person one relates to. This determines Danny's ultimate hostility toward Hasidism itself, so that when he rebels, he not only rebels against a religious movement but against his father, who is its representative. The worship of God gives way, in the first flush of enthusiasm, to his admiration, if not worship, of a substitute god, Sigmund Freud.

As the novel progresses, Danny the intellectual wizard, *Wunderkind*, finds himself increasingly boxed in by the restrictive ghetto mentality of the Hasidim. He sees that his father "Intellectually . . . was born trapped. I don't ever want to be trapped the way he's trapped" (p. 191).

Ultimately, though, *The Chosen* is a paradigm of two visions that have not only sundered Judaism but have affected other areas of life—the split between head and heart. The Saunderses seem to have an excess of head in their (paradoxical streak of zealousness and emotional) makeup; but the Malters have heart *and* head: They are in balance. For Reuven is not only an outstanding student of Talmud but he "has a head" for mathematics and symbolic logic. Like his father, he also has a spark of tolerance that illuminates his own knowledge of human essences as opposed to ritualistic forms.

Reuven's studies are "brain" disciplines—logic, mathematics, philosophy—yet it is he who finally turns out to have more "heart" than the brilliant son of a Hasid. Danny, on the other hand, having been raised in the tradition of the *Ba'al Shem*, should have been a "heart-and-joy specialist." Yet it is he who is all brain. And this produces a keen irony, since Hasidism, a movement that was originally a revolt against arid scholasticism became (as portrayed in *The Chosen*) transformed into its opposite. Piety, joy, even learning (a latecomer to Hasidism) becomes pietism, rote learning, memorization.

In this split between head and heart, Danny Saunders shows a brilliant flare for Talmudic explication. Yet Reb Saunders, addressing Reuven Malter in Danny's presence, complains, "the Master of the Universe blessed me with a brilliant son. And He cursed me with all the problems of raising him. Ah, what it is to have a brilliant son! . . . [But] There was no soul in my . . . Daniel, there was only his mind. He was a mind in a body without a soul" (p. 263). Too late: Danny has already "chosen" his own path, and Reb Saunders—plausibly or not—realizes at last that it is impossible to turn back now and give his son the love (or heart) he might once have given him, an act which may well have tempered Danny's mind.

Reuven is not exactly a *graubbe yung*, a moron, himself. For in one of the terminal scenes, he proves himself a master of many Talmudic brain twisters—and this, ironically, even when he *cannot* answer one difficult proposition which the teacher himself is unable to resolve! There is enough sanity in Reuven, though—presumably the heritage his father has passed on to him—to bring him to the realization that words themselves have little meaning unless they are rooted in life. If necessary, Reuven will show that he is capable of proving a formidable rival to Danny's father in his ability to untie knotty Talmudic propositions. Yet he also knows that this hardly makes a Jew, much less a compassionate human being. For brilliance, whether in Talmud or in other mental acrobatics, may as often blind the brilliant with their own brilliance as enlighten. The major irony, then, is that Hasidism—the brand portrayed in Potok's novel—though presumably a religious movement of the heart, has become transformed into its opposite. . . .

• • •

In any effective fiction it is the process rather than the outcome that is more important. This is especially true in *The Chosen*. For in this novel Chaim Potok gives us as keen an insight into the split between head and heart, tolerance and fanaticism, the strictures of tradition against the impulses of *rachmonis* (pity) as has appeared in the Jewish-American novel in a long time.

check for line-ups

Possible corrections

✓ galley 17, near foot: "...I said, wondering..." Or: that been moved about eating in the hospital..."

✓ 24 - check conversation with Billy's father
check 23 ed R. & D. conv.

✓ — Choose a friend

✓ 38 - "many" to "some" - top of galley - in able

→ — Do we have to get approvals on the quote on galley 79?

✗ change "sidecurls" to "earlocks" @ beg. of bk. [see galley 80, if you're going to change "sidecurls"

✓ galley 81 - around ½ - "Bevin" or "Bevan"?

→ — Can I use family colophon on ded. pg.?

Handwritten editorial notes on the author's personal notepaper.

THE CHOSEN:
DEFINING AMERICAN JUDAISM

Kathryn McClymond

> He's not like the other Jewish-American novelists being read by the
> general American public. He's an entirely new breed. The critics won't
> know what to do with him.
>
> —anonymous critic quoted in Leslie Field,
> "Chaim Potok and the Critics"

Like many Americans, I first read Chaim Potok's *The Chosen* as an adolescent. High school and college programs across the country assign this novel
because it describes two young men "coming of age" during a dramatic and
pivotal moment in Jewish and global history. These are important elements
of the story, but I've come to appreciate other dimensions of this novel—
dimensions that speak more directly to the relationship between literature
and the study of religion—and it is these dimensions that I want to highlight
in the following pages.

The Chosen is Potok's first book. Published in early 1967, it has also
been adapted for the screen (1980) and the stage (1999). Potok wrote the
novel while working on his doctoral dissertation in Jerusalem. He explained, "I wrote *The Chosen* in the morning and my doctorate in the
afternoon" (a humbling piece of information for all of us who struggled
with the dissertation alone).[1] *The Chosen* is highly autobiographical, drawing from Potok's childhood in New York. Yet despite the personal quality
of the book, it demonstrated broad appeal among Jews and non-Jews. *The*

Chosen quickly became a best seller, remaining on the *New York Times* best seller list for ten months, and it continues to be popular forty-odd years later. While Potok went on to write many more novels, as well as plays, short stories, children's books, and nonfiction, *The Chosen* is his most well-known work. It tells the story of Danny Saunders and Reuven Malter, two Orthodox Jewish young men growing up in Brooklyn in the 1940s. As the book opens, Danny, the brilliant son of a Hasidic rebbe, despises Reuven, the son of an academic who has developed a reputation for using secular textual-critical methods in his study of Talmud. During an intense baseball game, Danny almost blinds Reuven by intentionally hitting a ball directly into Reuven's face. The boys are thrown together as a result of this event, and they quickly become close friends despite the initial antagonism and their cultural differences. Several personal crises occur throughout the story, and the novel is cast against the backdrop of the end of World War II, unfolding revelations about the Holocaust, and deeply divisive attitudes toward Zionism. But the sustained focus of the story is on Danny's relationship with his father, the rebbe. Reb Saunders, the highly revered leader of a local Hasidic community, is raising Danny in silence. That is, he does not speak to his son except when they argue Talmud on Shabbat. At the climax of the story, Reb Saunders explains why he chose to parent in this seemingly heartless way. As the book closes, the reader, through Reuven's eyes, literally watches Danny turn a corner. Danny moves into a new life, more understanding of his father's methods and committed to upholding traditional observance, but unsure of how he will incorporate the experiences of his childhood into his adult life.

While *The Chosen* has consistently held wide popular appeal, critical reviews have been more mixed. In fact, many of its initial critical reviews were rather negative, and Chaim Potok has never risen to the ranks of other modern Jewish novelists included in collections about Jewish American literature—writers such as Philip Roth, Bernard Malamud, and Saul Bellow.[2] Most standard lists and anthologies of classic Jewish American writers omit Potok's name entirely, or he is characterized as a "popular" writer, as in Arnold J. Band's recent book *Studies in Modern Jewish Literature*: "One finds a group of books of less critical acclaim but of clearer Jewish resolution, books that have enjoyed enormous popularity and have had significant impact on American Jewish life . . . [including] *The Chosen*."[3] There are several understandable reasons for this. Potok's characterization of Jewish life in New York in the 1940s is sentimental. Baruch Hochman of the magazine *Commentary* characterized the novel as a "wish-fulfillment fairy tale which concludes with the familiar, sugary projection of desiderated relationships."[4] In addition, Potok's characters are problematic—Potok romanticizes them. No one is really bad or evil; individuals are just misguided or misunderstood. David Stern of *Commentary* charged, "Characters display no real understanding of the dilemmas which they have been chosen to exemplify," and he complained that Potok's characterization is "heavy handed and even careless."[5] To complicate matters further, Potok's interesting characters are almost all men; women barely figure into the story line of *The Chosen* at all. Reuven's mother has died before the novel opens, but we never learn how or why, and Reuven never seems to think of her. The only significant woman in the Malter household is the housekeeper, and Danny Saunders's mother functions as little more than a housekeeper in her home; she is entirely absent from parenting. Danny has a sister, but she appears primarily to prompt discussions of arranged marriages within the Hasidic community.[6] Finally, in sharp contrast to Bellow's and Roth's writings, neither of *The Chosen*'s protagonists expresses any sexual desire or frustration throughout the novel, despite the fact that we meet them relatively early in their adolescence and follow them through their college years. The dramatic tension in *The Chosen* is almost entirely intellectual. The central conflict develops as Danny gradually considers rejecting the inherited position of tzaddik within his small community, choosing instead the dangerous world of Freud and psychoanalysis.

The points I have just listed have raised problems for many of Potok's critics, and as a result he is often recognized as a well-known popular writer but not necessarily a writer deserving critical acclaim. But I want to argue that there may be another, more deep-rooted reason why Potok's work is often not received well by scholars of Jewish American literature. Potok's lack of overwhelming critical acclaim—and his striking success with popular audiences—is, in part, due to how he positions Judaism in relationship to mainstream American culture. I will lay out this argument in the following pages. First, I will indicate some key content and structural elements of the story that relate to this point. Second, I'll situate the book in the broader context of contemporary Jewish American literature. Finally, I'll argue that *The Chosen*, as Jewish American literature, raises several interesting issues from a religious studies perspective. Potok's characterization of Judaism in *The Chosen* differs markedly from characterizations by other authors of that period. In addition, critical interpretations of and responses to the novel reveal a theological stance taken by literary critics in the mid-twentieth century—a theological stance driven by a particular (and monolithic) understanding of traditional Judaism's place in relationship to mainstream America. Potok's presentation of Judaism differs markedly from what critics expected and perhaps wanted. He characterizes Judaism *not* as a tradition in opposition to mainstream American culture, but rather as an arena that had to be integrated into mainstream American life. By contrast, the trend in Jewish American literature at this time was to present Judaism in opposition to mainstream culture; one could not be traditionally Jewish and American. Becoming the latter seemed to require rejecting the former. This, I suggest, is a theological stance. Since Potok did not position traditional Judaism in relationship to mainstream American culture in the same way that writers such as Roth and Bellow did, critics who had specific notions of what Jewish American literature was *supposed* to be dismissed Potok's work as simplistic, naive, and sentimental. But popular readers accepted the multiplicity of Jewish identity suggested in Potok's novel, and they often saw themselves in Potok's protagonists. As a result, popular readers—Jews and non-Jews—embraced *The Chosen* as a novel that told their own American story.

The Chosen

Potok sets *The Chosen* in the Williamsburg neighborhood of Brooklyn in the 1940s. He tells his story in the first person, through the eyes of Reuven Malter, the teenage son of David Malter, a professor at a local yeshiva. From the very beginning, Potok uses Reuven's perspective to position communities in relationship to one another. In the opening pages, Reuven situates himself for the reader: "I attended the yeshiva in which my father taught. This latter yeshiva was somewhat looked down upon by the students of other Jewish parochial schools of Brooklyn: it offered more English subjects than the required minimum, and it taught its Jewish subjects in Hebrew rather than Yiddish. Most of the students were children of immigrant Jews who preferred to regard themselves as having been emancipated from the fenced-off ghetto mentality typical of the other Jewish parochial schools in Brooklyn."[7] Within the first two pages of the book Potok sets up an unexpected opposition. It is not the Hasidic Jews who are "alien" to mainstream America. Rather, the more liberal Orthodox community is "alien" to the Hasidic community. The reader is drawn into the complexity of Jewish American life. In this particular corner of American Judaism Reuven is marginalized, not for being too Jewish in the eyes of non-Jewish Americans but for not being Jewish enough. Potok reorients the reader so that he sees the world from the perspective of Reuven, who is committed to Orthodox Judaism but also to some level of participation in American life. This brings him into conflicts with other Jews, most significantly the Hasidic world of Danny and Reb Saunders. Here Potok differs markedly from the more critically acclaimed Jewish American writers, who focused on the angst of rejecting one's Jewish identity as a necessary prelude to living a full American life. In *The Chosen*, the problem is how to work out one's Jewish identity in light of being an American—but never to leave one's Judaism behind.

At the same time that Potok explores the conflicts between two Jewish communities—Danny's Russian Hasidic community and Reuven's more liberal Orthodox world—he situates these conflicts in the broader context of American life. Many scholars have noted that Potok begins his story in wartime, in the spring of 1944, and opens the novel on the quintessential American field of conflict: the ball field. "I use the openings to make the statement concerning the central metaphor of the novels," Potok explained. "The central metaphor of *The Chosen* is combat of various kinds, combat on the baseball field, combat in Europe, and then what happens when the combat in Europe is actually brought home to Brooklyn because of the Holocaust and the subsequent hunger to create the State of Israel."[8] Potok's opening scene suggests that all of these arenas of conflict are interconnected. In the first few pages, Reuven explains that the Second World War prompted some teachers in Jewish parochial schools "to show the gentile world that yeshiva students were as physically fit as any other American student, despite their long hours of study. They went about proving this by organizing the Jewish parochial schools in and around our area into competitive leagues" (11). But Potok doesn't use the baseball game primarily to distinguish Jews from gentile America. Rather, he uses the game to contrast Reuven's Jewish community with Danny's. Reuven's league is coached by a gentile public school gym teacher who uses military language to inspire and motivate his players. Danny's league is led by a rabbi who sits on the sidelines throughout the game with his nose buried in a book. Reuven's team members "had no particular uniform, and each of us wore whatever he wished" (14). Danny's Hasidic team members, by contrast, "were dressed alike in white shirts, dark pants, white sweaters, and small black skullcaps. In the fashion of the very Orthodox, their hair was closely cropped. . . . They all wore the traditional undergarment beneath their shirts, and the tzitzit, the long fringes appended to the four corners of the garment, came out above their belts and swung against their pants as they walked" (14). This baseball game does not represent a competition between Judaism and America, but rather a conflict between two different kinds of Judaism. As Potok explained in a later interview, "In that baseball game you have two aspects of Jewish Orthodoxy in contention. You have the Eastern European aspect, which prefers to turn inward and not confront the outside world. You have the Western European more objective scientific aspect within the core, within Orthodoxy, that is not afraid to look at the outside world that produces scientists. These are in interaction with one another inside the core. That's the baseball game." [9]

Potok's writing style is broadly inclusive. Throughout the story, Potok takes pains to make sure that non-Jewish readers can follow the events described. Daniel Walden, a well-known scholar of Potok's work, comments that Potok "makes that very particular world [Hasidism] seem eerily familiar to non-Jews." [10] Potok defines Hebrew and Yiddish terms as he uses them, and he offers a basic primer on several elements of Orthodox Jewish life, such as the history of the Hasidim, the basics of *gematria*, and Talmud study. At the same time, his style is simple and direct. Through Reuven Malter the reader is included in the most private moments, receiving occasional explanations as necessary. We are brought into the very inner sanctum of Hasidic family life and a rebbe's Shabbat afternoon Talmud study. As Sanford Pinsker observes, "Potok's Hasidic boys playing baseball, their earlocks and *tsitsis* flapping as they round third base, strike a wide audience of Jews and non-Jews alike as an entertaining way to learn about the ultra-Orthodox." [11] As a result, Hasidic Judaism increasingly becomes less foreign to the reader as the story progresses.

However, at the same time that Potok invites non-Jewish readers to feel comfortable in his 1940s Jewish world, he also includes elements that would probably be meaningful only to Jews. For example, the book is organized into eighteen chapters, eighteen being the numerical value of the Hebrew word for life, *chai*. He introduces each major section of the book with excerpts from religious texts—the Proverbs, the *Zohar* (a mystical text), and the Talmud—without providing explanations of the textual sources, let alone the excerpts themselves.

Most interestingly, in the juxtaposition of one father's household with the other, Potok sets up a kind of rabbinic encounter for the reader. Careful readers will note that the two fathers never talk with each other. In fact, they are never even in the same room or geographic space. They are, geographically and culturally, worlds apart. Yet the two sons move in and out of these two worlds, jockeying back and forth between the opposing positions these two scholars promote. It is as if the young men—and, by extension, the reader—are being exposed to and asked to evaluate two schools of thought, two *beit midrash*. Reuven learns from Danny's father in his "house of study," the three-story brownstone that functions as the Saunders home and the synagogue for the local Hasidic community. Alternatively, Danny learns from David Malter in his modern version of a "house of study": the public library. Here Danny is first introduced to Freud and psychoanalysis under Professor Malter's watchful eye. The two young boys move back and forth between the rebbe's study and the public library, traveling geographically and symbolically between two worldviews. The conflicting views of the two fathers culminate in their disagreement about Zionism. At one point Professor Malter shares his pro-Zionist views with his son, Reuven. When Reuven later shares these views with Reb Saunders, the rebbe explodes. This creates an interesting reading experience. Literally, with the first edition of the book open, we read Professor Malter's arguments for Zionism on the lefthand page (186) and then Reb Saunders's critique of Zionism on the facing page (187). The reader is witness to a variation on a great rabbinic debate, played out in the layout of the pages as well as the plot of the novel.

These conflicts, whether easily identifiable by non-Jewish readers or addressed with more nuance to Jewish readers, always come back to the core problem: Danny's increasing alienation from the life expected of him as Reb Saunders's son. The manner in which this problem is worked out sets *The Chosen* (and, in fact, most of Potok's writing) apart from what was being critically acclaimed as important Jewish American literature in the mid-twentieth century. I turn now to a brief discussion of that phenomenon.

Jewish American Literature

In general, Jewish American literature is traced back to the late 1800s. This first wave of writing was steeped in the experiences of immigrants, particularly European immigrants and their struggles building new lives in America. The next wave, roughly the period between 1930 and 1945, happily left immigrant culture behind and looked to America for hope in the face of crises such as the Depression and the Holocaust. Lewis Fried remarks, "Assimilation was a welcome fact of their American existence." [12]

Most scholars, however, agree that the heyday of modern Jewish American literature began in the 1950s, and references to great Jewish American literature most often take us back to this period. Saul Bellow, Bernard Malamud, and Philip Roth came onto the scene and dominated Jewish American fiction for decades to come. No list of Jewish American writers was complete without their names. More important, the themes these writers addressed and their orientations toward Judaism were embraced as the definitive expression of midcentury Jewish American experience and, therefore, midcentury Jewish American writing. For example, one critic commenting on Roth's work remarked that he is "one of the first American Jewish writers who finds that it [Judaism] yields him no sustenance, no norms or values, from which to launch his attacks on middle-class complaisance." [13] Over time, the most critically acclaimed Jewish American writers, almost without exception, depicted liberal Judaism as opposed to mainstream American culture and values, promoting either a rejection or a secularization of Judaism. Gerhard Falk notes that these writers "opposed their Jewish heritage and treated it with contempt, disdain and calumny. . . . Roth, and so many other Jewish-American writers, contributed mightily, not only to the secularization of Judaism and America in general, but also to the de-mystification of the Jewish tradition." [14] Another critic generalizes, "Our best writers are 'mad crusaders,' hoping for a transcendent ideal—art, potency?—to replace the tarnished ones they embraced in their youth." [15] Irving Malin offers a broad definition of Jewish American writers: "I would try to isolate 'Jewish' stories as those that witness, even in disorted [sic] or inverted ways, traditional religious and literary moments. . . . They demonstrate that their creators seek to escape from exile, to break old covenants, and to embrace transcendent ideals." [16]

Generally speaking, critics identified the great Jewish American writers as those who were in conflict with traditional Judaism. This is in sharp contrast to the Yiddish fiction tradition (as exemplified by Chaim Grade), which looked back to the old world, not necessarily as a utopian society but as a foundational community. Grade is best known for his novels *The Agunah* and *My Mother's Sabbath Days* and for the short story "My Quarrel with Hersh Rasseyner" (later adapted for stage and film). Grade is an apt figure for comparison with Potok because he, too, left Orthodox Judaism, but his writing moved in a different direction. Like many other classic Yiddish writers, he witnessed the decimation of Eastern European Jewry, and because his work is steeped in both the Eastern European experience and its destruction, it is difficult for many non-Jewish American readers to identify with.

Chaim Potok's work is much more accessible to American Jews and non-Jews alike. As a result, some argued that Potok, while a popular writer, was not a particularly good writer. Certain evidence, however, contradicts this view. First, *The Chosen* was nominated for a National Book Award when it was first published. Leslie Field notes that Potok's novel was reviewed in prestigious magazines such as the *New York Times Book Review*, *Times Literary Supplement*, *Saturday Review*, *Christian Science Monitor*, *Commentary*, and *Harper's*, an impressive feat for a first novel.[17] In addition, the book received positive reviews from respected critics such as Hugh Nissenson, Granville Hicks, and Karl Shapiro. Mark Van Doren went so far as to declare, "Chaim Potok is in my opinion the most powerful story teller living, in this or any other country."[18] Clearly, certain critics—as well as general readers—found value in Potok's work.

Another possible response is to recognize Potok as a strong American writer but not a particularly Jewish writer. This response raises even more serious problems. First, Potok has been widely recognized as an author dealing with and writing out of deeply personal Jewish experiences. Consequently, *The Chosen* received the Edward Lewis Wallant Award in 1967, an annual award that acknowledges contributions in Jewish fiction. In 1985 SUNY published a volume on Potok as part of its Studies in American Jewish Literature series (edited by Daniel Walden), and other collections dedicated to his work have followed. Potok was a committed Jewish writer, addressing explicitly Jewish content and speaking powerfully to certain Jewish audiences.

I would argue that the problem was, first of all, the *kind* of American Judaism Potok wrote about. Simply put, Potok's Jews are different from Roth's and Bellow's Jews. For example, Potok's characters' most intense personal crises play out in the intellect, not the body. Danny Saunders's adolescent rebellion expresses itself in surreptitious reading at the local library—hardly the scintillating and titillating world Roth describes. In addition, Potok's adolescent rebellions do not inevitably lead to permanent alienation between family members. We do not have here the adult men of "My Quarrel with Hersh Rasseyner," who run into one another after years of separation and spend the afternoon seriously debating God's character, even his existence, in light of the devastation of the Holocaust. While Danny and Reuven make choices that disappoint, pain, and even anger each other and their families, the conflicts center on different interpretations of religious identity, not their fundamental allegiances, and no irreparable breaks occur.

Second, Potok writes with the understanding that there are multiple Judaisms in midcentury America, and he highlights this diversity by focusing on Orthodox communities. In doing so he destroys the myth of a monolithic midcentury American Judaism, and he "decenters" the stream of Judaism that Roth, Malamud, Bellow, and many others made familiar. Barbara Meyerhoff has offered language that may be helpful in understanding the significance of this. She distinguishes between the "Great Tradition" and the "Little Tradition." The former is described as "the formal Jewish law, study, and shared history that make Jews one people, *klal Israel.*" Of the latter, Meyerhoff writes, "For Eastern-European Jews and their descendants, which includes most American-Jewish writers, this folk culture or domestic religion is *Yidishkayt.*"[19] Bonnie Lyons, building on Meyerhoff's terminology, argues, "What is central to the issues of the Jewishness of American-Jewish literature is the inheritance of *Yidishkayt.*"[20] In other words, although there are multiple Judaisms, one stream of Judaism dominates Jewish American literature: the domestic Yiddish culture of Eastern Europe. Potok, by contrast, is drawing from the "Great Tradition" or rabbinic stream of Judaism, focused on Torah study, Jewish law, and Jewish global history, woven into an American experience. Potok himself makes this point in slightly different language:

> My experience is so entirely different from that of Roth's. While we write about Jews, even the Jews that we write about are different, conceptually different. . . . Bellow really knows Yiddish literature. But it would stop there; he wouldn't be able to go beyond the Yiddish into the rabbinic, the heavy content of rabbinic tradition. . . . Interestingly enough, I feel closer to someone like Joyce, who really did, in terms of models, precisely what I'm trying to do. Joyce was right at the heart of the Catholic world and at the same time at the heart of western secular humanism.[21]

For Potok, the kind of Jew he writes about resonates more strongly with the kind of Catholic Joyce was writing about than with a different type of Jew.

Finally, because Potok draws on a different stream of American Judaism, he describes a different kind of relationship between Orthodox Judaism and mainstream America. Potok does not assume that Jewish and American identities are mutually exclusive. As S. Lillian Kremer notes, "Whereas the assimilated American Jews of the fictions of Saul Bellow and Philip Roth retain only peripheral connection to Jewish institutions, Potok's characters, like those of Joyce, are at the core of their cultural and religious heritage. They preserve the languages, traditions, and beliefs of Orthodox Judaism, even when they enter the secular professional world. Unlike most of the characters in the writings of Bellow, Malamud, and Roth, who leave the religious life for the secular, those of Potok's novels bring the secular life into the religious." [22] Potok's characters integrate their core Jewish and American identities rather than choosing one over the other.

I would argue that many of Potok's critics have missed this. They judged Potok's writings in light of dynamics that more accurately reflect liberal forms of Judaism and mainstream America. That is, they assumed a fundamental conflict between a monolithic modern Judaism and mainstream American culture. For example, Sanford Marovitz describes Potok's protagonists as being caught between "the threats and temptations of secular America in contrast to the security offered by their nuclear communities"—but he misrepresents Potok here. [23] The threats and temptations Danny and Reuven face do not come from secular America but from crises *within* their "core communities": the influx of textual-critical methods into yeshivas, the worldwide devastation and theological challenges of the Holocaust, and the deeply passionate stances for and against Zionism. Marovitz—and many others—assumed that Potok's Hasidic Judaism related to mainstream America in the way that Roth's and Bellow's liberal Judaism related to mainstream America. Fictional representations of Orthodoxy were asked to display the same themes and conflicts as fictional representations of "peripheral" Jewish experience—or to conflate Orthodox Judaism with Eastern European Judaism. As Potok's Orthodox world was rejected as a valid expression of American Judaism, so too was Potok's writing marginalized and dismissed as romantic and sentimental. At least in part because of this, he is not included in most critics' lists of influential Jewish American writers.

It is striking that the popular reading public, including non-Jews, read Potok differently than these critics, and perhaps more in line with the way Potok understood his own work. Notably, despite the fact that both Jews and non-Jews shared an experience of alienation in the 1960s, critics of Jewish American literature appropriated alienation as a distinctively Jewish American quality. Potok's characters do experience alienation, but he does not suggest that their experience is unique. On the contrary, even when cast in a traditional Jewish setting, the alienation Potok describes is something most Americans at that time could identify with; thus, readers of all backgrounds could see themselves in Potok's world. Potok managed to convince mainstream American readers that the personal religious crises that Orthodox, even Hasidic, Jews struggled with were not unlike their own. It was not the *content* of the conflicts that resonated with them, as the content was specifically Jewish: modern methods of biblical criticism, the Holocaust, and Zionism. Rather, it was the *scope* and *tenor* of the conflict. Potok received letters to this effect from his readers: "What non-Jews are doing—if I can get it from the letters they are sending me—is that they are simply translating themselves into the particular context of the boys and fathers and the mothers and the situation that I'm writing about. So instead of being a Jew, you are a Baptist; instead of being an Orthodox Jew, you are a Catholic; and the dynamic is the same."[24] Gershon Shaked comments, "In his [Potok's] fiction, it is the struggle for meaning and self-knowledge in the multiple entanglements of twentieth-century cultural confrontations that is central, though the actors who share in that struggle are all Jewish."[25]

More important, Potok painted a complex picture of the diversity within American Judaism and, as a result, a nuanced conception of the choices presented with regard to competing identities. Literary critics who focused on the Bellow-Malamud-Roth depiction of American Judaism focused solely on abandoning traditional Jewish identity. The choice these critics perceived was between being a traditional Jew and being a secularized American, implying that one could not be both. Potok understood that American life required choices—as suggested by his novel's multivalent title—but he presents more complex options. First, Danny and Reuven face differences *within* Judaism. The central conflicts within *The Chosen* are conflicts between Jews with different understandings of what it means to be Jewish. Potok suggests a spectrum of Jewish belief and practice, dramatized most strikingly in the imposed separation of the two boys by Danny's father. This resonated with American Christians, who were struggling with their own divisive issues in the sixties and seventies. Potok makes clear that even within the small world of Brooklyn Orthodox Judaism, there are strong conflicts of opinion among members—how much more, then, can one expect to find conflicts of opinion within the broad spectrum of Christian Americans?

In addition, Danny and Reuven never consider abandoning their Jewish identity; rather, their choices center on how to integrate their religious identities with secular modernism, in what Potok himself termed "core-to-core" confrontations. These choices play out in very concrete ways in *The Chosen*. Most obviously, at the end of the book, Danny shaves his beard and earlocks, choosing to look one way while the rest of his community looks another. He also breaks off a long-standing engagement in an arranged marriage. Reuven develops an interpretive response to a problematic Talmud passage using textual-critical methodologies, a strategy rejected by traditional Orthodoxy. In all of these examples, Potok speaks to general readers wrestling with how to integrate their religious identity into secular modernism.

Problems always arise when one tries to characterize an entire category of literature—one tends to homogenize. For example, Bonnie Lyons opens her essay "American-Jewish Fiction Since 1945" with a partial list of luminaries in the Jewish American canon. She then closes the essay with the following comment: "Contemporary American-Jewish fiction is then a coherent body of work; that is, there is something gained by grouping the individual writers and works in this way. . . . There are shared ideas about both life and art. Some of these ideas run counter to those of most American fiction; in particular, the American-Jewish vision of the individual as embedded in history and the family directly opposes the typical American conception of the American Adam, the solitary individual beginning a new day."[26] Lyons follows these generalizations with the obligatory caveat, but her point has been made: Jewish American fiction can be characterized in one way, but non-Jewish American fiction should be characterized in another. The two are necessarily distinct from each other.

Potok challenges this neat bifurcation. *The Chosen*, blatantly autobiographical, unveils a world of conflict, not between Judaism and America but within Judaism. It describes localized conflicts within families and between particular communities, challenging broad-brush characterization of mid-century Jewish experience. To categorize Potok as a "romantic" or a "sentimentalist" makes it easy to dismiss his portrayal of Jewish experience as false. Such a move suggests broad assumptions about what makes some experiences "Jewish American" and others not. This, I would argue, is an issue of concern to the study of religion, because it indirectly defines who and what is acknowledged as belonging to specific religious communities. What is (and is not) Jewish American? Such questions bring us to the heart of the work of religion and literature.

Religion and Literature

What do these comments about *The Chosen* have to contribute to the study of Judaism or to the study of religion more broadly? In this concluding section I'd like to outline some potential contributions at several levels.

It is common to think first of literature as a medium that includes religious themes or metaphors or as a context in which representations of specific religious communities are presented. As many scholars have noted, *The Chosen* offers a rare glimpse into a traditionally private community, Russian Hasidic Jews in New York. Through the novel Jews and non-Jews alike were introduced to a branch of Eastern European Judaism that exists on the margins of mainstream American life. This exposed readers to an unfamiliar world—Hasidic history, traditions of study, and domestic observance. At the same time, it demystified this world to some extent and spoke universally to concerns shared by Potok's readers. The novel demonstrated that while the particularities of Hasidic experience may be foreign to most Americans, the underlying concerns and conflicts were identical to other Americans' conflicts. It suggested that people across various religious communities wrestled with questions of how to live as modern Americans within traditional religious frameworks.

At another level, Potok intentionally sought not just to inform his readers but also to transform them. Potok specifically rejected the idea of writing for entertainment, asserting instead that he saw himself "as a novelist with a mission." He said repeatedly that the act of reading could be a transformative experience, describing how reading Evelyn Waugh's *Brideshead Revisited* had transformed him: "It absolutely changed my life.... I lived inside that book with more intensity than I lived inside my own world.... When I closed the book, I was *overwhelmed* by my relationship to that book. I remember asking myself, 'What did he do to me? How do you do this kind of thing with words?'"[27] Potok has also referenced James Joyce's *A Portrait of the Artist as a Young Man*: "*Portrait*, which was almost as much a part of my growing up as were the Bible and Talmud, is resident in the deepest springs of my being."[28] Potok, like many other authors, believed that literature had the power to transform individuals, to change their orientation to the world, and to instill moral virtues in their character. As Sanford E. Marovitz notes, "He intentionally conveys a sense of moral truth in his fiction and wishes it to serve as a means of guiding his readers, especially American Jews, toward developing some form of meaningful commitment in their lives."[29]

At still another level, Potok's work indirectly raises questions about representations of religious experience in America. As we have seen, the tendency among critics of Jewish American fiction was to highlight a certain kind of Jewish American experience, one chronicled in the writing of authors such as Roth, Bellow, and Malamud. By highlighting this stream of fiction, *without noting divergent streams of writing*, critics were not simply evaluating fiction. They were also glossing over the diversity of Jewish experience in America. Orthodox, particularly Hasidic Orthodox, communities were treated as throwbacks to the past, remains of the initial waves of Jewish immigration, but certainly not as representative of modern Jewish life. Such treatment conveys not only a certain perspective on traditional Judaism but also assumptions about the trajectory of modern Judaism, implying that the future of Judaism is assimilation.

It should be mentioned that, at the time, such assumptions were well founded. Jonathan Sarna, in his recent landmark book *American Judaism*, reminds us that in the 1940s and 1950s "Orthodox Judaism was actually losing ground." Sarna cites a 1952 study documenting that the existing Orthodox population was aging and "only twenty-three percent of the children of the Orthodox intend to remain Orthodox; a full half plan to turn Conservative."[30] Given these statistics, it may not be surprising that Jewish American literary criticism focused on more liberal, even "peripheral," Judaism as it identified its literary heavyweights. But such predictions about Orthodoxy now seem to have been premature. Alan Dershowitz, in his controversial book *The Vanishing American Jew*, notes that Hasidic and Orthodox "enclaves" persist in America, and he claims that "differential birth and assimilation rates suggest that what remains of the Jewish community by the middle of the twenty-first century will consist primarily of ultra-Orthodox Jews."[31] These staggering rates of assimilation and birthrate projections demonstrate that Orthodox communities are growing much more quickly than any other branch of Judaism.[32] Despite the dire mid-twentieth-century projections, Dershowitz's data indicates that Orthodoxy is alive and well. This may require us to rethink monolithic canons that marginalize traditional expressions of Judaism.

Current religious studies work on American religious life is grappling with similar issues. Increasingly, scholars are recognizing the diverse religious streams that were present at the birth of this nation, and they are revising histories to express the complexity of this religious diversity. No longer do we generalize about America as heir to the Puritans; instead, scholars such as Catherine Albanese draw attention to the multiple communities that contributed to the religious makeup of early America.[33] More recently, scholars have been documenting the global religious diversity present in America today. For example, Diana Eck's Pluralism Project at Harvard University draws attention to the wealth of immigrant religious communities within American metropolitan communities.[34]

Potok's literary treatment of Orthodox Jews resonates with these more complex approaches to American religious history. Conversely, by omitting Potok's work from the great canon of mid-twentieth-century Jewish American fiction, the myth of monolithic religious history is perpetuated. Smaller traditional Jewish communities get dismissed as out of date, irrelevant, and perhaps even backward, and thus are indirectly labeled as insignificant to the understanding of developing Jewish life in that time. Such a characterization not only oversimplifies Jewish American fiction; it belies the diversity of Jewish American religious experience and the complexity of Jewish American identity.

I do not want to oversimplify here. As mentioned early in this essay, there are numerous good literary reasons why Potok may not be included with Roth, Bellow, and Malamud among the great literary figures of mid-twentieth-century Jewish American fiction. But we need to be aware of what is at stake in such a list, and we need to be aware of the potential cultural forces at work when such canons are created. Critical and public responses to Potok's novels, beginning with *The Chosen*, may also reflect differing preferences—perhaps unconscious at some levels—for how American Judaism should be defined. In this context, the establishment of literary canons is an intensely theological pursuit.

We have recently celebrated 350 years of Jewish life in America. It seems appropriate at this time to reflect not just on the historical presence of Jews in this country but also on how we characterize that presence. As Americans become increasingly aware of the many religious communities being nurtured in the American landscape, it is important to highlight the complexity *within* each religious tradition as well. In this task, Jewish American literature has much to contribute. Jews continue to have widely divergent experiences of integrating their Jewish and American identities, experiences that Potok could not even dream of. A heterogeneous critical approach to Jewish American literature will represent and speak to the complexity of Jewish American life in a way that offers meaning to Jews and non-Jews alike.

NOTES

1. Mike Field, "Potok Has Chosen to Create Worlds from Words," *Gazette*, November 14, 1994, http://www.jhu.edu/~gazette/1994/nov1494/potok.html.
2. Potok's name and work do not appear in many volumes about Jewish American literature. See, for example, Sanford Pinsker, *Jewish-American Fiction, 1917–1987* (New York: Twayne, 1992).
3. Arnold J. Band, *Studies in Modern Jewish Literature* (Philadelphia: Jewish Publication Society, 2003), 409. Note that the reference to Potok appears in the chapter "Popular Fiction and the Shaping of Jewish Identity." Potok is omitted entirely from the list at the beginning of Bonnie K. Lyons's "American-Jewish Fiction Since 1945," in *Handbook of American-Jewish Literature: An Analytical Guide to Topics, Themes, and Sources*, ed. Lewis Fried (New York: Greenwood Press, 1988), 61.
4. Quoted in Field, "Potok Has Chosen," 5–6.
5. Quoted in ibid., 8.
6. For a slightly different take on Potok's treatment of women, see Joan Del Fattore, "Women as Scholars in Chaim Potok's Novels," *Studies in American Jewish Literature* 4 (1985): 52–61.
7. Chaim Potok, *The Chosen* (Greenwich, Conn.: Fawcett, 1967), 10. Subsequent citations to this edition will be given in the text.
8. Elaine M. Kauvar, "An Interview with Chaim Potok," in *Conversations with Chaim Potok*, ed. Daniel Walden (Jackson: University Press of Mississippi, 2001), 67.
9. Harold Ribalow, "A Conversation with Chaim Potok," in Walden, *Conversations with Chaim Potok*, 13.
10. Daniel Walden, introduction to *Conversations with Chaim Potok*, ix.
11. Sanford Pinsker, "The Crucifixion of Chaim Potok," *Studies in American Jewish Literature* 4 (1985): 40.
12. Lewis Fried, "American-Jewish Fiction, 1930–1945," in Fried, *Handbook of American-Jewish Literature*, 35.

13. Irving Howe, "Philip Roth Reconsidered," *Commentary*, December 1972, 22.

14. Gerhard Falk, "Jewish-American Literature," http://www.jbuff.com /c021501.htm.

15. Quoted in Irving Malin, *Jews and Americans* (Carbondale: Southern Illinois University Press, 1965), 4.

16. Ibid.

17. Field, "Potok Has Chosen," 5.

18. Quoted in ibid., 8.

19. Quoted in Lyons, "American-Jewish Fiction," 62.

20. Ibid.

21. Quoted in S. Lillian Kremer, "An Interview with Chaim Potok, July 21, 1981," *Studies in American Jewish Literature* 4 (1985): 96.

22. S. Lillian Kremer, "Dedalus in Brooklyn: Influences of *A Portrait of the Artist as a Young Man* on *My Name Is Asher Lev*," *Studies in American Jewish Literature* 4 (1985): 27.

23. Sanford Marovitz, "Freedom, Faith, and Fanaticism: Cultural Conflict in the Novels of Chaim Potok," *Studies in American Jewish Literature* 5 (1986): 138.

24. Chaim Potok, quoted in Ribalow, "Conversation with Chaim Potok," 5–6.

25. Gershon Shaked, "German-Jewish and American-Jewish Literature," in Fried, *Handbook of American-Jewish Literature*, 403. Shaked, however, argues that this is closer "to the Hebrew and Yiddish literature of the turn of the last century than to German or American-Jewish literature of this century," thus implying certain criteria for inclusion within the category of American Jewish literature (ibid.).

26. Lyons, "American-Jewish Fiction," 85.

27. Quoted in Walden, introduction to *Conversations with Chaim Potok*, viii. In personal conversation, Rabbi Gerald Wolpe noted that Potok, like many others of his generation, was also deeply influenced by Milton Steinberg's *As a Driven Leaf*.

28. Chaim Potok, "The First Eighteen Years," *Studies in American Jewish Literature* 4 (1985): 101.

29. Marovitz, "Freedom, Faith, and Fanaticism," 342.

30. Jonathan D. Sarna, *American Judaism: A History* (New Haven: Yale University Press, 2004), 278.

31. Alan M. Dershowitz, *The Vanishing American Jew: In Search of Jewish Identity for the Next Century* (New York: Touchstone, 1997), 23.

32. Ibid., 24–27.

33. See, for example, Catherine Albanese, *America: Religions and Religion*, 3rd ed. (Belmont, Calif.: Wadsworth, 1999), and Albanese, *Nature Religion in America: From the Algonkian Indians to the New Age* (Chicago: University of Chicago Press, 1991).

34. For more on Diana Eck's work with the Pluralism Project, see http://www.pluralism.org.

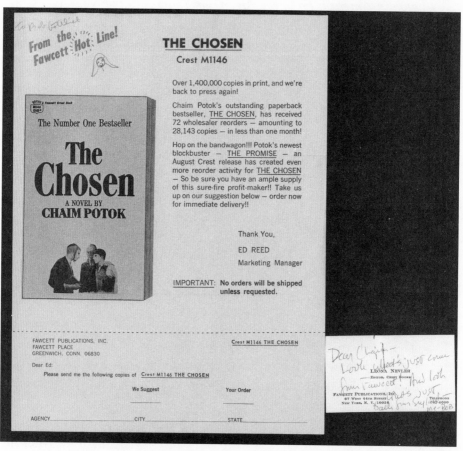

Fawcett promotional flyer for *The Chosen* paperback edition,
with a personal note from Robert Gottlieb.

CHOOSING THE CHOSEN:
A REAPPRAISAL OF *THE CHOSEN*

Hugh Nissenson

University of Pennsylvania
December 15, 2002

During the summer of 1973, just before the Yom Kippur War, Chaim Potok and I attended a conference of Israeli and American writers in Jerusalem. Late one afternoon, Chaim and I went for a cup of coffee at a café on King George Street. An old man, sipping a glass of tea alone at a table by the window, reminded me of Ernest Hemingway's story "A Clean, Well-Lighted Place." Chaim and I acknowledged to each other that Hemingway had had a formative influence on the development of our respective writing styles. Clarity and brevity of expression were our ideals.

In 1967, I had reviewed Chaim's first novel, *The Chosen*, for the Sunday book review section of the *New York Times*. It was a revelation to me. After all these years, I remember my response. Here was something different—a novel about Orthodox and Hasidic Jews living in Brooklyn toward the end of the Second World War that was written in a contemporary vernacular rather than in rhymes derived from Yiddish, like stories and novels of Bernard Malamud, for example.

Chaim's narrator, Reuven Malter, spoke in an authentic American voice. The novelist's first task is to find a voice appropriate to his story. Chaim dramatized a world about which I, a godless Jew with a minimal Jewish education, knew nothing. He peopled that world with characters that came alive on the page. The novelist's first task is to animate a cast of characters. I was impressed by *The Chosen*'s structure; each portion contributed to the effect of the whole. There wasn't a superfluous scene. The compelling narrative moved inexorably toward a classical Aristotelian climax, in which a recognition scene and an unexpected reversal of character occur. The novelist's first task is to make up a good story.

Three first tasks? The novelist has at least six first tasks, and they must more or less be accomplished simultaneously. They all require technical mastery of style, point of view, theme, structure, characterization, and plot. Chaim had technique; he was a craftsman. But that wasn't enough for him. He wanted to be considered an artist. Was he?

I recently reread *The Chosen* for the first time in thirty-five years. Well, Chaim was an artist. *The Chosen* is harmonious in all its parts. Reading it is an aesthetic pleasure; it's a well-wrought artifact. That book remains in the mind like the memory of actual experience. It gives the illusion of life.

Time has turned *The Chosen* into a historical novel. It captures that moment in the inner life of American Jews when they awakened to the nightmare of the Holocaust. The long shadows of gas chambers, sealed boxcars, and crematoria fall across the sunny streets of Williamsburg, where Reuven Malter and his friend Danny Saunders are growing up.

Cynthia Ozick recently reminded me that *The Chosen* has become a classic for young adults. "That way," she said, "lies immortality." Chaim pulled it off! His work lives after him.

A friend in New York teaches *The Chosen* to a junior high school class. The kids are not predominantly Jewish—there are several Muslims, some Episcopalians, one Jehovah's Witness. The kids are nuts about the novel. They talk about it outside of class. My friend says, "They relate to its depiction of the teenager's identity quest. They see that it's pertinent to their own lives."

Chaim's style is more derivative of Hemingway than I had recalled. The dialogue, particularly:

> "That ball could've killed me!" Schwartzie was saying. . . . "My God, did you see that ball?"
>
> "I saw it," Mr. Galanter said grimly.
>
> "That was too fast to stop, Mr. Galanter," I said in Schwartzie's defense. . . .
>
> "God, that ball could've killed me!" Schwartzie said again.

It's a catchy melody. Chaim and I belong to the disappearing generation of American novelists who learned to write from Hemingway. Our struggle with his influence forged our respective styles. We fell in love with the American language because of his prose. At that café in Jerusalem, Chaim and I discovered that Hemingway led us to read Mark Twain, who with Charles Dickens in the nineteenth century invented and perfected the genre of which *The Chosen* is a part: the first-person narrative of the coming of age of an adolescent male. *The Chosen* is a riff on *Huckleberry Finn*, like *Catcher in the Rye* and *A Separate Peace*. I wrote in that genre myself: my first novel, *My Own Ground*, is a chronicle of a Jewish boy growing up on the Lower East Side of New York in 1912.

The Chosen is a wonderful piece of Americana. It opens with the best-written baseball game in our literature. You all remember the scene: two teams of religious Jewish kids on a sandlot in Williamsburg; a hot summer day. Orthodox versus Hasidim; their payis fly, tzitzit dangle. A rabbi heads one of the teams: "A man disentangled himself from the black-and-white mass of players and took a step forward. He looked to be in his late twenties and wore a black suit, black shoes, and a black hat. He had a black beard, and he carried a book under one arm. He was obviously a rabbi, and I marveled that the yeshiva had placed a rabbi instead of an athletic coach over its team."

Chaim's deadpan style in his opening scene juxtaposes disparate details: a rabbi and an athletic coach, a Hasidic kid and his fastball, sports jargon and Yiddish. The effect is gently humorous. Chaim wrote with humor—not the first task of a novelist. Maybe it should be.

Chaim closely observed and recorded the details of physical experience. He sure could write baseball:

The next pitch left Schwartzie's hand in a long, slow line, and before it was halfway to the plate I knew Danny Saunders would try for it. I knew it from the way his left foot came forward and the bat snapped back and his long, thin body began its swift pivot. I tensed, waiting for the sound of the bat against the ball, and when it came it sounded like a gunshot. For a wild fraction of a second I lost sight of the ball. Then I saw Schwartzie dive to the ground, and there was the ball coming through the air where his head had been and I tried for it but it was moving too fast, and I barely had my glove raised before it was in center field. It was caught on a bounce and thrown to Sidney Goldberg, but by that time Danny Saunders was standing solidly on my base and the yeshiva team was screaming with joy.

The scene moves like a shot. Chaim propels it with verbs of action: "snap," "pivot," "dive," "bounce." He makes mental images out of specific visual details: "I knew it from the way his left foot came forward and the bat snapped back and his long, thin body began its swift pivot."

That left foot brings the sequence into mental visual focus. The game continues. Reuven says, "I saw [the ball] coming at me, and there was nothing I could do. It hit the finger section of my glove, deflected off, smashed into the upper rim of the left lens of my glasses, glanced off my forehead, and knocked me down."

Once again, a specific detail—"the upper rim of the left lens of my glasses"—gives us the picture. Chaim was a talented painter. *The Chosen* is composed of thousands of vivid pictures made from words. Chaim's prose makes you see. Joseph Conrad says his only task as a novelist is to make the reader see. You visualize the whole ball game—and the accident that initiates the book's plot.

Two adolescent boys fall platonically in love, are parted, and reunited. Yes, Reuven and Danny are in love. They're not aware of it, but they are. Chaim subtly dramatizes the true nature of their relationship; he does it obliquely— by innuendo. After months apart, the kids come together; Danny speaks to Reuven, and Reuven says, "I felt a little shiver hearing his voice."

While rereading *The Chosen*, I was struck by its implicit homoeroticism. Women scarcely exist in this world. Neither does overt sexuality. The novel is a classic bildungsroman about budding intellectuals. Two brilliant male teenagers learn something of life and, as a result, assume adult identities—Reuven will become a rabbi, Danny a psychologist. But they've learned nothing about sex. They never think or speak about it. Their emergent sexuality is entirely sublimated into their respective intellectual pursuits.

I use the word "sublimate" advisedly. Chaim was a Freudian. Along with Hemingway, Freud was a crucial intellectual influence for many American writers of our generation. Freud was, to paraphrase Auden, our climate of opinion. Reuven and Danny sublimate their developmental homosexual attachment; they resolve to some extent their respective Oedipal conflicts. *The Chosen* is a kind of Freudian romance. Freud's books change Danny's life. He encounters in their pages one of the transformative discoveries of mankind: the existence of the Unconscious. The hidden workings of the Unconscious is a major theme of the novel. Danny's recognition of its power liberates him from his domineering father.

Danny's father, Reb Saunders, is a famous Hasidic rebbe—a holy tzaddik, a righteous man—who led his congregation out of Russian bondage to the Promised Land, America. Danny says of him, "Six million Jews have died. . . . He's—I think he's thinking of them. He's suffering for them."

The suffering rebbe deliberately inflicts suffering on his son "to make certain his soul would be the soul of a tzaddik no matter what he [does] with his life." The rebbe thinks something like this: Daniel—my beloved son! A Talmudic genius! But all mind! He needs a loving heart. The rebbe tells Reuven, "Better I should have had no son at all than to have a brilliant son who had no soul." He inflicts on Danny what his father inflicted on him as a child. He says,

> "When I was very young, my father, may he rest in peace, began to wake me in the middle of the night, just so I would cry. I was a child, but he would wake me and tell me stories of the destruction of Jerusalem and the sufferings of the people of Israel, and I would cry. . . . My father himself never talked to me, except when we studied together. He taught me with silence. . . . One learns of the pain of others by suffering one's own pain. . . . [Pain] destroys our self-pride, our arrogance, our indifference toward others."

The rebbe is rationalizing his father's cruelty—and his own toward Danny. Reb Saunders is, in fact, an unconscious sadist who compulsively abuses Danny the same way his father abused him. The rebbe's lack of self-awareness about his unconscious motivation enriches his characterization. Chaim's revelation of the rebbe's hidden depths gives him vivid verisimilitude. His complex character is Chaim's most memorable creation.

Reuven is initially repelled by Reb Saunders. Then fascinated by him. He's riveted by the rebbe's Talmudic disquisitions—his only communication with his son. These explications are brilliant set pieces:

> "Hear me now. Listen. How can we make our lives full? How can we fill our lives so that we are eighteen, chai, and not nine, not half chai?

Rabbi Joshua son of Levi teaches us, 'Whoever does not labor in the Torah is said to be under the divine censure.' He is a nozuf, a person whom the Master of the Universe hates! A righteous man, a tzaddik, studies Torah, for it is written, 'For his delight is in the Torah of God, and over His Torah doth he meditate day and night.' In gematriya, 'nozuf' comes out one hundred forty-three, and 'tzaddik' comes out two hundred and four. What is the difference between 'nozuf' and 'tzaddik'? Sixty-one. To whom does a tzaddik dedicate his life? To the Master of the Universe! La-el, to God! The word, 'La-el' in gematriya is sixty-one. It is a life dedicated to God that makes the difference between the nozuf and the tzaddik!"

Chaim is the only novelist I know who could have written that. He was an original. His textual explications in *The Chosen* are an innovative narrative element in the American novel.

The novel's intricate structure relies on the use of doubles—characters who are distorted mirror images of each other, related but disparate. Chaim's technique is reminiscent of Dostoevsky's *The Double*, Poe's "William Wilson," Twain's *Pudd'nhead Wilson* and *The Prince and the Pauper*, and Conrad's "The Secret Sharer." For a while, Reuven and Danny metaphorically exchange fathers, who become their new spiritual mentors. Mr. Malter introduces Danny to Freudian psychology; Reb Saunders teaches Reuven about gematria. The switch imparts a geometric symmetry to the complex structure of *The Chosen*.

The two fathers are ostensibly polar opposites, but both have been traumatized by the Holocaust and share a common, unquestioning faith in God and Torah. It is the pattern of their religious observances that differentiates them.

Isaac Bashevis Singer wrote in *The Slave*, "But now at least he understood his religion: its essence was the relation between man and his fellows." Judaism in *The Chosen* is dramatized by intense, ritualized human relationships: teachers and students, a tzaddik and his son, a rebbe and his congregation. They interact with each other according to Jewish law and tradition. They relate to God the same way. Reb Saunders's congregation rejoices in God's Torah but not in his world. Or in him. Saunders's Hasidim are not religious ecstatics; they pay lip service to Baal Shem's joyful mysticism but seem incapable of experiencing it. Reb Saunders's relationship to God is utterly submissive: " 'How the world drinks our blood,' Reb Saunders said. 'How the world makes us suffer. It is the will of God. We must accept the will of God.' "

God never comes alive as a character in *The Chosen*. He is not felt as a presence in the fictive construct, as he is, for example, in *The Magician of Lublin* when he unexpectedly answers a sinner's prayer. Singer was a fantasist—and something of a mystic as well. Chaim was a naturalist; the eruption of the uncanny into everyday life is absent from his work. But, like Singer, Chaim was a religious artist, and the essence of his religion was the relation between man and his fellows.

Reb Saunders submits to God. Saunders's double, Mr. Malter—Reuven's father—rebels against him. Malter teaches Talmud at an Orthodox high school. He wears a yarmulke and upholds God and the Torah, but uses scientific exegesis in his study of the sacred texts. He's sympathetic to Reb Saunders's religious fanaticism. Malter says, "The fanaticism of men like Reb Saunders kept us alive for two thousand years of exile. If the Jews of Palestine have an ounce of that same fanaticism and use it wisely, we will soon have a Jewish state."

Malter is a fanatic Zionist; he jeopardizes his health for the cause. When he learns about the Holocaust, he renounces the immemorial religious messianic expectation of redemption for secular messianic nationalism. He wants to force the end of exile by the use of force. He says, "I am tired of waiting [for the Messiah]. Now is the time to bring the Messiah, not to wait for him."

Chaim created in Malter the archetypal Zionist of the postwar generation. He promulgates a new secular faith: Jewish history culminates in the State of Israel; Israel's creation through force of arms redeems Jewish history and makes it all worthwhile. Malter keeps saying over and over that the creation of Israel gives meaning to the death of the six million Jews: "We [are] a people again, with our own land. We [are] a blessed generation."

In *The Chosen*, Chaim obliquely presents another transformative event in Jewish history—the end of our exile.

Chaim was prescient. *The Chosen* was published in 1967. Remember that Mr. Malter tells Reuven, "It is strange what is happening. . . . And it is exciting. Jack [a businessman he knows] is on the Building Committee of his synagogue. Yes, he joined a synagogue. Not for himself, he told me. For his grandchildren. He is helping them put up a new building so his grandchildren can go to a modern synagogue and have a good Jewish education. It is beginning to happen everywhere in America. A religious renaissance, some call it." This from a character who at the same time, because of the Holocaust, renounces his belief in supernatural redemption.

In spite of everything, all the main characters—Malter, Saunders, Reuven, and Danny—cling to traditional Judaism. Danny eventually accepts Freudian psychology but rejects Freud's atheism. Reuven becomes a biblical scholar who is willing to apply the methodology of modern textual criticism to the Talmud but not to the divinely inspired Torah.

I once asked Chaim how he thought such a bifurcation was possible for committed intellectuals. He said, "We do it all the same. We compartmentalize." Chaim argued that most people separate their intellectual beliefs from their faith. They resist the attempt to synthesize them, and they're emotionally and intellectually satisfied by this compartmentalization.

Chaim's imputation of paradoxical beliefs to his characters humanizes them. They're unconsciously conflicted—like you and me. But *The Chosen* is a romance. Its characters' conscious and unconscious conflicts are easily and happily resolved. Danny's suffering sensitizes him to human suffering, as his father hoped it would. Its unintended consequence is to develop Danny's interest in psychology. In an Aristotelian reversal of character, Reb Saunders not only accepts but affirms Danny's decision to become a psychologist rather than take his hereditary place as tzaddik. His son will become tzaddik to the world. The rebbe asks Danny's forgiveness for his silence. Danny weeps. Reuven weeps with him. Silently. The motif of silence reverberates throughout *The Chosen*. It implicitly insinuates the silence of God during the Holocaust.

Just who are the "chosen"? The novel's title refers first to Danny, predestined by his father to take his place. And then to the Jewish people, who are conceived by Chaim to play an essential metaphysical role in human and cosmological history. The Jews and their Torah are to him the agents of redemption, the long-awaited transfiguration of mankind and the universe.

It's a tribute to Chaim's artistry that secular readers like myself suspend disbelief in his metaphysics and respond to the universal significance of the drama of two religious Jewish kids growing up in Williamsburg during a crucial time in Jewish history. We care about them—and all the major characters— as people.

However, I feel that their self-absorption in their closeness has become more problematic during the thirty-five years since *The Chosen* was written. Chaim was prescient to predict a Jewish religious revival. But he couldn't forsee that a number of Orthodox Jews, here and in Israel, would embrace a new belief that combines eschatological messianism and virulent Israeli nationalism. They have chosen themselves as redemptive agents, enjoined by God, to force an end to history and violently initiate the Messianic Age. These are religious Jews who have learned nothing from our history—nothing from the Sabbatean and Frankist scandals.

The Chosen evokes a more innocent time. It is fixed in our memory by Chaim's talent—his mastery of the novelist's craft, all those narrative elements that he simultaneously manipulated to achieve the unified effect of a work of art.

Chaim's death is an irrevocable loss to his loved ones, to his friends, and to American literature. But his work lives. Thirty-five years ago, I wrote in my review of *The Chosen* in the Sunday *Times*, "We rejoice, and even weep a little. . . . While Reuven talks, we listen because of the story he has to tell, and long afterward it remains in the mind and delights."

I stand by those words tonight.

Thank you.

 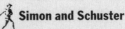
SS959
Newsp sched.

Simon & Schuster promotional ad for third print run.

PHOTOGRAPHS AND OTHER ARTIFACTS
FROM THE MOTION PICTURE

Photo from the film set, featuring Robby Benson (Danny Saunders) and Barry Miller (Reuven Malter).

Photo from the film set, featuring Potok (Talmud teacher) with
Robby Benson (Danny Saunders) and Barry Miller (Reuven Malter).

Photo from the film set, featuring Rod Steiger (Reb Saunders) and Robby Benson (Danny Saunders).

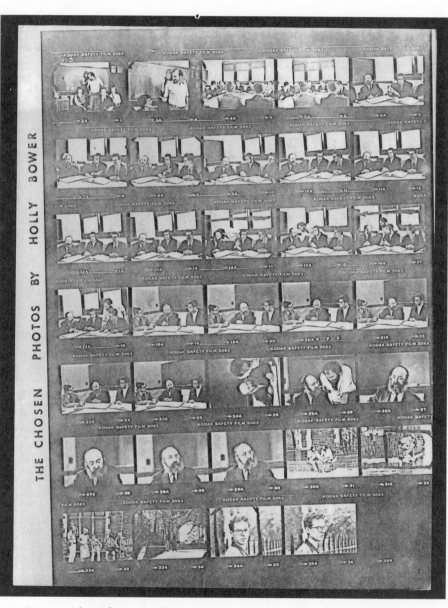

Contact sheet from the film, featuring Jeremy Paul Kagan (director), Robby Benson (Danny Saunders), Barry Miller (Reuven Malter), and Potok (Talmud teacher).

4.

7   As Reuven walks toward second base, he mocks being scared and then laughs back at Schwartzie.

8   Galanter yells to Reuven.

> GALANTER
> Malter. There's a war on.
> Remember?

> REUVEN
> Yessir.

9   A grounder is hit to the shortstop who throws it to Reuven who steps on his base and then whips the ball to first.

10   The FIRST BASEMAN catches the ball, then turns his head toward the wire fence.

> FIRST BASEMAN
> Here they come.

11   Reuven turns his head toward the fence.

12   FROM HIS POV we SEE the opposing team, also fifteen high school boys. Unlike Reuven's team, they are all dressed alike: They wear dark black pants, white shirts, and black ~~coats~~, and they all have small black skull caps on their heads. Each one's hair is closely cropped except around the ears where long curls (peyes) tumble down the sides of their faces. One boy stands out in the group -- DANNY SAUNDERS -- sandy haired, lean, intense. He is a loner. The other boys seem intimidated by him. A BEARDED MAN in his twenties wearing a black suit, black shoes, a black hat and a black beard stands with the team. Under his arm he carries a rather heavy ~~leather bound~~ book.

[handwritten: suit jacket (they play without the jackets)]

13   Both teams stare at each other.

[handwritten: unnecessary & unlikely; does not need to be heavy]

14   CLOSEUP - REUVEN

> REUVEN (V.O.)
> Even though Danny and I lived within only a block of each other neither of us knew the other existed until that day. To me where Danny lived was like the other side of the world; his block was filled with Hassidic Jews. They all wore black clothes, their men all wore beards and ~~according to their beliefs kept their heads covered and~~ never cut the hair by their ears. Danny's father was their 'Rebbe,' their leader.
> (MORE)

[handwritten: Reuven also always keeps his head covered; he was not mention this as a difference between the groups]

(CONTINUED)

[next pg.]

A page from the screenplay, with editorial notes by Potok.

DAY/DATE	SCENE #'S PAGE COUNT	DESCRIPTION	TALENT	BACKGROUND	PROPS/SPEC. EFX.	LOCATION
DAY 1 DAY 2 DAY 3 8/4/80 8/5/80 8/6/80 MON. TUES. WED.	1-92 14 & 6/8 Pg.	EXT. NEW YORK SCHOOL PLAYGROUND - DAY (June 1, 1944) The Baseball game. Reuven gets hit.	DANNY RUEVEN MR. GALANTER SCHWARTZIE DAVEY GOLDBERG BEARDED MAN UMPIRE 1st BASEMAN STUNT DOUBLE FOR REUVEN	2 S/1 10 Ball Players 14 Hassidim(inc.Dov) 3 Adults 3 Drivers Glasses and peyes for background	Softball equip- ment. Reuven's glasses. Schwartzie's glasses. Galanter's Hank- erchief. Leather-bound book. Scoreboard. Knee pads, etc. for falls. SPECIAL EFX.: Reuven's glasses break. VEHICLES: 12 Cars (3 moving) MISC. Crane - 26' Louma 2nd day only Steadicam-2 days Hi-speed camera Plexiglass pro- tection for camera. Doubles on clothes (Shoot Super for Sc. 96)	Henry Street Between Baltic and Kane Streets Brooklyn, New York

A page from the shooting schedule for the film.

EMPLOYMENT OF DAY PLAYER

Company __THE CHOSEN FILM COMPANY__	Date __8/11/80__	

Date Employment Starts __On or about 8/12/80__ _9/4/80_   Name __Chaim Potok__

Part __TALMUD TEACHER__   Address __20 Burwick Rd. Merion, Pa. 19131__

Production Title __"THE CHOSEN"__   Telephone No. __(215) 878-5426__

Production Number __---__   Social Security No._____

Daily Rate __Scale__   Legal Resident of What State_____

Weekly Conversion Rate __Scale__   Citizen of U.S._____

Married_____   Quota No._____

Date of Birth_____   Date of Entry U.S._____

The employment is subject to all of the provisions and conditions applicable to the employment of DAY PLAYERS contained or provided for in the Producer-Screen Actors Guild Codified Basic Agreement of 1967 as the same may be supplemented and/or amended.

The Player (does) (does not) hereby authorize the Producer to deduct from the compensation hereinabove specified an amount equal to _____ per cent of each installment of compensation due the Player hereunder, and to pay the amount so deducted to the Motion Picture and Television Relief Fund of America, Inc.

PRODUCER THE CHOSEN FILM COMPANY   PLAYER _Chaim Potok_

By _[signature]_

Day Player employment sheet for the film,
listing Potok as "Talmud teacher."

INTRODUCTION TO THE ALBION-ANDALUS STAGE EDITION OF *THE CHOSEN*

Aaron Posner

In my midthirties I found myself wondering what I meant when I called myself Jewish. I referred to myself as Jewish quite often, often jokingly . . . when I would make a Yiddish-y sound getting up, or when my stomach was behaving in a particularly Jewish manner. But I had begun wondering what exactly I really meant by calling myself Jewish.

Being a director and playwright, I decided I would try to figure out this question by bringing a great piece of Jewish literature to the stage. So I started reading . . . Isaac Bashevis Singer. Bernard Malamud. Philip Roth. Sholem Aleichem. Chaim Potok. And then, I went no further. I knew I had found what I was looking for.

I had read *The Chosen* in junior high school. I remembered there was a baseball game, and that was about it. In reading it as a searching adult, I was struck by so many things—the stark and powerful prose of the storytelling; the raw force of the core conflicts; the endlessly complex humanity of all the characters; and, finally, the universality of the story. Yes, it was deeply and uniquely Jewish, but it also had such depth and resonance that it was clearly built to connect to *all* audiences open to hearing its story.

I'd met Chaim a few times in the theater community in Philadelphia, where we both lived. I had even thought of approaching him to ask for his advice on Jewish literature for me to adapt. After reading *The Chosen* again, I knew I didn't want to ask for his advice, but rather for his permission to adapt this inspiring and challenging novel to the stage.

We met in his incredibly friendly but intimidating study, which was lined with books—tomes, even, of serious literature, Jewish history and philosophy, and, of course, many volumes of his own works translated into many different languages. I told him I was only a marginal Jew at best. This revelation did not seem to faze him. I told him my main idea for putting this story onstage: Two fathers. Two sons. Just the heart of the tale and the conflict, nothing extra or unnecessary.

The approach clearly appealed to him. It was, I think, a theatrical equivalent of the style and energy of his own writing. He was never flowery, never pyrotechnic. He was far less interested, it always seemed to me, in style than in substance. He wrote for a reason, and he wanted his stories to be heard and considered deeply. He told his stories, I believe, in the most direct, efficient, forceful way he could. I tried to take his lead and let that sensibility direct the adaptation.

The collaboration was inspiring and challenging in all the best ways. I felt a great responsibility to be true to the heart and soul of his characters as we transported them from one medium to another. We worked closely together to shape the play and find theatrical ways to bring his world to life onstage. Unlike many novels, *The Chosen* was remarkably hard to cut, since it is so tightly and economically constructed. There were also moments that were not in the book but that we felt needed to be part of the play, including a heated argument about a passage in the Talmud, and the response of Reb Saunders to the Holocaust. Chaim added these episodes seamlessly and elegantly. He was, in every way, an extraordinary collaborator.

He only called me once to tell me I had done something terribly wrong. I had made the ending overly sentimental . . . and he hated it. He wrote with such full and genuine heart that anything that tipped toward sentimentality was utterly anathema to him. Needless to say, we changed it. . . .

A final story: there is one big idea in the play that is only implied in the book—a core teaching from the Talmud that means, roughly, "both *these* and *these* are the words of the Living God." In other words (to be slightly less Talmudic about it), more than one thing can be true at the same time. Answers are neither simple nor singular. Both these . . . and these.

This idea came into the play during a long conversation I had one evening with Chaim and his wife, Adena. We were talking about the set for the original production at the Arden Theater in Philadelphia. There was a banner designed for the set and we wanted Hebrew text on it. But what . . . ? We talked about a number of possibilities. The conversation got complex and went to the core of the conflicts in the book. At one point Adena, in response to what we were talking about, said: "*Elu ve-elu*" . . . These and these—the beginning of this core Talmudic teaching. I asked what the words meant, a conversation ensued, and this concept of multiple truths became a central idea of the play, woven all the way through it.

I am proud of much of the work I have had the opportunity to do in the American theater over the past twenty-five years and more. I have told a great number of stories in a huge variety of ways. But there is no story I am more proud or more honored to have had the opportunity to share with hundreds of thousands of theatergoers, all over the world, than *The Chosen*.

The play asks a lot of those wishing to perform it. It asks you to engage with the world with the same fierce intelligence, heart, and spirit that Chaim poured into its creation. It asks you to be courageous in your willingness to grapple with core conflicts that go very deep, and it asks you to be generous of spirit and bring everything you are to flesh out these characters. I have seen many productions, from 1,000-seat regional theaters to JCC basements. If the actors are willing and able to tell the story simply, passionately, and truthfully, then the audience gets taken on an extraordinary journey.

Best of luck with the journey, and thanks for entering this world. . . .

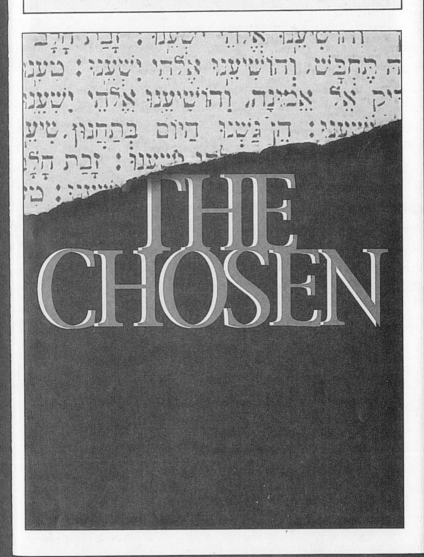

Playbill cover.

CREDITS

A NOTE
ABOUT THE AUTHOR AND THE EDITOR

CHAIM POTOK was born in New York City in 1929. He is the author of nine novels, including *The Chosen* (1967), *The Promise* (1969), and *My Name Is Asher Lev* (1972), as well as five plays, three children's books, and two works of nonfiction, including *Wanderings: Chaim Potok's History of the Jews*. An ordained rabbi, he served as an army chaplain in Korea and received his PhD in philosophy from the University of Pennsylvania. He died in 2002.

RENA POTOK has published articles, reviews, and poems in *Religion & Literature*; the *Bryn Mawr Review of Comparative Literature*; *Borders, Exiles, Diasporas*; *Contemporary Women Poets*; and *Jewish American Women Writers*. She is the editor of *Hills of Spices: Poetry from the Bible* and *The Collected Plays of Chaim Potok*. She received her PhD in Comparative Literature and Literary Theory from the University of Pennsylvania, and teaches English literature and composition at Saint Joseph's University and Villanova University.